A GAME OF CHANCE

Jon Osborne has been a newspaper reporter for a decade, most recently for the *Naples Daily News* in Florida, where he covered everything from bake sales to triple murders. He is a veteran of the United States Navy. He is currently at work on his third thriller.

Also by Jon Osborne

Kill Me Once

JON OSBORNE

A GAME OF CHANCE

arrow books

Published by Arrow Books 2012

2 4 6 8 10 9 7 5 3

First published in Great Britain in 2012 by
Arrow Books
Random House, 20 Vauxhall Bridge Road,
London SW1V 2SA

www.rbooks.co.uk

Addresses for companies within The Random House Group Limited can be found at: www.randomhouse.co.uk/offices.htm

The Random House Group Limited Reg. No. 954009

A CIP catalogue record for this book is available from the British Library

ISBN 9780099550891

The Random House Group Limited supports The Forest Stewardship Council (FSC®), the leading international forest certification organisation. Our books carrying the FSC label are printed on FSC® certified paper. FSC is the only forest certification scheme endorsed by the leading environmental organisations, including Greenpeace. Our paper procurement policy can be found at: www.randomhouse.co.uk/environment

Typeset by SX Composing DTP, Rayleigh, Essex
Printed and bound by CPI Group (UK) Ltd, Croydon, CR0 4YY

For Jacob, my brand new little man

ACKNOWLEDGEMENTS

Writing a book is truly a team effort – and I'm thankful to have the best team in the business helping me out.

First thanks goes to my awesome literary agent, Victoria Sanders, without whom none of this would be possible. Also to Chris Kepner and Bernadette Baker-Baughman, Victoria's dual right hands and outstanding literary agents in their own right. Thanks, guys, for everything. On the foreign rights front, a big thank you to Chandler Crawford and Jo Grossman for all their hard work on my behalf.

Georgina Hawtrey-Woore is a superstar editor in all respects. If I had all the silk purses she's woven from sows' ears over the years, I'd have a lot more silk purses than I'd know what to do with. Thank you also to the rest of the sterling staff at Random House UK, especially Selina Walker, Susan Sandon and Ruth Waldram.

As always, Laura Osborne has been my rock and my sounding board – which is weird because I didn't know rocks could be used as sounding boards. Thanks, honey, for always being there. Thanks also to my parents, Richard and Della; my children, Madison, Justin and Khloe; my sisters and their husbands, Kathy and Steve; Elizabeth and Cliff and Julie and Mark; and my nieces and nephews – Patrick, Molly, Annie, Nathan and Elyse.

A GAME OF CHANCE

PART I

OPENING GAMBITS

'It's just you and your opponent at the board and you're trying to prove something.'

Bobby Fischer, American-born World Chess Champion who famously defeated Russian grandmaster Boris Spassky to win the prestigious title during a highly contentious 1972 match held in Reykjavik, Iceland that gripped the world's attention and which at the time was considered to be nothing less than a Cold War propaganda battle.

CHAPTER ONE

Friday, 11:15 p.m., Manhattan

The man on the phone had told her it would be a scavenger hunt of sorts.

And also that he'd be watching her the entire time.

'One mistake and you'll never see your kids again,' he'd promised.

Stephanie Mann pulled her threadbare coat even tighter around her slender body as she stood shivering in the doorway of a convenience store on West 85th Street. Part of the bone-numbing chill ripping like poison-tipped razor blades through her central nervous system came from the fear and adrenalin flooding her veins. Part came just from standing outside on the sidewalk on a New York City night in April.

A light, misting rain that seemed perversely intent upon sucking the remaining warmth from everyone's bodies plastered a few strands of Stephanie's long dark brown hair to her forehead. She brushed them away but ten seconds later they were right back where they started. Not exactly Key West weather. Hell, it wasn't even Newark.

Worse, the coat didn't do a damn thing to shield her

from the cold. For all the warmth the tattered garment provided, it might as well have been stitched together from flimsy sections of the Sunday newspaper. It was old and frayed badly around the edges, second-hand. Like everything else in her life since Don had decided that it was perfectly OK to leave her alone with two children, no job and not even a high-school diploma to show for it. Was it any wonder the state had taken the kids away from her in the first place? How was she supposed to pay for anything?

Stephanie's anger warmed her up briefly. Even though they'd been together for fifteen years, she and Don had never taken the time to make it official by taking that long (and supposedly romantic) walk down the aisle and getting married, so her legal options seemed somewhat limited now. She supposed she could go after the cheating bastard for child support if she really pushed the issue. But just *how*, exactly, did you get money for kids who weren't even with you any more?

Stephanie tightened her jaw. Whatever. Poor people didn't go to court for civil matters, anyway. Criminal matters, yeah, all the time. Go to any downtown court-house in any big city around the country on any given weekday and you got what basically amounted to a low-class version of skid row's greatest hits.

Lawyers, clothing, transportation – everything cost money. Lots of it. And Stephanie couldn't afford even a decent coat.

Then – from out of nowhere – a lucky break. Or so

she'd thought initially. The first bit of good fortune that had come her way in the past six months, if not longer.

When Stephanie had opened her eyes that morning and found the prepaid cellphone sitting on the coffee table in the condemned apartment building that she and her kids had been calling home, she couldn't believe her eyes. Weak from hunger, she'd thought she'd hit the jackpot.

Rubbing the sleep away from her eyes to clear her vision, she'd yawned, stretched her arms high overhead and had straightened on the couch. There the phone had been.

Foolishly, Stephanie hadn't stopped to consider how it had even gotten there in the first place. Hadn't stopped to wonder *who* might have put it there or *why* they might've put it there. Sleep had been fogging her brain still.

Stephanie shook her head. Stupid in retrospect, no doubt about it. Because the locks on the front door were among the few things in the apartment that actually worked any more and the only people other than herself who still had a key were her kids.

Sadly, though, Stephanie hadn't stopped to consider these things. Not even for a moment. Instead, all she'd been able to think about was selling the phone and maybe getting something to eat that day. Something to take the edge off the incessant hunger that clawed at her.

Hot tears sprang up into Stephanie's eyes at the depressing realisation of just how far she'd really sunk since Don had left her. Just about as low as a human being could possibly go. She wished like hell she'd never even met the back-stabbing liar, wished like hell that she could somehow travel back in time to the night when she'd stupidly agreed to slow dance with him in the cramped, stifling-hot gymnasium of St Bonaventure's High School in Queens, all the while ignoring the nagging little voice in the back of her mind that was telling her to stay as far away from Don and his liquor-coated breath as she could possibly get. She also wished like hell that she'd never so much as *touched* the phone. But she had done those things. And now she was paying the price for it on all counts.

As soon as Stephanie had picked up the phone that morning, it had rung in her hand. Startled, she'd almost dropped it to the floor.

Most people said that they saw key events from their lives flash before their eyes in moments of great fear. For Stephanie, however, it had been lunch at Subway. Maybe even dinner at McDonald's. Dare to dream big, Rockefeller.

Cellphones weren't the hot commodities on the streets they'd once been – even ten-year-olds carried them around these days – but Stephanie had felt certain she could get at least twenty bucks for it. Maybe even twenty-five, if she was really lucky. Enough to get her through the next couple of days, at least.

The number on the caller ID had showed a 212 area code, which meant that it originated in New York City. Force of habit had driven her to flip open the phone and place it to her ear. A male voice tinged with a slight foreign accent had come across the line.

'Now, listen to me very carefully, Stephanie . . .' the caller had said.

The cellphone had been frozen to her ear the entire time he'd been speaking. His tone had a lullaby quality to it. No histrionics, no yelling, no empty threats. Just a mundane list of tasks for her to accomplish and she'd get her kids back again. Simple, right? By the time he'd finished speaking, everything had *seemed* to make perfect sense.

Right now, though, it didn't make a *lick* of goddamn sense whatsoever. There wasn't one part of his instructions that didn't sound completely insane. But in her split-second decision to pick up the phone she'd given herself no choice.

Stephanie looked up and down the busy street bustling with people, knowing that the man on the phone was probably out there somewhere right now, watching her. She tilted up her chin and scanned the illuminated skyline, using a hand to shield her eyes from the spitting rain.

Was he there in the warehouse across the road? Tucked away on the seventieth floor of the massive bank building next to it? Could that be him right there? A shadowy figure silhouetted in one of the building's windows and looking down at her from his lofty post above? Just like everybody else in the world looked down at her? Or was he in the all-night eatery twenty yards to the left of those two structures? Could he actually be one of the patrons of the eatery? Munching casually on a gyro with all the fixings while he carefully studied her every move?

Wherever he was, Stephanie could practically *feel* his perverted gaze upon her right now. Raping her like the twenty-dollar whore she hadn't quite yet sunk to becoming – not that she hadn't given the option some serious consideration in her weaker moments. After all, hunger could be an extremely powerful motivator. Hunger didn't leave room for moral judgements. Hunger didn't differentiate between right and wrong.

A hard shudder ran down the length of Stephanie's back at the nauseating thought of selling her sex. A beat cop strolled past no more than thirty feet away, but what could she do about it? Nothing. The man on the phone had told her exactly what would happen if she dared seek assistance from the police.

'It's something of a medical procedure,' he'd explained calmly, not even the slightest hint of a quiver affecting his deep voice. 'What I'll do first is tie your children down on some type of hard surface. They'll be face up and spreadeagled – naked, of course – with gags shoved in their mouths. Naturally, we can't have any passing Good Samaritans hearing their cries for help and trying to save the day. From there, I'll take a sledgehammer to their bodies, starting with their feet.'

Horror had flooded through Stephanie's mind at the ungodly imagery – like a replay of the movies she'd always enjoyed watching. She'd clutched the phone, not daring to speak, too shocked even to whimper. He'd told her not to hang up. It would only make it worse.

She was too afraid to listen, too afraid not to. Gentle laughter tickled her ear. He was enjoying this. 'Then I'll smash the bones in the feet until they've been turned into powder,' he continued. 'From there, I'll move up to their shins, and then to their kneecaps, and then to their femurs. And so on and so forth, all the way up their worthless little bodies until I crush their worthless little ribcages and their worthless little hearts stop beating.'

Stephanie had gasped then but the man on the phone had cut her off at once.

'Don't interrupt me,' he'd hissed. 'Let me finish. When their worthless little hearts stop beating, that won't be the end of it. Not by a long shot. When their worthless little hearts stop beating, I'll simply restart them with an injection of adrenalin. You're a big movie fan, right? You've seen *Misery*, haven't you? Now think more along the lines of *Pulp Fiction*. Not a very pleasant image, is it?'

He'd paused before continuing then, almost as though he were savouring the thought like a glass of fine wine, relishing the way the ugly words tasted on his lips. 'In any event, each time they pass out from the pain I'll simply bring them back to consciousness with another injection of adrenalin, followed at once by an injection of neuromuscular-blocking drugs. These drugs paralyse the body, Stephanie, but allow the brain to be fully aware of the pain I'll be administering on the deepest, most visceral level possible. Of course, I plan to take care of your son first so that his little sister can watch and have some idea what to expect. After all, we wouldn't want to catch her off guard, now would we? Of course we wouldn't. Where would be the fun in that? Anyway, by the time I'm finished with them, I expect that your children will be little more than flesh bags full of dust.'

Outside the convenience store, Stephanie's knees buckled hard at the haunting memory of the man's gruesome words. She fought the urge to collapse and die right there on the sidewalk. Jack and Molly were just fourteen and eight years old respectively. They hadn't had a chance even to live their lives yet. And now some maniac was threatening to snuff them out in the most disgusting manner imaginable. Somehow she knew he was telling the truth, that he'd do what he said he'd do. That it wasn't just some awful joke.

She gritted her teeth until her jaw began to ache. No way. Not this time. Jack and Molly deserved more than that from her. For once in their lives, her children deserved for her to be strong.

Taking in a deep breath to steady her jangled nerves, Stephanie pushed open the door to the convenience store and struggled to stay calm despite the fact that her pulse was pounding like crazy. No matter how hard it was for her to accomplish, though, she knew she needed to stay in the moment here, to stay completely focused on the task at hand. Either she did this or her kids died. It was as simple as that.

A computerised doorbell echoed throughout the space as she entered the store, but no one bothered to turn around and look at her. *So far, so good.*

A quick glance around the store told Stephanie there were about a dozen people inside. An Indian clerk with a red dot in the centre of his forehead was attending to a line of customers three deep. A fourth customer was filling out a thick stack of lottery tickets. A stubby pencil worked furiously in his stubby hand.

Five feet away from the lottery addict, a fat man with a dark woollen cap pulled low over his ears stood next to an end-cap loaded down to the point of collapse with a dizzying variety of snack foods. Ring Dings. Beef jerky. Pork rinds. Somehow sweating profusely despite this miserable weather, he seemed to be debating the respective merits of Twinkies and Pringles, holding up first one packet and then another, almost as though he were weighing them. After several moments of careful consideration he finally went with the Twinkies and joined the other customers in line just as a thin trickle of sweat leaked past his right ear and down his unshaven cheek. Stephanie empathised with him.

There were six aisles inside the store. Of course, the one she needed was located squarely in the clerk's line of sight. Her heartbeat slammed powerfully against her emaciated ribcage as she made her way down the first aisle to a pegboard lined with boxes of condoms and turned her shoulder to block the clerk's view. Like it or not it was time to check off the first task on her supremely weird little list. Again, what choice did she have in the matter? Either she did this or her kids died.

Drawing another deep breath, Stephanie felt her lungs expand fully and reached out a trembling hand, slipping an economy-sized package of Trojans into her purse as surreptitiously as she possibly could. Fire & Ice, with dual-action lubricant inside and out to deliver warming and tingling sensations to both partners. It had to be that brand and that brand only. The man on the phone had been *extremely* clear about that particular detail. Had said that no other brand in the world would do.

Thankfully, the clerk didn't even look up as she left the store. His attention was trained like a laser on the fat man and his precious box of Twinkies, for which the customer was paying with loose change. Stephanie didn't blame the clerk in the least little bit for his vigilance. After all, he wouldn't want to miss out on a single penny in this crippled economy. Poor as she was herself, she understood that harsh little fact of life better than most. It was precisely the reason why she was being forced to steal the first item on her nightmarishly odd shopping list right now.

The fat man's voice filled her ears as she passed by the counter again. He was using his chubby fingers to carefully separate coins from the lint in his pocket, his fingernails encrusted with grime. 'A dollar twelve, a dollar seventeen . . . oh, wait a minute, here's a quarter . . .'

Stephanie tried not to cry as she stepped back outside into the cold night. If she'd been caught on video, so be it. She'd deal with the repercussions later. Jail was probably a lot better than the place where she was staying right now, anyway. At least in jail they had food.

Still, guilt and shame heated up her cheeks. She'd never before stolen anything, not in her entire life, no matter how desperate her circumstances had gotten. Now, in addition to being an unfit mother, she was a petty thief as well. Before she could stop it happening, Stephanie's mind flashed back to her high-school days. Ironically, she'd been voted 'Most Likely to Succeed' right before she'd been unceremoniously kicked out of the best Catholic school in the borough of Queens for becoming pregnant with Jack. *If they could only see me now.*

Missing her children badly, Stephanie walked quickly away from the store with her head down, studying all the tiny little cracks in the sidewalk and doing her best to avoid eye contact with any other living soul in the wave after wave of pedestrians that streamed past her down the busy street. Two blocks down, she opened the pilfered box of condoms and put one of the small square packages into her pocket. Then she leaned down and handed the rest of the box to a homeless man who was huddled underneath a tattered blanket and shivering violently against the unrelenting cold. Just like the man on the phone had told her to do, though God only knew for what purpose.

The homeless man glanced up at her briefly, looking puzzled.

And then he smiled at her, his teeth perfect.

'Well done, Stephanie,' he said, coughing. 'Now get home as quickly as you can. Your children have very little time left.'

Stephanie stared down at him in horror, not quite sure she'd heard him correctly. 'Wh– what did you just say?'

The homeless man lifted a hand from beneath his tattered blanket and waved it in the air irritably, shooing her away. A fat black insect crawled on his left arm. A beautiful gold Rolex sparkled on his left wrist. An elaborate diamond ring glinted on his pinkie finger. 'Go now!' he urged. 'There isn't much time left! They'll be dead soon! The monster said he's going to kill them!'

Then he cackled: a horrible, jarring sound.

Stephanie's mind almost caved in on itself. Her vision blurred, then cleared again in a flash. Obviously this homeless man was part of the sadistic game she was being forced to play, but was it the same man from this morning's phone call? The same man who'd threatened to hurt her kids? To *kill* them?

The rain intensified, and then the heavens opened up completely, drenching them both. 'But I don't have any money.' Stephanie's voice caught. She could feel the rain beating against her face, seeping through her threadbare coat, as she raised her voice in a frantic effort to be heard above the thunderous downpour. 'How much time do I have left? I live thirty blocks away from here. How am I supposed to get there?'

A sharp look of annoyance creased the man's face just as a loud crack of thunder boomed above, shaking the buildings around them all the way down to their foundations. Two seconds later, a brilliant flash of lightning exploded overhead, ripping the night sky in two and leaving the heavy smell of electrically charged air hanging in the atmosphere. The storm was very close now. Almost directly above them.

'You have a condom in your pocket!' the man shouted. 'There are ten thousand cabs working in this city on a Friday night. I'm sure you can figure it out from there. Use the only currency you possess.'

Stephanie turned blindly and ran for the street. No more time for talking. Her children needed her. And for once in her life, she would be there for them.

She reached the street in a matter of seconds, twisting her right ankle awkwardly on the rain-slicked kerb in the process. An agonising jolt of pain rocketed up her leg but she ignored it. She couldn't think about herself any more. She needed to think only about her children now.

Stephanie stumbled farther into the rain-drenched street and looked up at the ominous sound of an approaching engine bearing down on her. A Yellow Cab nearly flattened her right there in the middle of West 85th Street.

The angry driver slammed on his brakes and sounded his horn at the same time, his vehicle squealing and fishtailing to a stop just inches away.

Stephanie's heart leaped into her throat as she instinctively brought down her palms on the hood of the cab as hard as she could, as though she could somehow stop the huge yellow beast through physical strength alone. She staggered backward three feet, her rubber-soled tennis shoes slipping wildly against the slick road surface. The heat of the engine warmed up her hands and reconnected her to a reality she didn't want any part of.

The vehicle's windshield wipers were turned up full-blast and whisking away the rain with a tortured electric whine that filled Stephanie's ears with a maddening buzzing sound. Through the frenetic wipers she locked stares with the irate driver. An African man. Judging from the colourful hat on his head, probably from Nigeria or Chad or Tanzania or something like that. Not an American.

The driver rolled down his window and stuck out his head. His bloodshot brown eyes bulged angrily from their sockets. The pale blue jugular vein on the left side of his throat pulsed crazily, all thick and fat with blood, straining hard against his brown skin. 'What the fuck, lady!' he roared. 'Watch where you're going! I could have killed you! Get out of the fucking road!'

African accent. Definitely not from America.

Stephanie hurried around to his window. The muscles in her thighs quivered as badly as the muscles in her vocal cords, barely able to support her own weight, barely able to form intelligible words. Tears slid down her cheeks and mixed with the pounding rain. 'Please, sir,' she croaked. 'I need your help. The lives of my children depend on it.'

The look of rage on the driver's face melted away, replaced gradually by a look of concern. For the first time in months, Stephanie allowed herself to feel a brief glimmer of hope. Perhaps the driver wasn't as heartless as he'd first seemed. Perhaps he'd help her out, after all. Perhaps he was one of the few good men in a world overrun with bad men. Bad men like the one with whom she'd spoken on the phone that morning. 'What do you need?' the driver asked her.

Stephanie told the man the address of the condemned apartment building, struggling to stay coherent. It wasn't easy. 'I need to get there as quickly as possible,' she pleaded. 'But I don't have any money to pay you with.'

The driver shook his head and began rolling up his window. Caring individual or not, he wasn't running a charity here. And no doubt he'd heard the same story a million times before. It was probably par for the course in his line of work. 'Nope,' he said. 'I'm sorry, lady, but I really don't have time for this shit right now. So get the fuck away from my car, OK? Nobody ever has any money. Everyone just wants something for free. Why doesn't anybody ever work in this country?'

Stephanie fumbled in her pocket and brought out the condom. Sickening as it was for her to realise, she now understood *exactly* what the rubber was for. The man on the phone had obviously thought things out very carefully – right down to the tiniest detail. The condom was her cab fare.

'I'll take care of you on the way over there,' Stephanie said, the words like acid on her tongue. Fresh shame heated up her face again. *Just about as low as a human being could possibly go.* 'I swear to God. Please, sir, you're my only hope.'

The driver glanced to his left, and then to his right. Headlights cut through the night from the passing traffic on the road, glowing yellow eyes staring straight ahead from gigantic metallic demons sent from Hell to hunt Stephanie down and claim her eternal soul. The sidewalks looked largely deserted now as only a few pedestrians were left seeking shelter from the incessant rain still pounding out a deafening staccato drumbeat against the sea of cement all around them. Stephanie blinked hard against the surreal imagery. To her eyes, the rain seemed almost to be dancing, happy to see her at this lowest point in her life.

Then the driver hit the door locks and said, 'Get in.'

The driver wouldn't let Stephanie out of the cab until she'd finished him off. Gagging from the chemical taste of the condom in her mouth, she felt his body finally tense. When he was drained completely, he pushed her roughly off of him. 'Now, get out,' he ordered. 'Fucking whore! I have work to do.'

Stephanie scrambled out of the cab and ran for the condemned apartment building, wiping at the sides of her mouth as she went. More lightning flashed in the dark sky above, illuminating the construction equipment and vehicles that would tear down the building in just two short weeks to make room for a new luxury high-rise. Stephanie had no idea where she'd stay when that happened. Maybe an old friend would take her in. Maybe she could find a room at a women's shelter. Wasn't important now.

The unit that she and her children had been staying in was on the fourth floor but since there wasn't any power left running to the building any more the elevator wasn't an option. It was only now that she remembered her children shouldn't even be here – they'd been taken into foster care. But the man had been adamant: she needed to hurry home to save them.

Stephanie flung open the door to the fire-escape stairwell with a violent bang and raced up the concrete steps as fast as her furiously pumping legs would carry her, slamming her shin painfully against a floor-waxer hidden in the darkness. Another white-hot jolt of pain flashed through her body but she ignored it again. It was pitch black inside the stairwell as she counted the steps in her mind. Two flights of stairs for every floor.

On the fourth floor, she felt for the door there and threw it open hard. Breathing in ragged gasps, she stepped into the long dark corridor.

Several loud clicks echoed at once in the narrow hallway. A split second later, bright floodlights blinded her.

Stephanie blinked rapidly against the powerful lights, stunned. She tried to move but her feet felt as though they'd been nailed to the floor. For one terrifying moment her lungs stopped working altogether. Her ears rang. Her world swam out of focus. A veil of confused tears clouded her eyes. In the very next instant, someone very strong emerged from the darkness and grabbed her from behind around her thin waist, began wrestling her down to her apartment. Stephanie kicked at him violently but it was no use. His vicelike grip didn't budge. She tried to scream but a large hand immediately clamped down over her mouth. It smelled of expensive cologne.

Reaching her apartment ten seconds later, the man from the darkness reared back with a loud grunt and kicked open the door in a deafening explosion of splinters, destroying the termite-infested wood with ease and dragging her inside. Stephanie looked around frantically. More floodlights had been set up in a semi-circle around a space cleared out on the living-room floor, directly in front of the broken-down television set. But the lights in the living room weren't as harsh as the ones out in the hallway. They were soft, muted.

Perfect light to work by.

Steel tethers were screwed into the floor.

Stephanie fought him as hard as she could, but her abductor proved much too powerful. Thick, sinewy muscles powered rough hands that tore at her clothing. A violent kick to her ankles swept her legs out from beneath her and brought her down hard to the floor. Before Stephanie knew what was happening, thin ropes cut painfully into her wrists and ankles, attaching her to the tethers. Tightening now, restricting her circulation. A gag was shoved halfway down her throat.

Breathing hard in short, animalistic bursts, her assailant leaned down and yanked Stephanie up viciously by her hair. Pure agony spread swiftly throughout her trembling body. Warm breath that smelled faintly of cloves tickled her left cheek. Duct tape was wound into place over the gag.

Wrapping around her head now. Three times. Four. Five. *Zip, zip, zip.* Around and around the back of Stephanie's skull the duct tape went. Then the man ripped it off the roll with a quick flick of his powerful wrist and smoothed down the jagged edge with his thumb. His Christmas gift had been wrapped to his satisfaction.

Five minutes later, Stephanie was completely naked and tied spreadeagled to the floor, unable to move, unable to speak, almost unable to breathe.

Still grunting from the intensity of his efforts, her assailant rose to his feet and towered over her, backlit by the floodlights. Stephanie's eyes widened in horror when she saw that he was wearing a tuxedo. Gold cufflinks glittered at his wrists. His silver hair had been parted perfectly on the left side of his head. A dazzling smile crossed his handsome face.

And then he lifted a sledgehammer.

'Good evening, Stephanie,' he said. 'Rude as this may seem, however, I'm afraid our introductions will have to stop there for now, as this night marks checkmate for you. I think you know what's coming next. Try not to scream.'

With that, he lifted up his arms and brought down the sledgehammer with all his might, starting at her feet. The primal scream that started somewhere deep within Stephanie's raw throat was lost completely in the gag. Her last thoughts were of her babies.

CHAPTER TWO

Darkness. Sweet darkness. Cold and deep and dark and lovely and painless.

In her traumatised mind, Stephanie is playing with her children in the park. Jack is pushing Molly on a swing and Stephanie is seated on the swing next to them, bending and unbending her knees. Not really seriously swinging, more just pushing herself back and forth. Enjoying the day.

The sun is warm and bright in the clear blue sky above but a cool breeze is keeping them comfortable, rustling through their hair. Songbirds whistle their pretty melodies in the swaying branches of the maple trees all around them, tall shoots of green ringing the park. Thirty yards to their right, a cotton-candy vendor is whipping up colourful fluffy treats on hollow paper cones for the excited children huddled around him. Laughter everywhere.

Stephanie looks over at her own kids and smiles. Jack is still pushing Molly on their swing – they're taking turns. Every mother's dream. Two little angels.

Up and down Molly goes, her long blonde hair trailing behind her in the breeze like dazzling rays of golden sunlight. At the apex of one her swings, Molly looks down at Stephanie and calls out to her in her sweet little voice. To Stephanie's ears, it sounds as though an angel is singing. 'Watch out for the bee, Mommy,' Molly says, giggling from the delicious feeling of all the silly butterflies fluttering around in her taut little tummy. 'He's going to sting you right on the arm.'

Stephanie looks down at her arm and swats at the bee but by then it is already too late. Its stinger bites deep into a vein on her left arm and injects her with a small dose of its poison. Yelping, she throws back her head and stares directly up into the blazing ball of fire in the sky.

Stephanie blinks again, harder this time, more rapidly, completely confused. The sun is much too close right now. Much too bright. Like it has fallen out of the sky. The light in her eyes is blinding. *So very blinding*. She can't make out a single thing.

Gradually, the sun morphs into a spotlight. Then a man's body blocks it out. Straightening, he turns and places a syringe down on the coffee table.

Pain. Dull and hot and throbbing and terrible. Like nothing else Stephanie has ever experienced before in her entire life.

Retrieving his sledgehammer from the couch, the man turns back around and smiles down at her gently, displaying two rows of perfectly white teeth. 'Ah, there you are, sleepyhead,' he says. 'Ready for round two yet? Your feet are completely destroyed, but now it's time for us to work on your shins. Don't be alarmed – this won't hurt one little bit. I promise.'

When the sledgehammer flies down again with such terrifying speed that Stephanie's horrified involuntary reaction squeezes all the remaining breath from her badly constricted chest, the dense block of metal makes solid contact with her right shin and shatters the bone instantly in a dozen places. Her eyes flutter wildly for a moment before they roll up completely into the back of their sockets. Blissfully, she passes out from the pain after just one blow this time.

But Stephanie knows she'll wake up again very soon. There isn't any other option. The man in her apartment will make sure of it.

He's *promised* her as much.

CHAPTER THREE

Wednesday, 11:46 a.m.

If possible, the dead body smelled even worse than it looked. And its looks weren't likely to win a beauty contest anytime soon.

The latest victim's name was Stephanie Mann. An anonymous caller to the New York City Police Department had reported the death – never a good sign. Because whenever an anonymous caller got involved in this sort of thing it usually meant that the possibility of getting any help at all from the general public was reduced practically to nil.

Thankfully, though, the NYPD had called the FBI almost immediately after arriving on the scene. The lead responding detective had obviously known instantly what she was looking at (and apparently hadn't wanted to touch the bloody mess with a ten-foot pole). Still, that speedy exchange of information had somewhat limited the degree of contamination to which the crime scene had been subjected, so that was certainly a good thing. Handled correctly from here, there was even an outside chance that it might be salvaged as though it were a freshly discovered murder scene: the next-best thing to the feds showing up first.

Peeling wallpaper, curled and yellowed at the edges from water damage, covered all four buckled walls of the living room. The electricity in the condemned structure wasn't hooked up any more because the building was scheduled for demolition in two weeks. But the dusty slants of springtime sunshine flooding into the room provided plenty of light to see by.

What they illuminated wasn't pretty.

Rat-chewed garbage bags, piled high and leaking wet refuse, littered the north-west corner of the apartment where two walls met. A blocky television set sat on a rickety TV stand that bowed and sagged underneath its heavy weight. It had been shoved up against the south wall, the prongs of a frayed power cord still plugged into the socket. Exposed electrical wiring hung dangerously close to the ragged fibres of a puke-stained carpet below: an almost certain fire just waiting to happen had there still been any juice running through the building's tired old veins. Directly above the TV, a grimy window had been hammered shut with a series of thin, rusty nails that poked out in all directions, promising a future full of tetanus shots for anyone foolish enough to brush up against them at the wrong angle. The inner city's version of an ADT security system: the poor man's alternative to owning a Rottweiler or pit bull terrier to protect what rightfully belonged to you and yours.

And right there in the middle of it all – on a freshly polished coffee table no more than three feet away from Stephanie Mann's destroyed body – sat a pristine copy of Swiss International Chess Master Richard Forster's *Amos Burn: A Chess Biography*. Standing beside it like a miniature mute sentry who'd been paid quite handsomely to ensure that no harm befell its prestigious client was a brass-cased nine-millimetre bullet.

Special Agent Dana Whitestone did a double take. Even among all this mess the bullet looked hopelessly out of place: a stranger in a strange land. Dana blinked and looked a third time. The bullet hadn't budged.

Queasiness gripped Dana's stomach and squeezed hard. For the first time in the string of unspeakably grisly murders that she and her partner Jeremy Brown had been investigating (up to this point with a spectacular lack of success that had been duly and joyfully noted in all the local newspapers), the killer they were after had chosen a co-star to share the harsh spotlight with the latest book he'd selected to represent an historical chess figure.

But *why*?

Dana grimaced and felt the beginnings of a world-class headache coming on. Although she didn't understand the exact meaning of the bullet yet, she *did* know that its addition probably meant just one thing: their man was getting bolder. Also never a good sign, because he'd been far too bold already. Bold enough to send the entire city into the kind of panic it hadn't felt since the days of the Son of Sam.

For its part, the mammoth nine-hundred-and-seventy-two-page tome detailing the remarkable life of the long-deceased English chess master Amos Burn made other doorstoppers look inconsequential. In sharp contrast, the tiny bullet gleaming in the bright sunlight next to it seemed almost lost against the book's massive size – an insignificant tourist gazing up in awed wonder at the breathtaking majesty of one of New York City's countless skyscrapers.

Dana let out an exasperated breath, already dreading the latest crash-course in chess that she'd have to struggle through. Though she'd been a casual player of the game since college – knowing all the pieces and how they moved – she was out of her depth when it came to playing strategy. To make matters worse, she and Brown were obviously going up against a master here. A master who'd once again gone on the offensive with the kind of senseless violence only employed by a man who had nothing left to lose.

Or a man who'd had nothing to start off with.

Reading the book would take Dana at least a week – probably longer if she wanted to actually *understand* anything in it – but she knew she'd need to do just that if she and Brown were to have any hope of finally catching a killer who'd thus far proved so terrifyingly cunning and elusive that it chilled her blood. As for what part in the killer's deadly little game the bullet played, Dana had no idea – not yet, anyway. Up to this point, their man had been outplaying them at every turn. Making them look like fools, amateurs.

Still, with luck, the words inside the book would finally help shed some light on the mystery that she and Brown had once again arrived too late to solve. If they were fortunate maybe they could save the next person who the killer had scheduled for execution. And hard as it might be for her to wrap her mind around, Dana knew that was *exactly* what each of these murders had been: executions.

In this instance, their failure to do their jobs properly had cost Stephanie Mann her life. Who knew who'd be next? It was anybody's guess from here, and that was the problem. The killer they were after didn't display any discernible pattern with the *targets* he chose. He did, however, display quite a distinct pattern with the *location* of his murders. But how did you profile someone like that when his target pattern changed each and every time?

'A little more light reading for us, Dana? Looks like a real page-turner this time. Can't wait to dig in.'

Dana closed her eyes and shook her head in annoyance. Like everyone else in the room processing the scene, Jeremy Brown had dressed in full protective gear so as to not contaminate the apartment. Make that contaminate it any further. By comparison, this dump made roach-infested no-tell motels look like glittering penthouse suites at the Four Seasons.

Filthy or not, though, everything in the apartment would need to be bagged, tagged and sent down to FBI Headquarters in Washington DC for analysis. And fast. Everything from the foul-smelling garbage bags to the broken-down television set to the chess book itself. There was no time to go to court and get an injunction against tearing down the building, so the entire apartment would need to go piece by painstaking piece. From there, the process of evidence analysis would probably take weeks – if not *months* – to accomplish. It was like shaking fifty different jigsaw puzzles into one gigantic box and then attempting to create a single clear picture from them all.

In other words: nearly impossible. Although an inter-agency task force had been assigned to the investigation due to the mounting number of murders connected to the case, Dana and Brown were ultimately in charge. It was them who'd get most of the credit if they managed to stop this guy, but also most of the blame if they failed. So far there'd been no credit, but *plenty* of blame. Patience down in DC was running thin and Dana knew that her and Brown's heads were on the chopping block if they didn't start making some serious progress in identifying the killer. An unfortunate way to think about such things, perhaps, but appropriate nonetheless.

Dana stretched her neck and turned to her partner. The paper masks tied over their faces matched the paper shoe-covers on their feet and made them look like a pair of ER surgeons discussing the best way to save a patient's life. Sadly, there wasn't anyone left here for them to save. Their patient was already very dead.

Dana nodded down at Stephanie Mann's mangled corpse, which had been stripped naked and tied spread-eagled to the living-room floor by thin ropes looped through thick steel tethers. The pressure of these bonds had turned the skin around the woman's wrists and ankles a sickening black. 'What do you make of that?'

Dana asked. Until the pathologist showed up, she and Brown would need to puzzle out on their own the forensics end of things.

Brown stared at the woman's decaying body. Most of it looked purple, crushed. There was no face left. The overwhelming smell of rotting flesh that had slapped them in the face as soon as they'd walked in the front door only seemed to be getting worse. 'Looks like somebody went to town on her with a blunt object,' Brown said, letting out a slow breath that inflated the portion of the paper mask covering his mouth. 'Some kind of hammer, maybe. The brutality of the murder and the chess book on the table indicate this game's been wrapped up. The needle marks on the victim's arms suggest she was an intravenous drug user of some sort – if not a current one, then definitely at some point in the past. No idea what the bullet means. But if our man's pattern holds, he'll start up another game in a few days. What do you estimate as the time of death? When did all this happen?'

Without the pathologist on scene yet, Dana forced herself to study Stephanie Mann's naked corpse again, paying close attention to the forensic details and resisting the urge to gag at what she saw. Wasn't easy.

Tiny, squishy-looking maggots wriggled in the woman's mouth, nose, eyes, ears . . . all the natural openings in her body. Stephanie Mann's abdomen looked badly distended, reminding Dana of the shocking photographs of starving Ethiopian children she'd seen while leafing through the pages of the *National*

Geographic magazines she'd been so fond of as a kid back in the early 1980s. Seemed like ten lifetimes ago now.

Dana took a mental snapshot of the disgusting image and went over it again in her mind, briefly wishing that she'd chosen a different occupation to which she could dedicate her life. Librarian, maybe. That seemed safe enough. After all, there hadn't usually been a whole lot of rotting meat to be found in any of the libraries she'd visited in the past. But Dana *hadn't* chosen to become a librarian. Instead, she'd very deliberately chosen to become a special agent with the Federal Bureau of Investigation, had known full well from the very start what she'd been getting into. What's more, she'd actually struggled to get here. Had fought tooth and nail to graduate at the top of her class at the Academy fourteen years earlier and embark upon her career of hunting down serial killers.

And Dana loved her work. Every single minute of it. After all, there were a lot of very sick people out there who didn't hesitate for a nanosecond while mindlessly harvesting the lives of innocent people, so it naturally followed that there also needed to be people like her who were willing to lay down their own lives in order to stop the heartless monsters.

She just hoped it wouldn't come to that.

Dana shook her head to chase away the thought and willed herself back into investigator mode. She operated far better there than in any other mode, anyway. Just ask her Bureau-appointed psychiatrist. Unlike librarians,

Dana had come across plenty of rotting meat in her lifetime. So much of it that she could never quite get its lingering smell out of her hair and skin and fingernails, no matter what kind of new soap she tried or how many blisteringly hot showers she took at the end of each exhausting workday.

There were five general stages of decomposition with dead bodies: fresh; bloat; active decay; advanced decay; and dry remains. Judging by the maggots and the woman's horrifically swollen belly, Stephanie Mann had reached the bloat stage now. From the look of things, active decay wasn't very far behind. 'She's been dead about three days now,' Dana said in response to Brown's time-of-death question, looking up again to see if the pathologist had made it on-scene yet. No luck. 'Maybe four. The gas build-up hasn't ruptured the skin yet but microbial proliferation is obviously under way. Sulphhaemoglobin has travelled throughout the circulatory and lymphatic systems. That's what is giving her body its marbled appearance.'

Though it was a clinical assessment – as clinical as it got – anger nonetheless coursed hotly through Dana's veins, replacing the nausea. Though Brown was right – though the killer's latest game did indeed appear to be over now – she had very little doubt that there were more murders to come.

Lots of them. Bloody, vile, vicious murders.

Though it wasn't always the case, Dana got the distinct impression this particular killer wouldn't stop murdering until he'd been caught. No, he'd keep on killing until she and Brown could figure out his pattern at the *beginning* of his sick little games. Or, at the very least, somewhere in the middle. Not at the end, when it didn't do them – or the people who were dying in some of the most horrific ways that Dana had ever witnessed – the least damn bit of good.

Dana gritted her teeth. In her whole career she'd never worked on such a frustrating case. She wanted to be the one to stop this killer, however long it took. Her desire to catch him burned inside her. The more he got the better of them, the more her resolve strengthened.

Dana looked around the room again and sighed. There were mountains of potential evidence to process here. To *further* complicate matters, the apartment had clearly been used by a constant stream of the homeless ever since the building had first been condemned two years earlier. The DNA inside the living room alone probably belonged to dozens of people, if not more.

Not a promising start at all.

If the apartment had ever been used for the buying, selling or using of drugs – a real possibility, considering the network of scabbed-over needle marks peppering Stephanie Mann's bruised and battered arms – that number could theoretically stretch into the thousands. And with an average of six weeks for each double-helix breakdown, not only was the time simple enough to calculate, it was squarely against them here. Like everything else.

While harried lab techs down in DC carried out their

tedious work as quickly as they could, Dana and Brown's unknown subject – what all the actors in the Friday-night TV crime dramas so blithely referred to as the *unsub* – would be free to murder again and again to his heart's content.

But what was this killer's *purpose*? *Why* was he murdering these people? What *goal*, exactly, was he trying to accomplish with all this? Nothing seemed to make any sense to her.

Dana knew that serial killers rarely varied their methods, usually murdering in roughly the same manner each time. Some were trying to relive – and in the process relieve – a childhood trauma. Others attached specific identities to their targets, often seeing in their victims' faces their own mothers, or perhaps a lover who'd spurned them in the past. But this guy was mixing things up at every juncture. Age, gender, social status – none of it seemed to matter to him.

Hell, maybe he just *liked* to kill.

For the past five months now, Dana and Brown had been on the ice-cold trail of a serial murderer whom the press had gleefully taken to calling 'The Chessboard Killer'. Apparently, it made no difference whatsoever to the headline-whoring media that there was already a killer on record who'd been dubbed the exact same thing. The important thing to them was that the name sold newspapers – lots of them – and so that was the name they'd decided to use. *Again*. Like just about everything else in this life, in the end this story was all about money.

Alexander Pichushkin – a Russian maniac who'd murdered at least forty-eight people in south-west Moscow's Bitsa Park before he'd finally been captured in 2006 when surveillance cameras had taped him accompanying his final victim on a busy train platform at the park – had at one point during his questioning claimed it was his intention to kill sixty-four people: one for each square on a chessboard. Unfortunately for Dana, Brown and the victims of this latest incarnation of a Chessboard Killer, their current unsub appeared to be taking Pichushkin's grisly idea several chilling steps further by recreating some of history's most famous chess games in their entirety and marking down the capture moves with his kills.

Clever bastard. Dana couldn't *wait* to meet him.

The first game they'd investigated had taken place the previous year and had paid homage to Siegbert Tarrasch, a world-class chess player from Prussia who'd died in 1934 and who'd once written the line 'Chess, like love, like music, has the power to make men happy.' When FBI agents stationed in the New York City field office hadn't been able to make head or tail of that case, Dana and Brown had been called in from Cleveland by FBI Director Bill Krugman to investigate. Not long after, they'd taken their positions as co-presidents of the head-scratchers' club.

Still, at least they'd made *some* progress.

They'd found Tarrasch's words in the preface to his book *The Game of Chess*, which had been discovered lying next to the dead body of Paul Winslow, a thirty-four-year-old African-American man from Yonkers who'd had the distinct misfortune of representing the unlucky final victim in the 'Siegbert Tarrasch' game back in November. From there, Dana and Brown had managed to link a series of unsolved murders similar to that of Winslow to a specific grid of streets in New York City. Using pushpins on a map, they'd figured out the unsub's pattern by running the locations of the unsolved murders through a powerful computer that decoded numerical sequencing. Exhaustive research eventually led them to the shocking realisation that the pushpins on the map matched up perfectly with the capture moves in Siegbert Tarrasch's very first recorded game.

And so had begun Dana and Brown's own nauseating game of cat-and-mouse. Problem was, Dana didn't quite know which animal they were supposed to be portraying in this contest. She sure *felt* like the mouse most of the time.

Occupying his position as the cat in this ghastly equation, the killer's checkmate move in that first game had been horrifying, to say the least. Like the others before him, Winslow had been 'desensitised'.

Which was to say that all five of his senses had been removed.

Winslow's fingers, ears, nose, tongue and eyeballs had each been sliced away with what forensics personnel later determined was a series of scalpels. Apparently, the surgical instruments lost their sharp edges after a while when they were used for their intended purpose: carving up flesh. More sickening still, forensic pathologists had also determined that Winslow had been alive the entire time his senses were being removed.

Dana shuddered and felt a stippled wave of gooseflesh ripple up her arms. She couldn't even begin to imagine what that must have been like for Winslow, the excruciating pain the man must have experienced. Although she'd been surrounded by death her entire life and could certainly be considered no stranger to the brutality of cold-blooded murder, Dana had always secretly hoped to die in her sleep when her time came. Didn't everyone?

After that first game, their unsub had gone on to recreate famous games of four other chess masters throughout history, including Bobby Fischer, Judit Polgar, Peter Leko and Anatoly Karpov. Each checkmate move had been more gruesome than the last, and a book featuring the respective player the killer was honouring at the time had accompanied the final crime scenes, marking the conclusions of the games. Something of a road map to what he'd accomplished. But by the time the chess books had made their appearances at the culminating murder scenes – basking in the warm glow of the spotlight so lovingly created for them by their unhinged director – it had been far too late for Dana and Brown to do anything about it. Far too late for them to stop the killer. And while their unsub had steadily ramped up the ferocity of his kills with each successive game, he hadn't gotten sloppy yet. At least, not sloppy enough to trip himself up. With all their resources, with all their expertise, it was frightening how this one had consistently gotten the better of them.

With luck, though, all that would change soon. At least, it had *better* change soon. Because none of the normal investigative routes that Dana and Brown had followed so far had turned up a thing.

They'd already amassed reams of paperwork on the hundreds of members of the dozens of chess clubs scattered throughout the enormous city, but to no avail. Enthusiasts of the genteel game didn't often display the murderous tendencies of a killer. What many of them had displayed, however, was a peculiar amount of interest in the unsolved cases of the Chessboard Killer. But who could really blame them? It was fascinating material. The kind of stuff that sold a lot of newspapers.

For the club players themselves, the mystery seemed almost *fun* to ponder, an interesting puzzle for the brain to solve. Dana and Brown were constantly being inundated with emails, letters and phone calls from well-intentioned players speculating on which games the killer was recreating. But in the end the players had proved every bit as clueless as the FBI.

Dana turned to her left and watched a young forensic photographer lean over the massive chess biography. The man took shots of the book from several different angles while three other photographers snapped away in the rest of the apartment. Ten feet away and closing the gap with each one of his careful steps, a stone-faced videographer conducted a grim walk-through of the scene, complete with a running commentary.

'Living-room floor. Victim lying naked and secured to the floor by thin ropes looped through thick steel tethers. Wounds clearly visible.'

The videographer advanced even closer to Stephanie Mann's smashed body and leaned down, hovering there for a moment before running the camera lens slowly along the entire length of her traumatised corpse, starting at her feet and working his way up from there, almost like a tender lover who was intent upon appreciating every last inch of his beloved's form. 'Multiple injuries to victim's facial bones. Cranium crushed. Brain leakage in the upper left quadrant. Clear insect activity in all orifices.'

Dana shuddered again and shifted her gaze back to the photographer shooting the chess book. 'Do you have enough documentation yet?' she asked. It was extremely important that everything in the apartment should be photographed before being boxed up and shipped down to the DC lab for further forensic examination. Photographs always made for prime evidence in trial cases.

Dana stopped herself mid-thought and gave herself a swift mental kick in the pants. Of course, it might help to actually *catch* this guy first before they started making any trial plans.

The photographer took several more shots before straightening up and letting his expensive camera dangle from a thick nylon strap around his neck. 'Yes, ma'am,' he said. 'It's all yours.'

Dana thanked the man and turned back to Brown. 'So, do you want to do the honours, or shall I?'

Brown lowered his eyebrows in a scowl and Dana frowned back. Her partner didn't look so hot right now. Brown's face – at least as much of it as she could see above his paper mask – had gone very pale. A thin sheen of sweat glistened on his forehead just beneath his hairline. Tiny broken capillaries were visible in the whites of his exhausted eyes.

Rough as Brown looked, though, Dana certainly empathised with him. After all, no matter how long they did this job it never seemed to get any easier. Their professional lives were full of violent death, almost on a daily basis, and that wasn't the most serene way to live.

'You do it, Dana,' Brown said. 'I think I might have brushed my hands against the television set earlier and contaminated my gloves.'

Dana nodded, knowing that Brown wasn't deferring to her because he didn't have the stomach for it but rather because of Locard's Exchange Principle.

French forensic scientist Edmond Locard had first postulated his groundbreaking theory in the late 1920s, opening up a brand-new toolbox full of investigative goodies for use by law-enforcement agencies all around the world. Locard's Exchange Principle held that every contact left a trace. From hair to clothing fibres to the dirt on people's shoes, some sort of transference was nearly unavoidable. So if Brown had picked up anything on his gloves from the television set he didn't want to transfer it to the chess book.

A hands-on examination of the body itself was out of the question here. In its pulpy state, that job was far better left to the pathologist – if and when the decidedly unpunctual woman ever decided to show up. One wrong move and Dana and Brown could easily destroy evidence that might never be recovered again. They couldn't afford to lose even the tiniest scrap of evidence at this stage.

Dana glanced down at her own gloves to make sure they were clean before lifting the book off the coffee table. Much more appetising than dealing with Stephanie Mann's brutalised corpse, no doubt about it, but still enough to fill her insides with a cold dread. The killer had touched this book, and therefore by extension was now touching *her*.

The mammoth book felt heavy in her hands as Dana opened its front cover and turned the pages, starting at chapter one and working her way methodically through to the back.

Her breath caught in her throat when, exactly halfway through, a photograph of a child's smiling face fluttered down to the ratty carpet.

CHAPTER FOUR

Dana's heart skipped three beats in a row inside her chest. Brown sucked in a sharp breath beside her.

In the school photograph, the grin missing its two front teeth belonged to a boy of about five or six years old. Probably a kindergartener. Maybe a first-grader. Not much older than that.

Tousled brown hair with a cowlick topped off an adorable face that had a deep dimple on either side of the boy's smiling mouth. Doe-brown eyes shone with the pure excitement of picture day at school. No doubt there was a plastic comb tucked away somewhere in the back pocket of his corduroy jeans. After all, he'd certainly want to look good for his mom when she got the proofs back from the photography studio. From there, the photos would be sent out to the entire extended family. Hell, his grandma's fridge alone would be covered with them from the freezer on down, occupying a special place of honour among all her early-bird dinner coupons and take-home church schedules.

Neither Dana nor Brown said a word for several long moments. Tension crackled in the air between them.

Brown spoke first. His normally assured voice

trembled. 'Christ, Dana,' he breathed. 'We've got to get this out to the media *now*. This could be the killer's next intended victim. Probably is.'

He blew out a slow lungful of air before continuing, puffing out his paper mask again. 'That is if the poor kid isn't dead already.'

Dana's vision swam out of focus. Her ears rang. Before she could stop it, her mind slammed back to the previous serial-killer case she and Brown had investigated – the first one they'd worked on together as a team. In that investigation, the Cleveland Slasher had murdered five little girls, all of them under the age of ten. 'Not again,' she whispered hoarsely.

Dana shook her head violently to chase away the terrifying thought. Of course that wasn't happening again. *Couldn't* be happening again. Nathan Stiedowe was dead. She'd killed him herself. He was gone for ever and he was never coming back. He could never hurt anyone again. Dana had made damn sure of that when she'd put two bullets into his kneecaps and another into his gut.

Still, for a moment there she couldn't help but wonder . . .

Dana shook her head again. The thought was absolutely ridiculous. She didn't need to be afraid of Nathan Stiedowe any more. Her brother wasn't coming back to finish off what he'd started. *Couldn't* come back. He was *dead*. She'd watched him die from no more than five feet away. Had *enjoyed* watching the bastard die.

When Dana's vision finally cleared, her gaze homed

in on the tiny script located in the lower right-hand corner of the photograph:

Grafx, '04

'It's an old picture,' she said, refocusing her vision to make sure she was telling the truth. 'It's not recent. This picture was taken seven years ago.'

Brown finally saw the writing for himself. He lifted an arm and wiped at his profusely sweating forehead with the back of his right wrist. 'That's the largest school-photograph company in the country. They did my own school pictures when I was a kid.'

'Mine too.'

Hard as it was for her to do, Dana forced herself to stay in the moment, to process the information and not go hurtling back into her shattered past. There wasn't time for that now. A boy's life could be on the line here. Probably was. She took in another deep breath. It helped.

Despite her initial shock at seeing the photograph, after a moment or two of further thought Dana realised that she shouldn't have been all that surprised by the discovery. Not really. Psychopathic serial killers like this one almost always challenged law enforcement directly at some point. It was part of their collective MO, part of their shared psychosis.

Although the nine-millimetre bullet and the boy's photograph were new additions to the collage of horrifying images that mapped out the Chessboard Killer's twisted outlook on the world, the chess book itself wasn't. Instead, much like the other books discovered in this long-running series of brutal murders, the biography of renowned English chess master Amos Burn seemed to be *this* killer's version of a letter to the police. His way of teasing Dana and Brown. Of taunting them. Of daring them to match wits with him. By placing the bullet on the table and the boy's photograph inside the chess book's pages, he'd just underscored that grisly challenge.

Challenge accepted.

Dana bit down gently on her lower lip – an unfortunate habit she'd formed in grade school and hadn't quite gotten over yet – while she tried to think things through. Wasn't easy. Still, she knew that while psychopaths like the one she and Brown were after at the moment tended to be much more organised than their sociopath counterparts – believing themselves smarter than everyone else in the world and completely invulnerable to capture – it was *precisely* that kind of narcissism that usually led to their downfalls. Sooner or later he'd make a mistake, but how many more victims needed to die before he did? They couldn't afford to let him keep calling all the shots. They *had* to get a break, and soon. The media were angry, New Yorkers were angry – frightened and angry – and it was up to Dana and Brown to put a stop to all this.

A few years back, Dana had attended a symposium on serial killers conducted by the staff of the FBI's famed Behavioral Analysis Unit. She'd learned a lot. Almost as much as she'd learned in her days as an eager-beaver student back at the Academy, back when she'd been just another wide-eyed, bushy-tailed kid who'd fervently believed that each murder could be solved if only you put enough time and energy into the investigations.

Unfortunately for Dana, however, she wasn't a kid any more. Far from it. Like it or not, she was old enough now to understand that sometimes the good guys lost these heartbreaking games – a little too often for her taste.

The symposium had hammered home the point that serial murder was neither a new nor a uniquely American phenomenon. Serial murderers had been chronicled around the world dating back to ancient times. And while it certainly received far more than its fair share of attention in the headlines, this type of murder was also a relatively rare phenomenon, estimated to account for less than one per cent of all murders committed in any given year. Still, there was a macabre interest in the topic that far exceeded its scale, generating scores of articles, books and movies on the subject each year.

The broad-based public fascination with serial killers had begun in the late 1880s, when Jack the Ripper had ruthlessly murdered five prostitutes in the Whitechapel area of London. Since then, much of the general public's knowledge about serial murder had come from Hollywood, which had never exactly been known as the world's most *reliable* source of information. Titillating storylines had been created to heighten the interest of audiences rather than to accurately portray serial murder. But fact and fiction were two very different things.

Dana reached into her purse and removed a sterile pair of tweezers from their plastic casing before leaning down to pluck the boy's photograph off the carpet. She held it up so that both she and Brown could see it, then turned and placed it on the coffee table, directly next to the chess biography.

Turning back to the crime-scene technicians in the room, she raised her voice so that everyone in the apartment could hear her clearly. 'OK, guys,' she said. 'Listen up, and listen up good. I want plenty of shots of this photograph on the table. Does anyone here have a laptop with an Internet connection?'

The photographer who'd been shooting the chess book raised his hand. 'I do, ma'am.'

'Great. Could you download a couple of shots to your laptop and email them to us?'

'Of course. Not a problem at all. What's your email?'

Dana gave the man her and Brown's email addresses. 'Make them good shots,' she said. 'No fuzziness. Plenty of detail.'

'You got it.'

As the photographer readied his equipment, Dana plucked the bullet off the table with the tweezers and deposited it into a plastic evidence bag before sliding the chess book into an oversized Manila envelope and tagging both pieces of evidence. She'd deal with the little boy's photograph in just a minute, after the forensic photographer had completed his assigned task to her satisfaction.

When she'd finished cataloguing the bullet and the chess biography Dana turned back to Brown and felt the familiar and addictive thrill of the chase begin to grip her innermost being. This was the part of the job she *never* grew tired of: the chance to level the playing field. The chance to even up the score on behalf of the weak and innocent. The chance to actually do something meaningful with her life.

'We'll get the photograph out to the media in just a bit,' she said, 'but first I want to see if we can identify the boy in the picture. For all we know, this could be some kind of trick, something planted to distract us. Maybe we're getting closer to him now. Maybe he's feeling the heat. I don't know. But what I *do* know is that I don't want the entire city getting into even more of a panic over this. If we're wrong about the Chessboard Killer going after kids now – if he has some other angle to his game – then the public-school system is going to shut down cold for no good reason. No mother in her right mind would ever send her child out into harm's way if there's even the slightest possibility of abduction, so we need to be absolutely certain of this first.'

Brown nodded. 'Good point. And we'll need to find out if the picture is connected to Stephanie Mann in some way.'

Brown turned and grabbed a passing uniform by the shoulder. Although the NYPD had initially resented the

FBI's appearance on the case, petty jealousies had been put aside for the greater good. Too many people had died for the boundary-protecting to continue. One of the only good things to have come out of the case. 'Do we have an NOK on Stephanie Mann yet?' Brown asked.

The silver-haired officer – obviously a long-time veteran of the force judging by the insignia on his sleeve – shook his head. 'Not yet, sir. We ran her Social Security number but there's no living family we can find. Both her parents died in a car crash in 1996. Never married.'

'Any kids?' Brown asked.

'Not that we know of, sir.'

Brown nodded. 'Well, keep working on it. Get back to me as soon as you find out anything.'

'Yes, sir.'

When the uniform had moved away, Brown turned back to Dana. 'What's bugging me is why the killer put the photograph inside the book in the first place. Seems like a pretty dumb move to leave that door wide open. And what's up with the bullet? He's never done anything like this before, never left behind this much evidence. Other than the books, he's kept pretty much to himself the entire time. It's been a successful pattern for him so far. Why risk exposure now?'

Dana shrugged. It was a good question, but one to which she didn't have the answer. 'I don't know,' she admitted. 'Maybe he's fucking with us. Maybe he's getting bored with our lack of progress. Maybe he wants to point us in the right direction this time. Could be anything, really. We know a lot about the psychology of killers, but there's still plenty we don't know. It's an evolving science.'

Brown nodded. Although he'd been an FBI agent for almost as long as Dana had, he'd initially worked in securities fraud before transferring over to serial homicide a few years earlier. So just as Dana's mentor, Crawford Bell, had taught her, she was now teaching Brown.

Dana felt a lump form in her throat at the thought of Crawford. She tried to swallow it but that didn't work. For one terrifying moment, she almost let herself give in completely to the memory of him, of the unspeakable manner in which her mentor and former partner had died. But she compartmentalised the thought quickly. She needed to. If she let herself remember Crawford now, she was pretty sure she'd break down and start crying her eyes out right there in the middle of the apartment. Not exactly the best way to inspire confidence among the troops.

She knew Crawford would understand if he were still alive.

Dana took in a fresh lungful of air and finished composing herself. Luckily for her, Brown was a wonderful student in every respect, putting aside his ego whenever it was necessary to catch a killer – which hadn't always been the case with some of the other law-enforcement personnel she'd worked with over the course of her career. Hell, Brown was a wonderful *man* in general.

She just wished he hadn't lied to her about his past.

Brown asked, 'Still, why would the killer want to make things more interesting for himself, Dana? He's been getting away scot-free up to this point. Why flirt with getting caught now? I still don't understand it.'

Dana brushed off the thought of Brown's dishonesty, which had been more a sin of omission than one of commission. Now was not the time to mourn what might have been. Not when a child's life could be in danger.

'Serial killers are narcissists by nature,' Dana said, pulling off her gloves with a loud elastic snapping noise. 'Deep down inside, they *want* to be recognised for their efforts. Want us to know just how smart they are.'

Dana balled up her gloves in her right hand and used her other one to tuck a loose strand of short blonde hair behind her left ear, feeling a disconcerting sense of déjà vu. Much like sadists, intelligent killers were certainly nothing new to them, either. She and Brown had faced much the same problem while chasing down the Cleveland Slasher the previous year. That maddening case had nearly driven Dana into early retirement – not to mention complete insanity – but now she was more determined than ever to catch killers. To catch the bad guys who hurt innocent people. If not her, then who? The Bureau had invested a lot of time and money in her career, and she felt the need to pay them back. Besides, without the FBI in her life, what else did she have left?

Not much. Especially not with what she'd learned recently about Brown's past. Not too long ago she'd thought her partner the kind of man with whom she might be able to spend the rest of her life. Not so much any more.

Brown's voice brought her back. 'So, where should we go from here?'

Dana checked her watch. The next step in processing crime scenes was to interview possible witnesses, but since this building's last resident had been rudely evicted by the Chessboard Killer that wasn't an option here.

'All we can do now is go with what we've got,' Dana said. 'Let's head over to the photography studio and take a look, make sure we're not chasing a false lead.' While they waited for the NYPD to come up with a next of kin on Stephanie Mann, they needed to explore all other avenues of investigation. Time was of the essence here and they couldn't afford to waste a single minute. People were still dying and that needed to stop. *Now*. 'I doubt the killer himself works for or frequents the place, but for some reason or another he wants our eyeballs in that direction. Let's accommodate him.'

'What if it's a trick, though?' Brown asked. 'Like you said earlier – what if it's a diversionary tactic of some sort? What if he's setting us up?'

Dana shook her head, knowing in her gut that it wasn't likely. In her heart of hearts, she knew that the Chessboard Killer wanted to stretch out these bloody games for as long as possible. It was how he got his sick thrills. How they *all* got their sick thrills. So there was no way in hell he'd shoot his load right out of the gate. Didn't suit his style. No, he'd wait until the timing was exactly right so that he could inflict the maximum amount of collateral damage right along with the big reveal.

'I don't think so,' Dana said. 'Not yet, at least. He put the photograph in the book and the bullet on the table because he wants us in the game from the beginning this time. Wants to go head-to-head with us now. It's actually a good thing for us. Maybe we won't be operating completely blind this time.' All take and no give.

Brown removed his paper mask and crumpled it up in his fist, shoving it deep into his pocket. His expression had gone grim now as his own anger boiled up inside him. The frustrations of the case had clearly gotten the better of him, too, and Dana knew exactly how he felt. It was almost as if they'd been banging their heads up against a thick concrete wall the entire time.

'I just hope we're up to the task this time,' Brown said, shaking his head in disgust. 'I'm getting sick and tired of this shit.'

Dana stared back down at Stephanie Mann's battered corpse, which crime-scene personnel had now freed from its tethers and were readying for removal from the apartment. She frowned. 'What are you guys doing?'

The lead tech glanced up. 'Dr Carlton just called and said she got caught up with something else. Told us to meet her over at the lab.'

Dana grimaced as the man zipped Stephanie Mann into a blue body bag made of industrial-strength rubber that had CORONER'S OFFICE stencilled in perfect white letters across the front.

Stephanie Mann's empty eye sockets seemed to stare back at Dana, almost as though the murdered woman were attempting to say her final goodbyes to a world that had never really cared about her in the first place. Then, as the zip closed, her face disappeared completely.

Shifting her gaze back to Brown, Dana blew out a slow breath and said, 'Me, too, Jeremy. I'm getting sick and tired of this shit, too.'

CHAPTER FIVE

The day only got worse from there.

As soon as they left the condemned apartment building, Dana and Brown were met immediately by an army of press surging up against a hastily constructed police line. Dana shook her head in irritation and cursed under her breath. 'Goddamn it.'

Great. Same faces; different day.

While she and Brown would need the media's help at some point during the day if they failed to turn up any promising leads over at the photography studio, the simple fact of the matter was that Dana really didn't feel like dealing with them right now. Right now, they were just getting in her way.

As usual, the loudest of them all was Nick Brandt from the *New York Post*, a tabloid-style journalist who'd almost single-handedly resurrected the 'Chessboard Killer' moniker. Brandt's considerable stomach bulged against a wrinkled white dress shirt, unbuttoned at the neck. Short sleeves exposed Popeye forearms covered in thick black hair. The uneven ends of an unfashionably skinny tie hung four inches above his protruding belt line.

Dishevelled from head to toe, Brandt was the very

picture of a bare-knuckle reporter straight out of a central-casting call for a modern-day reboot of *All The President's Men*. He was the kind of guy who asked no quarter and gave none – *ever*. Didn't even give a penny. Way too cheap for that. Sweating heavily, he was stealing quick peeks down the blouse of Lisa Morales, a former model turned television personality who'd increased Channel Two's ratings by thirty per cent through sheer virtue of her tight-fitting racy outfits. More eye candy than any sort of real journalist.

Next to Brandt and Morales stood Raymond Garcia, the twenty-seven-year-old investigative reporter wunderkind from the *New York Times*. A nice guy most of the time but given to occasional fits of petulance whenever he suspected Dana and Brown of holding out on him. Garcia's trademark red bow tie stood out against a blue shirt and yellow braces, harking back to a long-ago era in the ink-slinging business. In the wintertime, Garcia was exactly the kind of earnest young man who favoured wearing tweed jackets with leather patches stitched into the elbows. Dana wouldn't have been in the least bit surprised to find out that he owned a pipe of some sort, probably a meerschaum.

Twenty other reporters joined these three to complete the boisterous crowd, bumping shoulders and jostling each others' cameras out of position in the squirming fray as they tried to clear some space for themselves and ensure the best angles for their own shots. Worse, still more reporters were making their way up to the police line with every passing second, parking their cars at haphazard angles out on the busy street and hurrying up to the commotion with pens and notebooks in their hands.

Dana loved New York City like few other places – had started to consider it her second home – but there was nothing quite as maddening as the press in the Big Apple. Cleveland couldn't hold a *candle* to this sort of display. Whenever Dana dealt with the press in New York City, it always reminded her of feeding time at the zoo. And the monkeys looked *very* hungry today, indeed. *Starving*, even. And when it came to this particular story, they were downright *insatiable*. No matter how much information Dana and Brown fed them, they never stopped clamouring for more. Not that Dana blamed them for their zeal. After all, when it came to writing about serial killers and the details of their horrific crimes, it didn't come much juicier than this. Exactly the sort of headline-grabbing story that could make or break your entire career.

Despite Dana's irritation with the reporters' presence, she tried not to let it show as she and Brown walked quickly down the cracked sidewalk and directly into the barrage of shouted questions that rained down on them from all directions. Flashbulbs popped and television cameras whirred. Boom microphones attached to the ends of long aluminium poles were lowered just over their heads.

'Agent Whitestone, Agent Brown! Nick Brandt, *New York Post*. Has the Chessboard Killer struck again?'

'Where's the public information officer?' Raymond

Garcia chimed in. Upon hearing his voice, Dana knew at once that today must be one of Garcia's bad days. Maybe his editors were on his ass about something. Maybe his underwear was riding up on him. Dana didn't know. But she *did* know that he didn't seem to be in any sort of mood to walk away without prying out some new information. 'We need answers, Agent Whitestone,' Garcia went on, his voice carrying the whiny edge of a spoiled child's. 'We *deserve* answers. It's our right as members of the press. Our tax dollars pay your salaries. Quit avoiding us. How many more people need to die before the FBI finally stops this maniac?'

For her part, Lisa Morales just stood there looking pretty. It was what she got paid to do, and she was damn good at her job.

Dana and Brown kept their heads down and ducked quickly into the narrow alleyway running along the west side of the decrepit apartment building. Brown pulled back a length of broken chain-link fence and held it open for Dana before slipping in himself through the criss-crossed metal. Fortunately, several uniformed cops moved forward at once to hold back the panting press corps. Thank God for small favours. If nothing else, Dana didn't want the media to find out what model of car she and Brown were driving. Up to this point in the investigation, they'd already had to switch vehicles six times, and it had begun to make life a little harder on them than it should have been.

Besides, Dana knew for a fact that it was much more

advantageous to ignore altogether the questions from the media than it was to feed them yet another statement chock-full of evasion but sorely lacking any real substance. Not to mention her intense dislike of Nick Brandt, a dislike that had started to border on hatred. The guy had gotten all the way underneath her skin, and it had come to the point now where Dana could hardly stand the sight of him any more. And who could blame her? Brandt had made something of a personal crusade out of skewering her and Brown in print, and Dana didn't especially enjoy being referred to as 'the Queen of Doublespeak'. For his part, Brown probably didn't care very much for his characterisation as her faithful lapdog, either. It was one thing to want information – like Raymond Garcia had said, it was the reporters' right as members of the press and their tax dollars *did* pay her and Brown's salary – but it was something totally different to be a complete jerk in the way you went about it. So no more grist for Brandt's mill. Not today, at least. His less-annoying colleagues would just have to suffer right alongside the loudmouth. As far as Dana was concerned, one bad apple had spoiled the entire barrel.

'The vultures got here quick this time,' Brown said, shaking his head and checking his watch as they walked deeper into the alleyway before coming to a stop next to a broken-down old generator spilling an impressive collection of copper wiring from its guts. 'I swear to God, sometimes I think they can smell a dead body from clear across town. A lot of these guys would make kick-ass feds. Are we still recruiting?'

Dana was just about to answer him when the cellphone in her pocket rang. She held up a finger to Brown and motioned for him to wait while she dug it out.

Flipping open the phone, she placed it to her ear. 'Whitestone.'

A woman's voice came across the line, clear and strong. 'Dana, it's Maggie Flynn in DC. How are you doing today?'

Dana stuck a finger in her right ear to block out the sound of traffic zipping past on the busy road forty yards away. Though faint, the discontented grumblings of the press were still audible even here, too.

Dana had worked with Flynn, an FBI lab tech, during the Cleveland Slasher case, and they'd later struck up a bond at a Bureau Christmas event. Though it wasn't technically procedure, Flynn usually kept an eye out for the evidence in Dana's cases. Normally those sorts of things were handled like bread in a grocery store: first in, first out. But like so many other things in life, it wasn't necessarily *what* you knew, it was *who* you knew. Not always the fairest set-up in the world, to be sure, but it could prove useful at times. Like right now.

'I'm fine, Maggie,' Dana said. 'How are you?'

'Great. Listen, I think we might have found something interesting for you here.'

'What's that?'

Flynn cleared her throat. 'A possible pattern the Chessboard Killer used in one of his games; a pattern we hadn't realised before.'

Dana sucked in a sharp breath. An electric jolt of anticipation shot through her.

If a new pattern had been discovered in one of their killer's games, it could turn out to be a huge break for them. A monumental one. From there, she and Brown could probably compile a brand-new psychological profile on the killer – one that would with luck narrow down the pool of possible suspects, which currently numbered several million citizens of New York City. Sadly, the profile they had right now looked eerily like an exact version of the list of misconceptions that Dana had been warned against at the symposium: white male; late thirties or early forties; above-average intelligence; social misfit. In other words: almost as worthless as the paper that it had been printed on. 'What's the pattern?' Dana asked.

Flynn shuffled some papers on her side of the connection. 'It's in the Bobby Fischer case,' she said. 'The one where the killer murdered all his victims with a nine-millimetre handgun. Do you recall that one?'

Dana's skin crawled. Just four floors above her head rested a nine-millimetre bullet in a plastic evidence bag, waiting patiently for shipment down to DC for further forensic examination. Was the killer deliberately trying to tie the two cases together for some reason? And, if so, for *what* reason?

Dana fought off a sudden chill despite the unseasonably warm weather. A high-pressure system working its way up the eastern seaboard had turned yesterday's black skies a brilliant blue, almost as if to tease the residents of the Empire State into believing that summertime was almost here. But Dana knew the pleasant weather wouldn't last much longer. It never did in April in New York City. Sooner or later, the Big Apple would be plunged right back into the kind of frigid early-spring temperatures that made New Yorkers' fingers ache and their toes curl up, even through their heavy gloves and boots.

And of course Dana recalled the Bobby Fischer case. How could she ever forget it? During that game, their killer had put a bullet into the back of a seventeen-year-old boy's head with a Russian-made Makarov pistol, smashing the poor kid's skull like a dropped eggshell. Not to mention into the skulls of eight other people: one for each bullet that the gun held.

'That's something I'll never forget, Maggie,' Dana said. 'What's the link?'

Flynn cleared her throat again. 'Well, while the gun that he used was the same in each one of the killings, judging from the bullets we recovered from the bodies, he alternated ammunition.'

'What do you mean by that?'

Just then, a loud bang exploded in Dana's ear. Spinning around frantically, she swept her terrified gaze up and down the long alleyway, behind trash cans, overhead to the ledges of the buildings sandwiching them. Her heartbeat thudded painfully. Her vision clouded, then cleared again in a flash. All movement around her slowed to a halt.

But Brown only lifted an eyebrow at her.

Maggie Flynn came back on the line a moment later. 'Sorry about that, Dana. I dropped the phone.'

Dana let out a nervous laugh and tried to ignore the pounding of her pulse. She was getting paranoid, she knew that. But could anyone blame her? With all the killings she'd witnessed in her lifetime, there was certainly plenty for her to be paranoid about. That was what you got when a vicious serial killer had targeted you personally – as Nathan Stiedowe had done to her.

'Anyway,' Flynn went on, 'in the first murder in the Bobby Fischer case, the ammunition came from a company known as American Eagle. Located out of San Francisco. Ninety-five grain, full metal jacket casings. In the second murder, the ammunition came from a Texas company called PS Grand. Brass-cased bullets with boxer primer. In the third murder, it was the American Eagle ammo again. And so on and so forth, all the way down the line.'

Dana widened her pale blue eyes. Still, she forced herself to rein in her excitement. Above all else, she knew that she needed to stay level here, to not go off half-cocked and expect too much. Although she wanted desperately to believe this could be just the major break they'd been waiting for – the one that would finally crack this maddening case wide open – she knew for a fact that such hoping wasn't a good idea. From uncooperative witnesses to unreliable data to just plain bad luck, there was no point in counting your chickens before they'd hatched.

That said, sometimes catching a killer really *could* be just that easy.

Dana's mind whirred as her investigative brain sprang into action, processing the new information. 'We could subpoena the ammunition companies' sales lists,' she said quickly, finally allowing herself to become excited with the idea. 'The killer might be in there somewhere. If we're lucky, it might even be just a simple process of elimination from there. It'll take some time and plenty of paperwork, but we really don't have very much else to go on right now. It could prove a worthwhile effort.'

Flynn's response brought her back down to earth. 'Maybe, Dana, but don't forget there's quite an active secondary market out there for ammunition. Gun shows, swap meets, unscrupulous online vendors with their headquarters located overseas – a hundred other places like that where ammunition is bought and sold without much of a paper trail to follow. We'll delegate the task of combing through the companies' sales lists to some Academy students, but although this lead sounds promising it probably won't yield any immediate results.'

A fresh surge of annoyance engulfed Dana. When were they ever going to catch a break in this case? A *real* break? One that didn't come with a list of caveats longer than her arm?

Dana tried not to sound grouchy. It wasn't easy. 'Thanks, Maggie. That *does* sound promising, but I'm not going to lie to you – I was hoping to get something I could work with right *now*. I've got real problems over here. And there's a bunch of innocent people here who have it a lot worse than I do. One boy in particular.'

'How's that?'

Dana drew a deep breath. As quickly as she could, she brought Flynn up to speed on her and Brown's recent discovery of the boy's photograph tucked away inside the pages of the chess biography on Amos Burn.

Flynn clucked sympathetically when she'd finished. 'That's horrifying. But hang in there, OK? If anyone can solve this case, I know it's you. Everyone down here in Washington has a lot of faith in you.'

'Thanks, Maggie. That helps.'

'Don't mention it. Anyway, not to change the subject too drastically or anything, but are you still coming to the Christmas party this year? I'd really love to see you again.'

Dana's mind barely processed the question. Her brain was already somewhere else. An unformed thought tickled the back of her skull. But then started to slip away.

Dana exhaled in frustration. The older she got, the less it seemed that she could count on her powers of what had once been almost total recall. The photographic memory that had always been her professional trademark in life, her greatest claim to fame in the world of law enforcement, had been reduced to a simple hit-or-miss proposition now. Sadly, this time it was a miss. And then some.

She just hoped that someone didn't die because of it.

'My attendance at the Christmas party depends

entirely on whether or not we can catch this guy first, Maggie,' Dana said. 'Yes if yes – and no if no.'

'What if I put in a good word for you with Santa Claus? Would that help you out any?'

Dana sighed. The unformed thought was totally gone now. Maybe it would come back later. Maybe it was gone for ever. Only time would tell.

Too bad time was the one thing they didn't have here.

'If I have to wait that long before we catch this guy, the only thing I'll be getting for Christmas is a nice big fat sack of coal,' Dana said. 'It's only April now.'

The FBI lab tech groaned. 'That reminds me – I still need to file my tax returns. Have you done yours yet? Deadline's only a week away, you know. I wouldn't want Uncle Sam coming after me. The IRS building is right down the street. Hell, I can practically see it right from my window. It wouldn't take the government very long to find me. I'm just a sitting duck over here.'

Flynn paused. Then, with a sigh, she added, 'That's what it's all about in the end, isn't it, Dana? Death and taxes. Nothing else even stands a chance.'

Dana felt the entire weight of the world resting on her slender shoulders. She needed a hot shower desperately, something to loosen up the twisted muscles in her back. She also needed a vacation somewhere warm. A fruity drink and a sandy beach were probably just what she needed at the moment. Just lean her body all the way back in her nylon beach chair, stick her toes in the warm sand in front of her and swirl a plastic straw around in a rapidly melting strawberry daiquiri, letting all her many troubles simply drift away out to sea on a soft ocean breeze. She'd happily pay *double* taxes if she and Brown could erase the first part of that death-and-taxes equation and finally put the Chessboard Killer out of commission once and for all. She'd consider it money well spent.

'Sure seems like it sometimes,' Dana said. 'Death and taxes are everyone's best friends. They're the only constants anyone can count on.'

She waited a beat, then added, 'Hey, Maggie? Is there any way you could overnight me the autopsy photos in the Bobby Fischer murders? I'd like to take another look at them now that we've got this new information to work with.'

'Of course, Dana. I'll do it just as soon as we hang up here.'

Dana chatted with Flynn for another minute or two before switching off the phone and turning to Brown. He was keying something into his own cellphone.

Brown flipped it off and put it into his pocket when Dana cleared her throat loudly in order to get his attention. He looked at her expectantly.

Dana was just about to fill him in on what Flynn had told her when the unformed thought she'd been struggling with suddenly came back. Her blood ran cold.

A look of concern flashed across Brown's handsome face. He reached out and touched her shoulder lightly. 'Are you OK, Dana? All the colour drained out of your face just now. What's going on?'

Dana stared up at her partner. At five feet, four inches

tall, she stared up at practically everybody. Adrenalin pumped hot through her veins. All the tiny little hairs on the back of her neck stood up. She found it difficult to breathe.

Dana shook herself and shuddered for the third time in just the past hour. She knew this sensation. She knew it well. She'd felt it before. Something of her very own 'spidey sense'.

And whenever she felt it, it usually meant someone was about to die a horrible death.

'What is it?' Brown demanded. 'Just tell me already.'

Dana tried to calm her shaking hands. No use. They wouldn't stop trembling.

She paused to fix the idea in her mind before finally sharing it with him. 'I think we may have been looking at these murders the wrong way the entire time,' she said, her voice barely louder than a whisper.

Brown arched an eyebrow at her. 'What do you mean?'

Dana closed her eyes and let herself go with the idea. To hell with it. If she was wrong, so be it. She'd deal with the fallout later if and when it came to that.

'I think we might be dealing with *two* serial killers here, Jeremy,' Dana said, holding Brown's stare. 'Not just one. And, if I'm not mistaken, I think they could be working together.'

PART II

ADVANCING PAWNS

'When you see a good move, look for a better one.'

Emanuel Lasker, German chess player, mathematician and philosopher who reigned as World Chess Champion for twenty-seven years.

CHAPTER SIX

Wednesday, 12:58 p.m.

The winner of their final match was decided with the simple flip of a very uncommon coin in the ornate marble-tiled lobby of the Fontainebleau Hotel in downtown Manhattan.

The proceedings were largely ceremonial, of course. Little more than pomp and circumstance, really. Both men had long ago agreed to see these matches all the way through to their inevitable conclusions no matter what the outcomes of the flips. It was what they always did. The very nature of their games. The very nature of their beast. At the very heart of what both were trying to accomplish here.

Sergei Michalovic removed his right palm from the top of his left hand and held the result over the table so that the man seated on the other side could see. Positioned against faint blue veins and pale white skin stretched tight across prominent bones, a stunning depiction of Lady Liberty rendered in breathtaking bas-relief glinted in the soft light overhead. She was holding a flaming torch in one hand and an olive branch in the other. War in her right hand, peace in her left.

Michalovic grinned like an excited kid on Christmas morning who'd just discovered a shiny new bicycle stashed beneath the tree. Exactly what he'd asked for but hadn't actually expected to receive. A joyous occasion if ever there were one. Something to be welcomed with open arms. Michalovic had plenty to smile about, too. Like each one of their games, this most current affair would no doubt prove to be an all-out war. A very *bloody* war. And since he would win again this time – twice in a row now, following a couple of very painful losses – he knew that peace didn't stand a snowball's chance in hell.

Michalovic's dazzling porcelain veneers nearly blinded his opponent across the table. 'Heads,' the Russian pronounced with satisfaction.

Through a lot of hard work on Michalovic's part – not to mention more than a little assistance from a nineteen-year-old Columbia University undergrad with the sort of gravity-defying body that, were it not for his enormous wealth, he wouldn't have been able to get within even arm's-reach of – the sixty-something's slight foreign accent had almost completely disappeared now. Which would prove quite important throughout the ups and downs of this final match.

'It looks like I'll be the victor again this time, Edward,' Michalovic went on cheerfully. 'That's certainly no reason for you to lose heart, though. Every dog has its day, right? Isn't that what you Americans say? I swear to God – your people have the most wonderful expressions. I love each and every last one of them dearly.'

Edward J. O'Hara III smiled back at his adversary. He could almost *feel* the luminescence emanating from his own face. Was he actually *glowing*? He wouldn't have been in the least bit surprised to find out that he was. Honestly, how much more *fun* could this possibly get? Days like this one were precisely what he lived for. Once again, all the hopes and dreams of a brand-new season had put an unmistakable spring in his step and a gleeful smile upon his ruddy face.

'Is it the people you love, Sergei, or is it their wonderful expressions?' O'Hara asked.

'Why, both, of course.'

'Of course.'

O'Hara leaned back in his chair and ran his gaze thoughtfully over Michalovic's chiselled countenance, studying his opponent carefully. The Russian's winsome grin had no doubt cost him somewhere north of a hundred thousand dollars and, from the looks of things, it appeared to have been well worth it, too. It really was very good work, very natural-looking.

O'Hara made a mental note to get the name of Michalovic's dentist before the two of them parted company today. No doubt the veneers would cost him a hell of a lot more than would a shiny new bicycle, but the quality of the work probably justified the hefty expenditure. After all, it took a great deal of money to buy the good things in this life, didn't it?

Of course it did. It also took a great deal of money to buy the *bad* things in this life.

O'Hara sat up straighter in his seat and felt his skin

tingle with an almost erotic charge. The bad things that he and Michalovic bought were very bad, of course. But they could also prove quite advantageous when it came to the context of their special little games. For it was the bad things they bought that provided them with the tools necessary to get their respective jobs done, completely unimpeded by the shackles of any irritating financial constraints.

O'Hara leaned forward in his chair and lifted his handcrafted five-hundred-dollar-a-glass port to his lips before taking a careful sip and setting the crystal stemware back down on the linen-covered table, luxuriating in the taste of the expensive wine. 'By the way, please try to remember that you're the winner in name only so far, Sergei,' he said, straightening back up in his seat. 'There still remains the unresolved matter of the ten million dollars that's on the line here. We certainly can't forget about that. After all, we're not communists.'

The Russian chortled gently at the Irish-American's good-natured joke. How very satisfying it was for him to finally share company with a man who actually *got* him for once in his life. Didn't happen very often – and that would have been putting it mildly. And he knew for a fact that O'Hara wasn't at all concerned about the money. Not really. The five million dollars each of them had put up for the winner of this contest were strictly for fun. A little added bonus. Something to spice up their games that much more.

Not that their games needed any more spice, of course. Still, why should he and O'Hara settle for anything less than the very best? Why not employ all the bells and whistles at their disposal right from the very start this time? It wasn't as if they couldn't afford it. Quite the opposite, actually.

Both players were already very rich men – two of the wealthiest people in the entire world, in fact – so the ten-million-dollar prize reserved for the winner of this contest couldn't have bought them a single thing they didn't already possess. Certainly not the quality of the smiles plastered across their faces at the moment. Right now, it was Christmas morning on both sides of the table, and Michalovic liked that. He liked it a lot. Just the way things ought to be.

Michalovic smiled thinly across the table at his opponent. 'Why all the sudden worry, Edward?' he asked, clucking his tongue softly. 'It's not as though our *own* lives will be on the line here. Far from it. What would be the point in that? No, once again we'll be playing with house money on that count. Just like we always do. So just sit back and let it all unfold naturally, would you? Try to *enjoy* this.'

With that, Michalovic slipped the glittering twenty-dollar gold coin he'd used for the game's positioning flip back into the pocket of his expensive Armani dress slacks and twisted his torso to release a troublesome kink that was knotting up his lower back. Although in tremendous physical shape for a man of his age, the Russian was getting older now, and he realised that harsh fact of life a little more with each passing day. Therefore, he knew that he and O'Hara needed to make this last match one to remember. One for the ages. One for the history books. They might never get another chance like this again. So right from the very start this time, both himself and the man seated across the table – who at sixty-four years old was certainly no spring chicken himself – would need to push in all their chips and let them fall where they might. Winner take all.

Watching his opponent's movements, O'Hara lifted his bushy eyebrows and stared at his Russian counterpart. 'Not even a cover for it, eh, Sergei? Aren't you at all interested in protecting your investment?'

Michalovic narrowed his soft green eyes. 'Come again?'

O'Hara focused his own bright blue eyes in response, never having been the kind of man to be stared down very easily, not even by a monster like Michalovic. O'Hara's eyes were so clear as to appear almost transparent. Almost as though there was no soul stationed behind them.

'Come, now,' O'Hara went on, tutting. 'You're not really going to sit there and tell me that's not the Fenton example of the 1933 Saint-Gaudens Gold Double Eagle you've just tucked away in your pocket, are you?'

Michalovic looked surprised for a moment, and then he smiled again. Not much eluded the Irishman's hawkish gaze, did it? And that was precisely what he loved so much about the man. Furthermore, O'Hara had been right on the money with his astute observation – just like he always seemed to be. Good for him. After all, O'Hara would need to be at the very top of his game if he were to have any chance of besting a man of Michalovic's considerable skill level. And, besides, the coin in Michalovic's pocket was *exactly* what O'Hara had judged it to be.

Much like each of the men seated at the table, the 1933 Saint-Gaudens Double Eagle had a fascinating history behind it. A history that could never be erased no matter how much money was thrown in its direction. President Theodore Roosevelt had commissioned the original design in 1907, but Franklin D. Roosevelt had stopped the release of the 1933 edition when he'd taken the United States off the gold standard during the Great Depression. At one point, King Farouk of Egypt had owned the coin that currently nestled in Michalovic's pocket, eluding in the process the frantic confiscation efforts of the United States Secret Service, which had considered it stolen property rightfully belonging to the US Mint.

When Farouk had been deposed during a bloody military coup orchestrated by the charismatic rebel leader Anwar Sadat in 1952, the coin had appeared briefly on the market before disappearing once again. Forty years later, the British coin dealer Stephen Fenton had showed up with the Saint-Gaudens on the streets of the financial district in New York City, looking to sell. Unfortunately for Fenton, however, his little ploy hadn't worked out quite the way he'd planned. For it was then that – after a great deal of covert planning on its part – the Secret Service had finally nabbed the Saint-Gaudens in an elaborate sting operation.

From there, the celebrated coin's strange journey had only grown curiouser and curiouser. While Fenton and the United States government waged a fierce legal battle that would drag on in court for years, the specimen now resting in Michalovic's pocket was stored for safe keeping in the World Trade Center's treasury vaults until just two months before the terrorist attacks of 11 September 2001 – narrowly avoiding destruction on that infamous day. Fenton and the government had finally agreed to auction off the coin and split the proceeds down the middle.

Taking into account the standard fifteen per cent buyer's fee and the twenty dollars that the US Mint had demanded to replace the money it believed had been stolen from it all those years ago, the total cost of the Saint-Gaudens at its 2002 auction had eventually risen to a staggering seven million, five hundred and ninety thousand and twenty dollars. Over the course of the heated auction – which had taken nearly an hour and a half to complete – the unseen buyer had chosen to remain anonymous, making his expensive purchase through a proxy bidder in an effort to shield his identity from the prying eyes of the public.

Apparently, though, the mysterious buyer wasn't quite so anonymous any more. Not to O'Hara, at least. As a matter of fact, he was seated right there on the other side of the sturdy mahogany table.

Michalovic winked at the man whom he considered to be his first real friend in his new homeland. 'There's no point in buying toys if you can't play with them,

Edward,' he said, smiling more broadly now. 'Come on – you know that every bit as much as I do. It's what this great country of ours is all about. Hedonism. Luxuries. *Living*.'

'It's also about dying, Sergei,' O'Hara reminded the Russian gently. 'Don't ever forget about that. Anyway, let's have a look at the coin, shall we?'

Michalovic hesitated for a moment before reluctantly reaching back into his pocket to retrieve the Saint-Gaudens, resisting the urge to curse beneath his breath as he did so. In some ways, he knew, owning the Saint-Gaudens was like taking your brand-new baby for a carriage stroll through the park on a beautiful spring day. For some reason or other, everyone in the world thought they had the right to *touch* the goddamn thing with their germ-infested hands. Still, Michalovic didn't want to appear rude, so he leaned forward across the table and handed the coin over to O'Hara, who took it and immediately began to examine the glittering coin with a well-practised eye.

Michalovic leaned back in his chair again and steepled his fingers in front of his body while O'Hara manhandled his baby with dirty hands, trying to ignore the intense feeling of unease flooding through him. 'It's certainly a beautiful specimen,' he said, trying to sound casual about the whole thing but no doubt falling far short. 'One of the most beautiful coins in the entire world. There's certainly no denying that fact. And what you said earlier about life also being about dying is true as well, Edward. Then again, life is considered so much more valuable here in the United States, isn't it? Much like the Saint-Gaudens itself: a commodity to be treasured, not to be thrown away onto the trash heap of history without a second thought. Sadly, that's exactly what happens where I come from. But the two of us shall never spend lives thoughtlessly unless we're absolutely convinced of such an action's inherent goodness. I truly believe in my heart that what we're doing here is an honourable thing.'

O'Hara looked up from his careful examination of the Saint-Gaudens and nodded solemnly. 'As do I, Sergei. As do I.'

Michalovic leaned forward again while O'Hara resumed his careful appraisal of the coin. With an irritated sideways glance and an impatient gesture he shooed away a waiter who seemed unduly concerned with the level of their drinks. The tuxedoed man practically ran out of the lobby. Just another pawn in the game of life who couldn't help but quake in the presence of kings.

And Sergei Michalovic knew that was *exactly* what he and Edward O'Hara represented here in the United States. *Kings*. Their money made them nothing less.

The billionaire Russian shipping magnate had moved his base of operations out to the more inviting shores of America just two years earlier, but already he felt like a true citizen. Here things were much simpler when it came to dealing with and managing his vast and varied financial concerns. Simpler and altogether more appealing.

These days, there were for Michalovic no more smoky boardrooms full of men whose sweating and red-splotched faces he could hardly bear to look at. No more stuffing envelopes full of cash in order to grease the wheels on a particularly sticky transaction. No more hiring armed guards to stand watch over his bed every time he laid down his head to sleep at night – in either his sprawling Moscow estate, which featured no less than sixteen fountains decorating the glittering property, or in his much more conservative dacha out in the rolling countryside, where the day's water still came each morning from an antique outdoor hand-pump, regardless of the weather.

There were still back-room deals to be cut, of course: many, *many* back-room deals to be cut. But here in America that sort of thing lacked the cloak-and-dagger thrill of the Motherland back home, where getting caught in the act might mean having your throat slit in the dead of night by rough, no-nonsense men whose financial concerns were diametrically opposed to your own. In America, however, such dealings were almost trivial by comparison, conducted right out there in the open, with the details often hammered out in the harsh glare of the lights of television cameras that had been trained on the proceedings so that anyone who wanted to see could watch and discuss freely. That was capitalism for you and, as far as Sergei Michalovic was concerned, it was the very best economic system in the entire world.

Survival of the fittest. The cream always rises to the

top. The proof of the pudding could be found in the eating. The way it *should* be. And in a financial landscape populated by countless giants, he was among the biggest giants of them all.

The Russian found his best smile again at the comforting thought, then broadened it even further at the delicious anticipation of what lay ahead for himself and O'Hara. His dazzling grin provided a perfect complement to his athletic build, generally easygoing nature and carefully coiffed silver hair.

Back home in Mother Russia, where the Communist Party had experienced a frightening resurgence in popularity following the hopelessly failed policies of glasnost, these back-room dealings were usually considered to be tampering with the financial infrastructure of the country, to be going against the greater good. But here in America, it had simply become known as 'lobbying'.

Yes, life was definitely *good* in the United States, wasn't it? It certainly was. And it was about to get much, *much* better.

Or, at the very least, much more *interesting*.

These days, instead of stuffing envelopes full of financial incentives for use in the secretive and often deadly behind-the-scenes transactions that usually showcased the worst denizens and practices of Moscow's seedy underbelly, Michalovic simply wrote cheques to whichever politicians he thought might keep his best financial interests in mind once they'd been elected to public office.

Though the total cost varied from time to time, the individual price tags always remained roughly the same. Twenty-five grand for a state senator. Fifty grand for the governor. A hundred thousand dollars to gain favour with a member of the House of Representatives. For a quarter of a million dollars, you could buy yourself your very own junior United States senator – store him or her in your hip pocket for later use at the appropriate time – and for a quarter-million more you could purchase a senior one lock, stock and barrel. Bargain-basement prices, really, when you looked at things through the crystal-clear lens of unlimited wealth. And while the system wasn't quite perfect as it stood currently, the only real hitch that Michalovic could see was that the campaign contributions weren't tax-deductible. Not yet, anyway. Then again, you needed to remember who possessed the power to actually *change* those laws.

Politicians. The very same politicians whose campaign coffers Michalovic had grown so accustomed to stuffing.

Reaching underneath his chair, Michalovic straightened with a slight groan and slid across the table a box he'd wrapped by hand in plain brown butcher's paper and had tied up with a length of coarse string. 'A little gift for you, Edward,' he said, winking mischievously. 'Just a little something to welcome you to the table and start off the game right – even if it was *you* who happened to have the misfortune of drawing Black this time.'

O'Hara looked up from his intense appraisal of the

infamous Saint-Gaudens and casually slipped the glittering coin into one of his *own* pockets before reaching out across the table to take the box that the Russian was offering. Pulling the string on top that had been tied into a rudimentary bow, he once again marvelled at just how far he'd come in this life following a decidedly rocky start.

The descendant of Irish immigrants who'd come over to the United States in 1852, O'Hara had, through a series of both legal and illegal manoeuvres, expertly parlayed his father's modest local holdings into one of the largest real-estate corporations in the country since the old man's untimely death thirty years earlier – a death he soon planned to finally avenge.

If nothing else, Edward J. O'Hara III had always been a man with a *very* long memory.

That aside, O'Hara knew he'd done quite well for himself by anybody's standards, even when taking into account his relatively humble upbringing. Still, there was no way he felt anywhere near satisfied yet. As much as he possessed – in terms of both power and financial resources – he knew there was plenty of room for more.

And where was the surprise in that? Coming from a lineage of people who'd needed to flee their home country because of the devastating Irish potato famine more than a century and a half earlier – leaving behind their possessions and loved ones in a desperate rush to find a better life in America – he knew there was *always* room for more.

Still, however unsatisfied with his present standing in

the world he might be, O'Hara actually had plenty to be proud about when it came to his long and distinguished career. He'd started out small and had grown his businesses patiently until he now found himself one of the richest men in the entire United States. As a matter of fact – according to the latest *Forbes 400* list of America's richest people – he was now the three hundred and eighty-fifth wealthiest person in the country. Not too bad for a former street tough who'd had to fight for every single nickel he'd ever earned. And with his recent acquisition of nine new parking garages scattered throughout the five boroughs of New York City, he was already positioning himself to rise even higher when the next *Forbes* list came out in June.

O'Hara wasn't a billionaire like Michalovic quite yet, but he was close enough to comfortably run in the same social circles without arousing feelings of jealousy or contempt. It was the best of both worlds, really. He could safely swim with the sharks while quietly bolstering his own position. Completely confident in their financial superiority over him, the billionaires he mingled with tended to pay him little if any attention at all, considering him a minimal threat at best. But that was exactly where their biggest mistake lay, precisely what would lead to their ultimate downfalls. Someday, O'Hara knew, the situation would be reversed. Someday it would be *him* at the very top of the heap, the Great White who dominated the nurse-shark competition all around him with row after row of his sharp, jagged teeth. And why not? As far as O'Hara was concerned, it was the only sensible option, the only choice that seemed to take logic into the equation. For in his world, second-best had always only meant that you were the first loser.

It had been that way ever since his father's unscrupulous business partners had tried to muscle the old man out of his rightful share in a vacant lot in the Bronx that had eventually been turned into a city park through the magic of eminent domain. Armed with hungry bellies, baseball bats and bicycle chains, a teenaged Edward and a few of his like-minded friends had paid each one of his father's business partners late-night visits in order to remind them that the O'Hara family would not be pushed around so easily. While it hadn't been the most romantic introduction to the business world, O'Hara had nonetheless always considered it his debut in the arena of high finance, his first bold plunge into a financial tank teeming with bloodthirsty predators who seemed intent upon sucking dry every last one of his precious liquid resources. So far, the only real difference that O'Hara could see between the streets and the boardrooms seemed to be the fact that the men involved favoured wearing immaculately tailored designer suits rather than dirty blue jeans while they stabbed each other viciously in the back with their sharp knives.

The brown wrapping paper fell away from the package to reveal a hinged container of Cuban Cohiba Behike cigars – the rarest and most expensive cigars in the world. O'Hara widened his eyes in genuine appre -

ciation. Long a cigar aficionado, he knew that these Behikes were an extremely limited edition, with just four thousand of them produced back in 2006. To his knowledge, no one had even *smoked* one yet, preferring instead to save the pricey tobacco for their own personal collections, or perhaps to be used as an investment that would almost certainly turn a tidy profit at a later date.

With a price tag of four hundred and forty dollars a cigar, O'Hara also knew that Michalovic would have needed to pay at least ten times that amount to secure a box on the lucrative and very secretive black market in Europe. The American government's embargo on Cuban goods made it the only way to obtain the items concerned. Instituted in 1960 and strengthened in 1962 by Fidel Castro's communist government, the embargo made even the simple *possession* of the cigars quite illegal in the United States.

Then again, he and his good friend Sergei Michalovic had never been the kind of men who'd ever been especially concerned with following the law should it happen to pose a direct conflict with their best financial interests, had they?

Of course not. Here in America – in the land of the free and the home of the brave – you were only as guilty as your bank account said you were. And O'Hara's bank account said that he was guilty of absolutely *nothing* – with the obvious exception of playing like a finely tuned fiddle the system that had fought for so long to keep him and his loved ones under its oppressive thumb.

And perhaps – just *perhaps* – the Irish-American had also been guilty of a minor case of shoplifting just now.

O'Hara smiled, knowing full well that Michalovic had seen him pilfer the Saint-Gaudens. He'd taken the thing right from underneath the Russian's nose. But O'Hara also knew beyond a shadow of a doubt that Michalovic would rather *die* than mention it. Doing something like that would be unheard-of for men of their high station. For in their closed world of high finance – where the rich got richer with every passing tick of the clock over at the New York Stock Exchange and where the poor were simply swept out with the rest of the ticker-tape trash littering the floor at the end of each business day – even the slightest *appearance* of financial need could be enough to strike you dead where you stood. Blood in the water that would almost certainly trigger the attack instinct in all the other predatory sharks gathered around you.

O'Hara reached into the inside pocket of his Gucci blazer and slipped on his tortoiseshell reading glasses to better study the label on the box of Behikes. Forty cigars, which meant he now owned exactly one per cent of the world's total output of this particular vintage. He immediately decided – right then and there – that he'd eventually need to own at least fifty-one per cent. And soon. He gave himself three months to accomplish the feat. Much like the competition that he and Michalovic were once again in the process of embarking upon, it was a *game* to him. Still, holding the position of minority shareholder in anything was not an arrangement in which he'd ever been particularly interested.

O'Hara lifted his gaze until it met that of the Russian seated on the other side of the sturdy mahogany table, simultaneously reaching past the pilfered Saint-Gaudens in the left-hand pocket of his jacket for a small wrapped box of his own.

'Thank you, Sergei,' he said, sincerity etched in his expression as he slid the box across. 'This is extremely generous of you, and it just so happens that I've got a little surprise here for you, too.'

The Russian took the box and peeled back the professionally done gift wrap, being very careful to avoid tearing the paper. He'd find a use for it later. Though he was rich now – even richer than his dear friend Ed O'Hara (whom he understood to simply be testing him by pocketing the expensive coin) – Michalovic, too, had grown up poor, and old habits died hard.

Michalovic threw back his head and laughed heartily when he saw what was inside. Sparkling in the soft light coming from a beautiful crystal chandelier suspended over their heads, a solid gold cigar-cutter rested in a glass-topped, cushioned wooden container.

Still chuckling, Michalovic said, '*Touché*, my dear Edward. I can see you're already anticipating my moves. That's something I'll certainly have to watch out for in the coming weeks, but it also means you'll make a very worthy opponent for me. Then again, that's not exactly surprising, is it? What's the score now, anyway? Three games apiece?'

O'Hara smiled back but shook his head with a steely glint reflecting in his translucent blue eyes. 'No, Sergei,' he corrected. 'With the completion of our last match, the score now stands at three games to two – in my favour. Fear not, though. As long as everything goes smoothly for both of us, according to the coin flip the score will be evened up to three games apiece in about a month. Since this contest marks our final match in this current series, when it's complete perhaps we can begin planning a new game for us to play together, if that arrangement sounds agreeable to you. Checkers, perhaps?'

Both men laughed.

Pleasantries and ceremonial gifts duly exchanged, Michalovic stood up and stretched his back until O'Hara heard a vertebra pop. 'Now,' the Russian said, 'as you prudish Americans no longer seem to allow smoking in public places, what do you say we recess to my suite upstairs? As we won't be speaking directly very much for the next several weeks, I think it should give us an excellent opportunity to go over the rules of the game just once more while we partake of a couple of your very fine cigars.'

O'Hara nodded and rose to his own feet on the other side of the table. From every corner of the gleaming lobby, guests of the prestigious hotel cast furtive glances at them as O'Hara swept an arm gallantly in front of his portly body in a gesture of respect that the Russian had done far more than his fair share to deserve. 'That sounds like an absolutely splendid idea to me, Sergei,' O'Hara said. 'As always, smoke before fire. Please lead the way, comrade.'

CHAPTER SEVEN

Jeremy Brown's lips moved but no words came out. It looked as though he didn't know what to say.

Neither did Dana. If she was right, they were facing a whole new nightmare.

All the colour had gone out of Brown's face. He took a deep breath and finally asked, 'What makes you think we're dealing with two serial killers here, Dana?'

Dana couldn't stop her hands from shaking. Still, now that the words were out of Brown's mouth – redirected at her instead of originating *with* her – she realised that she didn't have much to offer him by way of an explanation other than her gut feeling. And gut feelings, though sometimes effective in catching killers, didn't provide them with much of a starting point. 'Forget it,' she said. 'I spoke too soon. I didn't stop to think things through. My mistake.'

Brown narrowed his eyes. Though usually the same colour as his name, they somehow seemed several shades darker at the moment. 'Who was that on the phone just now?'

'Maggie Flynn in DC.'

'What did she have to say?'

Dana drew a deep breath and filled Brown in on

Flynn's discovery that two different kinds of ammunition had been used in the Bobby Fischer killings. Dana wished she'd taken the time to think things through properly before she'd dropped a bombshell suspicion like that on him – but she hadn't. Instead, she'd blurted it right out even before she'd had a chance to process it herself – and now she didn't know what to do with it. Still, now that the cat was out of the bag, she would have to find a way to put it back in. 'It's probably nothing,' Dana said. 'I wish I'd never said it. Let's just go with the hard evidence that we have, OK? Let's just follow up with the boy's photograph.'

Brown put his hands on his hips and stared down at her, looking irritated. Dana sighed, but she didn't blame him at all for his annoyance. Truth be told, she would've been every bit as irritated with him had the shoe been on the other foot. Probably more so.

When her partner spoke again, there was an unmistakable edge to his voice, and that surprised Dana. Brown wasn't normally the kind of guy who lost his cool. It was one of the things she'd always liked best about him. No matter how difficult circumstances got, Brown usually managed to keep his head.

But that particular guy was nowhere to be seen right now.

'You can't drop something like that in my lap and expect me to just forget about it, Dana.'

'Well, that's what I'm doing. I'm sorry.'

For several awkward moments, Brown looked as though he wanted to say something else to her –

something rude that he'd probably wind up regretting later on. But then the moment passed and he composed himself. 'It's not that crazy an idea,' he said after a moment, softening his tone. 'There have been cases in the past where serial killers have worked together. Why not this time?'

Dana closed her eyes and tried to rein in her frustration. Although she understood Brown's consternation at her refusal to pursue the idea, she too was getting annoyed now. She just couldn't help herself. In her heart of hearts, though, she knew that Brown was probably right. Gut feeling or not, at least they needed to consider the possibility. But knowing that didn't do a damn thing to lessen her irritation.

'Why not this time?' Brown repeated.

Dana opened her eyes again and shook her head in an effort to chase away the question, but her mind nonetheless drifted back to her earliest days at the Academy, back to the time in her life when she'd become an expert in serial murder practically at Crawford Bell's knee – the most prolific profiler the FBI had ever known. Almost as though he were flipping a switch in her brain from somewhere high above, the case histories he'd taught her flooded back.

In 1829, William Burke and William Hare had teamed up to murder sixteen people in Scotland. In the 1990s, Paul Bernardo and Karla Homolka had killed a string of victims in Canada, including Homolka's own sister. In Labette County, Kansas, the entire Bender family had gotten together to murder at least twenty guests at their inn from 1872 to 1873. The daughter of the Bender clan, Kate, a self-proclaimed psychic, pretended to communicate with the dead while guests relaxed in a comfortable leather chair. Another member of the Bender family hid behind a curtain before popping out to bludgeon the victims to death with a series of sharp hammer blows to the head. From there, it had been a simple matter of throwing the corpses down through a trapdoor in order to get rid of the evidence. Out of sight, out of mind.

Still, was that really a possibility here? Could she and Brown honestly be dealing with two serial killers stalking the streets of New York City, working together? What were the chances of that? Although it happened sometimes, it was rare enough almost to the point of being unthinkable.

Then again, chess was a two-player game. Not to mention the sheer *number* of people who'd died so far.

Dana massaged her neck while she tried to think things through. The sad fact of the matter was that she didn't have any idea how many killers were involved here now, and that scared her. Above all else, though, she knew that she and Brown couldn't afford to play fast and loose with other people's lives. It just wasn't fair to the victims – past and future – unless they could somehow figure out a way to remove the last category from the sinister equation.

Dana breathed out slowly and made her decision. She just wasn't comfortable with the theory of two killers yet, even if it had originated with her. 'I'm barking up the wrong tree,' she insisted. 'Please, let's just forget about it and go with what we've got. Let's just go with the photograph.'

Brown ran a hand through his short auburn hair and continued to stare down at her. Shaved close to his head in a buzz cut copied straight out of the FBI regulation handbook, the hair at his temples had already gone grey despite the fact that he was just thirty-five years old – only a few years younger than Dana. Dana's partner looked as though he'd aged ten years in just the short time since she'd known him, but that wasn't very surprising. The FBI had always had a knack for turning young, bright-eyed agents prematurely old after just a few years on the job.

Brown broke the silence a moment later and surprised her again. 'No,' he said.

Dana lifted her eyebrows at him. 'Excuse me?'

Brown rolled his muscular shoulders. The vein on the left side of his throat pulsed just above his white shirt collar. 'I said no, Dana. I'm not going to just forget about it. Not this time. I think you're onto something here, so let's give it a chance. We need to. We owe it to the people we're being paid to protect.'

Dana started to protest further, but soon found that she just didn't have the energy for it. One man or two, the Chessboard Killer was draining her reserves of strength. But to avoid any further unpleasantness between herself and Brown, she revisited in her mind the idea of two serial killers working together.

Maybe it wasn't such a crazy notion after all. Dana

had certainly seen stranger things over the course of her career. *Much* stranger things. Besides, she respected Brown's intuition, even if she didn't always respect her own. So if he thought the theory worth exploring, it probably was. He deserved to be taken seriously. It was the least she could do for him after what he'd gone through for her in the Cleveland Slasher case. After all, there weren't too many men out there who'd have taken a bullet in the chest that had been meant for her and then proceeded to ask her out on a date a few weeks later with a genuine smile plastered across their face, as Brown had done.

'OK,' she said, raising her hands in a gesture of defeat. 'We'll look into it a bit more. But to tell you the truth, Jeremy, I don't have the faintest idea of what we can do about it other than to create a new profile.'

Brown scratched his ear. The pulsing vein in his neck had calmed down a bit, and Dana was happy to see that. It was progress, however slight.

After a short pause, he asked, 'Maybe we should go to the press with this? Try to smoke these guys out of their holes that way?'

Dana fidgeted with the sleeve of her navy-blue blazer. It wasn't a bad idea in theory, but she knew that going to the press could often prove a double-edged sword – especially with Nick Brandt performing his aggravating little dog-and-pony show over at the *New York Post*. The increased publicity – as if this case needed any more publicity – might work to finally drive the killer or killers out of hiding, but it might also drive whoever was committing these unspeakable crimes even deeper into hiding. And could they really take that chance at this point in the case? They were already playing catch-up as it was. Already up to their ears in a sea of clues that they didn't understand. Besides, they had no way of knowing for sure just how many killers were involved here now. It might be one, it might be two, and it just as easily might be twelve. Who knew? Not only that, this line of thinking was brand new to Dana. She hadn't had time to process all of it yet.

Still, Dana forced herself to stay with the idea of multiple killers, while at the same time reminding herself to tread lightly. Better safe than sorry. She didn't want another innocent person to die another horrible death simply because she'd been wrong with one of her gut feelings – least of all the boy whose photograph she'd tucked away into her jacket pocket. So caution needed to be the rule of the day here. 'Let's have a think about this first,' Dana said. 'For all we know, I could be completely off base with it. We'll keep it in the backs of our minds for now, but we'll continue operating as though there's just one killer involved. At least until we find out something else that points to the possibility of two killers. Deal?'

Brown breathed out harshly in frustration. 'Whatever you say, Dana. You're the boss.'

Dana bristled before she had a chance to stop herself. 'Hey, that's not fair. Don't be a jerk about this. This isn't my fault.'

Brown rolled his eyes and shoved his hands deep into

his pockets. 'I didn't say it was your fault, Dana. And I'm not being a jerk about it. But I stand by what I said about you being the boss. It's par for the course with us, isn't it? You making all the decisions?'

Dana stared at him as though she was trying to drive a hole right through him. Brown wasn't the only one frustrated by this case, so if she was going to tread lightly here he'd sure as hell better, too. 'What's up your ass?' she snapped. 'Do you have something you want to say to me?'

Brown held her blazing gaze for several measured beats before finally dropping it after a brief stand-off that accomplished nothing. 'Nope,' he said. 'Not a thing. So let's just head over to the photography studio, OK? I'm getting a headache over here.'

Dana continued staring at him for several more seconds before realising just how stupid they were being. She finally dropped her gaze to the ground and funnelled the intense annoyance she felt flooding through her body into her toes, clenching and unclenching them inside her shoes. Still, irritated as she might be at the moment, Dana knew there was no point in fighting with Brown. They were on the same side here. However hard it was for them to accomplish, they needed to save whatever vitriol they could muster for the Chessboard Killer, whether it was one man or two. *That* was who represented the bad guy in this situation, not them. So it was foolish to quarrel like two spoiled children who weren't getting their own way. It only made them look like the bumbling amateurs the press and the general public had been making them out to be. To avoid that, she'd need to watch her step from here on out and remain professional at all costs. The victims deserved nothing less from them. Whatever personal problems she and Jeremy were dealing with couldn't be allowed to interfere with the investigation, no matter how tempting such a diversion might be. The families of the Chessboard Killer's victims had every right to answers that Dana fully aimed to provide them with. It was her *job*, for Christ's sake. Brown's, too.

To Brown's headache remark, she responded, 'You and me both, partner. You and me both. Got any aspirin on you?'

Brown didn't acknowledge her attempt at lightening the mood. Didn't even crack a fake smile. Just waved it off with an irritated sweep of his hand.

Dana raised her own hands again. 'So much for teamwork, I guess. Anyway, let's get out of here and head over to the photography studio, see what we can drum up there. It's got to be better than the two of us sitting around this alleyway all day sniping at each other.'

Brown cast a sideways glance at her as he brushed past her on his way back toward the entrance to the alleyway. His eyes flashed angrily in the bright sunlight streaming down from above. 'Whatever you say, Dana. Like I said before – you're the boss.'

CHAPTER EIGHT

Sergei Michalovic and Edward O'Hara took a private elevator reserved for hotel administrators and select guests up to the Presidential Suite of the Fontainebleau Hotel, chatting amiably the whole way.

Unlike some of the other presidential suites that Michalovic had stayed in, this particular one actually lived up to its lofty billing. To his knowledge, no fewer than five commanders-in-chief had stayed here in the past while holding the nation's highest office, including three in a row: Gerald Ford, Jimmy Carter and Ronald Reagan. What was more, rumour had it that none other than Barack Obama himself was scheduled to stay in this very same suite sometime during the next few months, though it was a rumour that Michalovic hadn't yet been able to confirm independently.

When they'd arrived at the doorway of the suite on the thirtieth floor of the venerable hotel, Michalovic reached into the back pocket of his slacks and withdrew his alligator-skin wallet before sliding a plastic key-card through the electronic reader on the set of massive double doors leading into his sumptuous accommodation. The light blinked green and he stepped aside to let the American in first. 'After you, Edward,' he said, bowing to his opponent with a flourish. 'In Russia, it's customary that guests should always enter the room first.'

O'Hara stepped inside the suite and looked around, admiring the view and not knowing then that *actual* Russian custom – pilfered unashamedly from the Japanese – held that the most powerful man in attendance should always enter the room *last*. Even with his privileged lifestyle, though, the pure luxury of it all was enough to take away O'Hara's breath. At four thousand square feet, the five-bedroom suite was easily twice the size of most ordinary people's houses, featuring a veranda that wrapped around the entirety of the building and offered a panoramic view of New York City's Central Park thirty storeys below. In the centre of the living room stood a marble chess table featuring handcrafted pieces carved out of solid ivory. Like the chess set itself, every other item decorating the plush room had been manufactured from the finest materials available.

O'Hara paused and shook his head in disbelief at his own uncharacteristically boyish amazement. With the amount of money he and Michalovic had – roughly equivalent to the gross domestic product of most Third World countries – they certainly weren't *ordinary* people by any stretch of the imagination. The finer things in life were *normal* for men of their high station. 'Very nice, Sergei,' O'Hara said, meaning it. 'I've never stayed here before but I shall make it a point to do just that very soon. It's absolutely exquisite.'

Michalovic waved a manicured hand in the air. 'Consider it done, Edward. When this latest competition of ours is over, I shall arrange for a week's stay here in this very same suite for you and one of your favourite mistresses. Before you say anything to the contrary, you should first know that I won't take no for an answer, so it would be a complete waste of your breath to even consider refusing.'

With that, Michalovic walked the length of the suite and slid open the glass doors to the veranda before turning back to O'Hara. On the busy street below, car horns honked and children laughed. The soft smell of a false springtime in the city floated in the warm air and a slight breeze fluttered Michalovic's impeccable silver hair as he stood in the doorway. 'Now,' the Russian said, 'I do believe we'd agreed to go over the parameters of the game just one more time while we sampled a couple of your Behikes. In anticipation of this moment, I have also arranged for a bottle of Havana Club rum to be sitting on ice out on the veranda. I think it will go quite nicely with the cigars.'

A few moments later, the men of means settled into their comfortable leather chairs and used Michalovic's brand new cigar-cutter to snip off the ends of two Behikes. Lighting up their expensive cigars and sipping on their fine rum, Michalovic and O'Hara shared a companionable silence while surveying the always interesting goings-on in Central Park thirty storeys below. Street vendors loudly hawked their knock-off wares to anyone who'd listen to them, amateur musicians strummed their instruments clumsily, and a man dressed as a clown delighted a small crowd huddled around him by juggling sharp knives.

Casually puffing on their contraband tobacco, Michalovic and O'Hara broke the silence after a few moments and revisited the moves that each would make in the coming weeks. As he'd be representing White in this final contest, it was Michalovic who'd be going first this time. *Smoke before fire.*

Michalovic cleared his throat and motioned to the network of streets just beyond the edge of the park, a system that had been laid out in a near-perfect grid. 'OK,' he said, 'so the outline of the board stretches from A Street to H Avenue from west to east, and from First Street to Eighth Avenue from south to north. Each city block represents one square on the board and each capture move has a time limit of three days. Each non-capture move has a time limit of twenty-four hours. As we'd like to make this final game as authentic as possible, we'll endeavour to use our pieces against one another this time when executing our capture moves, while at the same time retaining the right to take care of business for ourselves. In addition to the newspaper advertisements that we'll take out, I shall also chart our moves on the chessboard that you saw out there in the living room. If you'd be so kind as to humour me, I'd like to take this opportunity to invite you to accompany me for the positioning of the pieces following each one of our capture moves – our own private little ceremonies to mark our progress along the way. And it's from this very same suite's living room that we'll begin our race for the final target. The economic summit in Manhattan is still on for the twenty-third of this month, and the chairman of the Securities and Exchange Commission is still scheduled to be in attendance as the keynote speaker. Other than that, though, as always, none of the predetermined moves should be altered in any way. Doing so shall result in the automatic disqualification of the offending party and the forfeiture of all monies involved. Agreed?'

O'Hara nodded. 'Of course, Sergei. As always.'

The American real-estate developer blew out a huge cloud of fragrant blue smoke before continuing, savouring the sweet scent of the expensive tobacco in his nostrils and once again marvelling at just how far he'd come in life after his hardscrabble youth on the mean streets of Brooklyn – a hard-nosed childhood that had more often than not left him with skinned knees and black eyes to show for his ambition. But instead of ever feeling shame for his many wounds, O'Hara had worn his fighting spirit *proudly* around his neighbourhood. Each scrape, every little bruise, was simply a badge of honour that served to inform everyone in his world that he was *exactly* the kind of person who'd gladly go to *war* for whatever he wanted. But things were certainly different for him right now, weren't they?

They sure were.

After all these years of scratching and clawing his way to the top, O'Hara could finally sit back and enjoy the fruits of his labour. Hell, he'd *earned* that much. And perhaps a fifty-one per cent ownership stake in the cigars had been far too low an estimate to shoot for. Perhaps he should set his sights on something higher, something a little harder to accomplish, like owning every last Behike in the entire world. And why not? It would take some time and work, certainly, but there weren't many people in existence who could stop him from accomplishing a task once he'd really set his mind to it – though the jury on that particular verdict remained out when it came to the distinguished-looking man seated next to him.

Still, O'Hara had successfully completed far trickier missions in the past, including recently wresting away majority control in a string of supermarkets in the Bronx from the stubborn family that owned them and hadn't been especially interested in giving up that control.

Although he'd used a network of go-betweens to act as shields in that instance, the basic strategy that O'Hara had employed had been much the same as the one he and his hungry friends had used fifty years earlier when dealing unceremoniously with his father's bullheaded and thoroughly uncooperative business partners. If there was one lesson in this life that Edward J. O'Hara had learned very well, it was that people tended to take you more seriously when you delivered your messages to them along with a few broken bones.

A wave of warmth washed through O'Hara's veins at the pleasant memory. Not even the family's seventeen-year-old daughter had been exempt from the negotiations during those talks and as a result she was now lying in a Manhattan hospital bed, still recovering from her very serious injuries.

O'Hara smiled inwardly at the recollection of how his men had shaved off the girl's long, flowing blonde hair in the course of completing their assigned task – subsequently presenting him with a wonderful photograph of her humiliation as a prized memento of the occasion. But then he shook his head and forced himself to concentrate on the matter at hand, berating himself for his lack of focused thought. Although the negotiations had once again gone in his favour in that instance, it was neither here nor there at the moment. He wasn't giving the present subject the attention it deserved, and that was a dangerous sign. Above all else, he knew that he needed to remain in the game here, both mentally and otherwise. It was absolutely imperative when dealing with a man of Sergei Michalovic's volatile nature. Though the Russian had an easy smile, O'Hara knew that his friend could be every bit as ruthless as himself when the situation called for it. And then some. But he was better – and Michalovic would learn that one day very soon.

O'Hara forced his thoughts back onto the proper track. 'In any event,' he went on, 'as the ten-million-dollar prize for the winner of the contest is being held in escrow by our previously agreed-upon third party, dispensation of the funds is assured. Non-capture moves shall be communicated through the classifieds section of the *New York Times*. Capture moves, of course, should be relatively obvious to the other man. Remember: the report can appear no later than the "B" section of the newspaper. It appears that young Raymond Garcia is working our particular beat, thus putting his costly Harvard education to good use by transcribing our historic deeds into words that should ensure the easiest consumption by the unwashed masses. The "B-section-or-sooner" rule should also serve to ensure that our capture moves are splashy enough for a game of this magnitude. When the game is complete, we shall meet once again in the lobby of the Fontainebleau Hotel for the final coin flip to determine which man shall take ownership of the other's five million dollars – with *me* flipping the coin at that point in time, of course. Does that sound about right to you?'

Michalovic smiled. 'Right as rain, my dear Edward. Right as rain.'

The Russian paused and took another long drag on his Behike, then gestured absent-mindedly with the cigar. 'So, now that's settled, is there anything else we need to discuss? Anything else we need to say?'

O'Hara shook his head and stood up. 'No, Sergei,' he said. 'I think that should just about cover it for the time being. This isn't our first game, so I'm not anticipating any problems. Therefore the only thing I've got left to say is that I'm very sorry, but I'm afraid we're going to have to break with Russian custom this time. As you'll be representing White in this contest, it's *you* who shall have the honour of going first on this occasion.'

Michalovic slipped his barely smoked Behike into his

half-full glass of expensive rum and rose to his feet, once again delighting in the similarity between his and O'Hara's physical height. The two men were matched evenly from head to toe, that much seemed clear, and that knowledge filled him with great warmth. After all, if this wasn't to be a fair fight, what point was there in even having a fight at all?

The cigar made a slight hissing sound as it was extinguished in the liquid. Gripping O'Hara's mitt in a firm handshake, Michalovic held the American's stare. 'Very well, Edward,' he said. 'It's all settled, then. Good luck to us both – and may God have mercy on our souls.'

CHAPTER NINE

Wednesday, 3:02 p.m.

While Sergei Michalovic and Edward O'Hara sipped on their fine rum and puffed on their expensive cigars across town – revelling in their privileged lifestyles like a couple of hogs buried up to their ears in slop – Jack Yuntz surfed the Internet after school as his little sister napped peacefully in her bed fifteen feet away, snoring away softly beneath a poster of Justin Bieber.

The poster of the teen heart-throb wasn't the only item in his and Molly's shared room that testified to Jack's little sister's tender years. Far from it. Pokemon cards were stacked up high on her bedside table, threatening to spill over with even the slightest bump of a corner. A foil Pikachu smiled out from the top of the stack – supposedly one of the rarer cards in the set and Molly's most highly prized possession. A frilly green dress with a wide sash slung across the middle was draped over her bedpost. A *Dora the Explorer* bedcover kept her warm while she slept with a teddy bear resting comfortably in her toothpick-thin arms. Molly's very own little baby to love and care for. The very picture of innocence if ever there was one.

Pity her innocence wouldn't last much longer.

Jack sort of wanted to wake Molly up so that they could head over to Central Park – where he'd become something of a minor celebrity thanks to his remarkable talent for playing speed chess – but she was resting so deeply and he'd had such a rough day already that he just didn't have the heart for it.

Jack looked over at Molly again and tried to quell the sudden, intense swell of anger that he felt rising up inside his narrow chest at the mere sight of her. Didn't work.

Her adorable blonde ringlets framed the face of an absolute angel, all tiny lips and little ears and a cute wee button nose. The smooth pink skin on her cheeks looked eminently kissable, and her small chest rose and fell gently with each one of her slow, easy breaths. He clenched his jaw so hard that he nearly chipped a tooth in the back of his mouth.

The heartless motherfucker!

How could anyone ever leave a face like that? A face that beautiful? That precious? Much less someone who'd been responsible for her existence in the first place?

Jack loosened his jaw and forced himself to calm down. Above all else, he needed to stay composed here, to save whatever rage he had stored up inside for when the time was exactly right. When that time came, that was when he could spring out from the shadows and unleash his revenge upon the unsuspecting world with a ferocity that it had never witnessed before – not even in its worst nightmares.

Just wait until Don Yuntz saw what Jack had in store for him.

The slight, auburn-haired boy took several deep breaths and felt his pulse begin to slow a little. There. That was better. Just a bit longer now until he could make everything right again. Just a few more hours and he could finally even up the score once and for all.

Jack knew that he wasn't anywhere near strong enough to take down his father by force – not yet, anyway – but that was perfectly OK with him. Instead, he'd simply use his remarkable brain to exact his revenge on the sperm donor who'd had the gall to actually refer to himself as a *father*, tousling Jack's hair affectionately and kissing Molly's warm cheeks each Father's Day after they'd borrowed money from their mother in order to present the asshole with his obligatory gift of Old Spice cologne. Jack's brain had always been his strongest muscle, anyway. His most lethal weapon. And on that level – if none other – Don Yuntz presented no match for him. Not even close. It was all Don's fault, everything was his fault – and he needed to pay. Jack would make sure of that.

Jack shook his head and looked around the small room again, trying his best to count his blessings. Sadly, it was a lightning-quick inventory, for there weren't many blessings for him to count.

Molly was Number One, of course – always had been and always would be. But after his little sister, what else did Jack have left? Not much. Especially not with the way their father had betrayed their poor mother worse than old silver-loving Judas had betrayed Jesus himself.

Jack cracked his knuckles in disgust and swallowed the fresh rush of bile burning his throat. Although his upbringing had been a staunchly religious one – thanks in large part to his mother's own god-fearing background – he didn't feel the slightest twinge of guilt buzzing around inside his brain for what he once would've considered an unforgivable act of heresy punishable by nothing less than death itself. After all, Jack hadn't always been an atheist. Far from it. As a matter of fact, there'd been a time in his life not very long ago when he'd been an extremely pious boy, mostly using his nightly praying time to beseech God to help out his mother, to cut her a break for once in her wretched life, to help her get back on her feet long enough to recover custody of her children. But any such religious convictions were gone now, had left him that very morning, as a matter of fact. After what he'd seen, he could no longer believe in a concept as ridiculous as God – not with a capital 'G' and not with a lower-case one, either. No god in the cosmos would have ever signed off on the atrocity he'd witnessed with his very own eyes.

Early that morning, at about five a.m., Jack had snuck out of the midtown foster home where he and Molly were staying at present and had proceeded to take the Six train across the city by himself in order to visit his mother. Jack hadn't wanted any company for the trip, so he'd left Molly sleeping alone in her bed. This was between himself and his mom and not another living soul. Some things in this life were meant to be private, and this happened to be one of them. Besides, Jack hadn't seen his mother in weeks now, and he'd had a present that he'd wanted to give her personally. Something to let her know that he still loved and cared about her, no matter what. But when Jack had pushed open the broken front door to his mother's apartment an hour later, he'd been greeted instead with the worst shock of his entire life. Something that had completely and utterly destroyed his belief in God.

His mother's body had been smashed in and strapped to the floor. Dozens of squirming white maggots had been feasting on her purple flesh. Huge black flies had buzzed around her head. Her once-beautiful blue eyes hadn't been there any more. The overwhelming smell of rotting meat had nearly caused him to vomit up the contents of his stomach through his oesophagus.

In that instant something had broken inside Jack's mind, and he knew he'd never be the same again.

Despite her face being smashed beyond recognition, he knew that it was his mother. Distasteful as the action had been for him, Jack had forced himself to lean down and kiss his fingers before pressing them softly against her broken cheek prior to exiting the condemned apartment building, leaving behind the present he'd brought for her. It was the last thing of his that Stephanie Mann would ever have, and he'd wanted her to take it with her into eternity – wherever that might be.

By the time he'd made it outside to a payphone and the police dispatcher had picked up on the other end of the line, his entire body had gone numb. He hadn't identified himself to the woman at the downtown call centre, though, not even when the insistent bitch had demanded that he should do just that.

Jack's reasoning for this was simple enough: he didn't want to get involved in this mess. Not officially, at least. He'd leave that part up to the professionals assigned to the case – not that they seemed to be doing a very bang-up job so far. Still, the chess book he'd seen lying on the coffee table next to Stephanie Mann's murdered body meant that his mother would be famous soon. The infamy of the notorious serial killer who'd snuffed out her life ensured that much. And at the time Jack had wanted to stay as far away from that as he possibly could.

He didn't feel that way any more, however.

Turning back to his computer, Jack pecked at a few keys while Molly snored away contentedly. His little sister was lost in her own dream world now, a dream world in which puppies and butterflies frolicked in rolling green pastures stretching on for as far as the eye could see. A dream world in which their mother was still alive. But Jack lived in the *real* world now, and he knew he wasn't ever going back to the other one again. *Couldn't* ever go back. Still, he wanted to let Molly enjoy her ignorance while she still could. Pretty soon, she'd need to grow up.

Steering the computer's web browser over to Google, Jack typed 'Chessboard Killer' into the search bar and clicked on the 'latest results' tab before leaning back in his chair. Just as he'd suspected, news of his mother's gruesome death had already reached the Internet. In this age of the 24/7 news-cycle, the vultures didn't circle for very long. Instead, they'd begun gorging themselves upon his mother's rotting flesh just as soon as they'd smelled it. The goddamn jackals.

CHESSBOARD KILLER STRIKES AGAIN
Nick Brandt
New York Post
A source inside the NYPD confirmed today that the Chessboard Killer has claimed yet another victim – this time a woman who'd been living in a condemned apartment building over on the West Side.

The police source said Stephanie Mann, 30, suffered 'substantial' injuries, but declined to comment further on the specific nature of the woman's wounds.

According to the source, a chess book featuring one of the game's greatest players was discovered at the scene, though the source declined to comment on its title. The Chessboard Killer has left behind such books at the scenes of each of his slayings, which have been modelled on famous chess contests of the past. His own calling cards to ensure that he gets credit for his bloody handiwork.

FBI Special Agents Dana Whitestone and Jeremy Brown – who have been investigating the case for the past five months now – refused to answer any questions from the press on the matter. Instead, the federal agents simply departed the scene without providing so much as a single comment to the assembled media.

Story still developing. Check back often on the *New York Post* website for updates.

New York City's only *reliable source of information.*

CHAPTER TEN

As Dana and Brown weaved their way through the heavy afternoon traffic clogging up the downtown city streets, Dana got the distinct feeling that Brown wanted to break the silence and talk about their little tiff. But now wasn't the time for that. They were on the clock here. The boy in the photograph – wherever he might be right now – was probably counting on them to save his life. So whatever personal stuff she and Brown were dealing with would just need to wait.

Twenty minutes later, Dana drove their latest fancy car courtesy of the FBI's motor pool – a pale blue 2004 Ford Focus, featuring a heavily dented front fender – into the parking lot of Grafx Photography Services on Lindale Road in the Meatpacking District of Manhattan. Dana slid the car into a vacant parking space and turned off the engine before hopping out. Brown joined her. As they walked across the parking lot without uttering so much as a single word to one another, Dana tried to ignore the intense feeling of uneasiness between them. Wasn't easy.

Reaching the entrance to the building, Brown pulled open the door for her and stepped aside to let her in first. 'Age before beauty,' he said, smiling.

Dana didn't smile back. He'd had his chance to lighten the mood back at the condemned apartment building and he'd blown it.

Dana shot a sideways glance at him as she entered the building. 'More like pearls before swine.' She couldn't help it. Cliché or not, it expossed her feelings perfectly.

An electronic doorbell chimed directly above Dana's head as she stepped inside the doorway and looked around. Though it might have been the largest producer of school photographs in the entire country, the New York City office of Grafx wasn't much to write home about. A medium-sized lobby with about a dozen chairs positioned around the room, no one sitting in them. *Redbook*, *Sports Illustrated* and *Today's Mother* scattered on the tabletops. Artificial plants shoved into the corners. A rack of pamphlets hanging on the wall, most of them order forms for school photographs.

Fifteen feet away from the front door, a scratched plastic divider separated the service counter from the rest of the lobby. The young woman seated behind the closed divider was murdering the gum in her mouth. An intense look of concentration coloured in her pretty face as she renewed the paintwork on blood-red acrylic nails that were at least three times too long to be any practical use. Huge silver hoop earrings dangled from either side of her head, lost in the soft tendrils of bleached-blonde hair that hung from her scalp. Next to her, the most recent issue of *Cosmo* had been flipped open to display an article with a headline screaming *Satisfy Your Man In Bed The Old-Fashioned Way!*

The receptionist looked up at Dana and Brown with a calculated lack of interest until Dana flipped open her badge and held it up against the plastic. The woman stopped painting her nails. She stopped torturing the gum in her mouth. She slid open the scuffed divider. 'Yes?' she asked.

Dana slipped her badge back into the inside pocket of her blazer and removed the plastic evidence envelope containing the boy's picture, at the same time wondering what the article had meant by satisfying your man the 'old-fashioned' way. She shook away the thought and held up the picture. 'We need some information on this photograph,' Dana said. 'It's urgent. Is there a manager around?'

The young woman nodded and rose to her feet, pointing to a door on Dana's right. 'Yes, ma'am,' she said. 'If you'll just go around to that door there, I'll let you in and take you to Mr Finklestein. His office is in the back.'

Dana and Brown did as they were instructed, waiting patiently for the door to open for them before following the young woman past a series of machines that were cranking out thousands of photographs, almost all of them school pictures. The workers, most of them Hispanic and wearing hairnets, didn't even look up as they passed. The sharp smell of processing chemicals stung Dana's nostrils as they made their way even deeper into the cavernous space. *Odd*. She'd thought this kind of stuff had gone digital years ago.

Several moments later, the receptionist finally came to

a stop in front of a door with an engraved plaque on it that read *Jacob Finklestein, Acting Manager*.

Dana shook her head in mild contempt. Apparently, Jacob Finklestein, Acting Manager, had gone to the great trouble and expense of having a plaque engraved for his office door even before he'd had the interim tag removed from his title. Dana knew the type all too well. There were too many of them all around the country. Dozens of them in the FBI alone.

The young woman turned around to face her and Brown. 'Let me just go in first to make sure that Mr Finklestein isn't busy,' she said. 'He doesn't like being disturbed when his office door is closed. It's one of his rules.'

Dana rolled her eyes and cast a sideways glance at Brown, who shrugged in return.

Dana and Brown waited outside the office while the receptionist knocked lightly on the door and went in. The conversation coming through the partially open door was audible even above the low whine of the photograph-processing machines.

'What is it, Shelley?' Dana heard a man ask in a high-pitched nasally voice. 'I'm busy here. You *do* know that there's an intercom on your desk that connects to this intercom right here on *my* desk, don't you? Remember how I showed you how to work it the other day?'

The receptionist sounded nervous, and for some reason or another that irritated Dana. What *didn't* irritate her these days? 'I'm sorry, Mr Finklestein,' the young woman said. 'I forgot. Anyway, there's some kind of cops here or something. They said they need some information on a photograph.'

'Cops?'

'I don't know. One of them had a badge.'

'Were they wearing uniforms?'

'No, I just – I don't know.'

'Were they wearing uniforms, Shelley?'

Dana tightened her jaw and felt a fresh swell of annoyance flare up. She'd heard quite enough already. She didn't like bullies. Never had. Pushing open the door of the office, she was ready to unload both barrels on Jacob Finklestein, Acting Manager, but was instead surprised to find herself suddenly fighting back laughter.

Finklestein's horn-rimmed glasses sat precariously on the end of his long, slender nose, threatening to fall off at any given moment. A large pocket-protector crammed full of pens and pencils was displayed prominently on the front of his short-sleeved white shirt. The collar of the shirt was buttoned down, as though it might somehow start flapping like a tiny pair of wings and fly off into the distance if it wasn't secured properly. A wide black tie that had gone out of style sometime around the late 1970s encircled his impossibly thin neck.

Finklestein had gone mostly bald from front to back, but the unruly red hair remaining on his head looked long enough to provide a decent comb-over should he ever decide to go that route. Even from his seated position behind his massive desk, Dana could tell that he was every bit as short as she was.

Dana drew a quick breath and composed herself. Finklestein was a jerk, obviously, but the truth of the matter was that he had a lot working against him. So the irritation she'd felt when she'd been listening to the way he'd been speaking to the receptionist subsided at once. Dana wasn't going to be a bully, either. Removing her badge from the inside pocket of her blazer again, she advanced farther into the office and flipped it open as Brown entered the room behind her. 'My name is Agent Whitestone,' she said, then turned and gestured to Brown. 'This is Agent Brown. I'm sorry to barge in on you like this unannounced, but I was wondering if we might have a few moments of your time.'

Finklestein rose to his feet and nodded to the receptionist. 'Thank you, Shelley. That will be all for now.'

The young woman left the office and shut the door behind her. When she'd gone, Finklestein lifted his eyebrows at Dana and Brown, splaying his small hands on the cluttered surface of his ridiculously oversized desk: Napoleon surveying his vast empire, which in this case amounted to a cramped office located at the back of a photograph-processing plant, empty cardboard boxes stacked high in one corner. 'So, what can I do for you guys?' he asked. 'I'm Jacob Finklestein, by the way. Acting manager.'

Dana suppressed a smirk and handed across the desk the plastic evidence bag containing the boy's photograph. 'Please don't touch the picture directly,' she said, 'even through the bag.' If there were any prints on the photo, she didn't want Finklestein smearing them when he handled the bag. 'Anyway, can you tell us anything about this photograph? Anything at all?'

'Like what?'

'Like where it came from, where it was produced – that kind of stuff.'

Finklestein pushed his heavy eyeglasses up on his face and lifted the bag until it was no more than two inches away from his nose. He studied it closely. 'It's a Plimpton model,' he said, as though only a complete idiot wouldn't know something like that.

'What's a Plimpton model?' Brown asked, ignoring the man's tone.

Finklestein looked up from the bag and repositioned his eyeglasses on his face, and Dana found herself wishing she had a tiny screwdriver she could loan him. Finklestein probably spent half his days pushing his glasses back up. 'The Plimpton model is a manufacturing process we used to use back in the days when we were experimenting with a way to catalogue all the pictures we took. We wanted to make it into a McDonald's sort of thing. You know, fifty-five million served and all that?'

Dana's heartbeat fluttered. This could be just the major break they'd been waiting for. 'You *catalogued* all the pictures?' she asked. 'How so?' Most companies catalogued their work, she knew, but she hadn't thought of that until just now.

Finklestein waved a hand in the air, still acting like the pompous know-it-all that Dana had already figured him out to be. He used his other hand to return the boy's photograph across the desk, and Dana noticed that his fingernails had been bitten right down to the quick. He was probably a nervous wreck most of the time whenever he was out of sight of his underlings and safely ensconced behind his closed door. 'We catalogued them by date, by school district, that kind of stuff,' Finklestein said.

'Where do you keep the records?' Brown asked. 'We'll need to take a look at them.'

Dana's excitement intensified. If all went well for them, she and Brown could probably identify the boy with a few simple strokes on a keyboard. The boy's photograph and the information about his school would be in the database. From there, it could be just a simple matter of time and legwork before they finally caught the Chessboard Killer and nailed him to the nearest available cross.

'Records?' Finklestein broke into Dana's thoughts. 'What records?'

'The hard data,' Dana said, frowning at the question. 'If you can trace this photograph to a specific school district, it would be a huge help to us.' She held up the evidence bag. The toothless grin of the boy inside nearly broke her heart again. 'This child's life could be in danger, Mr Finklestein.'

Finklestein was shaking his head the entire time she was speaking. 'Trace it?' he said. 'I'm afraid we simply can't do that. We discarded the Plimpton model five years ago, Agent Whitestone. Destroyed all the records. Not only did it become a privacy issue, it was way too much work to be worth it in the first place. Didn't make financial sense. And the boys upstairs don't like it when things don't make financial sense. They don't like it one little bit.'

Dana's heart sank at Finklestein's words, all the way down to the pit of her stomach. 'So you don't have *any* records left?' she asked wearily.

Finklestein shook his head matter-of-factly. He seemed almost pleased to be imparting this bit of discouraging information. 'Nope,' he said. 'We got rid of all the records two years ago.' He paused, and pursed his lips. 'Besides, Agent Whitestone, all this stuff went digital *years* ago. To be perfectly honest with you, I'm a little bit surprised you didn't know that already. Sounds to me like the FBI needs to come out of the Stone Age and step into the twenty-first century. Might help you finally catch this Chessboard Killer guy.'

Dana stared at him. Her skin flushed hot. All the little hairs on the back of her neck stood up. 'Excuse me?' She'd never mentioned the Chessboard Killer to Finklestein. Neither had Brown.

Finklestein dropped his gaze to his desk and toyed with a heavy metal stapler. 'What?' he whined defensively. 'I just saw your picture in the newspaper, that's all. In the *New York Post*. Don't worry about it, Agent Whitestone. I'm definitely not your guy.'

Dana turned on her heel and stormed out of Finklestein's office. Brown followed close behind. She'd been that close to booking the guy – his smug remarks had just about tipped her over. She was frustrated enough at running up against another dead end. But she wasn't going to let a jerk like him get the better of her. He wasn't worth her career, however tempting the thought might be.

So instead of socking the weasel in his mouth, Dana simply slammed the door shut behind them, knocking off Finklestein's grandiose plaque and sending it clattering down to the tiled floor.

CHAPTER ELEVEN

Wednesday, 4 p.m.

Sergei Michalovic couldn't wait to get to work, so he didn't. What was the point? He might as well get this contest off to a swift and lethal start.

The first move in the game proved exceedingly easy, practically effortless. The exhaustive preparation and research that had gone into both sides of the board meant that Michalovic was ready no matter which colour the coin-flip decided he would play. From here, the manoeuvres should be as simple as shooting fish in a barrel.

Then again, there were always glitches in these games, weren't there?

Of course there were. Always one or two unwilling participants doing their damnedest to gum up the works and sully the simple perfection of the game, regardless of how much research and preparation he and O'Hara had put in. Besides, how was the act of shooting fish in a barrel ever supposed to be *easy*, anyway? To him, it sounded like a complete mess from beginning to end.

Still, it didn't matter. As they said here in America, it

was the squeaky wheel that got the grease. And – financially speaking – Michalovic had enough grease to lubricate an entire theme park full of roller coasters, which seemed quite fitting considering that he and O'Hara were once again about to embark upon their own personal thrill ride of sorts. *Admit two, and two only.*

Michalovic leaned back in his comfortable executive chair, picked up the phone sitting on his massive glass-topped desk inside his luxurious office suite on the eighty-third floor of the Trump Towers and punched in a number. Ten minutes later he'd successfully rented out an apartment at 19016 Fourth Avenue in Manhattan.

Michalovic placed the phone gently back into its elaborate cradle when the deed was done, shaking his head in amazement at the pure ease and simplicity of it all. Having once been destitute himself – destitute to the point of being forced to seek out his nightly dinners in alleyway trash-bins infested with rats, maggots and other kinds of unspeakably disgusting vermin – he knew that arranging for housing so swiftly was a rare privilege indeed. But as they also said here in America, money talked and bullshit walked.

More than that, Michalovic's money *shouted.*

Yes, America was indeed the finest country in all the world, no doubt about it. At least, for men of his and O'Hara's unique tastes.

Five minutes later, Michalovic picked up the phone on his desk again. This call went to one Betty Arsenault, a single mother of three who'd advertised her need of a job recently on the popular Craigslist website. Time to move the first pawn.

She answered after five rings, just a moment or two before Michalovic lost his taste for waiting and cut the connection from his end. To say that the Russian wasn't a man accustomed to abiding by other people's schedules would have been the understatement of the century. In the background of the call, a screaming child was demanding to be picked up, hitting a pitch that Michalovic would have thought quite impossible for a human voice to reach had he not heard it with his own ears. 'Be *quiet*, Mark!' a woman reprimanded harshly, only adding to the general chaos of the already ear-splitting phone call. 'Mommy's on the phone here.' Her hand over the receiver did little to lessen the noise.

To Michalovic, the woman said, 'Hello?'

A low buzz of excitement hummed in Michalovic's brain like a dose of pure heroin. The woman's voice sounded soft, seductive. The perfect voice for the first perfect move in this decidedly perfect final game. But the first move in chess was also the most dangerous one, wasn't it? Damn right, it was. The first move set the tone for the rest of the game and somewhat limited your options going forward. Though the issue remained the subject of hotly contested debate among scholars and world-class players, prevailing wisdom held that White enjoyed a slight inherent advantage in these competitions, with those who went first winning fifty-two to fifty-six per cent of the time in matches that were held between players of a more or less equal skill-level. And while others who moved in their lofty circles might not see it yet, Michalovic had witnessed O'Hara's ruthless competency first-hand. And then some.

Weak-willed the man was not. He certainly wasn't weak-stomached, either. Not by a long shot. It took guts to slide a razor-sharp knife across the throat of a twenty-three-year-old prostitute you'd kidnapped only hours earlier, administering the killing cut while standing on the pristine white carpet of your own living room, as O'Hara had done in their last match-up. The Irish-American hadn't blinked even once as torrents of blood had spurted forth from the young woman's severed jugular vein, spraying in a fine mist all over his immaculate white carpet and sprinkling the keys of his all-white Steinway grand piano with dots of bright red. Instead, he'd simply held Michalovic's stare the entire time with a mischievous twinkle sparkling in his own clear blue eyes.

That cold-blooded manoeuvre had marked the check-mate move in their last encounter, elevating their grisly competition to the next level and landing on the front page of the *New York Times*, though the city's bewildered law-enforcement agencies were still trying their best to identify the killer. *Good luck there*, Michalovic thought. O'Hara *always* covered his tracks in these games. *Meticulously.* It was just one of the many factors that made him such a great player, such a worthy opponent . . . and such a fitting final target for this culminating game.

In any event, it had been quite the spectacular finish, to say the least. But now the time had finally come for Michalovic to even up the score. Ruthless though O'Hara might be as a competitor, Michalovic was certainly no slouch himself when it came to carrying out the capture moves. Just *wait* until O'Hara saw what he'd scripted for him behind his back.

Michalovic cleared his throat quietly. 'Is this Betty Arsenault?' he asked. 'The Betty Arsenault who lives at 551 Second Avenue, Unit 12?'

On the other end of the line, the woman's voice immediately took on a suspicious tone, and who could blame her? Although among the glitziest metropolitan areas in the entire world, New York City was also home to some of the biggest weirdos Michalovic had ever had the misfortune to lay eyes upon.

'Yes,' Arsenault said. 'This is she. Who may I ask is calling?'

Michalovic reached out a hand and lifted the metal ball on the right side of the Newton's Cradle that was sitting on the corner of his massive desk before letting the shiny sphere fall again, smiling once again at the pure ease and simplicity of it all while he listened to the soothing sound of metal clacking against metal. Much like the workings of the Newton's Cradle itself, this phone call would set into motion a series of events that wouldn't let up until the game was complete or an outside force intervened to interrupt the proceedings. Perhaps an uncharacteristic mistake by his dear friend O'Hara? Or how about some much-belated progress by the bumbling federal agents assigned to their case five months earlier? Only time would tell.

'Miss Arsenault, my name is Pierre LeBlanc,' Michalovic said, deliberately using a French name to throw the woman off-track should she happen to be the rare sort of person who could identify what little remained of his accent as Russian. Still, most Americans weren't exactly what he would describe as *Cosmopolitan*.

Betty Arsenault shushed the unruly child again. 'What can I do for you, Mr LeBlanc?' she asked, obviously trying to disguise her impatience. The kid was still complaining loudly in the background and clearly shredding his mother's every last nerve. The joys of parenthood.

'Well, Miss Arsenault, it's not about what you can do for me, but rather about what *I* can do for *you*,' Michalovic said smoothly.

'What do you mean by that?'

'What I mean by that is that I'm calling you with a job offer,' Michalovic said without further preamble. 'My company, Settle Systems Group, a computer-technology outfit that's listed on the NASDAQ, noticed your advertisement on the Internet, and after a great deal of research by our human resources department we think that we may have found a suitable position for you. That is, of course, assuming that you're still looking for employment?'

Arsenault's voice jumped an octave in Michalovic's ear to indicate her interest. 'Yes, sir, Mr LeBlanc,' she said, all suspicion gone now. 'As a matter of fact, I *am* still looking for a job. What sort of position did you have in mind?'

Michalovic leaned back in his office chair and twirled a heavy fountain pen between his slender fingers. Like every other material item he possessed, the pen was no ordinary artefact by any stretch of the imagination.

The writing implement was a Diamante, of which just *one* was produced each year. It contained more than thirty carats of diamonds and featured nearly two thousand DeBeers-certified '4C' diamonds set into a solid platinum barrel. Even the nib itself had been fashioned out of eighteen-carat gold. To top it all off, a diamond cabochon – a highly polished, not faceted, gem.

Price tag? One point two eight million dollars.

To Michalovic's mind, worth every last penny of it, too. Not only did status symbols such as the Diamante let your opponents know that you were in a financial position to buy and sell them just for fun, but also that you were *exactly* the kind of person who wouldn't hesitate to do just that.

By this time Michalovic could no longer hear the insufferable child in the background and he was extremely grateful for that. Perhaps the woman had ushered it into a back bedroom, where it belonged. Michalovic shook his head in disgust. Had the child been his *own* son, the boy would also have been nursing a nasty welt on his backside to remind him of the importance of keeping his big fat mouth shut the next time Daddy was on the phone. Spare the rod and spoil the child.

Then again, *nobody* knew how to parent these days, did they? Not in this country, at least. In Russia, though, it was a different story altogether. In Russia, they knew how to *discipline* their children.

Michalovic's left hand went unconsciously to his left ear and to the mass of scar tissue there that had come courtesy of his father when Michalovic had been just eight years old. Michalovic's father – a boozy old lout of a man whose fondness for cheap vodka had been rivalled only by his even greater fondness for cheap women – had once held his son's ear to a stove-burner glowing bright red as punishment for Michalovic having received poor marks in school. Even then, though, Michalovic hadn't really been angry with his father. Even way back then, he'd known it had just been business – an act of love, really. Or, at the very least, an act of *concern*.

To Arsenault, Michalovic said, 'The position we have in mind is administrative in nature, ma'am. Mostly paperwork, but there's a good deal of answering telephones involved too. Though it doesn't happen very often, also the delivery of packages from time to time. We try to keep that sort of thing to the bare minimum, though. We don't like our employees to feel as though we're taking advantage of them.'

'May I ask how much the position pays, Mr LeBlanc?'

Michalovic paused, knowing that he needed to be very careful here. He'd made silly mistakes in these games in the past by offering compensation that was well beyond the normal levels for the work involved, but he was determined never to make that mistake again. You live, you learn. 'Twenty-four thousand dollars a year,' he said.

The excitement in Arsenault's tone deflated quickly. After a moment or two of pregnant silence, she finally let out a slow breath and said, 'I'm sorry, Mr LeBlanc. I don't mean to sound ungrateful for the job offer, but I've got three children here that I need to support by myself and that's barely more than my government unemployment cheque provides me with at the moment. Are you sure you can't go just a little bit higher than that?'

Michalovic grinned. Negotiating with neophytes such as Arsenault had always been a source of pleasure to him. Had *he* been in the woman's position, he would have lied immediately and informed his opponent that he had three higher job offers on the table already. It was Negotiating 101, really. Not that he expected *Arsenault* to know that, of course. Still, trying to negotiate payment in this economy wasn't always the wisest move. You took what you could get when you could get it or else you and your family went hungry as a result. It was as simple as that.

'*I*'m very sorry, Miss Arsenault,' Michalovic said, 'but I'm afraid I'm not authorised to offer you a single penny more. There is, however, a unique job-related benefit involved should you happen to accept the position we're offering.'

Arsenault's interest perked up at that. 'What kind of benefit, Mr LeBlanc?'

Michalovic breathed in deeply. This was the second tricky part of the approach. Good deal or not, most people were naturally reluctant to pull up stakes, common as those stakes might be. 'Free rent in our relocation initiative,' he said, trying his best to disguise the heightened anticipation in his voice. He was pretty sure he had Arsenault hooked with the job offer, but now he needed to reel her in: not always the easiest element in the procedure. Some of these fish could prove to be surprisingly slippery when you thought you had them securely on the line. 'Settle Systems Group is experimenting with a pilot programme where we pay employees' housing costs at lodgings of our choosing,' Michalovic went on. 'Our company wants to nurture a family environment not only because we think it's good for business but also because we sincerely believe in our mission. Your rent is guaranteed for two years as long as you agree to the move – and also to a non-competitive contract of that same length, of course.'

Michalovic could almost *hear* the woman doing the mental math on the other end of the line. From his exhaustive pre-game research he knew that Arsenault's three-bedroom apartment on Second Avenue cost her two thousand dollars a month, so if she accepted the job offer, her free-rent bonus would raise the value of her employment contract to a much more appetising forty-eight thousand dollars a year. Not too shabby for an unemployed single mother of three who was currently receiving just four hundred and twenty-one dollars a week from the federal government.

There were, however, a few more logistical matters to which Michalovic needed to attend before he could land this particular fish.

'What about health care?' Arsenault asked. 'Like I said before, I've got three children here that I need to support by myself.'

'Completely covered,' Michalovic answered.

'And moving costs?'

'Covered as well,' Michalovic said.

'I've got four months left on my current lease, Mr LeBlanc . . .'

Michalovic sat up straighter in his chair. A hot buzz of adrenalin coursed through his veins. One more step and the deal would probably be sealed. Only one way to find out. 'Settle Systems Group is prepared to buy out the remainder of your lease, ma'am,' he told her. 'Our company is committed to taking care of our employees every single step of the way. We value them that much. They're the absolute lifeblood of our entire operation.'

Arsenault paused for what seemed an eternity then. Finally, she cleared her throat quietly and asked, 'Where would we need to move to?'

Michalovic stopped twirling his pen between his fingers and returned the Diamante to its heavy marble holder on his desk, breathing in deeply again. *This was it!* From the look of things, his new opening gambit was working like a charm. Almost as bold as the famous 'Ruy Lopez' opening, which had been named after the Spanish priest who'd first analysed the classic chess sequence way back in 1561. Still, he wasn't counting his chickens just yet.

Or his fish.

'Well, Miss Arsenault,' he said, forcing himself to choose his words carefully, 'you wouldn't need to move very far away at all. Just two blocks north from where you're living now, as a matter of fact. As we already have a moving company on retainer, you wouldn't need to lift a finger yourself. Everything will be completely taken care of for you.'

Twenty minutes later, Sergei Michalovic dispatched a FedEx courier to Betty Arsenault's cross-town apartment with three copies of her new employment contract for her to sign: one for her, one for him and one for the company's files.

The final phone call of the afternoon went to an advertising account executive who worked for the *New York Times*. As bright late-afternoon sunlight streamed in through his enormous floor-to-ceiling reinforced-glass office windows, Michalovic leaned back in his comfortable executive chair and ran his fingertips through his perfectly styled silver hair while dictating the contents of the classified ad whose true meaning would be understood by just one other person in the entire universe:

> E. 302828206, 551 2 A 12/19016 4 A A 19. Your move. S.

Translation: Betty Arsenault's Social Security number in reverse, moving from 551 Second Avenue, Unit 12, to 19016 Fourth Avenue, Apartment 19.

Or, in algebraic notation, simply *e4.*

And, with that seemingly innocuous opening move, so began the recreation of the most famous game in the history of chess.

Slightly tweaked, of course, for men of Michalovic and O'Hara's unique tastes.

PART III

'It is impossible to keep one's excellence in a little glass casket, like a jewel, to take it out whenever wanted. On the contrary, it can only be conserved by continuous and good practice.'

Adolph Anderssen, German chess master who was considered the world's leading player in the 1850s.

CHAPTER TWELVE

Wednesday, 4:22 p.m.

Dana and Brown left Grafx and began what was supposed to be a short drive over to NYPD headquarters located at 1 Police Plaza in Lower Manhattan.

Jacob Finklestein had set Dana's teeth on edge, and she knew that she didn't do her best thinking when she was angry. If nothing else, she needed a timeout to clear her head, however brief.

Instead of the much-needed breather she was after, though, she and Brown only ended up getting snarled in an irritating hour-long traffic jam over on Broadway caused by a broken water main, further exacerbating the already nerve-snapping tension in Dana's brain.

Finally, *blissfully*, extricating themselves from the godforsaken mess with the help of an understanding traffic cop on horseback, Dana at long last slid the Ford Focus into an empty parking space at the home of New York's Finest before downshifting the vehicle into park mode and switching off the engine.

In the seat next to her Brown flipped closed his cellphone as she did so and turned to face her. 'I just emailed the picture of the boy to an FBI sketch artist I worked with out in LA,' he said. 'Thought it might be helpful to get one of those "what do they look like now?" drawings started. He said he'll have it back to me ASAP, make it his top priority. He's getting to work on it now.'

Dana nodded. An age-progression sketch was a smart idea. The boy in the photograph had to be a teenager now – he was sure to look a lot different. 'Good call,' she said. 'Seven years is a heck of a long time, especially when you're a kid.' She paused, wishing she'd thought of it herself, but happy that she had Brown around to pick up her slack. They made a good team, at least professionally. Always had, ever since the beginning. 'So, you ready to go do this or what?' she asked.

Brown raised his eyebrows. 'Ready as I'll ever be, I guess. Let's get back to work.'

Dana and Brown got out of the Focus and headed for the headquarters building a hundred yards away. With nearly thirty-eight thousand uniformed officers patrolling the mean streets of Gotham, the NYPD represented the largest municipal police force in the United States – and a good thing, too. One need look no further than the Chessboard Killer for evidence of the fact that crime in New York City wasn't quite like crime anywhere else in the country. The crimes here seemed harsher, baser, *bloodier*. More than that, the city was widely regarded as a veritable *breeding ground* for serial killers. Always had been ever since the days of the Son of Sam.

Stepping inside the sprawling police headquarters building a few moments later, Dana and Brown walked quickly up to the front desk, Dana's low heels clicking and echoing against the marble-tiled floor while harried-looking officers escorted one handcuffed offender after another to and fro around the huge building. Fifty feet to their right, relatives of the offenders queued up in long lines to post bail and spring the silver shackles fastened around their loved ones' wrists: the American justice system at work right there out in the open for all to observe – now you see them, now you don't. At least, for the non-violent criminals.

Several stacks of papers and two telephones sandwiched the officer seated behind the receiving desk. The large flat-screen television hanging on the wall behind him was tuned in low to CNN. A teary-eyed reporter with thick rivers of black mascara streaking down her pretty face was struggling through a report on the recent horrific mass shooting out in Arizona that had left six people dead and thirteen more injured – including Congresswoman Gabrielle Giffords, whom preliminary reports now placed in critical condition at a Tucson-area hospital.

Dana shook her head in disgust. Obviously New York City wasn't the only place in the United States up to its eyeballs in violent crime. From small towns to big cities around the country, each geographical area was dealing with its own murderous problems.

Fresh-faced and clean-shaven, the officer seated behind the receiving desk couldn't have been much older than twenty-two or twenty-three. Hardly more than a rookie, really. Thankfully, though, he'd chosen to go the exact opposite route of the young man out in Arizona, opting to dedicate his life to the *protection* of innocent lives rather than the indiscriminate slaying of them.

The young officer's navy-blue uniform was immaculately pressed, his short brown hair was shorn neatly into a crew-cut and the shiny gold badge pinned to the front of his button-down uniform shirt made Dana think he'd stayed up until the small hours the previous night polishing it again and again until it shone just right in the fluorescent lights hanging above his head. Dana had very little doubt that the earnest young man's shoes had received the same meticulous attention but she couldn't see them from where she was standing.

Brown flipped open his own badge and identified himself and Dana. 'Agent Brown, Agent Whitestone,' he said. 'We need to get some fingerprinting done.'

Though the FBI and NYPD had been working closely together on this case for some time now, the young officer seemed surprised by the visit from the feds. He fumbled for one of the phones on his desk, inadvertently knocking it over before picking it up again. His boyishly handsome face reddened slightly as he smiled shyly at Dana. 'Of course,' he said. 'Let's see here.'

He opened up a directory and scanned the listings with a long index finger, and Dana couldn't help but notice that *his* fingernails – quite unlike those of Jacob Finklestein, Acting Manager – were beautifully maintained. She wondered briefly if he'd ever had a manicure, but then decided he probably hadn't. Didn't seem to suit his style.

After several moments of intense searching, the young officer finally looked up from his directory again and said, 'That would be Detective Rodriguez's department, extension two-one-two. Let me just give her a call for you guys real quick to see whether or not she can help you out.'

Brown smirked at Dana as the young officer tried to make small talk with her while they waited. Five minutes later, though, the tables were turned. Now it was *Dana*'s chance to smirk. Brown's eyeballs nearly popped out of his head when he got his first look at Detective Mariel Rodriguez. To be honest, though, Dana really couldn't blame him that much. The woman was a real knockout.

Rodriguez strode into the lobby with her long brown hair flowing behind her. A short beige skirt encased impossibly long legs. Her slender feet were shod in a pair of fashionable black dress shoes featuring four-inch heels – a good two inches higher than Dana's own sensible heels. Not that Rodriguez needed any of the extra height, of course. Dana pegged the thirty-something detective at about five-nine already. A white blouse complete with understated ruffles showcased a swanlike neck that had a silver chain hanging around it. To top it all off, she had one of the most beautiful faces Dana had ever seen.

When Rodriguez smiled at them, Dana wasn't at all

surprised to see that she had perfect teeth. Some women really did have everything.

The NYPD detective widened her big brown eyes in surprise. 'I'm Mariel Rodriguez,' she said in a thick Brooklyn accent. 'You're Agents Whitestone and Brown, right?'

Dana smiled at the woman. 'Yes, ma'am.'

Rodriguez smiled back. 'Wow, it's a real pleasure to meet you two. I've been following the Chessboard Killer case closely, like everyone else in the world, I'm sure. Anyway, you guys need some fingerprinting done? Something connected to the case?'

Dana winced internally at Rodriguez's labelling of the investigation. Still, thanks in large part to Nick Brandt over at the *New York Post* and a few of his less responsible colleagues, even law enforcement had begun referring to their killer by the unimaginative moniker that had been first used for Alexander Pichushkin. Dana had never liked the idea of nicknaming killers, had always feared it might encourage murderers to think more highly of their disgusting work, lead them to believe they were accomplishing something of note by their slaying of innocents. But, once applied, nicknames weren't easily erased.

Dana filled in the NYPD detective on what she and Brown needed since her partner still didn't appear capable of making his tongue work properly. 'Thanks so much for taking the time to see us, Detective Rodriguez. I really appreciate this, and the sooner we can get this done, the better. Time is of the essence here.'

Rodriguez nodded, all business despite her supermodel appearance. Dana respected that. 'Of course,' Rodriguez said. 'Come with me. I'll have you in and out of here in less than twenty minutes. Promise.'

Pivoting on her well-turned ankles, Rodriguez turned and led Dana and Brown through a labyrinth of halls. As she'd done during her and Brown's previous visits to NYPD headquarters, Dana marvelled at the sheer size of it all. Certainly a far cry from Cleveland, where everything seemed downright miniature by comparison. If you didn't know your way around this place you'd wind up walking around in circles for days.

After a series of lefts and rights that Dana tried her best to keep track of mentally, they finally came to a stop outside a set of massive double doors with *Fingerprinting* stencilled in big block letters across the glass.

'This is it,' Rodriguez said, opening up the door to the lab and stepping aside to let Dana and Brown in first. 'This is my little playground, where we catch all the bad guys who are stupid enough to leave their fingerprints behind. Believe it or not, that would be just about every last one of them.'

Dana stepped inside the lab and looked around. Even by law-enforcement standards, the fingerprinting facility was impressive – like something straight out of the movies. Three other detectives wearing thin rubber gloves and paper masks tied over their faces attended to a variety of tasks while Rodriguez led Dana and Brown over to a long metal counter in the far south-east corner.

'Might not look like much, but this here's my baby,'

Rodriguez said, coming to a stop in front of the counter and patting the top of a small cubical plastic box. 'In this case, bigger isn't necessarily better. Quite the opposite, actually.'

'What is it?' Brown asked, at last uttering his first words to the stunning fingerprint expert.

'This,' Rodriguez said, 'is a machine that employs the cyanoacrylate fuming method to develop latent prints. Better known as the superglue method.'

Dana stepped past Brown and handed Rodriguez the plastic evidence envelope containing the boy's photograph. There was no time for small talk. 'This is what we need analysed, Detective Rodriguez. Please be extremely careful with it. It's one of the very few pieces of solid evidence we have.'

Rodriguez nodded and took the envelope. Sliding open a drawer beneath the counter, she removed some rubber-tipped tweezers from their plastic casing and extracted the boy's photograph before placing the picture inside the machine and shutting the door. She pressed a small red button and a tiny motor purred to life.

Rodriguez leaned down and checked a digital readout on the box before straightening back up. The ensuing air current she created sent the light scent of her perfume floating up into Dana's nostrils – 5th Avenue by Elizabeth Arden. Nice choice.

Rodriguez said, 'As I'm sure you're both well aware, there are three different types of prints: visible, impression and latent. Visible prints are simple enough to understand – you can actually see them with your own eyes, no enhancement needed. You can also photograph them directly. Impression prints can usually be photographed under special lighting conditions—'

'Why not try that first?' Dana cut in. 'Wouldn't that be quicker?' She didn't want to sound rude, but neither was she in the mood for a lecture right now. She and Brown couldn't afford to waste a single second.

Rodriguez smiled easily at Dana, seemingly unfazed by the interruption, and Dana got the distinct impression that the NYPD detective wasn't the type of woman ever fazed by *anything*. 'Yes and no, Agent Whitestone,' Rodriguez said. 'We *could* do that, but then we'd have to walk about half a mile to get to the room with the special lighting conditions I was talking about. If you hadn't noticed on our walk over here, this place is just about the size of five football fields. Maybe even bigger. Anyway, since you guys are in a hurry here, I figured we'd just go on the assumption we're dealing with invisible, latent prints. Either way, if there's a print on the photograph it'll show up here in this machine.'

'Makes sense,' Brown said.

Dana rolled her eyes.

'Anyway,' Rodriguez went on, 'there are also three general techniques we use to make latent prints visible to the naked eye: physical, chemical and instrumental. The cyanoacrylate fuming method is a chemical technique. Since we're using this machine, in this case it's also an instrumental technique.'

Dana sighed. She knew all this stuff already, but she

reminded herself that Rodriguez had dropped whatever she'd been doing previously in order to help her and Brown out. For that reason alone the woman deserved to be listened to carefully and treated with respect. So if she were going to be in class anyway, Dana figured she'd play the part of the brown-nosing student to the best of her abilities. You caught more flies with honey. 'Latent prints are left from the oil on people's fingertips, right?' she asked.

Rodriguez nodded, obviously pleased for the chance to talk about her work. 'Yep,' she said. 'Actually, *all* fingerprints are left that way, Agent Whitestone. But it's not quite that simple. You see, fingerprints are composed of several chemicals exuded through the pores. They're left on virtually every object that's touched. The primary component of fingerprints is ordinary sweat, but since sweat is mostly water it dries out after a fairly short time. The other chemical components of fingerprints are primarily solids, and those chemicals usually remain on surfaces for much longer periods.'

'What kind of other chemicals?' Brown asked. Dana shot a sideways glance at him. Looked like she had competition for the part of teacher's pet.

'Organic compounds, mostly,' Rodriguez said. 'Amino acids, glucose, lactic acid, peptides, ammonia, riboflavin – that kind of stuff. There are also inorganic chemicals present, including potassium, sodium, carbon trioxide and chlorine.'

'So how long does the chemical technique take?' Dana asked, wanting to speed the process along.

Rodriguez opened the door of the plastic box and squeezed a few drops of superglue into a small tray before shutting the door again and pressing another button. 'Not long at all,' she said. 'Not in this case, at least. The basic concept behind the chemical technique is simple enough to understand: apply something – in this case, superglue – that will react chemically with the constituent chemicals present in fingerprints. The resulting reaction gives the fingerprints a new chemical composition, and this composition makes the prints visible by producing a sticky white material that forms along the ridges of the fingerprint. From there, we should be able photograph any prints if they're present. But to enable such a reaction to occur, first we need to convert the superglue to its gaseous form. That's what my little baby here is for.'

'How so?' Brown asked, effectively taking the lead in brownie points. Dana sighed again. They were racing against the clock here, but you couldn't underestimate the human element in investigations. As with just about every other job in the world, you needed to be nice to the people you were working with if you wanted to get their best from them. Still, Brown might have been being a little *too* nice. He knew his stuff, too.

'Well, Agent Brown, there's a small heater inside this box. When the superglue reaches its boiling point – usually between forty-nine and sixty-five degrees Celsius – it begins to boil away into the surrounding atmosphere. That's what exposes the fingerprints,' Rodriguez said.

'So is the process under way now?' Brown asked. Thankfully, it looked as though he was finally ready to move on, too.

Rodriguez nodded. 'Yep, and that's precisely why bigger isn't better in this case. The smaller the tank, the quicker the results. And since our tank here is just about as small as they come, we're already ahead of the game.' Rodriguez made another adjustment on the box by turning a small dial to the left and added, 'I've also got the air inside the tank circulating continuously now, so that should cut down on our waiting time even further. Now all we need to do is give it a few minutes or so. If there's a print on this photograph, it'll show up pretty soon.'

From that point, the three law-enforcement officials simply stared at the photograph inside the airtight tank like three kids huddled around a fishbowl. After about five minutes or so, Dana's breath quickened when a clearly visible print began to form on the photograph.

'Bingo,' Rodriguez said.

'Now what?' Brown asked. The excitement in his voice was clearly evident, and Dana knew exactly how he felt. She was excited now, too. Next to catching a killer standing over a dead body with a bloody knife in his hand, fingerprints were just about the best hard physical evidence you could hope for. And this was the first time they'd had a fingerprint to test. It could be the break they were looking for.

Rodriguez opened the tank and used the tweezers to remove the boy's photograph before blowing on it lightly to accelerate the drying process. 'Now we just take a picture of the fingerprint, convert it to its digital form and run it through Interpol,' she said.

Rodriguez paused while she studied the print on the photograph. After a moment or two, she frowned and said, 'Hmm. That's odd.'

Dana's stomach flipped over. She didn't like the sound of that one little bit. 'What's odd?'

Rodriguez held up the photograph. 'Well, I'm sorry if I'm assuming too much here, Agent Whitestone, but I thought the Chessboard Killer was a man.'

Dana's stomach turned over again. 'He *is* a man, Detective Rodriguez. At least, that's the assumption we've been working on. Why do you ask?'

Rodriguez's frown deepened. Somehow, it only made her look prettier. 'Well, it's just that the size of this fingerprint looks way too small to belong to an average man. To me, this almost looks like a *woman*'s fingerprint.'

A chill went through Dana, right to the bone. But she couldn't possibly wrap her mind around the idea that their killer might be a woman. It was all just too much to handle. First they'd thought the killer was a man, and then two men, and now a woman? What was next – a three-headed alien from outer space? With the way this nightmare investigation was going, Dana wouldn't have been in the least bit surprised to find out that was the case. 'Run the print through Interpol,' Dana said, wanting to swing into action to counteract the confusion racing through her brain. Then she calmed down and thought about it. There was a reasonable explanation for this, disappointing though it would be if it were true. 'Maybe the print belongs to Stephanie Mann herself. The photograph might have been in the apartment on the night she was murdered. The perp could've slipped it into the chess biography just for kicks.'

Rodriguez did as she was instructed, photographing the print and feeding it through a digital scanner before uploading the image to the Interpol database.

After several tense moments, the fingerprint expert looked up from her computer again and shook her head sadly. 'No hits,' she said. 'Doesn't belong to Stephanie Mann, either. The ME has already uploaded her prints to the database. I'm afraid the print we have here doesn't match up with *anyone* in the database, though. I'm very sorry, guys.'

Dana waved away Rodriguez's apology and felt her temples begin to throb again. The headache that had started out early this morning back at the condemned apartment had carved out a permanent home in her skull now and didn't appear likely to move away anytime soon. 'Don't be, Detective Rodriguez,' Dana said. 'There's nothing at all for you to be sorry about here. This is still way more than we had to work with before. Thank you for your time. This is a huge help to us – it really is.'

Dana turned to Brown and pressed her lips together. 'Are you ready to go?'

Brown gave her a puzzled look. 'Sure. Where next?'

Dana breathed in deeply. 'To the media. I think it's

time we went public with this. I really don't see any other option at this point.'

Brown was all business now himself, and Dana was happy to have her partner back. If she were to be completely honest about the whole thing, she'd have to admit she'd felt just the tiniest bit jealous watching the way he'd fallen all over himself in an effort to impress Mariel Rodriguez. 'Right behind you,' he said.

Dana and Brown thanked Rodriguez again and left the lab through the same huge glass doors they'd entered. Stepping out of the sprawling building and into the late-afternoon sunshine five minutes later, Dana shielded her eyes with one hand and flipped open her cellphone with the other, punching in a number while they stood on the concrete steps out front with streams of people filing past.

A familiar voice answered after just one ring. 'Ray Garcia, *New York Times*.'

Dana took in a lungful of air through her nostrils and caught the unmistakable smell of a hot-dog cart thirty yards away. Her stomach grumbled loudly, reminding her that she and Brown hadn't eaten a single thing all day, but she forced herself to ignore it. There wasn't any time for eating now. It was a luxury they just couldn't afford. As quickly as she could, Dana filled in Garcia on her and Brown's recent discovery of the boy's photograph tucked away inside the pages of the chess biography of Amos Burn. Of all the reporters they'd dealt with over the course of this investigation, Garcia was the one Dana trusted the most, the one with whom she felt the most comfortable. Even though he could behave childishly at times – especially when he thought he wasn't getting enough information from them – at least the guy was fair, which was a hell of a lot more than she could say for Nick Brandt over at the *Post*. 'How long before you can get the photograph up on your website?' Dana asked.

'How long will it take you to get the picture over to me?'

'Five minutes.'

'Give me ten and it'll be featured at the top of our homepage.'

'Great. Thanks, Ray.'

'No, thank *you*, Agent Whitestone. Appreciate it. My bosses have been breathing down my neck non-stop about this case. It's almost like they've forgotten what it's like to be a reporter out in the field or something.'

Dana laughed without humour, knowing that it shouldn't be too long now before she and Brown started hearing about this case from their own bosses. No doubt FBI Director Bill Krugman was getting an earful about the slayings from the White House each morning during his daily debriefing sessions with the President. Sooner or later, those earfuls would be passed right along to her and Brown – with any sugar coating removed. 'Tell me about it, Ray,' Dana said.

Garcia grunted into the mouthpiece. 'So I'll watch out for the photograph in my email, OK?'

'Yep. Sending it over now.'

Dana cut the connection with Garcia and accessed her

email account from her cellphone before forwarding over to the *New York Times* the pictures that the forensic photographer had taken back at the condemned apartment building earlier that morning. She closed her eyes when the deed was done. For better or worse, things were about to change in a big way. She only prayed they changed for the better – for the boy's sake, wherever he might be right now.

Brown was working on his own cellphone as Dana slipped hers back into her pocket and sighed heavily. He didn't look up. 'I was eavesdropping, Dana,' he said, tapping a few more keys and furrowing his eyebrows in concentration. 'My artist has already finished up with the age-progression sketch, so I'm emailing it over to Garcia now.'

Pressing one more key, he flipped shut his phone and finally looked up. 'Anyway, now what? Where do we go from here?'

Dana held his stare, feeling helpless. Sadly, it was a feeling she was becoming all too familiar with lately. 'There's nowhere for us *to* go, Jeremy,' she said, trying to keep the frustration out of her voice but no doubt falling miserably short. 'That's the whole goddamn problem. Now we just wait.'

Brown pursed his lips. 'Wait for what?'

Dana shook her head. 'I don't know. Something. Anything.'

'You sure that's a good idea?'

Dana ignored his tone. She really didn't feel like fighting with him again right now. 'You got a better one?'

Brown dropped his gaze to the cement and kicked at a stray penny that someone had dropped. 'Nope.'

Dana stared down at the penny. The coin was facing heads-up. Abraham Lincoln's profile stared grimly ahead into the distance, no doubt wondering how he was going to deal with that pesky slave situation once and for all. Dana knew pretty much how he'd felt right now. There didn't seem to be any easy answers here for her and Brown, either. 'You'd better pick that thing up,' she said, nodding down at the coin.

Brown looked at her quizzically. 'Why? You trying to supplement your income here or something?'

Dana shook her head. 'Nope. But I have a funny feeling we're going to need all the luck we can get in this case.' She paused, knowing that luck wasn't going to cut it. Not even close. 'While we wait, though, we should go back to the start, whiteboard everything we've learned so far, see if we can't finally find a crack in this wall that's been put in front of us.'

Brown nodded. 'Sounds like a plan to me.' Leaning down, he picked up the penny and slipped it into his pocket before straightening back up. He smiled thinly. 'Every little bit helps, right?'

Dana didn't smile back. 'Let's hope so, Jeremy. Because if this doesn't work, I'm afraid that I'm fresh out of ideas.'

Brown closed his eyes. Exhaustion carved deep grooves into his face. 'Me, too. Anyway, so when do you think we'll start hearing about all this from the bigwigs down in DC?'

Just then, Dana's cellphone rang in her pocket. She dug out the phone and looked at the name on the caller ID: *Bill Krugman*.

Dana's stomach went sour. Flipping open the phone, she covered the mouthpiece with her right palm and shifted her stare back to Brown. 'Looks like we'll start hearing about it right now.'

Brown winced.

Dana breathed in a fresh lungful of air and placed the phone to her ear. When she heard what Bill Krugman had to say, she winced too.

CHAPTER THIRTEEN

Wednesday, 5:15 p.m.

Two hours after his first Internet search of the day, Jack Yuntz refreshed the browser on his computer and was shocked to find himself staring directly back into his own face.

His breath caught in his throat at the sight of his first-grade photograph splashed all over the homepage of the *New York Times*. What the fuck was *this*?

Jack swallowed hard to clear away the fear-spawned lump that was blocking his throat and making it nearly impossible to breathe. His whole body shuddered. His entire world swam out of focus. His ears rang as though someone had just jammed a huge copper bell over his head, then clanged the hell out of it with all their might.

Jack blinked rapidly and looked at the image on the screen again. There he was, looking right back at him - self. He could barely resist the urge to rub his eyes in disbelief.

Jack leaned forward in his chair until his nose practically touched the computer screen, studying the image of his own face even more closely. The only difference in the eyes right now was that the ones on the screen weren't blinking back at him in incredulity. Luckily, though, everything else had changed with the passage of time, rendering the age-progression sketch positioned next to his first-grade photograph basically useless. The artist had missed his mark by a mile.

Jack's toothless childhood grin had been filled in as he'd grown. The unruly cowlick in his brown hair had finally been tamed. His once pale white skin dotted with tiny brown birthmarks had darkened considerably over the years. And his face, somewhat round back then, had been reshaped by high, delicate-looking cheekbones that belied his newly hardened soul.

Jack shook his head hard in outright amazement, as though he could somehow chase away the surreal image if he shook his head hard enough. He didn't want to believe what he was looking at right now. Who would? It was just plain *disturbing* seeing your own face – however different it might look now – plastered across an Internet page belonging to one of the biggest and most famous news outlets in the entire world. He just hoped the police hadn't discovered he'd been in his mother's apartment that morning. Because if they *had* discovered that and somebody out there somehow recognised him from the photograph on the website – however unlikely that might seem – then the chase would be on and they'd be tracking him down very soon.

If they weren't on their way over here already.

Jack's jaw tensed as the thought occurred to him. What if they suspected *him* of his mother's murder? Even *charged* him with it? He shook his head again, even harder this time. The thought was just too horrifying to even consider.

Jack scanned the website article quickly, his heartbeat thumping out of control the entire time he worked his way through the text.

He gathered this much immediately: the FBI thought he was missing. Not a good sign at all. Because if the feds thought he was missing, that meant they'd be out there looking for him and they wouldn't stop until they'd found him. After all, the FBI had never been an organisation especially inclined to give up very easily when it thought that it was hot on the heels of a killer.

The headline at the top of the article blared out in big block letters that scorched Jack's eyes:

> FEDS RELEASE PHOTO IN CHESSBOARD KILLER CASE, ASK FOR PUBLIC'S HELP
>
> By Raymond C. Garcia
>
> *New York Times* staff writer
>
> The FBI on Wednesday released a photograph it says was discovered at the scene of the infamous Chessboard Killer's latest murder.
>
> According to the Bureau, the Chessboard Killer took the life of Stephanie Mann, 30, sometime late last week. Although no official number of victims has been released, Miss Mann's slaying marks the notorious murderer's latest confirmed victim since his well-chronicled crime spree began last year.
>
> Lead investigator Special Agent Dana Whitestone and her partner, Special Agent Jeremy Brown – who

have been heading up the investigation for the past five months now, ever since being called in from Cleveland by FBI Director Bill Krugman to take the reins – are pleading for the public's help in identifying the boy in the photograph.

'It's literally a matter of life and death,' Miss Whitestone said Wednesday afternoon. 'If somebody out there even suspects they recognise this boy, I'm asking them to come forward now.'

Miss Whitestone noted that the photograph itself was seven years old.

'At the time this picture was taken, the boy in the photograph appears to have been five or six years old. That would make him twelve or thirteen years old today. Please bear that in mind when calling in with what you think might be new information.'

Miss Whitestone said that all tips would be kept confidential.

'The FBI, in association with the NYPD, is working diligently to bring this long, citywide nightmare to an end for the good people of New York City. Any help we can get from the general public is greatly appreciated.'

Anyone with information on the identity of the boy in the photograph is asked to contact the FBI, the NYPD or this newspaper column. Phone numbers and email addresses for each are listed below. The FBI is offering a $100,000 reward for information that leads to the arrest, capture and conviction of the Chessboard Killer.

Story still developing. Check back often for updates.

Lost in his reading, Jack was jolted back to the room by the sudden sound of his younger sister's sleep-fogged voice directly behind him. 'What's that you're looking at, Jack? Is that you when you were little?'

Jack's heart nearly exploded inside his chest. His stomach folded over on itself. A dizzying rush of adrenalin flooded through his veins. *Jesus Christ.* He hadn't even heard Molly get out of bed.

Jack closed the lid of his laptop and turned around quickly to tousle his little sister's hair with a trembling hand, trying his best to act as normal as possible. 'Yeah right,' he said in a shaking voice. 'Like *I*'d ever be in the newspaper. C'mon, Molly – what are you, crazy or something?' Molly couldn't know about what had happened to their mother. Not yet, at least.

Fortunately for Jack, his little sister didn't seem to notice his heightened emotional state. Thank God for small mercies. Like his mother had always said – those were the ones that usually counted the most in this life.

'I don't know,' Molly said, still rubbing at her eyes with a tiny balled-up fist in her ongoing effort to wake up. 'I just thought that maybe somebody wrote a story on you or something because of how good you play chess. You're the best one in the whole park.'

Jack let out a deep sigh of relief and felt his heartbeat begin to slow a little. *Fuck.* That was close. He'd dodged a bullet. For now, at least. But just barely. He knew he'd need to be a lot more careful from here on if he wanted to keep Molly out of this mess, though. 'Ha, I *wish* somebody would write a story about me in the newspaper, Mol,' he said. 'But it's not going to happen.'

'Why not?'

'Because I'm not good enough.'

'Well, maybe someday you *will* be good enough. *I* think you will be, anyway. In fact, I know it.'

Jack smiled gently at his little sister's faith in him. Even during the toughest times in his life, Molly always knew *exactly* how to make him feel better. It was just one of the many reasons he loved her so much. Just one of the many reasons he'd *die* for her, if need be. He just hoped it didn't come to that. 'Yeah, maybe someday I'll be good enough,' he said. 'But that day's definitely not today. I still have a long way to go. I still have a lot more work to do.'

'What kind of work?'

Jack shrugged. It was a good question, but one he didn't have the answer to. 'I'm not sure,' he admitted. 'I haven't figured that part out yet.' He paused and raised his eyebrows. 'Why? Do you *want* to see my picture in the newspaper or something? Want me to be a big-shot celebrity so that you can brag about it to all your little friends?'

Molly tilted her head in thought. After a moment or two, she nodded and said, 'Yeah, I guess so. That would be pretty cool. That way I could show it to Brittany and Allison at school. Ugh, I swear, they're always bragging about something or the other. Usually about something stupid, like their stupid dolls or their stupid hair ties or their stupid boyfriends. Like either of them even *have* a boyfriend.'

Jack shook his head in bemusement at the disgruntled tone of his little sister's voice, then paused again when the idea occurred to him. He knew he'd need Molly's help if he wanted to get away with what he planned to do next – which he most certainly did – but he didn't want *her* to know that. Not yet, at least. The farther he could keep her away from this mess – at least for the time being – the better and the safer for her. Still, maybe this conversation could pave the way for her eventual cooperation; ease her into this ordeal as gently as possible.

Jack swivelled back and forth in his desk chair and asked, 'How would you like to *help* me get my picture in the newspaper, Molly?'

Molly frowned at him and bit down softly into her lower lip. 'How would I do something like that?'

Jack stopped swivelling. 'Well, it would involve you keeping a secret. Do you think you could do something like that?'

'What kind of secret?'

Jack waved a hand in the air. 'It doesn't *matter* what kind of secret, Molly. Can you keep a secret or not?'

Molly screwed up her little face in righteous indignation. 'Of *course* I can keep a secret, you big dummy. I'm really *good* at keeping secrets. Everyone at school says so. Even Brittany and Allison.'

Jack rolled his eyes. 'Yeah, I'm so sure. Everyone at

school says that, huh? Even Brittany and Allison? Well, what about that time you told mom on me for breaking her favourite coffee mug? You didn't keep a secret very well that time, now did you?'

'That time was totally different.'

'How so?'

'I was just a kid then.'

Jack laughed out loud. He just couldn't help himself. For as long as he could remember, just being around Molly had always lightened his mood, and that was *precisely* what he needed at the moment. Above all else, he knew that he needed to approach his upcoming mission with a clear head, and if she were helping him to achieve that goal, well, then her partnership with him was already working, whether or not she knew it.

'OK, smarty-pants,' he said. 'Whatever you say.'

Molly put her little face up close to his. She was deadly serious about this. 'Honestly, Jack,' she persisted. 'I can keep a secret really, really good. I promise. You can trust me.'

Jack looked deep into his little sister's bright blue eyes. Pure innocence stared back at him. Molly was clearly annoyed with the 'tattletale' title he'd just hung on her, and from the looks of things she wanted to erase it as quickly as she possibly could. 'Do you *swear* you can keep a secret?' Jack asked, holding her stare.

'Yes, I swear.'

'Do you cross your heart and hope to die?'

Molly nodded. 'And stick a needle in my eye.'

'How about in both eyes?'

'Yep.'

'Do you swear to *God*?'

Molly paused. To all intents and purposes, she might as well have been called before Almighty God himself. In any event, the religion factor had obviously raised the stakes considerably for her, and judging from the look in her eye she wanted to be absolutely certain of her answer before committing to it. To her young mind, this could mean the difference between an everlasting life in heaven and an eternity of suffering in hell. After a moment or two of careful consideration, she finally let out a deep breath and said, 'Yes, Jack, I swear to God.'

Jack studied his little sister's face. There was absolutely no falsehood in her eyes at all. It was in that instant he knew he could trust her with his life. Good thing, too. Pretty soon he'd probably need to do just that. 'OK, Molly,' he said. 'I'm happy to hear that. Because we're all that each other has left now.'

Molly pursed her lips and shook her head in annoyance, shooting him a look that could have frozen water. 'No, we're not, Jack. You forgot about mommy.' Molly paused and wrinkled up her face some more. 'Don't *ever* forget about mommy, Jack. It's not nice, and besides, she's coming back for us pretty soon, you know. She said so.'

Newly hardened soul or not, Jack's heart broke a little bit at that. *The poor kid.* Molly would be devastated when she found out their mother wasn't *ever* coming back for them. *Couldn't* ever come back for them. Not today, and not on any other day for the rest of their lives. Still, *he* didn't want to be the one to tell her. Doing something like that would be like stabbing her in the heart himself. So instead of filling her in on what he knew he simply shook his head and said, 'Don't worry about it, Molly. I didn't forget about mommy. All I meant by what I said just now is that we're all each other has left right now.'

Molly's expression softened. Apparently she'd been reassured by his hasty correction. Again, thank God for the little mercies. Lifting his arm over her bony shoulder, she sat down in his lap. 'So,' she said eagerly, 'are you going to tell me your great big secret or not? What's it about, anyway? Do you like a girl or something?'

Molly blinked. Then she laughed happily and said, 'That's it, isn't it! You like a girl!'

Jack grinned. 'How'd you guess?'

Molly giggled some more. 'I could just tell,' she said, talking at the breakneck speed of an excited eight-year-old girl, her words bumping into each other before tumbling out of her mouth. 'I'm a very good guesser, too. I don't just keep secrets good. Anyway, what's her name?'

'What's whose name?'

'The girl that you like, you big dummy!'

'I can't tell you her name right now.'

'Why not?'

'Because you haven't met her yet.'

Molly's big blue eyes went saucer-wide. 'Am I going to meet her?'

'Yep. I think so.'

'When?'

'I don't know. Pretty soon.'

'*When?*'

Jack smiled. Taking his little sister off his knee, he walked over to their closet and retrieved his jacket from a hanger before slipping it on. Then he reached into the jacket's pocket and took out his hat, putting that on, too – but not all the way yet. When he was dressed properly for the night's activities, he turned back to Molly and said, 'I don't know. I guess you'll probably meet her at the same time I do.'

Molly stared up at him. 'What do mean by that? You mean you haven't even *met* her yet?'

'Nope.'

'Why not? Are you chicken or something?'

'Nope.'

'OK. So why did you put your coat and hat on just now, then? Are you going to meet her right now?'

'Nope.'

'Quit saying "nope", Jack. It's annoying. Anyway, if you're not going to meet her right now, where *are* you going, then?'

Jack pulled down the black ski mask over his face. 'I'm going to play chess, Molly. As a matter of fact, I'm going to be playing a *lot* of chess from now on.'

'Can I come with you?'

'Come with me where?'

'To the park.'

Jack smiled again through the ski mask. 'Nope.'

Leaving his little sister behind in the bedroom, Jack

shut the door after himself with a soft *click*. But he wasn't even halfway down the hall before the door opened up again. 'Hey, Jack!'

He turned around to see Molly standing there in the hallway. 'What?'

'I changed my mind.'

'About what?'

'About keeping your big secret.'

'Why's that?'

'Because I decided I can only keep it on one condition.'

'What condition's that?'

'You have to tell me the girl's name.'

Jack sighed in frustration. Still, there was nothing to be surprised about here. He'd known all along that his little sister wouldn't let him off the hook *that* easily. She was a natural-born busybody, always had been. So if he didn't tell her now, he knew she'd never leave him alone about it. She'd follow him right to his *grave* until she got the information she was after. Eight years old or eighty, women were all the same. 'OK,' he said. 'You win. Her name's Dana Whitestone. Satisfied?'

Molly's entire body quivered with the pure *ecstasy* of hearing a secret. After a moment or two, she nodded and said, 'That's a very pretty name, Jack. I can't wait to meet her.'

Jack nodded. 'Neither can I. She's gonna help us get our mom back. And she's going to hurt the people who took her away from us in the first place. She's gonna hurt them real bad.'

Molly frowned. 'How do you know that? Did she say that?'

Jack held his little sister's stare. 'Yep. Dana Whitestone said it right in the newspaper. And now that I've told you this, I guess we'll see how good you are at keeping a secret. You can't tell anybody about this, Molly. Not even Mrs Macklin.'

Molly twisted up her face. 'I don't even *talk* to Mrs Macklin. She's not my real mom. But you believe the woman who said she's gonna help us get our real mom back?'

'Of course I believe her.'

'Why?'

Jack gritted his teeth. 'Because if she's lying, then I'm going to hurt those people myself.'

CHAPTER FOURTEEN

Bill Krugman's angry voice exploded in Dana's ear as she and Brown stood on the concrete steps leading up to the entrance of the NYPD headquarters – the perfect end to a perfectly miserable day. 'What the *hell* are you two doing up there, Agent Whitestone? I just had the distinctly unpleasant experience of having my ass handed to me by the President yet again. Called me up special from his personal cellphone in order to do it. Apparently, the ass-chewing he gave me this morning in front of everyone wasn't enough to satisfy him. Wanted to make damn sure I understood just how much of a fuck-up agency he thought I was running. What's the status of the Chessboard Killer investigation? Give it to me short and sweet and keep any extraneous bullshit out of it. I've already heard about the Stephanie Mann murder, so there's no need to pass along any extra details about that one. I've already read the report genned up by the NYPD, already seen the crime-scene photographs up close and personal and in living colour. Can't wait until the President sees them tomorrow morning. Should be a real shit-show over in the West Wing.'

Dana bit down hard into her lower lip and resisted the

urge to shout back at her boss. She was frustrated enough as it was already, didn't need him piling on the pressure. Still, she knew that getting mouthy with Krugman at this crucial point in the case probably wasn't the wisest move for her career. Besides, he had every right to be angry with her and Brown. They were just spinning their wheels in the muck of New York City, had been doing so for the past five months now, kicking up mud that no doubt splattered across the lapels of Krugman's freshly pressed suit each morning all the way down in Washington, DC. And the sad fact of the matter was that Dana and Brown hadn't made a lick of progress in the investigation, not recently, at least. Most importantly, people were still dying horrible deaths. Hard as they'd tried to stop him – and they'd tried their damnedest – she and Brown hadn't been able to trip up the Chessboard Killer. Not even close. Not to mention the fact that the press was beating up on them a little bit more with each passing day, especially Nick Brandt over at the *Post*, bloodying their noses with each of their increasingly sensationalised stories that were finding their way to the front pages of every major newspaper across the city – and across the world – every morning. So, no matter how hard it might be for Dana to get to grips with the realisation right now, she knew that she and Brown had to admit that they weren't any closer to identifying the killer than they'd been five months ago, back when they'd first been assigned to this nightmare case.

Besides, Dana knew for sure that if she wasn't

extremely careful here she might very well wind up passing out basketballs in the FBI Academy gym down in Quantico on cold Saturday mornings. After all, she'd seen the same thing happen to more than one of her fellow agents who'd had the temerity to cross Krugman in the past. The man known to everyone around the FBI simply by his title of 'the Director' wasn't the kind of guy with whom you wanted to get lippy. So to assuage Krugman's obvious irritation with her and Brown's woeful lack of progress, Dana brought him up to speed on their recent discovery of a fingerprint on the boy's photograph, passing along Mariel Rodriguez's suspicion that the fingerprint might belong to a woman and hoping this new piece of evidence might be enough to calm Krugman's jangled nerves. Unfortunately, though, quite the opposite took place. Rather than being in the least bit mollified by Dana's hasty report, Krugman didn't seem at all impressed. 'A *woman*'s fingerprint?' he asked incredulously. 'How could some hack detective at the NYPD possibly know something like that without first getting a hit back from the Interpol database, Agent Whitestone? Ever stop to think that the fingerprint might belong to a smaller *man*? We come in all shapes and sizes, you know. Jesus fucking Christ, do I need to do *all* the thinking for you two?'

Dana closed her eyes and fought the sudden temptation to slam the cellphone down onto the concrete steps as hard as she could. She reminded herself that Krugman had a reason for being tougher on her than he was on most of her fellow agents. Bill Krugman had been Crawford Bell's closest friend. Had been ever since their days at the FBI Academy forty years earlier. They'd graduated together, risen up through the ranks together and had taken their places as the Number One and Number Two men in the entire agency together. So Dana was pretty sure that talking with her only reminded Krugman of Crawford each time they spoke. And Crawford had died an extremely gruesome death while he'd been helping her out on the Cleveland Slasher investigation.

Dana continued to fight back her irritation. It was a losing battle. If she were to be perfectly honest about the whole thing, though, she supposed she could understand Krugman's frustration with her. Quite apart from the association with Crawford Bell, he'd always backed her in the past, and she owed much of her continued career to him.

Krugman grunted into the mouthpiece when Dana didn't immediately answer his rhetorical question about doing all the thinking for her and Brown. 'Anyway,' he said, 'I apologise for shouting at you like that just now, Agent Whitestone, but I'm afraid you're not going to like the purpose of this phone call very much. I don't want to do this – honestly, I don't – but I don't have any other choice in the matter. As of right now, I'm officially putting you and Brown on notice. My hands are tied on this one, so please don't try to talk your way out of it. As it is now, I'm getting far too much heat from the White House and, as I'm sure you're well aware, shit rolls downhill. Always has and always will.

It's an ugly fact of life but one that's simple enough to understand.'

Dana frowned at Krugman's last statement, unclear of what he'd meant, exactly, about putting her and Brown on notice. Did that mean they *would* be passing out basketballs in the FBI Academy gym down in Quantico on cold Saturday mornings soon? Should she just go ahead and book her plane ticket right now, try to save herself a little money by ordering in advance? Or could it actually be something *worse* than that?

She closed her eyes while she ran through all the possible fates in her mind. None of them were very pretty. Only one way to find out what Krugman was talking about, though. 'What, exactly, do you mean when you say that you're "putting us on notice", sir?' Dana asked. She regretted the words just as soon as they'd left her lips.

Krugman's exasperated sigh echoed in her ear from more than six hundred miles away. His patience had clearly run out now, and the simple truth of the matter was that Dana was surprised it had lasted this long. She doubted whether she would've been half as patient had she been in his shoes. 'What I mean by that, *exactly*, Agent Whitestone,' Krugman said, speaking slowly and presumably through gritted teeth, 'is that if just one more dead body should happen to pop up during the course of this investigation – *just one more* – you and Agent Brown are officially off the case. You'll be reassigned. I'm completely serious about this. If some - one should happen to get a cold and die of pneumonia while they're reading paperwork on the Chessboard Killer's slayings, if someone should happen to break their neck while walking away from a crime scene . . . if a fucking *piano* should happen to fall on top of a crime-scene technician's head while she's walking down the street to pick up some sandwiches for the hungry troops. Just one more dead body and you and Agent Brown are gone. Off the case for good. No ifs, ands or buts about it. Do we understand each other?'

Dana's cheeks flushed hot. For a moment she couldn't form words, no matter how hard she tried to do so. Her lips, tongue and mouth had gone much too dry for that. Finally, she pulled herself together and slid her sandpaper tongue across her desiccated lips. 'Yes, sir. We understand each other perfectly. One more dead body and we're gone.'

The connection went dead at Krugman's end. Apparently, he was done talking with her for the day. Still, Dana didn't blame him. No amount of words would stop the Chessboard Killer. She and Brown needed to *do* it.

She just hoped they were up to the task. So far, though, things weren't looking so hot. And the stakes had just got a whole lot higher.

CHAPTER FIFTEEN

Wednesday, 5:51 p.m.

Jack Yuntz ducked out of the house without telling his foster mother where he was going. Honestly, it was none of her business. Although the woman was nice enough as far as foster mothers went, this was his and Molly's third foster home in just the past five months, and he really didn't expect to be living there that much longer.

Not after what would happen tonight.

Besides, becoming a foster parent wasn't too much different from becoming a substitute teacher in a sense – something that looked pretty good on paper but was not so great in real life. Once you were faced with the harsh realities of raising two kids who didn't belong to you – biologically, at least – the entire romantic concept went south quickly, even when you took into account the many generous state and federal subsidies that went along with it.

Cynical outlook on the set-up or not, Jack knew that just beneath the surface it wasn't that different from seeing one of those heartrending 'Feed the Children' ads on television at three in the morning, dutifully agreeing to sponsor a child for the low, low price of the equivalent of just a single cup of coffee a day while you brushed potato chip crumbs absentmindedly off your finger-smeared T-shirt, and then realising later on that you valued your daily coffee a hell of a lot more than you did some random child who didn't have the same blood as you running through its veins. At least, that was the way it felt to him sometimes. He was just glad they hadn't separated him and Molly. He didn't know what he would have done if that had happened. Something good to be said for the care system, he supposed.

At almost six p.m. now, it was cold enough outside to make Jack's black ski mask enough of a necessity not to draw too much unwanted attention to him. After all – with the FBI no doubt hot on his trail by now – he certainly didn't want to be recognised tonight by some no-good do-gooder out there intent upon collecting a reward. Thankfully, though, the ski mask provided the perfect camouflage.

An icy wind that seemed hell-bent on cutting him clean in half howled down the street and sliced through the stretchy fabric of Jack's mask like a million tiny razor blades while he walked down the street with his head down. A hurricane of loose papers and debris flew past: hot-dog wrappers; a coupon supplement from the Sunday newspaper; dust and little bits of concrete that stung his eyes and made them water. Shivering violently against the unrelenting cold, Jack fought back against the powerful gusts as best he could, but it was a losing battle the entire way. From the looks of things, the false springtime in New York City had run its course.

Jack's first stop fifteen minutes later was at Larson's Book Shop on Monterey Street. Heaving a sigh of relief, he stepped inside the scruffy brick building and stomped his feet in an effort to get the blood flowing again, happy to finally get out of the bitter cold. Gradually, he felt the sensation come back into his fingers and toes. Removing his ski mask, he luxuriated in the shop's heating that warmed his frozen cheeks.

Larson's was one of those old-fashioned family-owned independent bookstores that you didn't see around very often these days. But one of the good things about living in a place like New York City was that even the smaller stores usually had at least a handful of people in them at any given time of the day, allowing you to become just another face in the crowd. Larson's was no exception. In addition to the clerk standing behind the front counter – a 1960s-ish librarian type with huge grandma boobs, who wore her ornate Harlequin glasses on a thin gold chain around her impossibly fleshy neck – there were three other distinct groups of people milling about the store. A young hippie couple who smelled faintly of patchouli even from fifteen feet away nodded at each other knowingly while they examined a New Age cookbook that no doubt featured pot brownies somewhere in the appetisers section – or perhaps even as an entrée offering. Over by the magazine racks, a Travis Bickle clone decked out in a beat-up camouflage jacket – who could have passed as the grandfather of Arizona shooter Jared Loughner – studied the latest issue of *Field &*

Stream with an intense look fixed upon his scowling face. Twenty feet to Bickle/Grandpa Loughner's right, a middle-aged gay couple who reminded Jack of Robin Williams and Nathan Lane in *The Birdcage* fawned over a brand-new hardback copy of Man Booker prize-winner Hilary Mantel's *Wolf Hall* in the New Releases section.

Shoving his ski mask deep into his coat pocket, Jack made his way over to the corner of the shop that contained the chess-strategy books. There were about a dozen of them lined up in two neat rows on the fourth and fifth shelves. The most promising title leaped out at him immediately: *Chess For Dummies*.

Using his index finger, Jack slid out the book and felt a growing sense of anticipation. He couldn't think of a more appropriate selection for his father. But Don Yuntz's days of being a dummy and actually getting away with it would be over soon enough. It was the only way Jack knew how to make things right again.

Jack tucked the book under his right arm and turned his body sideways as he passed by the camouflage jacket again in an effort to avoid bumping shoulders with its wearer. Judging from the furiously knitted eyebrows and the tightly set jaw – not to mention the fact that the guy actually *smelled* like anger when you got up this close to him – Jack didn't figure he was the sort of chap with whom you would want to start a fight. An innocent shoulder-bump most likely would have been just enough to send him hurtling right over the edge.

Reaching the front counter, Jack stood before the old

woman stationed on the other side. She balanced her fancy eyeglasses on the end of her nose and peered down at the book he handed her. 'Interested in chess, are ya?'

Jack nodded and reached around to his back pocket for his wallet, slipping out his lone wrinkled twenty-dollar bill and holding it out to her. 'Yes, ma'am. I like it a lot. It's my favourite game.'

The woman didn't take his money right away. 'Any good at it?'

'Any good at what?'

'Chess.'

Jack shrugged, feeling dumb as he stood there with his arm still extended. This old bat sure was chatty. But his mind was already somewhere else. Somewhere far, far away. 'I don't know. I'm OK, I guess. I can hold my own when the conditions are right. I play in the park sometimes.'

'How long have you been playing?'

'About three years now.'

The woman glanced around the store and lowered her voice. She handed the book back to Jack but still didn't take his money. 'Put your money away, kiddo. This one's on the house. It's nice to see young people like you who still appreciate the finer things in life.' Nodding in distaste over to the patchouli-scented hippie couple, she wrinkled her nose. 'Young people like you who still realise the value and importance of personal hygiene.'

Jack held the woman's gaze for several measured

beats to make sure he'd heard her correctly. After several awkward seconds, he finally put his tattered banknote back into his wallet and returned it to his left rear pocket. He didn't know what to say. He hadn't expected this. 'Thank you,' he said finally. 'I don't have very much money these days.'

The old woman rolled her eyes. 'Heck, who does, child? Anyway, don't mention it. Now get out of here and go read your book. If you want to pay me back someday, just say hello to me in the newspapers when you become world-famous.'

Jack still felt weird as he continued to stand there. He tried to move his feet, but his shoes felt as though they'd been glued to the floor. Peace on earth and goodwill toward men just didn't fit into his current world-view right now. So it was just plain *odd* to make a real personal connection – however brief – when you were in the middle of plotting out the best way to murder another human being in cold blood and actually get away with it. 'What's your name?' he asked.

The woman raised her thin, plucked eyebrows. 'Excuse me?'

'Your name,' Jack said. 'You said that I should say hello to you in the papers when I become famous, so in order to do that I'll need to know your name first.'

She laughed. 'Oh, of course. I'd lose my head if it weren't attached to my shoulders, wouldn't I? Anyway, my name's Penelope Briggins, honey, but you can just call me Penny. Everyone else does. What's yours?'

'Garry.'

Penelope Briggins nodded. 'That's a fine American name you've got there, Garry. Don't do anything to spoil it, OK?'

Jack forced a smile, but didn't bother mentioning to her that his chosen alias had actually been picked to honour his all-time favourite chess player, who was most decidedly *not* American. 'I won't,' he said. 'And it shouldn't be too long now before I'm famous. One way or another, it'll probably happen soon enough.'

The old woman laughed again, jiggling her enormous breasts. 'Well, now, that's certainly the spirit, isn't it? Confidence never killed anybody, right? Anyway, I'll watch out for my name in the *New York Times*.'

Just then, the door to the bookshop banged open and a delivery man holding a thick bundle of newspapers secured by criss-crossed plastic straps entered. Several icy blasts of air entered behind him and swirled around the store before he closed the door again. Dropping the heavy papers onto the counter with a thump and a groan, he said, 'Hey there, Penny. Got a special edition here for you today. Missing kid.'

Jack looked down at the papers and immediately felt his heartbeat accelerate. There was his first-grade photograph again, displayed prominently on the top of the front page and accompanied by the age-progression sketch. The headline above the story read *FBI Seeks Public's Help In Unidentified Child Case* .

The clerk's voice cut through Jack's fear-induced haze a split second later. 'Thanks, Tom. Still freezing out there?'

'Colder than a witch's teat, Pen. I figured I'd better get my ass the hell inside where it's a little bit warmer.'

Jack tried to act as normally as he could while the clerk and the delivery man continued to engage in their pointless banter. He held up *Chess For Dummies* in his right hand and said, 'Thank you very much for the book.'

Still distracted by the delivery man's charms, Penny Briggins waved a hand briefly in the air without making eye contact with Jack again. 'Don't mention it, sonny. I hope you enjoy it. Anyway, have a nice day.'

'You too.'

Jack left the bookshop as quickly as he could and stepped back outside into the freezing wind, imagining that he could feel the clerk and the delivery man's accusing glares burning a hole through the back of his skull. But when he glanced through the window he saw that they were still laughing and talking together.

Jack's mind was still in a fog by the time he reached the convenience store a few minutes later to buy the sleeping pills and scissors he'd need for tonight's mission. Neatly stacked in two high piles next to the service counter, still more newspapers with his photograph and age-progression sketch looked to him like wanted posters that were calling out for his swift capture and even swifter punishment. On the subway ride across town, a commuter seated directly across the aisle was reading the *New York Times*. As Jack stared back into his own eyes again, he felt an unsettling rush of adrenalin flood through his body. He might just as well have been looking into a funhouse mirror that reflected the image of the person you *used* to be. Everywhere he looked, Jack was convinced he could feel people's harsh stares upon him, accusing him of a crime he hadn't yet committed. But no one said anything to him, and after a while he decided it was probably just his overactive imagination at work.

Jack breathed a deep sigh of relief when the subway doors finally slid open ten minutes later. As quickly as he could, he left the car and lost himself in the crowd streaming up to the busy street.

By the time he knocked on the apartment door on the fifth floor of a co-op building on 18th Street twenty minutes later – making sure that no one had seen him on his way up, of course – his pulse had begun to slow a little and the haze in his brain had cleared up somewhat. Overactive imagination or not, he was pretty sure that no one had recognised him. Not yet, at least.

A chain rattled and the door of the apartment opened up in response to Jack's knocking. Tilting up his chin, Jack once again found himself staring directly back into his own eyes – except they were many years older this time. The funhouse-mirror effect at work again but in the opposite time-travel direction now.

Forcing a smile, Jack tried to keep his voice steady even though the enormity of his situation was making it almost impossible for him to think or speak clearly.

Amazingly, though, his words came out much more confidently than he would have dreamed possible. 'Hey there, dad,' he said. 'Long time, no see.'

CHAPTER SIXTEEN

Dana flipped her cellphone shut and felt her mood darken like the ominous skies overhead. The once-bright sun had disappeared completely now and the storm clouds were rolling in, fast and threatening. The schizophrenic New York City weather at work again.

Standing just three feet away from her on the concrete steps leading up to NYPD headquarters, Dana's partner took one glance at the disgusted look on her face and shook his head. 'Bad news, huh?' Brown asked.

Dana nodded. 'And then some.'

'How bad we talkin'?'

'Well, let's just say we're on a very short leash from here on out.'

'How short?'

Dana held her thumb and forefinger an inch apart. 'This short. One more dead body and we're gone. Off the case for good.'

Brown winced. 'Ouch. Pretty short leash.'

Dana gave a humourless laugh. 'Yeah, I know. Anyway, c'mon. I'm starving. Let's get something to eat.'

Descending the steps, Dana led Brown over to the hot-dog cart stationed on the sidewalk thirty yards away. Only the finest cuisine for them.

Dana ordered a foot-long with mustard and onions, and Brown took his with ketchup and relish. As the old Greek vendor prepared their food he glanced up at Dana and said, 'Eh, what's this? Why such an ugly look on such a pretty lady on such a pretty day?' He pronounced the word 'pretty' as *pree-dy* and waved an arm in the air. 'A beautiful day for a beautiful lady like you to enjoy. What more could you possibly ask for? God has given us this day, and we should rejoice in it and realise that this day is good.'

Dana took the hot dog the man was holding out and frowned at his generous assessment of the deteriorating weather. Looking up at the black skies, she said, 'Doesn't look like a very pretty day to me. Anyway, what makes you think I'm sad?'

The old man laughed and wagged a finger in her face. 'Ah, don't try to fool me, young lady. I've got three daughters of my own back in Greece and I can always tell when they're sad. It's in the eyes. It's something you can never hide from a father, no matter how hard you try. We read the sadness in our daughters' eyes just as easily as a child reads a picture book. It's that simple to see. Besides, when you're still alive, *every* day is a beautiful day, isn't it? We must never take any of them for granted. It is an insult to God.'

Dana felt her cheeks flush hot. Even with Brown standing next to her, she couldn't resist the urge to open up to the chatty vendor. Something about the man's easygoing nature, about his soothing tone, relaxed her slightly. Besides, she *needed* someone to talk to right now. Someone who didn't know anything about her or her troubled past. Someone who didn't know all the details surrounding this maddening case. Someone who wouldn't judge her for what Dana knew to be her many faults. 'Work's not going so hot right now,' she admitted. 'Hell, half the time I can barely figure out if I'm coming or going any more.'

The vendor clucked his tongue. 'Ah, I know this feeling well.' He spread his arms open wide, showcasing the huge smear of mustard staining the front of his white apron. 'Just look at me. Back home in Greece I was an electrical engineer, a highly respected man. But here in America I run this hot-dog cart and save whatever pennies I can to send to my daughters back home. I know that work can be hard sometimes, young lady, but you need to remember that things could always be worse.'

Dana raised her eyebrows, surprised to hear about the vendor's high-level occupation back home in Greece. She herself had studied electrical engineering in college at Cleveland State University for exactly one week before dropping the maddeningly difficult major and beginning her coursework in criminal justice. 'Why would you leave your job back home to come here?' Dana asked. 'Don't you miss your daughters?'

The hot-dog vendor smiled sadly. 'Ah, yes, of course I miss them. I miss them very much. Every single day, as a matter of fact. But where else except here in America do you get the chance to start fresh every day? To turn a new page with each new morning God gives us? This country is the greatest in the entire world, young lady. Don't ever forget to count your blessings. There are always other people out there who have it far worse than you do.'

This was far better advice than Dana had ever received from any of her many psychiatrists, and before she knew it, a real smile was playing across her lips. For the first time in months she allowed herself to feel a glimmer of hope. Maybe she and Brown were just one step away from cracking this nightmarish case, just one step away from moving on to the next stage of their careers. For all she knew, the answer they'd been seeking might be just around the corner. But before she could find out, Dana would first need to *turn* that corner and see what was there.

She paid the vendor for their hot dogs before she and Brown turned away, and Dana was thankful she'd tipped the vendor twelve dollars on the eight-dollar tab before they'd left. Heck, he'd *earned* it.

Not that Dana thought she could ever repay the vendor for his kindness. Still, she knew that she needed to try. In order to do that, though, she and Brown would need to stop the Chessboard Killer dead in his tracks and prevent him from killing any more innocent people.

Innocent people like the old Greek man's precious daughters.

CHAPTER SEVENTEEN

There weren't a whole lot of preliminaries that went along with Jack's unscheduled reunion with his father. The look on the man's face was a strange mixture of surprise and listlessness when he saw Jack standing there in the hallway.

'Hey, son,' Don Yuntz said, scratching at his three-day-old whiskers while he drained the last of a can of Pabst Blue Ribbon before crumpling the thin aluminium in his hand – his signature move when he was really into his cups. He was wearing only an open white bathrobe and a pair of vintage boxer shorts that looked as though they'd most likely been purchased sometime back in the early 1980s. 'I take it you heard about your mother?'

Jack nodded. 'Yep.'

'Cops tell ya about it?'

'Mm-hmm,' Jack lied. 'Saw it in the paper, too.'

Don Yuntz shook his head in feigned sadness. Certainly a daytime Emmy couldn't be out of the question for this asshole. 'Yeah, the cops never bothered coming over here to talk to me about it,' his father said, still scratching at his whiskers with his nicotine-stained fingers. 'Guess they don't know we were ever together, considering the fact we never got married. Saw some -

thing about her death on the news earlier today, but I ain't chasin' after them. If they want to talk to me, they can find me themselves. I ain't doin' their jobs for them. Anyway, it's a goddamn shame. I always loved that woman. Fucking serial killer. Can you believe that shit? What a fucking way to go, huh?'

Jack's ears rang as he tried to keep his hands steady. Wasn't easy. They were shaking with such fear and anticipation that for a moment he was afraid his father might hear the scissors rattling in his back pocket. Then again, Don Yuntz was probably much too drunk to notice. Some things never changed. And thankfully the old bastard didn't seem to be aware of the special-edition newspaper that had just come out featuring Jack's first-grade photo on the front. A lucky break. 'Can I come in?' Jack asked.

His father stepped aside and swept an arm in front of his waist, letting out a small burp in the process and blowing the unpleasant odour in Jack's direction. 'By all means. *Mi casa es su casa*. Come on in, boy. Make yourself at home.'

Jack wrinkled his nose at the offending smell and entered the apartment. To put it mildly, his father's new living quarters were a mess. Still, what did you expect when you'd dumped your partner of sixteen years – a woman who'd borne you two children at the great sacrifice and expense of her own body – and had started dating a dim-witted twenty-two-year-old with no brains but plenty of washboard abs and perky tits to make up for it?

A small collection of empty Pabst beer cans – each one crushed in the middle – was piled up high next to an overstuffed recliner featuring a huge rip that belched fluffy white cotton out of the left armrest. The powder-blue couch stationed in the middle of the living room was littered with an assortment of household items. Discarded clothing; empty takeout containers; half a tub of yogurt with the spoon still inside; old *Vogue* magazines; even a plastic spatula covered with baked-on food stretched across its grooves.

The smell in the apartment was pungent, over-whelming, a combination of stale cigarette smoke and – as near as Jack's nostrils could figure it – old cheese. Advancing several steps into the room, Jack glanced to his left. Through an open bedroom door twenty feet away he saw his father's girlfriend. Wearing only brief white panties, she was sleeping on her stomach on the sheetless bed. A tantalising mound of exposed boob flesh peeked out from her left side. Errant wisps of long blonde hair covered the left side of her face. Still, even that wasn't enough to obscure her obvious beauty. Seeing how good-looking she was only made Jack even angrier.

Don Yuntz followed his son's gaze to the bedroom and barked out a short laugh. 'She can't hold her liquor worth a damn, but she's got one hell of a great ass, huh? Traded in on a newer model, I guess. No offence to your mother, of course.'

Jack didn't say anything.

His father grunted. 'Well, I guess maybe you're still too young to appreciate that kind of stuff, eh? Don't worry about it, boy, your time's coming soon enough.' He paused, then, after another burp, said, 'Anyway, have a seat, kiddo. Clear off a space for yourself on the couch there. I need to go get me another beer.'

Jack did as he was instructed while his father disappeared into the kitchen. He heard the man pop the tab on another Pabst. Moving aside a pair of his father's girlfriend's dirty panties – a black thong this time that looked as though it hadn't seen the inside of a washing machine in months – Jack sat down on the couch and sank low into the cushions, placing his copy of *Chess For Dummies* beside him and taking in several deep breaths, trying his best to ignore the revolting smell of the place. *Just a little bit longer now and he could make everything right again.* After that, it would all smell like roses.

On his way back from the kitchen, Don Yuntz finally pulled shut the bedroom door, cutting off Jack's view. The idiot had been absolutely wrong with his assessment of Jack's interest level in his new squeeze, though. Jack *was* old enough to appreciate the sight of a nice ass and some great tits. He was fourteen years old now, for Christ's sake. What fourteen-year-old male in their right mind *wasn't* interested in a nice ass and a great set of tits? And Jack's father's girlfriend had excellent examples of both to offer. But cheap thrills weren't what Jack was after here today. Not even close. No, he was after something much more expensive. The kind of thrills you could never give back to whatever invisible deity dispensed them once you'd purchased them with a chunk of your very own soul. There would be no cancellation of this transaction. All sales would be as final as they came.

Lowering himself into the recliner across from Jack, Don Yuntz took a long pull on his fresh beer and drained half the can in the process. Working the lever on the rickety recliner, he propped up his bare feet on the footrest and splayed his hairy legs three feet apart. 'So, are you having emotional problems over your mom's death or something? Need someone to talk to about it?' All heart, this guy.

Jack closed his eyes and concentrated the rage he felt into his hands, clenching and unclenching his fists at his sides. He breathed in deeply again and reminded himself to stay calm. There was absolutely nothing to be surprised about here. Nothing he hadn't expected. Right from the very start – ever since he'd first had the notion of killing his father in revenge for what had happened to his poor mother – Jack had known that this part would probably be harder than actually murdering the bastard in cold blood.

Check that. No way in hell would *cold* blood play any part in this. Not by a long shot. Jack had very little doubt his father's blood would prove very warm indeed. *Hot*, even. Only one way to find out.

Rolling his neck above his aching shoulders, Jack felt some of the tension knotting up his muscles subside a bit. Good. That was better. Above all else, he knew he needed to stay relaxed here, to go about this whole thing in the right way, no matter how hard that might be for him to accomplish.

First time on the killing floor or not, this needed to be a *professional* hit.

'So, do you need someone to talk to about it or what?'

Don Yuntz's voice brought Jack back into the living room. And even though small talk with his father was the last thing Jack had any interest in at the moment, he nonetheless swallowed back the bile he could taste in his throat and forced himself to play along anyway, knowing it was a necessary evil. After all, everyone knew that the key to disarming egomaniacs like his father was to make them feel comfortable, to play into their stupid pride. And Don Yuntz had plenty of stupid pride to play into; that much was for sure. It was one of his trademarks in life, one of his few claims to fame.

'Not really,' Jack said in response to his father's mind-blowingly insensitive question about his emotional state regarding his mother's horrific murder. 'I'm dealing with her death OK, I guess. About as well as can be expected, anyway. I miss her already, but I've still got you around, right?'

Don Yuntz nodded and tilted back his head, taking another healthy swig of his beer. 'Goddamn right you do, boy. Besides, death is a part of life, buddy. You can't have one without the other. Anyway, how's your little sister holding up?'

Jack shifted uncomfortably on the couch. 'Molly doesn't know about it yet. And I'm not going to be the one to tell her about it, either. She'll probably lose her mind when she finds out, though. She's always been a mama's girl. You know that.'

Don Yuntz waved a hand in the air. The Sigmund Freud of 18th Street. 'Well, don't worry about it,' he said, in the familiar and thoroughly aggravating tone that had always set Jack's teeth on edge since early childhood – the tone of a man who knew jack-shit about *anything* yet was absolutely convinced he knew *everything*. 'She's still young,' Don Yuntz went on. 'She'll get over it eventually. You'd be surprised, son. The human brain has a remarkable ability to heal itself. Learned that during my semester and a half at City College.'

Jack's father leaned back his head again and finished off the second half of his latest beer before holding up the empty can and dropping it onto the ever-growing pile beside him. 'Anyway, go get me another beer, would you? I'm running through these goddamn things like water today.'

Jack pulled himself up from the couch and did as he was instructed. Walking into the kitchen on shaking legs and hearing an odd sound echoing in his ears, he couldn't quite shake the eerie sensation that he was floating through a dream world right now. Everything looked fuzzy around the edges to him. Conversely, the sounds in his ears seemed greatly amplified, almost as though they were coming from somewhere deep inside a sound-magnification chamber.

Glancing over his left shoulder back into the living room, Jack imagined that he saw blood painting the apartment. On the couch. On the chair. Splattered across the carpet. Red *everywhere*. Soon enough, that would be *exactly* what this place would look like. Soon enough, the premonition currently playing itself out in Jack's mind would turn itself into a very bloody reality for Don Yuntz. There was no other option.

Jack knew this needed to be *murder*. Vicious, take-no-prisoners murder. Just like the murder that had taken the life of his poor mother.

Shaking off the thought for the time being, Jack made his way over to the refrigerator and tried his best to ignore the picture of his father and his new girlfriend that was pinned there with a little heart magnet. He was angry enough as it was already, didn't need any additional incentive for this.

This would be something he'd *enjoy*.

Jack opened the refrigerator door and peered in. Two empty cartons of Pabst stared back at him from the top shelf, sandwiching an unopened twelve-pack. Other than that, though, it was all condiments. An old bottle of Heinz with disgusting black ketchup gunked up around the cap. Half a jar of Hellmann's mayonnaise. A small jar of Grey Poupon mustard. Assorted sauce packages from Taco Bell. Apparently, his father's new girlfriend wasn't much of a cook. Then again, where was the big surprise in that? When you had tits like hers, cooking wasn't at the top of the list of things you needed to know how to do in this life. 'You want me to open up this new box of beer for you?' Jack called out.

'Do what you gotta do, boy,' Don Yuntz called back from the living room, flicking on the television set. 'And get rid of those empty boxes while you're at it, would you? Break down the boxes and put them in the trash can. Don't do a half-ass job of it, either. The garbage can's under the sink.'

Jack closed his eyes and again did as he was told. Still, if Don Yuntz thought he was there to play unpaid maid today, the drunken bastard was sorely mistaken about that.

Jack was there to play executioner.

Removing the empty cartons of Pabst from the refrigerator, Jack folded up the boxes before jamming them down into the garbage can on top of a pile of cracked eggshells. From out in the living room he heard the sound of a baritone-voiced news anchor launching into a report on the murderous rampage in Arizona. Apparently, the congresswoman who'd been shot was still alive, still clinging to life, though just barely. Don Yuntz wouldn't be anywhere near as fortunate, however. Not if Jack could help it.

Jack removed from his back pocket the sleeping pills he'd purchased at the convenience store an hour earlier and pushed five of them through their foil backing as quickly as he could. There. That ought to be enough to silence the loudmouthed asshole once and for all.

The sleeping pills were the capsule kind that held tiny multi-coloured granules inside. Jack pulled off the tops of the pills and arranged the contents in a small pile on the counter before pulling back the tab on his father's beer, which produced a metallic popping sound that startled the living shit out of him.

Jack's heart flipped over. His palms flooded with sweat. His pulse crashed in his wrists. He shook his head and breathed in deeply. Gradually, he realised that his senses felt sharper. More acute. More reliable. More in tune with the world around him. Almost as if they somehow knew they were gearing up for the biggest moment in Jack's brief lifetime. Not to mention the last moment in Don Yuntz's lifetime – a miserable, worthless lifetime that had already stretched on for far too long as it was.

Using his pinkie finger, Jack slid the medicine into the small horseshoe-shaped opening on the can's lid and put the empty capsules back into his pocket before swirling around the beer a little to dissolve the granules inside.

'What in the hell are you doing in there, boy? Hurry up with that goddamn beer already. I'm fucking parched out here.'

Jack jumped at the sound of his father's loud voice booming out from the living room. Beer sloshed out of the Pabst can and over his hand. He clamped down his teeth until his jaw began to ache. The motherfucker would pay for that. *Just a little bit longer now and everything would be made right again.* After that, Don Yuntz wouldn't be able to shout at another living soul ever again.

As calmly as he could, Jack returned to the living room and handed his father the beer, even though what he *really* felt like doing at the moment was taking the scissors from his back pocket and slitting the drunken bastard's throat right then and there. Nothing else in the world would've been more satisfying. Still, Jack knew the time wasn't right for that. Not yet.

Don Yuntz looked up at him and snorted as he took

the beer. ''Bout goddamn time. What in the fuck were you doing in there, anyway?'

Jack shrugged and walked to the couch, sinking down low into the cushions again and shrugging off his coat, knowing that he'd need his arms and shoulders free for what was coming next. 'Had to break down the empty boxes,' he said. 'Like you said – don't do a half-ass job of it. I didn't.'

His father rolled his eyes and lifted the fresh beer to his lips, sucking down several mouthfuls and wincing at the taste. He held up the can and examined the label. 'Tastes like shit. But I guess that's what you get when you buy the cheap stuff, huh?'

'Guess so.'

From there, Jack and his father simply watched television without speaking. Jack was immensely thankful for the break, however brief. For the exquisite mental relief. Because if he'd had to listen to *just one more* of his father's inane expositions on the state of the world, he was pretty sure he'd wind up slicing open his own throat too before the night was out. Probably would've been much less painful that way.

When the news finally wrapped up twenty minutes later and gave way to *CSI: Miami* – whose cast were using their superhuman tracking powers to hunt down a serial killer whose claim to fame came from his penchant for targeting the children of famous politicians – Jack glanced over at the recliner and saw that Don Yuntz was out cold, snoring softly with his head thrown back and his mouth wide open.

Perfect.

Jack stood up and took a quick look into the bedroom at his father's girlfriend. She too was fast asleep. Good. All systems go. Walking over to his father, Jack loomed above him. This was it. The moment he'd been waiting for ever since finding his mother's murdered body in her apartment earlier that morning. Now he was standing over the man who'd failed to love Jack's mother enough, to be faithful enough to her, to *protect* her enough from the animal who'd killed her.

Jack's world swam out of focus briefly before his vision cleared again. There were no two ways of looking at things. The simple fact of the matter was that Stephanie Mann had died because Don Yuntz had been unable to conduct himself like a civilised human being.

And now it was payback time.

Jack stared down at the man who'd been half responsible for giving him life. All the rage he'd felt upon first finding his mother's rotting corpse in her condemned apartment building boiled up inside him again. Still, Jack was surprised to not feel *any* other emotions coursing through him to compete with the rage. No fear. No trepidation. No *anything*. Just the absolute knowledge that what he was doing here was the right and honourable thing. Hell, Don Yuntz *deserved* this for what he'd put Jack's poor mother through.

Taking in a deep breath that filled his lungs almost to the point of bursting, Jack took the scissors from his back pocket. Thankfully, his hands remained as steady as a surgeon's as he leaned down over Don Yuntz's supine body and slid the blades between the man's open lips. They clicked softly against his father's teeth, but the man didn't stir. The drunken asshole was dead to the world right now. Soon enough, though, he'd be lifeless for real.

Right now, as a matter of fact.

Jack opened up the scissors inside his father's mouth. Before he had a chance to change his mind about everything – to chicken out of the biggest moment in his life and go running off into the night like some scared little girl deathly afraid of her own shadow – he squeezed his fingers back together hard, slicing off his father's uvula – the small, pink appendage located at the back of the throat that looks just like a miniature punching bag – with a sickening *schwick!*

Everything was a blur after that. Don Yuntz bolted upright in his chair, gargling on his own blood. His eyelids flew open to show brown eyes bulging with fear, like those of a farm animal in the process of being slaughtered. Confusion and disbelief flashed across his ugly face. An instant later, he retched violently, vomiting up his severed uvula in a disgusting shower of blood and flesh and puke that stained the front of Jack's clean white T-shirt.

In a frenzy, Jack stabbed at his father's face. At his body. At his hands. The scissors sank deep into an eyeball and pulled the bulbous orb halfway out when Jack drew back his arm for another attack. Don Yuntz's hands reached out for Jack's throat, but Jack stabbed at those some more, effectively repelling the man's frantic counter-attack. Jack's own eyes bulged wildly. His entire body shook. His heartbeat pounded. Finally, on the fifth or sixth stab, the scissors found their mark deep in Don Yuntz's neck. A horrible, animalistic cry of pain echoed through the room as the man collapsed back down into his recliner and clutched at his throat. More blood spurted forth from his severed jugular vein and splashed across the front of Jack's T-shirt again. Then Don Yuntz began to seize up.

Jack looked on in amazement as the veins in his father's throat stood out dramatically from his skin, straining hard, engorged with blood rushing toward his brain in a last-ditch effort to keep the worthless bastard alive. Then Don Yuntz's remaining good eyeball fluttered wildly for a moment before rolling halfway back into his skull. Choking, strangled noises came from his throat.

Thirty seconds later, it was all over.

Jack stood over his father, shaking like a leaf. The noise in his ears was deafening – as though metallic cymbals were crashing over and over right next to his head and drowning out every other possible sound. It was like no other sound that Jack had ever heard in his life. No matter how hard he tried, though, Jack couldn't quite tell the difference between what was real and what was imagination right now. Everything was too intense at the moment, too powerful.

But then reality kicked in. *Hard.*

Holy fucking Christ! He'd really done it! Had really

killed the motherfucker. The score had finally been evened up. Now all Jack needed to do was make sure he didn't get caught. In order to do that, he'd need Molly's help. He knew he could count on her.

The euphoria was still with Jack as he went into his father's bedroom. His skin felt as though it was on fire with the novelty of the kill, like orange flames were licking his skin. He stared down at his father's girlfriend. The stupid slut was still sleeping on her stomach on the bed, hadn't budged an inch. For several agonising moments, Jack gave serious consideration to killing her as well. And why not? The dumb bitch deserved to die every bit as much as his father did for what had happened to his poor mother. But then Jack shook his head and decided against it. Much as he would have enjoyed snuffing out this worthless little slut's life, his quarrel wasn't with her. Besides, life itself would take care of this one soon enough. It always did with whores like her.

Walking over to the closet, Jack slid open the door on the left side and located his father's belongings. The Nike shoebox in which his father kept his gun was only half-hidden beneath a pile of folded clothes. Reaching in, Jack slipped out the shoebox and removed its top with shaking hands before sliding the loaded Smith & Wesson revolver into his waistband and returning the box to its usual place underneath the clothes, trying his best to disguise the fact that he'd ever been there at all.

His heart still hammering, Jack made his way over to the bedroom door and paused to look back at his father's girlfriend. She was still asleep, still unaware of the murder that had taken place just thirty feet away while she slept. Good thing too. If she'd shown any sign of consciousness it would have been an instant death sentence for her.

Jack shut the bedroom door softly behind him and stepped back out into the hallway before glancing over at the recliner in the living room, wanting to take just one more look at what he'd done, to *savour* it.

But his heart stopped dead in his chest when he saw that his father wasn't there any more. 'What th—'

The words weren't even halfway out of Jack's mouth before his father's hands were suddenly around his throat from behind, squeezing hard. Sharp fingernails dug deep into Jack's flesh, tearing at his skin. Hot beer breath tickled his left ear. A strangled noise came from Don Yuntz's throat as he struggled to form words without the assistance of his uvula. 'Fginbstrd, allkkcklllu!' *Fucking bastard, I'll kill you!*

Jack struggled to stay calm, to stay conscious. It wasn't easy. The pressure of his father's hands cut off the blood flow to his brain, causing the edges of his vision to go black.

Wrenching his body around as hard as he could, Jack twisted until he was facing his father. The blood on Don Yuntz's hands around Jack's neck provided the necessary lubrication. Instinctively, Jack brought up his right knee hard between the man's legs, scoring a direct hit on his father's testicles.

Don Yuntz finally let go of his son's throat, bending

over to clutch at his crotch and moaning in pain. In one fluid motion, Jack retrieved the scissors from his back pocket and stabbed them into the same place in his father's throat that he'd hit earlier, only harder this time, deeper, more violently. Don Yuntz reached for the handles of the scissors as he collapsed to the floor and started seizing up again before his convulsing hands could remove the sharp metal blades from his neck. He flopped around wildly on the bloodstained carpet, smearing the walls of the hallway with bright red streaks of his own blood. Finally, he stopped moving altogether.

Jack stared down at his father, breathing harder than he'd ever breathed before. He rubbed at his neck where Don Yuntz had tried to choke him and cleared his throat forcefully. This time there was no confusion about his father's condition. The miserable bastard wasn't going to mount another surprise attack. Not now, and not ever again.

Still breathing hard, Jack made his way into the bathroom and washed himself as best he could. Staring at his own reflection in the grimy mirror above the sink, he suddenly felt very confused. He blinked rapidly, not quite understanding where the confusion was coming from. The blinking didn't help matters. The fog was inside his brain again. Invading it. Making it impossible to think clearly.

Jack splashed some cold water onto his face in an effort to snap himself back into reality. It didn't work at first, but after several tense moments the fog in his brain finally began to clear. Suddenly, Jack realised where his confusion had originated. There was something different in his eyes now. Something strange. He barely recognised himself any more. Finally, he understood *exactly* what was different about himself. The person he'd once been was dead now, too. As dead as his father. Maybe even deader. Jack's outside shell still looked the same, but the person on the inside was someone very new. Someone very different. A *bad* person.

A *killer*.

It was then that an unearthly calm settled over Jack and enveloped him in its comforting embrace, like a heavy funeral shroud. Slowly, a contented smile played across his thin lips.

Jack turned off the water and dried his hands on the front of his jeans before drawing a deep breath, steeling himself for what would come next. He knew exactly what needed to be done now. This game of chess wasn't over. Not yet. Not for him, at least. Not by a long shot. As a matter of fact, for Jack Yuntz this game had only just begun.

And he knew it was a game he would *win*. *Needed* to win. For Molly. For his mother.

For *himself*.

Looking hard at his reflection in the mirror again, after a moment or two of further appraisal Jack decided that he *liked* his new look. It suited him perfectly.

It was the look of a killer.

Jack cracked his knuckles in satisfaction. The time had come for the next move in this decidedly deadly little game. And if Dana Whitestone thought that she'd had problems before, boy, was the FBI agent ever in for a surprise. She didn't know the *half* of it. Not yet, anyway. But she'd find out soon enough. Just like Don Yuntz had.

The *hard* way.

CHAPTER EIGHTEEN

Thursday, 7:15 a.m.

The next morning, Dana turned off the faucets in the spacious shower of her ridiculously opulent suite at the Fontainebleau Hotel and pulled back the paisley-patterned curtain before emerging from a huge cloud of steam. She wrapped a fluffy towel around her body and another around her head, then slipped her feet into a pair of fancy cotton slippers that had been unsubtly monogrammed with the prestigious hotel's initials.

Of course, that was when a knock sounded at the suite's front door.

Dana looked around the bathroom for a robe. There wasn't one. She'd left her complimentary robe in a wet pile on the bathroom floor the previous morning and the cleaning lady had picked it up without leaving another in its place, probably out of spite. Dana didn't blame the woman in the least for her calculated 'oversight', though. Served Dana right for being such a slob in the first place.

The knocking sounded at the door again, louder this time. Dana cursed underneath her breath. Might be something important, though. No time for modesty now.

Dana left the bathroom and walked to the front door, leaving a trail of wet footprints soaking into the deep Berber carpet behind her. She was half-surprised to see that the footprints didn't show up monogrammed, too. For some reason she still didn't quite understand, the FBI had decided to put her and Brown up in the ritzy Fontainebleau Hotel rather than in something a little more economical – something, say, more along the lines of a Holiday Inn. It was no wonder the taxpayers were up in arms all the damn time over wasteful government spending. This place was about a gazillion times nicer than she and Brown had any need for – the FBI's equivalent of a politician's eight-hundred-dollar hammer or two-hundred-dollar toilet seat.

Dana opened up the set of double doors at the entrance to her impressive hotel suite and a FedEx delivery man stopped what he was doing mid-knock. His jaw went slack when he saw Dana standing there wearing nothing but a towel. Suddenly, Dana became painfully aware that the skin of her bare shoulders was still glistening from her shower.

The delivery man cleared his throat uncertainly, trying not to look at Dana's semi-nude body. 'Got a package here for you, ma'am,' he said to the floor. 'You'll need to sign for it.'

Dana reached out and took the plastic stylus the man was offering, scribbling her name hastily across a small box on a hand-held computer screen that reminded her of an elaborate Etch-a-Sketch. The delivery man handed her a large envelope in return. Taking it, Dana closed the doors to her suite and walked over to a freshly polished mahogany table positioned next to a huge picture window. She sat down on a padded wooden chair before pulling back the tear-strip on the FedEx envelope and tipping out its contents. Nine gory murder-scene photographs. True to her word, Maggie Flynn down in DC had overnighted the crime-scene photos Dana had requested from the Bobby Fischer killings.

One by one, Dana examined each of the photographs closely, trying to look at them with fresh eyes now that some time had passed. The photographs had been arranged in chronological order – Maggie Flynn's work again – according to when the subjects had died. Each successive picture was more gruesome than the last, and Dana was thankful that she hadn't eaten breakfast yet.

Bullet holes punctured the backs of the skulls of nine people. These were the killer's nine victims during the Bobby Fischer murders – an unlucky group that had included a seven-year-old boy who'd been abducted from his bed in the dead of night while his parents had slept just two rooms away in their comfortable Greenwich Village home, blissfully unaware of the nightmare world to which they'd awake the following morning.

Sadly, though, the little boy's murder had marked just the first in a long line of casualties. The bullet from a Russian-made Makarov pistol had penetrated the back of the boy's skull on the top right-hand side and had exited through his right eye. A day and a half later, the second victim's body had been discovered. Hannah

Birkman, an elderly Social Studies teacher at PS213 in Brooklyn for the past thirty-seven years who'd earned 'Teacher of the Year' awards no less than nineteen times over the course of her distinguished career and who'd once even merited a mention from none other than President Ronald Reagan during his State of the Union address to Congress way back in 1982, had been shot dead centre through the back of her skull. The bullet had taken off her nose on its way out.

Dana paused and made a mental note to check in with Flynn and find out the status of the bullet that had been recovered from Stephanie Mann's apartment, see if there might be some connection with these killings. She needed to cover all her bases.

Third in line during the Bobby Fischer slayings had been Aimee Barton, fiancée of Cleveland Indians baseball player Grady Sizemore and the envy of every single girl around the city. Barton had been shot two-thirds of the way down her skull on its right side, ripping off her right cheek in the process. The fourth victim had been Enzo Pangrazzio, an Italian immigrant who'd been shot execution-style through the bottom-left side of his skull. The bullet had torn off the left side of Pangrazzio's face before shattering a glass jar of pickles sitting on the kitchen counter of his tidy efficiency apartment in Queens.

Dana frowned as she continued to examine each of the photographs carefully, finding it odd that each of the bullets had penetrated different sections of the victims' skulls – and wondering just why the incongruity hadn't occurred to her earlier. It was almost as though it had actually been *planned out* that way.

Her stomach went sour at the thought.

Dana shook her head and once again imagined her alternative life as a librarian. She probably would've had three kids and the white picket fence by now had she gone that route. Maybe even a shaggy-haired dog that slept at her feet while she read the latest James Patterson thriller instead of *living* it each day.

Three whole weeks had passed after the first four murders in the Bobby Fischer killings, leading people to believe incorrectly that the bloody series of slayings had been wrapped up. They'd been proven tragically wrong, however, when Allison Haverty had turned up dead the following month with a bullet hole in the top-left portion of the back of her skull. Haverty had been shot from behind while she'd been walking home from a New York Knicks basketball game at Madison Square Garden following a nasty and very public fight with her long-time boyfriend, John Erickson, who'd inadvertently humiliated Haverty by proposing marriage to her on the big screen during half-time.

Ted, Todd, Tim and Terry Thompson had been next in line for execution. The Thompson quads had gained a certain measure of notoriety when their mother had grabbed national headlines for the rare multiple birth on New Year's Day in 1972. Even at the relatively ripe age of thirty-eight, the confirmed bachelors had still lived together in a dilapidated brownstone over on Allentown Drive. Each of the Thompson boys had been shot once through the back of his skull on the same night while they'd slept in their brownstone, thus becoming the sixth, seventh, eighth and ninth victims in the process.

Ted Thompson's bullet had gone through the centre of the back of his skull; much like the wound that had taken the life of Hannah Birkman. Todd Thompson's wound was to the top right-hand section of his skull. Tim Thompson's bullet had penetrated the lower left-hand portion of his skull. Terry Thompson's bullet had entered the lower right-hand area of his skull and had marked the end to that horrific series of slayings when a chess book – *Bobby Fischer: Profile of a Prodigy* – had been discovered at the scene. After that, the Chessboard Killer murders had simply stopped for a while – before the next game had started up the following month.

Dana frowned in confusion, still puzzling over the photographs. Finally, she reached out across the table and grabbed a heavy silver pen. On a thick pad of hotel stationery, she sketched out the locations of the bullet wounds in the backs of the victims' skulls for the first four murders, then did the same with the next five killings immediately underneath, breaking up the two series of murders since that's what the Chessboard Killer had done himself. When she'd finished sketching out the locations, Dana used the pen to connect the dots. She sucked in a sharp breath when the lines she drew appeared to spell out initials.

SM.

Dana glanced down at the slippers on her feet and

frowned again. The initials there – FH – clearly stood for the Fontainebleau Hotel. But what did SM mean? Stephanie Mann? Or was she simply seeing something that wasn't there at all? Was it just her overactive imagination at work again, or could she have somehow stumbled upon a worthwhile clue after all this time of groping around in the dark? Before Dana had a chance to puzzle it out further, though, her cellphone rang on the television stand next to the enormous fifty-five-inch Vizio flat-screen that it was supporting.

Dana walked over and picked up her outdated Motorola Razr cellphone, flipping it open and placing it to her ear. 'Hello?'

A female voice came across the line. 'Agent Whitestone?'

'Yes? This is she.'

The woman cleared her throat. 'I'm sorry if I'm bothering you, ma'am, but my name is Angela Slater. I'm a detective with the NYPD. Got a minute?'

Dana closed her eyes. In the background at the NYPD end, she could hear a man with a ridiculously deep voice loudly giving instructions on how to process murder scenes. 'Of course,' Dana said. 'What's up?'

Slater breathed out slowly. 'Well, like I said before, I'm really sorry to bother you like this, but I was told that you're the point of contact for any possible Chessboard Killer murders. Is that correct?'

Dana's stomach sank. 'Yes, it is. What's going on?'

Slater lowered her voice. 'Well, I think we might have come across another victim for you.'

Suddenly, Dana felt an overwhelming urge to cry. Was it *ever* going to stop? 'What makes you think that?' she asked.

'We've got a vic here with scissors in his neck,' Slater said. 'His girlfriend says she was sleeping in the apartment all night long but didn't hear any commotion. Just woke up this morning to find him dead outside her bedroom door. Seems to me like she's telling the truth, too. She's hysterical but she's the one who put in the call. Besides, to tell you the truth, I don't think she's the kind who's smart enough to make it all up, if you know what I mean.'

Dana frowned. 'OK, Detective Slater, but what makes you think it's the work of the Chessboard Killer? Murder isn't exactly an uncommon occurrence in this town, is it?'

Slater laughed humourlessly. 'Nope. Not by a long shot, unfortunately. But we found a book lying on the living-room couch at the scene. *Chess For Dummies.* From what I've read in the papers, that would fit in perfectly with his MO, wouldn't it?'

Dana sighed. Sadly, it *did* look like it was their man. 'Where are you guys?' she asked. 'I'll come right over.'

'Over on 18th Street,' Slater said. 'Just wrapping up the crime scene now. Wouldn't make any sense for you to come over here, though. The chief's got a hard-on for this one. The news media's already here and he wants to look like a big shot to them. His numbers are sinking in the polls and he seems to think this is exactly what he needs to bring them back up. He's instructed the boys outside not to let you guys in without a warrant. Anyway, not to pile it on or anything, but I'm afraid I've got some more bad news for you.'

Dana gritted her teeth. Bad news was the *only* kind of news they'd been getting in this case. And it certainly didn't help matters that the head of the NYPD had chosen *now* to become territorial. 'What's that?' Dana asked. 'What's the bad news?'

'The vic's name is Don Yuntz. Ex of Stephanie Mann, the murdered woman you and your partner dealt with earlier this morning. Hell of a way to find out the NOK, I know.'

Dana's insides lurched. 'Jesus Christ.'

'Yeah,' Slater said. 'Anyway, the chief says you guys can do one thing, if you want.'

'What's that?'

Slater shouted something to someone at the crime scene before she came back on the line. 'You can inform the children of Mann and Yuntz, if you want. Their names are Jack and Molly. Staying in a foster home over in Queens. You want the address? I've got it right here.'

Dana went back to the mahogany table and picked up the pen and stationery again. Flipping open the writing pad to a fresh page, she poised the pen over the paper and cradled the phone between her ear and shoulder, wondering if the mystery of the child's photograph tucked away inside the biography of Amos Burn had finally been solved. Could be Stephanie Mann's son. Only one way to find out. 'What's the address?' Dana asked.

Slater gave it to Dana. 'I've already called up the foster parents so they'll be expecting you.'

Dana flipped off the phone and tossed it onto the suite's couch in disgust, standing there for a moment and seething with anger. Then she went weak at the knees when Bill Krugman's words from the previous day echoed in her mind:

One more dead body – just one more – and you two are off the case.

CHAPTER NINETEEN

Twenty minutes later, Dana and Brown made the short drive over to Jack and Molly Yuntz's foster home in Queens. Dana's hair was still damp from her recent shower as she filled Brown in on the gut-punch phone call she'd just received from Detective Angela Slater of the New York City Police Department.

'Christ,' Brown said when she'd finished bringing him up to speed. 'So you think our killers might be playing two games at once now?'

Dana shook her head, choosing to ignore his reference to there being two killers at work. Although it did look more and more likely that they were dealing with more than one killer she still wasn't quite ready to accept it just yet. 'I don't know, Jeremy. But I wish to God we'd find out.'

Brown tightened his grip on the steering wheel, turning his knuckles white. He was driving this time. He nodded. There was no need for words.

Fifteen minutes later Dana and Brown were standing in the bedroom of Jack and Molly Yuntz, with Connie Macklin, the children's foster mother, hovering nearby in the doorway. Two single beds were spaced twenty feet apart. One of the beds had a stuffed teddy bear on it. A pink bow was tied into its hair. A frilly dress with a wide sash slung across the middle was draped over the bedpost. Next to it, a teetering stack of Pokemon cards had been piled up high on the bedside table, Pikachu smiling out from the top.

Dana felt a twinge in her heart at the overwhelming normality of the tableau in front of her. Didn't look all that much different from her own bedroom when she was a little girl. Still, that wasn't a childhood bedroom she would've wished on *anyone*. Instead of ever having been the place of comfort and warmth every child deserved, *Dana*'s childhood bedroom had become a place from which she could never escape, no matter how old she got or how many psychiatrists she visited.

Over on the boy's side of the room, an old iMac computer with a translucent green cover on the back sat on a prefabricated desk. A poster of the *Twilight* cast – featuring the beautiful Bella Swan flanked by teen heart-throbs Edward and Jacob – hung above his bed. Dana studied Jack Yuntz's face closely and felt a twinge of recognition. He'd changed a lot since he'd been a little boy, but enough similarities remained to convince her that he was the same child in the photograph they'd discovered in the chess biography of Amos Burn. The fingerprint might have belonged to him, but it was unlikely they'd ever find out. You needed probable cause and a search warrant for those things, and no judge in the world would sign off on further harassing a boy who'd just lost both his parents.

Dana cleared her throat quietly. As gently as she

could, she informed the children about their parents' horrific deaths.

Jack Yuntz appeared stoic when he heard the news. Like a statue. Probably in a state of shock. His little sister, though, proved a completely different story. The scream she let out curdled Dana's blood.

Dana knew that it was a scream that would stay with her for ever. A scream that had already *been* with her for ever. A scream that seemed chillingly similar to the heartbroken cry she'd let out as a little girl on the night she'd watched her own parents murdered in cold blood right in front of her eyes.

Connie Macklin rushed into the room, but the little girl stopped her with another scream, this one laced with raw anger. 'Get away from me!' Molly Yuntz screeched. 'You're not my real mother!'

Crestfallen, the woman turned and left the room. Dana's heart ached for her, but at the same time she knew there was no way to soften this blow for the children.

After all, how did you soften the blow of a fucking *sledgehammer*?

CHAPTER TWENTY

Jack Yuntz fought back the urge to start laughing hysterically when the FBI agents first entered his and Molly's bedroom. He felt like some kind of lunatic who couldn't control his actions, no matter how hard he tried to do so. This was all just too much to take. Still, the sad looks on the FBI agents' faces let him know they didn't suspect him at all in the matter of his father's death, so he was at least thankful for that much. For several tense moments, however – after Dana Whitestone had filled them in on the details of their parents' murders and had handed them her business card, telling them to call her if they ever needed someone to talk to about it – Jack had thought he might have to shoot them dead right where they stood. Just five feet away his father's gun rested beneath his pillowcase, and it wouldn't have been all that hard to pull off. But just then Molly's help had come into play, just as he'd known it would all along. When Molly heard what Dana Whitestone had to say, she lost her mind, right on cue – and he hadn't even had to prime her. The distraction proved just enough to take the FBI agents' attention off Jack, which was a lucky break for all of them.

More than an hour passed after the FBI agents had finally left their bedroom before Molly started to calm down a bit. Looking up at him with tear-filled eyes, she asked, 'Are *we* safe, Jack?'

Jack smiled down gently at his little sister and sat down beside her on her bed, putting a comforting arm around Molly's bony shoulder and playing the part of the concerned big brother flawlessly. It wasn't hard. He cared about Molly, he really did. Life sucked and he hated that she had to hurt like this. But he was going to make it better. 'Of course we are, silly,' he said. 'Didn't you hear what they said? They said they're going to put a twenty-four hour guard outside our house, so we're safer here than anybody else in the whole wide world right now.'

Molly sniffled softly and blew her nose loudly into an already soaked tissue. 'Can we go play chess in the park tomorrow?'

Jack smiled at her again. 'I don't think so. We can go to the park, but not to play chess. How about we just swing on the swings instead? Just like we used to do with Mommy?'

Molly looked up at him and cradled her teddy bear in her slender arms. 'Why don't you want to play chess any more, Jack?'

Jack shrugged. 'I don't know. It's not fun for me any more, I guess. I'm retired.'

'So you're *never* going to play chess again?'

'Nope. Never again.'

'Promise?'

Jack raised his eyebrows. 'Yeah, I promise. Why?'

'Do you swear to God?'

Jack studied his little sister's face. There was something different in Molly's eyes now. Like she knew something that he didn't. A nervous flutter rippled through the pit of his stomach. 'Yeah,' he said. 'What do you mean by that, anyway? Why are you so damn worried about whether I ever play chess again?'

Molly held his stare. Her bright blue eyes burned a hole right through him. 'Just promise me you'll never play chess again, Jack.'

Jack lifted up his hands in a gesture of defeat and stood up. Pacing the room, he said, 'Fine, Molly. I promise. I swear to God. I'll never play chess again. Feel better now?'

Molly curled up into a tight little ball on her bed and fiddled with the pink bow tied into her teddy bear's hair. Looking up at him again, she said, 'I just want to know you're safe, that's all. I don't want to lose you, too. You're all I have left now.'

Jack's mouth went dry. Tears filled his eyes. Her words slammed into his gut and took away his breath. He stopped pacing the room. Finally, he whispered, 'I'm safe, Molly. And I'll always make sure you're safe, too.'

Molly dropped her stare and fiddled some more with the bow tied into her teddy bear's hair. Letting out a deep breath, she said, 'Promise about that, too? Cross your heart and hope to die and stick a needle in your eye? *Swear* it?'

Jack nodded. 'Yes, Molly. I swear to *God*.'

And Jack meant it. For in that very instant he'd recovered his faith in the almighty creator of the universe.

After all, only God could ever have created an angel as beautiful and loving as Molly.

And only a demon like Jack could make sure she stayed safe for ever.

PART IV

COUNTERMOVES

'We cannot resist the temptations of sacrifice, since a passion for sacrifice is a part of a chess player's nature.'

Rudolf Spielmann, Austrian-Jewish chess player and writer who died in 1942.

CHAPTER TWENTY-ONE

Thursday, 11 a.m.

Edward J. O'Hara reclined in his exceedingly comfortable leather chair located in the grand wood-panelled study of his Upper West Side Manhattan brownstone and opened up the morning edition of the *New York Times*, at the same time humming softly to himself one of his all-time favourite tunes: 'You've Got To Hide Your Love Away' by John Lennon.

Having been a huge fan of the Beatles ever since he'd first heard 'It Won't Be Long' on the radio as a kid, O'Hara had been overjoyed when he'd learned that an apartment had become available in The Dakota, one of the city's most famous addresses and the place where Mark David Chapman – accompanied by his beloved dog-eared copy of *The Catcher in the Rye* – had gunned down John Lennon with four bullets in the back on 8 December 1980 while Yoko Ono had looked on in abject horror.

'Apartment' probably wasn't the correct word to use when it came to The Dakota, though. It was far, far more than that: a *palace*, really. Located at 72nd Street and Central Park West, the venerable building housed just sixty-five residences, ranging from four rooms all the way up to twenty. O'Hara's lodgings, of course, checked in at the uppermost end of that scale. Completed in 1884, The Dakota had been given its name due to the fact that – at the time – its location as far as the main action in New York City was concerned had been considered as remote as the Dakota Territory itself. In its earliest days, The Dakota had boasted a playroom and a gym on the tenth floor, a separate stable for tenants' horses and carriages, and tennis and croquet courts behind the building. The fabled courtyard remained there to this day, the preferred gathering place for those keen on picnics and quiet reading.

The exterior of The Dakota was breathtaking by anyone's estimation, featuring terracotta spandrels, towering gables, soaring balustrades and impeccably maintained grounds. For its part, the interior was no less impressive – especially inside O'Hara's residence.

With plenty of blood, sweat and tears – not to mention the outlay of truckloads of cash – O'Hara had made the apartment into his pet project, his pride and joy. Its twenty rooms had their floors laid in the most expensive woods available on the market, including oak, mahogany and cherry. Fourteen-foot-high ceilings were featured throughout. In the parlour, four Rembrandts hung next to three Picassos, two Van Goghs and a Georgia O'Keefe. Added together, the paintings alone were valued at nearly thirty million dollars. A handsome sum by anyone's measure.

O'Hara pressed his lips together in satisfaction.

Although he hadn't yet been able to obtain Lennon's actual living space, he was close enough for the time being to actually *feel* the singer/songwriter's legendary energy through the walls, and that would have to suffice for now. Meanwhile, he continued to negotiate with the current owner about the possibility of purchasing the prestigious property. The last offer on the table had been an even seven million dollars – a full two million dollars above the apartment's last selling price – and the Asian software tycoon who now owned the place had seemed to wobble a bit at that. Had wobbled, but hadn't fallen down. Not yet, anyway. But O'Hara knew that if he kept up the pressure he'd be living in Lennon's old digs by no later than the end of the year. After all, that was the name of the game in business, wasn't it? Pressure, pressure, pressure. And when that didn't work, you simply turned up the pressure a little bit more.

No, it shouldn't be long now at all.

By staying in The Dakota, O'Hara had already added his name to a star-studded list of past residents that included such famous actors as Judy Garland, Lauren Bacall and Boris Karloff.

Still, everyone knew that the real prize in The Dakota was Lennon's old apartment. It was the place that everyone wanted, the place everyone lusted after. From music nuts to fame whores to profit-minded investors with a cold, calculating eye trained squarely on the bottom line, Lennon's apartment represented the Holy Grail of New York City living. And why not? After all, could you imagine hanging your hat in the same place where the most famous member of The Fab Four had laid down his head to sleep at night, possibly dreaming up such classics as 'Instant Karma!', 'Whatever Gets You Through The Night', 'Watching The Wheels' and 'Mother' while he drifted off into dreamland? Seriously, how cool was that?

Very fucking cool indeed. Cool enough to make O'Hara actually consider murdering someone to get it. He just hoped it wouldn't come to that.

Opening up the newspaper directly to the classifieds section, O'Hara adjusted his tortoiseshell reading glasses and scanned the listings, keeping an eye out for Michalovic's correspondence. Halfway down the second page he found what he was looking for, right next to a ridiculously large advertisement pimping out the latest Broadway production of *Cats*:

> E. 302828206, 551 2 A 12/19016 4 A A 19. Your move. S.

O'Hara smiled, reading the code as effortlessly as a blind person might read Braille. While others might not understand what he was looking at right now, the string of seemingly random numbers and letters made *perfect* sense to him.

O'Hara closed the paper and considered his options. Ultimately, there weren't many, as the sequence of moves in this match had already been predetermined. Still, that didn't mean he couldn't add a wrinkle or two here and there when the mood struck. It seemed to him that Michalovic had done just that himself by murdering Don Yuntz and leaving behind a copy of *Chess For Dummies* in the man's apartment, so turnabout was fair play. But O'Hara's wrinkle would just have to wait for now. When the time was right, *that* would be when the Irish-American could spring his surprise move on the Russian and catch him completely off guard. After all, O'Hara wanted this to be a *surprise* attack – just like the one that had killed his father nearly thirty years earlier.

O'Hara leaned back in his chair and steepled his fingers in front of his portly body. The countermove he'd be playing in this game represented the first move in the Sicilian Defence – the natural reaction to an opponent who'd opened up with *e4*, as Michalovic had done. The Sicilian Defence had been mentioned in notes dating back to the late sixteenth century by the Italian chess players Gioachino Greco and Giulio Polerio, and it was combative in nature, which suited O'Hara's taste for competition just fine. And by advancing his *c*-pawn two squares, O'Hara would assert control over the *d4*-square and begin the battle for the centre of the board – just as his predecessor and model for this match-up had done fifteen years earlier in Philadelphia.

O'Hara sighed. To his mind, playing Black in chess had gotten somewhat of a bad rap. While most experts agreed that White had a slight inherent advantage in these affairs – with a draw for Black most often considered a win and an actual win considered a major upset – O'Hara had been playing the role of underdog all his life. Was *used* to it by now. He'd been playing catch-up ever since the beginning, ever since he'd needed to crack a baseball bat over the heads of his father's business partners in order to clarify his negotiating position all those years ago. And just look how that had turned out. Well enough for him to currently be in negotiations to buy out John Lennon's old apartment.

In other words: not bad at all.

Besides, inherent disadvantage or not, O'Hara's advance of a queenside pawn would give him a spatial advantage over Michalovic and operate as the basis for future moves on that flank, so it wasn't as though the conditions were *all* bad.

O'Hara leaned forward in his seat and slid open a drawer to retrieve his notebook for this latest game. Flipping through the pages, he finally came upon what he needed. A painting contractor in his employ by the name of Jack Aaron lived on the correct city block. Excellent. Just two or three phone calls should turn the trick.

Half an hour later, the deed was done. Not that it had been easy to pull off, of course. In the end, *six* phone calls had been needed to ensure that Aaron would begin work the next day two blocks south of where he lived – not to mention an extra two thousand dollars in the man's pocket. O'Hara grimaced at the additional outlay of cash. To say that he was a man who despised inefficiency and overpaying workers would have been a colossal understatement.

Taking in a deep breath, O'Hara attempted to control his irritation. Wasn't easy. But high blood pressure was the bane of his family, its mortal curse, having claimed his grandfather at the tender age of just thirty-nine. At sixty-four years old now himself, O'Hara would really need to start watching his health from here on out. His doctors already had him on forty milligrams of lisinopril daily – the maximum dosage allowable – but he didn't especially like taking it. It gave him heartburn. Just like not getting what he wanted gave him heartburn.

O'Hara leaned forward again and picked up the antique phone on his desk, knowing that he needed something to make him feel better about the morning's events. Thankfully, he knew exactly how to go about it.

The one hundred and fifty additional boxes of Behikes cost O'Hara nearly eighty grand by the time everything had been negotiated but he considered it money well spent. He now owned far more than half the world's entire stock of those particular cigars – just like he'd planned to from the very beginning.

For some reason, though, acquiring the additional cigars didn't quite alleviate O'Hara's annoyance. *Odd.* Frowning, he picked up the phone on his desk once more. With luck, *this* call would release the magic elixir. The man he was phoning had better pray it did. Otherwise, things could get very messy indeed.

The man on the other end of the line answered after four rings. 'Hello?'

'Sukiyama,' O'Hara said. 'Ed O'Hara here. How are you doing today?'

The Asian businessman seemed surprised by the phone call from his neighbour. 'I'm fine, Mr O'Hara. And you?'

O'Hara exhaled a deep breath. 'Not good, Sukiyama. Not good at all. Listen, what's it going to take to buy you out of Lennon's old apartment? Let's talk numbers here. I'm sick and tired of fucking around on this thing. Let's get this behind us already.'

The Asian software tycoon cleared his throat, clearly taken aback by O'Hara's brusque tone. 'But I've already told you, Mr O'Hara. The property is not for sale at this time. Maybe in the future, but—'

O'Hara cut him off. 'Ten million dollars. Take it or leave it. That's my final offer.'

Even for a multimillionaire such as Ahiro Sukiyama – a man who'd made his fortune by getting in on the ground floor of a largely overlooked wireless company in the early 1990s – the chance to double up on his investment in just four short months was too good to pass up.

'Sold,' Sukiyama said. 'I'll have my lawyers call your lawyers in the morning to work out the details.'

O'Hara nodded and flipped open Michalovic's gift to him. Snipping off the tip of a Behike, he fired it up and took a long drag. Now that he owned the lion's share of the cigars, there was no need to conserve them. 'That'll be just fine, Ahiro,' O'Hara said. 'Have a nice day.'

'You too, Mr O'Hara. I very much look forward to doing business with you.'

'Same here, Ahiro.'

The final call of the morning was made to the *New York Times*. As a cuckoo clock chimed out the hour over in the corner of his fine study, O'Hara relayed the series of letters and numbers to an advertising executive at the venerable newspaper in order to inform Michalovic of what he'd just done. Five minutes later, he hung up the phone and cracked his knuckles in satisfaction, feeling much, *much* better about his present state of affairs.

Your move, Sergei, he thought. *If I were you, I'd make it a good one.*

CHAPTER TWENTY-TWO

Saturday, 10:30 a.m.

The phone call from Bill Krugman removing Dana and Brown from the case had come just fifteen minutes after they'd left Jack and Molly Yuntz's bedroom in Queens: the final *coup de grâce*. The Director had been absolutely true to his word, hadn't been kidding about his one-more-dead-body-and-you're-gone ultimatum. And with the discovery of *Chess For Dummies* at the latest crime scene, Don Yuntz's murder had fit the bill to a *T*, regardless of whether or not the killer or killers were playing two games at once now. Not that Dana had ever believed Krugman would be anything less than deadly serious about his ultimatum. It just wasn't in the Director's nature to kid about *anything* – much less about something this horrific.

Now, two days later, Dana and Brown sat in a cramped white cargo van on Colfax Avenue across the street from Luigi's Deli in the heart of Manhattan, listening in as two of the most notorious gangsters in the United States brazenly discussed their illegal money-laundering and drug-dealing operations. During the phone call with Bill Krugman, Dana and

Brown had been reassigned, flip-flopped, effectively trading investigations with another set of FBI agents who'd been working the mob angle in New York City. Not what Dana had wanted at all, but what could she do about it? Besides, it beat the crap out of passing out basketballs down at the FBI Academy gym. Like the old Greek hot-dog vendor had told her – things could always be worse.

Still . . .

Dana shook her head and repositioned the powerful directional microphone poking through a small hole cut into the van's side, attempting to get better sound quality on the mobsters' conversation. It wasn't easy. The seemingly never-ending flow of both vehicle and foot traffic on the busy street offered up enough acoustical interference to make a Marilyn Manson concert sound more like the quiet reading room of a monastery. According to the microphone's advertisement, users of the equipment were *supposed* to be able to hear a turkey walking in the woods from a hundred yards away. Unless it happened to be a nine-hundred-pound turkey, though, Dana didn't see how that could possibly be true.

Before heading over to the deli, Dana and Brown had stopped off at the NYC field office to requisition a surveillance vehicle, leaving behind their battered Ford Focus in its place. Or, in this case, they'd picked up a ridiculous facsimile of a surveillance vehicle.

A few agents on duty at the NYC field office had raised their eyebrows at Dana and Brown when they'd walked in, obviously curious about the Chessboard Killer investigation and wanting to ask them how they felt about being reassigned, but thankfully no one had pushed it to the point of actually doing so. Dana doubted whether the answers she would've provided would have been phrased in the most politically correct of terms.

To make matters worse, the surveillance vehicle was an absolute *joke*. A very *unfunny* joke, at that. Unfortunately, though, the head agent in charge of the NYC office had assured them it was the only one available.

With high-tech eavesdropping gear lining both walls of the rear section of a van that had 'Jimmy's Plumbing' splashed on the side with all the subtlety of a gaudy neon sign flashing on the Las Vegas strip, Dana had initially feared that the entire set-up would be so painfully obvious to anyone who'd watched more than one crime-investigation movie in their life that they just as well might have painted FBI on the side to announce their presence.

But for the past twenty minutes now, she and Brown had hunkered down in the van and listened to Mario 'Bones' Garabaldi and Joey 'Fingers' Baldarama talk openly about their plans for expanding their illegal drug business. Not exactly the most observant guys in the world, to be sure, but where was the surprise in that? Last time Dana had checked, you didn't need an advanced university degree to become a low-life thug.

Dana glanced to her left at Brown. Both their careers had just taken a very weird turn, and the thoughts on both of their minds seemed crystal clear: how would they ever get back on the Chessboard Killer investigation? How could they ever *redeem* themselves?

Dana closed her eyes and cupped her headphones closer to her ears. To hell with it. They were here now, so they needed to put their time to good use and gather all the information they could. And the mafiosi were providing *plenty* of interesting conversation to listen to – that much was for sure – even if it felt to Dana as though she was starting another book when she hadn't finished reading the one she'd been in the middle of.

Silly nicknames aside, the way Mario Garabaldi and Joey Baldarama figured it the gangsters would simply acquire more seemingly innocent businesses across the city to use as fronts for pushing cocaine, heroin and crystal meth to the drug-addicted denizens of the world's most famous city – while at the same time concealing the source of their ill-gotten gains from the prying eyes of the tax authorities. It was the same old story. Nothing new in the world of crime to see from where Dana was sitting.

Dana pressed her lips together and tried to ignore the expanding pressure inside her skull. She and Brown had just stumbled out of one hornets' nest and directly into another. But what could they do about it? Krugman had stationed them here, so they were in the right place, though the timing seemed off. Right now, though, they should be doing everything in their power to track down the Chessboard Killer. Still, Dana wasn't in the habit of watching crimes unfold right in front of her eyes without doing anything about it – whether it was the crimes of a vicious murderer or of drug-dealing thugs. Truth be told, there wasn't much difference between the two. Murder and the Mafia had always gone hand in hand in perfect harmony.

Dana checked a dial on the recording equipment in front of her to make sure it was working properly. All systems appeared to be running smoothly, so that was good. At the very least, she and Brown could make *some* progress on collecting damning information to be used against Garabaldi and Baldarama in court – even with all the maddening noise pollution in Manhattan. So it wasn't as though their morning had been a complete waste of time. From here, whatever information they collected could be handed over to the district attorney who worked the mob cases in New York City.

Ten minutes of lowbrow conversation later – conversation littered with such gems as 'Our friend in Jersey' and 'Fuck 'em, they're animals, anyway', expressions that let Dana know that these two jerks had at least seen more than one Mafia movie apiece in their lifetimes – the gangsters completed their illicit dealings for the day. At any rate, those illicit dealings that they were stupid enough to conduct right there out in the open while the FBI listened in and recorded the moment for posterity.

Flicking their still-burning cigarettes onto the sidewalk, Garabaldi and Baldarama finally went back inside the deli. Dana removed her headphones and flipped off the recording equipment in front of her. Brown did the same in the seat next to her. *Another day, another dollar.*

Dana sighed. This was the part of the job that the public rarely got to see, lacking the glitz and glamour of the big screen. Unlike in the movies, however, being an agent with the Federal Bureau of Investigation wasn't all just death-defying shoot-outs, high-speed car chases and heart-pumping adrenalin rushes, where innocent lives hung in the balance around every turn. Far from it. Truth be told, the job could be mind-numbingly *boring* at times. Like right now.

From out of the corner of her eye, Dana watched Brown neatly wrap wires before stashing them in a drawer. She felt a pang in her heart when she saw the look of utter hopelessness in his eyes. It looked like he needed a hug, but Dana would be damned if she were going to be the one to give it to him.

The mild flirting that had taken place between her and Brown during the Cleveland Slasher case had eventually blossomed into a full-scale love affair, but two months earlier they'd decided to put their romance on hold and focus on doing their jobs. Hard as it had been for her to do, Dana had been the one to suggest the cooling-off period.

It certainly hadn't been easy on either of them, but they seemed to have been managing up to this point. At least, Dana had. She still had feelings for Brown, and she knew he still had feelings for her, but it was a complication in her life that she really didn't need right now, so she'd tried to convince him she wasn't as keen on him as he was on her. But although he'd used his words to tell her differently, that he accepted her decision to step away, his eyes had never lied to her even once.

Dana's cheeks flushed hot and she brushed off the thought with a quick shake of her head, feeling stupid, like a heartbroken schoolgirl blinded by unrequited love. There was no point in reflecting on the past here. No point in getting nostalgic about the whole thing. That was then and this was now, and her and Brown's situation had changed considerably since those first few giddy weeks of their romantic relationship. At least for Dana.

Punching in a series of keys on her laptop computer, Dana made a backup audio file of the mobsters' conversation and turned to face her partner. 'What do you say we check out that new Thai place we passed on our way over here for lunch?' she asked. 'I'm starving, and I think I'm in the mood for something exotic.'

Brown nodded. 'You've read my mind.'

Dana flipped closed the lid of her laptop and climbed up into the front compartment of the van before sliding behind the wheel. Cranking the engine into life, she slipped the vehicle into gear and eased the van out into the heavy traffic flowing down the busy street. As Brown settled into the passenger seat beside her and pulled on his seat belt, Dana didn't bother mentioning to him that his mind wasn't the only thing she'd read recently. Again, what would be the point? As far as Dana was concerned, there was absolutely nothing to be gained by cluing him in to the fact that she'd also recently read his jacket on file down in Quantico.

The jacket that informed her Jeremy Brown was still a married man.

CHAPTER TWENTY-THREE

Saturday, 9:15 a.m.

Following their respective opening moves, Michalovic and O'Hara took turns moving pawns. For Michalovic, it was Anna Baker, a social worker with a heart of gold and a bank account to match who lived with her six cats in a surprisingly modest apartment complex located at 832 C Street in Manhattan.

As it was Saturday now, Michalovic knew that Baker would be at home. With barely any family left alive and none living anywhere near her, the elderly woman *never* left her apartment any more unless it was to bring her cats into the vet for their monthly check-up or to go into work at her volunteer job with the city's Child Welfare Programme, a non-profit outfit underwritten by billionaire financier George Soros. Anna Baker even had her groceries delivered to her like clockwork each and every Friday evening at precisely seven p.m. by a young man wearing a backwards baseball cap, effectively eliminating the need for her to venture out into the dangerous city streets unless she chose to.

Pity she wasn't in charge of that particular decision any more.

In the most faithful definition of the term, Baker was old money, having made her fortune the old-fashioned way: by inheriting it. So it seemed odd that she'd gone to work for George Soros, a man who'd started off in his life with absolutely nothing but who'd rectified that problem far better than almost any human being who'd preceded him.

The thought of George Soros made Michalovic smile in bemusement at the paradox of America. Sometimes – no matter how hard he tried to understand it – this great country he now called home, the greatest in the entire *world*, just didn't seem to make any sense to him.

To make things even *more* interesting, Michalovic and Soros shared something of a similar background. But for all their similarities, there were many more differences between them. Soros – who'd become known as 'The Man Who Broke the Bank of England' when he'd reportedly made one billion dollars during the 1992 'Black Wednesday' currency crisis in the United Kingdom – and Michalovic had made something of a sport out of matching each other dime for dime when it came to political campaign contributions. While Soros most often financed the Democrats and other similar wishy-washy liberal causes, Michalovic preferred to finance the Republicans, the political party that actually *cut* taxes for the wealthy. Seemed like a pretty straightforward equation to him. Still, who was he to judge? Soros was obviously doing just fine for himself. And then some.

Soros, though, had very good reason for putting his

money where he did. After having survived the Nazi-occupied Hungary of his youth, he'd moved his base of operations to New York City in 1956 and had then proceeded to become one of the richest men in the history of the world. Even richer than Michalovic himself, which was certainly no small feat to accomplish.

For his part, though, Michalovic possessed no equivalent soft spot in his heart. Far from it. *His* heart was as hard as they came, as hard as steel – and every bit as cold. Had been ever since he'd been a young man hustling on the streets of downtown Moscow, selling fake handbags, knock-off perfumes, cheap watches and anything else he could lay his hands on to unsuspecting tourists. Right from the beginning, Michalovic had been interested in just one thing: making money. And lots of it. Thankfully, he'd proved extremely adept at that particular endeavour, which now allowed him the financial freedom to participate in his and O'Hara's exceedingly interesting games. The way Michalovic figured it, if anything went wrong in their games he'd simply *buy* himself out of trouble. After all, that was the American way.

Michalovic smiled to himself and phoned his next pawn from the driver's seat of his Rolls-Royce Phantom II. There was always something interesting to contemplate in this great country he was now living in, and right now he had something *very* interesting to think about.

Though Michalovic usually employed a trusted

driver to whisk him around the city streets and shield him from the aggravations of everyday life, that arrangement wasn't an option here. Apart from himself and O'Hara, *nobody* could know about what the two of them were up to, which brought to mind yet another wonderful American expression:

Loose lips sink ships.

Exceptionally appropriate for a shipping magnate such as himself.

When Anna Baker answered her phone, Michalovic almost felt sorry for the woman, knowing that her days on this Earth were now numbered. *Almost* felt sorry for her, that was – but not quite. The silly little woman had been given nearly every imaginable advantage in life, and it wasn't *his* fault if she'd chosen not to exercise those advantages.

'Miss Baker, my name is Pierre LeBlanc,' Michalovic said when the woman picked up the phone, using the same fictitious name he'd used with his first pawn, Betty Arsenault. Time for a little more make-believe. 'I'm a special assistant to Mr Soros. How are you doing today?'

The connection on Baker's end of the line sounded rife with static. No doubt the miserly old bat was trying to save a few pennies by going with a cut-rate telephone provider – not that she had any reason for doing so. With her money, she could have afforded to *buy* the goddamn phone company. 'I'm fine, Mr LeBlanc,' Baker said in a clear, strong voice that belied her nearly eighty-two years. 'How may I help you this fine morning?'

Michalovic swallowed back the bile he tasted in his throat and forced himself to stay calm. Unlike George Soros, this crazy old woman had no excuse whatsoever for giving a damn about the less fortunate. Hell, she deserved to die for that much alone. 'I'm fine, Miss Baker,' Michalovic responded. 'I only wish I could say the same thing for poor little D'Andre Williams.'

More static sounded in Michalovic's ear. Perhaps the old woman was fiddling with the cord on her end of the line. Whatever it was, though, it worked like a charm. When Baker's voice came across again, it sounded crisp and clean, save for the palpable note of apprehension in her tone. 'What do you mean, Mr LeBlanc?' she asked. 'Who is poor little D'Andre Williams?'

Michalovic turned his Rolls-Royce onto Fernway Street in downtown Manhattan and eased the car to a gentle halt at a stop light. From both lanes on either side of his classic vehicle, gawking rubberneckers admired his car while he explained to Baker what would be needed from her.

'D'Andre Williams is a six-year-old African-American boy who lives alone with his mother – a crack addict and sometimes a prostitute,' Michalovic said. 'Our non-profit has had reports of abuse, so Mr Soros would like for you to open a case file on him immediately. As it's the weekend, naturally you'll be paid extra for your work. Mr Soros would also like you to keep this particular file confidential, Miss Baker. He considers it a pet project of his and doesn't desire any unwanted attention from the press on the matter.'

Baker sighed impatiently. 'There's no need for any additional money, Mr LeBlanc,' she said, sounding like a stern old schoolmarm who was quite used to letting students know how events would proceed – not the other way around. 'I donate the entirety of my stipend back to the welfare programme anyway. All I care about is that unfortunate little boy. Where exactly does he live?'

Michalovic cleared his throat and gave Baker the address, where the conditions were exactly as he'd described.

'That's only a block north of here,' Baker said. 'I'll get over there right away.'

Michalovic nodded. 'Thank you very much, Miss Baker. You're a wonderful person to be doing this on your off time.'

Baker tutted. 'No, thank *you*, Mr LeBlanc,' she said. 'Besides, this is exactly the kind of stuff I live for.'

Michalovic waited until the connection had gone dead at Baker's end before responding. 'It's also exactly the kind of stuff you'll *die* for, you silly old bitch.'

And Anna Baker *would* die an extremely horrible death. Michalovic had no doubt in his mind about that. But she wouldn't be the only one. Not even close.

After all, this game was just *beginning*.

CHAPTER TWENTY-FOUR

Thirty minutes after wrapping up their first surveillance session of the day, Dana and Brown settled into their seats at the Thai restaurant known as '35' on Lispenard Street in the Tribeca area of Manhattan.

Dana paused and looked around the place. Typical Tribeca. Most of the diners were dressed in business-casual attire. Polo shirts and pressed beige Dockers for the men; lightweight flower-patterned sundresses for the women. Outfits that Dana presumed had been chosen in order to take advantage of the schizophrenic mid-April weather, which had once again reached nearly eighty degrees Fahrenheit on the mercury and which was forecast to rise an additional five degrees by three p.m.

The restaurant itself was a classy kind of place without overdoing it and slipping into pretentiousness, which Dana appreciated. Clean, efficient and discreet – much like the patrons themselves.

After several minutes spent hesitating between a variety of dining choices, Dana finally decided to go with the vegetarian fried rice platter and a green papaya salad starter. For his part, Brown selected the *ho mok pla*, a pâté of fish, spices, coconut milk and eggs steamed in a banana-leaf cup and topped off with a thick coconut cream. In other words: just about one of the most thoroughly unappetising choices Dana could think of.

Silverware and chopsticks clattered against plates in the background and mixed in with the low murmur of conversation at the other tables to provide a pleasantly mixed soundtrack for the scene. Although they were technically at work, the social surroundings reminded Dana so much of the dates that she and Brown had once gone out on that it produced a sharp twinge of loss in her heart. Loss of the intimacy they'd once shared. Loss of the personal companionship. Loss of the *trust*. She wanted to ask Brown why he'd never told he was still married, but she just didn't know how to go about it without blowing her cover. She'd flipped through his file down at Quantico in an uncharacteristic moment of weakness and now she didn't have the foggiest idea of how to bring up the subject without revealing her transgression. But now it seemed that they both had a secret that neither one of them appeared especially keen on being first to share.

Dana shifted in her seat and screwed up her courage. To hell with it. She'd bull ahead and find out what he had to say about the matter even if meant she needed to show her hand first. Who knew? Could be something simple, something he could easily explain away. A typo, maybe. A simple mistake of some sort.

Just then, though, Brown's cellphone chimed in his pocket, signalling an incoming text message and taking the wind out of Dana's sails. She let out a soft breath as he dug out his phone and studied the screen. After a moment, he turned down the corners of his mouth.

'What is it?' Dana asked, then immediately regretted the words. Might be something personal to him, something he didn't feel like sharing. If nothing else, she needed to remember that she and Brown weren't partners any more. Not in any romantic sense, at least. All because both of them were too chicken to address their feelings.

Brown glanced up from his phone and cast his stare around the restaurant. Returning his gaze to Dana, he leaned forward across the table and lowered his voice. 'I'm afraid I've been something of a bad boy,' he said, looking embarrassed.

Dana raised her eyebrows questioningly. 'What do you mean?'

Brown smiled mischieviously. 'I've got a line into DC about our former investigation. Guy I graduated from the Academy with.'

Dana's ears perked up at Brown's mention of the Chessboard Killer slayings. In the days since they'd been taken off the case, her mind had never drifted far away from the subject. But Bill Krugman had been extremely clear with his demand that they should remove themselves completely from the case and not even participate from the sidelines. After all, they'd had their shot – *several* shots, actually – and they'd blown them. The case was somebody else's baby now.

Still, Dana wanted to know what was going on.

Needed to know what was going on. She and Brown had spent far too much time and energy on the investigation to just forget about it altogether now. And as long as they didn't actively participate in tracking down the perpetrator of the horrific crimes, she didn't see the harm in staying in the information loop. 'What do you have?' she asked.

Brown shrugged. 'Nothing, really, I'm afraid. Just another dead end with the bullet we found at Stephanie Mann's apartment. No connection whatsoever to any of the other murders, including the Bobby Fischer slayings.'

Dana grimaced. Looked like the new agents heading up the investigation were running into the same brick walls that she and Brown had. In this case, though, misery didn't love company. Far from it. Dana didn't care *who* stopped the killings, she just wanted them to stop. And fast.

Five minutes later, the waitress came around and Dana and Brown gave the woman their orders before shifting the conversation back to work – this time to their own newly assigned investigation.

'So what exactly do we have so far on Garabaldi and Baldarama?' Brown asked. 'It's unlikely they're in charge of anything the mob's got brewing, but we really don't have any other leads to follow right now. What do we know about these guys?'

Dana shrugged. Sadly, what they knew about Garabaldi and Baldarama were just the very basics. Both men worked for the Gambino crime family, headed up by Joseph Tucci, who was one slippery son of a bitch, to say the least. As a matter of fact, over the past few years Tucci had started to make John Gotti, the notorious 'Teflon Don', look more like a cheap frying pan by comparison.

John Gotti had earned his nickname due to the fact that the majority of the charges against him hadn't stuck – with his trials most often ending in either hung juries or outright acquittal. Thankfully, though, that lucky streak had finally come to an end in the summer of 1992 when he'd been convicted of thirteen murders, conspiracy to commit murder, racketeering, obstruction of justice, illegal gambling, extortion, tax evasion and loan-sharking, enabling the FBI to let out a collective sigh of relief. If ever there'd been a more appropriate person in the history of crime to throw the book at, Dana couldn't think of who it might be. Following his convictions, Gotti had died in prison of throat cancer ten years later – an oddly ironic fate for a golden-throated man who'd always displayed a marvellous ability to charm criminals, law enforcement and the general public alike with his smooth-talking ways.

As always with the mob, however, the power vacuum that Gotti left behind hadn't lasted long. Joseph Tucci – the man now pulling the strings of the human puppets known as Mario Garabaldi and Joey Baldarama – had stepped directly into Gotti's ten-thousand-dollar patent leather shoes without missing a beat following his predecessor's spectacular fall from grace. If Gotti had been the Teflon Don, Joseph Tucci could just as easily have been called the 'Invisible Don' – considering that neither Dana nor Brown had laid eyes on him in person. But that was what you got with the mob these days. The power-players at the top of the organised-crime structure tended to keep their fingernails very clean, which made catching them red-handed nearly impossible.

The American Mafia, or *la cosa nostra* – literally translated as 'this thing of ours' from the original Italian – was an offshoot of the Sicilian Mafia. Along with the Gambino family, there were four other main mob families headquartered in New York City: the Luchese, Genovese, Bonanno and Colombo crime syndicates. Though each family operated independently, the five heads of those families, including Joseph Tucci himself, met regularly to conduct business and to carve up the city into separate geographical areas for each to exploit – not so very different from the way American political parties engaged in gerrymandering, with the Democrats and Republicans getting together every ten years to redraw voting districts.

The Mafia called this ruling body of theirs 'the Commission' and through a phone call back to the NYC field office Dana and Brown knew that it was scheduled to meet again tonight in a hunting lodge on the outskirts of Albany, the state capital located a two-and-a-half-hour drive away.

'What do you think about crashing the Commission's little party tonight?' Dana asked, nodding down at her unkempt attire – jeans, T-shirt and sneakers worn in an effort to look the part of the plumber she'd played today. 'I promise I'll wear something a little nicer.'

Brown rolled his eyes. 'C'mon – quit being so modest. You look great, and you know it.'

Dana ignored the flirtatious tone in Brown's voice. She didn't know what else to do. It was uncomfortable for her, and she wished it were just a little more uncomfortable for him. After all, married men shouldn't flirt. 'What about the Commission's meeting tonight?' Dana asked. 'Are you up for a road trip or what?'

A brief look of hurt flashed in Brown's eyes. 'Sure, Dana. Whatever you say.'

CHAPTER TWENTY-FIVE

In response to Sergei Michalovic's positioning of Anna Baker, Edward O'Hara telephoned Micah Brantley, a six-foot-nine former professional basketball player who'd once starred on the hardwood at Madison Square Garden for the New York Knicks. Might as well start big. And any way you chose to cut the mustard, they didn't come much bigger than Micah Brantley.

The unquestioned pinnacle of Brantley's tragically short career had come when he'd dropped fifty-one points on the Chicago Bulls during a 1998 play-off game that had propelled the Knicks into the championship round, which they'd eventually lost in a heated five-game tilt with the Los Angeles Lakers. From that dizzying high point in his life, however, things had gone downhill very fast for Micah Brantley, indeed, when his drug-induced spiral had really begun in earnest.

Around Gotham, Brantley's name was most often spoken in a tone that swung somewhere between awe and pity. Awe for his heroic exploits on the basketball court – the best since Michael Jordan, some said – and pity for the fact that he'd become just the latest in a long line of pampered athletic heroes who'd thrown away their enormous talents on a crippling drug addiction.

Crack, heroin, crystal meth, uppers, downers, in-betweeners – it didn't matter to Brantley *what* poison he pumped into his system, just so long as there was a steady supply of it to keep him in a constant state of altered reality. When three stints in drug rehab after popping positive on three separate mandatory NBA drug tests hadn't been enough to convince Brantley of the error of his ways, the league had finally thrown up its hands and walked away from the troubled superstar. And who could blame them? In the end, Micah Brantley had cost the league far more than he'd ever brought in – his once-in-a-lifetime night at Madison Square Garden notwithstanding.

Not that Brantley had any of his NBA money left any more, of course. When the league had imposed a lifetime ban on him following his third failed drug test, he'd quickly blown through the six million dollars remaining in his bank account. Just like most has-beens, however, the problem with Micah Brantley was that he didn't realise just how *far* from grace he'd fallen. In his drug-scrambled mind, he was still the man who'd drained a thirty-foot jump shot at the buzzer to lift the Knicks to victory and into the next round of the play-offs twelve years earlier. In reality, though, now he was just another broken-down shell of a person who lived in a one-bedroom, fifth-floor walk-up on Seventh Avenue with two other men – both drug addicts as well. Just another one of the eight million stories in the naked city, almost every last one of them pathetically bad.

On this fine April morning, Edward O'Hara decided

that the time had come to remind Micah Brantley of his new, lowly position in life. Someone needed to.

Even though it was nearly eleven a.m. by the time O'Hara dialled the former pro-ball player's number, Brantley proved none too happy to be woken up by the phone call. 'Who in the fuck is this?' he snapped into the receiver. 'Whoever it is, you'd better have a goddamn good reason for calling me. I was taking a fucking nap.'

O'Hara closed his eyes. Dealing with spoiled athletes was not his idea of a pleasant way to pass the morning. Still, he tried to be nice at first. 'Micah Brantley,' he said warmly. 'My name is Ed Montague. I was a big fan of yours when you played for the Knicks. Probably the biggest of them all. Hell of a game you had against the Bulls back in 1998. I was there, you know. Cheering you on every step of the way.'

'Ed *who*?'

'Montague,' O'Hara said.

'Is that name supposed to mean something to me?'

O'Hara switched gears. To hell with it. He didn't enjoy being cursed at by *anyone*, much less by an animal like Micah Brantley. 'My name had *better* mean something to you, Micah,' O'Hara growled, straightening in his chair and feeling his blood pressure rise. 'After all, I'm the only friend in the world you've got right now. The least you could do is know my name.'

Brantley snorted into the mouthpiece. 'Yeah, whatever. What do you want?'

O'Hara sighed, already weary of speaking with this

man. Cutting short the preliminaries, he got straight to the point. 'I want you to enter drug rehab again, Micah. This time it will work, I promise. As I own the facility that you'll be entering, I'll personally monitor your progress and foot all the bills from my own pocket. It won't cost you a single penny, so there's no need for you to worry about the financial end of things.'

Brantley laughed bitterly. 'What makes you think I *want* to go back into rehab? I'm doing just fine as it is.'

O'Hara rolled his eyes. Denial was the first stage of addiction. Everybody knew that. 'What makes me think you want to go back into rehab is the fact I'm *telling* you that you want to go back into rehab, Micah,' O'Hara said. 'It's as simple as that.'

'Fuck off.'

O'Hara shook his head. This was just getting tedious. 'Listen to me very carefully, Micah,' he said evenly. 'You'll do exactly what I tell you, exactly *when* I tell you to do it. You won't deviate even one iota from my instructions. Do we understand each other yet?'

Something in O'Hara's tone must have let Brantley know the Irish-American wasn't a man to be disobeyed or spoken to in such a disrespectful manner. Because when Brantley spoke again his tone still sounded combative but decidedly less defiant. 'Why in the hell should I do what you tell me to do?' he asked weakly, his earlier bravado almost completely gone now.

'Because I know your little secret, Micah,' O'Hara said, springing his checkmate move on the unsuspecting dolt. 'I know what you did when you were playing basketball at Syracuse University before turning pro. So either you'll enter my drug-rehab facility tomorrow or I'll go directly to the police with all the details. It's quite elementary, really. Do you understand what that word means, Micah?'

Brantley exhaled a short, hard breath that made it sound as though he'd just been punched in the gut. 'But I don't have no secrets, man,' he whined. 'I'm just trying to live my life the best I can with what I got left. It ain't much, believe me. So please just leave me alone. Leave the past alone.'

O'Hara laughed harshly. 'Leave you alone, Micah? Leave the past alone? You must be putting me on. You mean like how you left Melanie Anderson alone when she was pleading for you to spare her life after you and your friends took turns viciously raping her? Is that what you're talking about here, Micah? Because if it is, then I'm afraid I simply can't do that. Now, listen to me very carefully. I want you to get a pencil and paper. Do you have it yet? Good. Now, I'm going to give you a phone number and an address. The address is just two blocks south of your apartment. Call the number and speak with the woman who answers the phone. She's expecting your call in precisely ten minutes. Either you'll check into my rehab facility by eight o'clock tomorrow morning or else you'll receive a visit from the New York City Police Department. Cops don't like cold-case files, Micah. Gives them a hard-on to finally crack them. So that's the deal. Either you enter rehab tomorrow morning or I spill the beans on the rape and murder of Melanie Anderson. Do we understand each other now?'

All the remaining fight left Brantley's voice. 'Yeah, man,' he said. 'We understand each other perfectly. Eight o'clock tomorrow morning. I'll be there.'

O'Hara nodded. 'You'd better be, Micah. Because if you're not, you'll pray you were.'

CHAPTER TWENTY-SIX

The drive to Albany six hours later was unremarkable. Since both of them were lost in their own thoughts, neither Dana nor Brown said very much. What *was* there to say? Should they just remind each other again of the humiliation they'd suffered – in the eyes of Krugman, in the eyes of their fellow agents, in the eyes of *themselves*? It didn't stop Dana's mind running a loop on their previous case, though – going through every little detail, knowing it was no good. They hadn't been able to catch the killer: it was time to let it go. Let their colleagues have a shot. And good luck to them. But please God they caught the killer – killers – soon.

When she and Brown finally reached the outskirts of the state capital Dana was relieved to finally get out of the car and away from her self-torturing thoughts.

After several minutes of confusion over the exact location of the hunting lodge (Dana thought it was due north while Brown thought it might be in a more westerly direction) they finally figured out their bearings and began preparing for the task at hand.

Dana popped the lock on the recently retrieved Ford Focus's trunk, and she and Brown shrugged themselves into bulletproof Kevlar vests before slipping camouflage jackets over their chest-protectors in an effort to help conceal their presence in the woods. After all, this wasn't the kind of party you wanted to crash without first being prepared for any possible eventuality – including the possibility of being shot at. Dana and Brown weren't dealing with third-rate street hustlers here. As far as organised crime went, this was the cream of the crop, the very best of the best. Or the very worst of the worst. It all depended on your perspective, Dana supposed.

Dusk had already begun to darken the springtime sky by the time she and Brown picked a small clearing in the woods and plunged into the deep underbrush. The temperature outside had dipped to a chilly-if-more-seasonable sixty degrees by now, and Dana was grateful for the extra warmth that the jacket provided. Brambles snagged at the bottom of her jeans while they walked and the branch of a dogwood tree nearly poked out Brown's left eye, but other than that their half-mile trek was uneventful.

By the time they finally came upon a slight rise in the ground overlooking the hunting lodge in which the Commission's meeting would take place it was fully dark. Brown handed Dana a pair of ATN Night Scout binoculars featuring five times magnification, a two-hundred-and-fifty-metre range and a long-range infra-red illuminator. The same model that he'd be using himself. With luck, the binoculars would help shed some more light on the subject. Or, in this case, subjects. At least, they better had. They were expensive enough. Nearly five thousand dollars a pair.

Still, ridiculously expensive or not, the binoculars were top of the line all the way. From their ninety-millimetre lenses to the distance indicator in the upper right-hand corner to the negative-five to plus-five diopter adjustment, Dana knew it had been money well spent. The view the binoculars provided was tinged with green and grey – sort of like when you took a picture of a cat's eyes in the dark – but other than that the imagery came across crisp and clear.

Pressing their bellies against thc soft earth, Dana and Brown trained their high-tech binoculars on the hunting lodge a hundred yards away. As she peered through the eyepieces, Dana couldn't help feeling a bit like 'Buffalo Bill' in *The Silence of the Lambs.*

A chill ran down her spine at the weird thought. She shivered despite her jacket, knowing that she didn't need to be thinking along those lines right now. Not when she and Brown were hiding out in the woods and trying to get the drop on some very dangerous men who wouldn't think twice before killing them.

Dana tried to conjure up another movie in her mind – something more along the lines of *Bambi* – but it didn't work. All she could picture was the scene in the film where the hunters had killed poor Bambi's mom. The woodland setting, Dana supposed.

Dana shook her head to clear away the thought. Even though the Commission's meeting wasn't scheduled to begin for another hour, armed Mafia goons were already standing guard around the property, smoking unfiltered cigarettes and laughing at jokes that Dana couldn't hear but didn't imagine were very funny at all.

Ten minutes later, Brown used a hand signal to alert her to the fact that a long line of sleek black cars had begun to ease its way up the dirt road leading to the entrance of the hunting lodge. The vehicles bobbed up and down over ruts in the road, their headlights piercing the night all around them.

Crickets chirped in the forbidding woods and provided an eerie soundtrack as the leaders of the five ruling mob families in New York City emerged from their back seats one by one like conquering kings, helped along by solicitous drivers who hustled around the vehicles to open their doors. Dana shook her head in disgust. It was *The Godfather* all the way.

Carmine Tulio from the Luchese family emerged first, dressed in a silk shirt open at the neck to reveal a thick gold chain and a fuzzy blanket of curly black chest hair. Next came Bonaventure Abazzi from the Genovese family, wearing a lightweight hat and flower-patterned shirt that made it look as though he was about to embark upon a family vacation, not participate in the day-to-day operations of the organised-crime racket in New York City. After Abazzi came Fabricio Fabiano from the Colombo family, a short, fat man who – from the looks of things – had never once in his life met a meal he hadn't thoroughly enjoyed. The fourth man to emerge from his car was Anthony Lamana from the Bonanno family. At fifty-two years old and six feet, four inches tall, Lamana was the youngest of the five leaders and by far the most physically imposing specimen.

Then, finally, like a homecoming queen arriving fashionably late to the big dance, came Joseph Tucci from the Gambino crime family. In a valley full of monsters he was the biggest monster of them all and, judging by the looks on the faces of everyone there, Dana could tell that they all knew it too.

Dana adjusted the high-tech binoculars and brought Tucci's face into sharp focus, trying her best to remember what she could of the infamous gangster's appearance from the newspaper photographs she'd seen of him. Tucci was smoking a long cigar that had a fat yellow ring near the butt. Smoke curled up into his face and made him further squint his already narrow eyes. He wasn't classically handsome, but neither was he all that hard to look at. On a scale of one to ten, Dana probably would have given him a solid seven.

Most noticeably, though, there was a palpable air of danger surrounding Tucci. Dana supposed it only added to his legendary allure for the opposite sex. Tucci's reputation as a ladies' man had been well chronicled in the press – a fact that Dana couldn't imagine made his wife very happy.

Tucci's weather-beaten skin was stretched tight over his delicate bone structure, giving him a slightly haunted look that made Dana think that – although he was supremely confident – he also wasn't one hundred per cent comfortable with his position at the top. Instead, he seemed to be the sort of man who always felt the need to look over his shoulder, no matter how many armed bodyguards he employed.

A thin layer of silver hair on the top of Tucci's head couldn't hide the onset of male-pattern baldness – cracks in an armour he'd built up by becoming one of the mob's most feared killers at the tender age of seventeen when, in a local bar, he'd ruthlessly carved out the eyeballs of a rival gangster with a switchblade knife when the unfortunate man had had the temerity to look at his girlfriend the wrong way. And that had been just the beginning of Tucci's bloody career. Dana didn't know the exact body count he'd racked up, but it had to be in the dozens.

Then – just as quickly as they'd appeared – Joseph Tucci and his fellow mob bosses were ushered inside the hunting lodge to conduct their business. *Now you see them, now you don't.*

Pure boredom followed after that. The mob kingpins were inside the lodge for two solid hours, and Dana fought the urge to fall asleep the entire time. The crickets weren't helping matters any, singing their soft lullaby in an unsubtle attempt to woo her into dream-land. Even the armed sentries lost their good humour after a while, still smoking their unfiltered cigarettes but no longer cracking their stupid jokes.

Then the door of the hunting lodge opened again.

Dana shook the cobwebs from her brain and raised the binoculars to her eyes again, expecting to see the five mob bosses being escorted back to their vehicles with all the pomp-and-circumstance that had marked their arrival. Instead, Mario Garabaldi and Joey Baldarama left the building, dressed in what *appeared* to be matching polyester tracksuits and smoking their own unfiltered cigarettes.

The grogginess was gone now as Dana adjusted the viewfinder on the binoculars. What they revealed nearly stopped her heart.

Garabaldi and Baldarama were walking directly toward her and Brown's hidden position in the woods.

Everything seemed to unfold in slow motion after that. When the mobsters had cut the distance between them to a mere thirty yards, Dana placed her binoculars quietly on the ground beside her and flattened her body even closer against the ground. Only her eyes moved in order to keep Garabaldi and Baldarama in her line of sight. Brown did the same three feet to her right. His breathing slowed, hardly noticeable at all.

Ten seconds later, Garabaldi and Baldarama had reduced the distance between them to just twenty-five feet. A mosquito buzzed in Dana's ear, but she dared not swat it away. Instead, she forced herself to breathe as evenly as Brown despite the fact that her heartbeat was thumping out of control. From this distance, she could clearly hear the mobsters' conversation as they engaged in a little bit of light-hearted banter.

'Can you believe they actually make us go outside to take a piss?' Joey Baldarama asked disgustedly, undoing the drawstring on his jogging pants and proceeding to urinate on the ground. 'Who the fuck do they think they are, the kings of Egypt?'

'You mean leave one,' Garabaldi said, tossing his cigarette onto the ground and immediately lighting up another.

'What?'

Garabaldi snapped shut his gold Zippo and blew out a huge cloud of blue smoke. 'You don't take a piss, man, you leave one.'

Baldarama shook himself off and pulled his jogging pants back up before patting at his pockets. 'Whatever. Hey, you got a cigarette on you? I'm all out.'

Garabaldi reached into his pocket. The hand that came out wasn't holding a cigarette, though.

Dana muffled a scream in her throat as Garabaldi took one quick step forward, lifted a silver pistol to the back of Baldarama's head and blew out his fellow gangster's brains.

Dana couldn't be absolutely certain, but she was pretty sure that a small fragment of Baldarama's skull nicked her left cheek before falling away into the darkness.

CHAPTER TWENTY-SEVEN

Practice time, Sergei Michalovic thought.

He was in room 297 of the Catskills Inn on Lennox Avenue in the heart of downtown Harlem, wearing dirty blue jeans, a rumpled New York Yankees T-shirt and a pair of battered tennis shoes he'd picked up off a sales rack at a Salvation Army store on his way over here – certainly a far cry from the designer suits he was used to wearing. Still – somewhat camouflaged by his disgusting clothing though he was – he knew for sure that his white skin stuck out like a sore thumb around here, so he'd have to do this fast. Just get in, get out and get on with his life.

Though he'd paid for use of the filthy room for the entire night, the Catskills Inn was one of those establishments that also offered guests the option of paying by the hour – so that a customer could conduct a quick tryst with somebody who wasn't his wife, Michalovic supposed. A creaky double bed was stationed in the middle of the room. Ten feet away, a scarred wooden desk on which Michalovic had placed his oversized duffel bag full of tools was shoved into the corner. Other than that, though, there wasn't much to speak of by way of furniture in the room.

Peeling brown wallpaper covered the buckled-in walls. The carpet itself hadn't been swept in weeks, if not months. Thick black mould converged in an ever-growing mass in the corners of the walls near the waterlogged ceiling. A used condom sat on top of the overflowing trash can next to the bed.

Michalovic shook his head. He hadn't yet looked in the bathroom, but he doubted very much that he would've liked what he saw. If this main room was any indication, it too was probably full of cockroaches and the fat black ants that were munching on food crumbs left by previous renters of the room. Class place, all the way, no doubt about it. But it was perfect for his purposes. The kind of place where everybody minded their own business – even if they'd been requested to do otherwise by a murder victim using her dying breath to let out a blood-curdling scream.

Michalovic sat down in the uncomfortable wooden chair at the desk and toyed with the zipper on his duffel bag while he waited impatiently for his guest to arrive. He closed his eyes and tried to stay calm. The twenty-minute subway ride over here had been irritating enough. The entire time, he'd been sandwiched between a sleeping homeless man who – judging by the smell of him – hadn't taken a bath in at least a year and a young woman holding a screeching baby in her arms. To make matters worse, there was no air conditioning in the cut-rate motel room, so a light sheen of sweat had broken out across his forehead. The sounds of a fighting couple next door sliced through the paper-thin walls just as clearly as if he'd been sitting in the same room with them. Apparently, the woman was angry with the man for denying fatherhood of her latest baby, her fifth by the tender age of twenty-two.

The woman spoke first. 'If you're man enough to make a life, why the fuck ain't you man enough to take care of one, Malcolm?'

'Fuck you, slut,' came the casual reply. 'I ain't that kid's daddy. You slept with at least three of my homies that I know about, and I wouldn't be surprised to find out you slept with more than that. Did you fuck 'Twan too? He told me he hit it at Marisol's party. Shit, I bet you the kid's probably his.'

'Marcus is *yours*, Malcolm,' the woman sniffled, clearly on the verge of full-blown tears now. 'You know he is. Just look at his eyes. They're the same as yours. He looks just like you.'

Laughter cut through the wall like a switchblade knife. 'Look at his eyes? Shit, bitch, what in the fuck is his eyes supposed to prove? You'd better get yourself one of them DNA tests.'

Five minutes of this delightful slice-of-Harlem-life conversation later, the knock for which Michalovic had been waiting finally sounded at his door.

Michalovic glanced down at the Timex watch strapped around his wrist – another inexpensive Salvation Army purchase – and smiled. Ten-thirty p.m. on the dot. His guest was right on time.

Rising from his chair, Michalovic walked over to the door and opened it to find a thirty-something black woman wearing tight spandex bottoms, a low-cut blouse and no bra. Thigh-high vinyl hooker boots and a thick gold chain hanging around her neck completed her decidedly understated outfit. From the looks of things, she'd made a recent visit to the Salvation Army store, too. 'Are you Beatrice?' Michalovic asked.

The woman ignored his question and brushed past his left shoulder into the room. Turning around, she gave Michalovic the once-over, rolling her eyes while she smacked away at the gum in her mouth like a cow chewing on its cud. 'Fifty bucks for a blow job, a hunnerd for a half-and-half. You cool with that?'

Michalovic nodded and reached around to the back pocket of his jeans for his wallet. He held out a crisp one-hundred-dollar bill to the woman and resisted the urge to start giggling like an idiot. 'Of course,' he said. 'A bargain price, I'm sure.'

'So which one do you want?' the woman asked, taking his money and folding it in half with fingers that featured sharp acrylic nails at the tips.

Michalovic smiled sheepishly at her. 'Well, seeing as how I just handed you a hundred dollars, how about we go with the half-and-half?' he asked. 'I want to make sure I enjoy this.'

The woman leaned down and tucked the money away in one of her ridiculous boots. 'Fine. Let's just get on with it already. I got other clients I need to see tonight. Where do you want to do this? On the bed?'

Michalovic shook his head. The bed wouldn't do at all. He could practically *see* the chlamydia having a party on the soiled bedspread. 'No, I was thinking we might do it on the floor instead,' he said. 'I guess I'm feeling extra kinky tonight.'

The prostitute rolled her eyes again. 'Whatever, dude. It's your dime. Take off your clothes.'

Michalovic did as he was instructed, kicking off his battered tennis shoes and slipping his long limbs out of his civilian attire. A moment later he stood before the woman, naked and fully erect. And why not? This was exciting stuff, to say the least.

The prostitute stared down between Michalovic's legs and nodded in approval. 'Not bad for a white boy.'

Michalovic laughed. 'Thank you. And you? Do I get to see the wares before I sample them?'

'What?'

Michalovic shook his head. He should have known metaphors would have no place here tonight. 'Will you be getting naked as well?' he asked.

The woman took a step back and slipped her blouse over her head. Sagging brown breasts complete with oversized brown areolae stared back at him. 'So?' she said. 'You gonna come over here and touch me or what? Like I said before, I got other clients I need to see tonight. We need to get this show on the road.'

Michalovic smiled again and took a step in the woman's direction. She was absolutely right. It *was* time to get this show on the road. 'Yes, Beatrice,' he said. 'As a matter of fact, as you're about to find out, I'll be touching you all night long. I doubt you'll enjoy it very much, though. Please try not to scream. After all, we wouldn't want to disturb our neighbours next door, now would we? Those crazy kids are in love and they need to keep the atmosphere romantic. They're going to be parents again, you know.'

CHAPTER TWENTY-EIGHT

The mood in the car on the drive back to Manhattan twenty minutes later was much the same as the mood that had permeated the vehicle on the way down to Albany several hours earlier: *quiet*.

This time it was because Dana and Brown had both watched a man get his brains blown out – with a portion of his skull splattering against Dana's cheek – and they hadn't done a goddamn thing about it.

'What *could* we do?' Brown asked in exasperation, finally breaking the deafening silence in the car. He was behind the wheel of the Ford Focus again. 'SOP clearly spells it out: if engaging a suspect puts your life or any other innocent lives in danger, disengage and regroup. That's what we're doing here, Dana. We're disengaging and regrouping. Those goons would have turned on us if we'd have tried to apprehend Garabaldi, and you know it.'

Dana shook her head, knowing in her gut that Brown was probably right but unable to make herself feel any better about it. Standard operating procedure *did* say to disengage and regroup in those instances but, even for a stickler for the rule book like her, something about what had just happened didn't sit right with her. How could it? They'd let a man get away with *murder*. And no doubt it hadn't been his first. 'We could have at least *tried*,' she said.

Brown pursed his lips. 'Tried and *failed*. Listen, Dana, they had a goddamn *arsenal* down there. Didn't you see it? I sure as hell did. I counted at least five MAC-10s and another four assault rifles. God knows how many handguns. We've got two Glocks. How in the hell were we supposed to fight that kind of firepower? They would have taken us out in ten seconds flat if we'd have given away our position. I know what we did – or *didn't* do – doesn't feel right to you, but it was the textbook move.'

'You're not the one who caught a piece of a guy's skull in your face.'

Brown cracked a window and let some fresh air into the car. This time it was him who couldn't stand the tension. 'Think again, my friend,' he said in a clipped tone. 'I was three feet away from you the entire time, remember?'

Dana shifted in her seat and stared out the passenger-side window into the darkness. 'Whatever. Let's just stop talking for a little while, OK? It's obviously not getting us anywhere.'

After what seemed an eternity – but which in reality was probably only about ten minutes or so – Brown finally spoke again. 'So, are you going to call Krugman, or do you want me to do it?'

Dana sighed and shook her head. This was the part of the night she'd been dreading ever since agreeing to accompany Brown back to their car instead of going after Garabaldi with their guns blazing. Krugman was already pissed at her as it was. No doubt this phone call would only further foul his mood. While Dana and the Director had developed something of a bond at the end of the Cleveland Slasher case – when Krugman had informed Dana that Crawford Bell had always thought of her as a daughter – that bond had already been stretched to the point of snapping by her and Brown's failure to apprehend the Chessboard Killer. Still, even though this call wouldn't be an easy one to make, Dana felt as though she should be the one to make it. 'I'll do it,' she said. 'He already hates my guts, anyway. What's it going to matter if he hates my guts that much more?'

Dana sighed and called up the contacts list on her cellphone. She hit the little green telephone icon next to Krugman's name. Several rings passed without an answer, and Dana was pretty sure his voicemail was about to click on when Krugman finally picked up.

'Krugman here,' he said in his characteristically brusque tone.

'Sir, it's Dana Whitestone.'

Krugman laughed sourly. 'Yeah, I'm well aware of that, Agent Whitestone. I've got caller ID, you know. Anyway, what's up? What's going on?'

As quickly as she could, Dana filled the Director in on what had just transpired out in the woods. When she'd finished bringing him up to speed, she delayed what she knew would be his thunderous response by asking, 'Should we bring Garabaldi in for Baldarama's murder, sir? I'd say the case we've got is pretty cut-and-dried. Brown and I will testify, of course.'

Surprisingly, the backlash that Dana had been expecting didn't materialise. Instead, she heard a car door shut on the other end of the line, prompting her to check her watch. Eleven p.m., which meant Krugman was probably just wrapping up his work for the day – a workday that for him always started at precisely five a.m. A moment later an engine purred to life in the background and Krugman said, 'No, I don't think so, Agent Whitestone. Let's let the murder ride for now. I want to bring down the whole Tucci family, not just one of its goons.'

Dana let out a relieved breath, thankful that Krugman hadn't bitten off her head. Still, even though he'd let her know they'd most likely let a few minnows go in order to get to Tucci, the idea of letting a thug like Garabaldi skate on yet *another* murder burned in her throat like a bad case of acid reflux. 'So, if you don't want us to bring Garabaldi in yet, what *do* you want us to do?' Dana asked.

Krugman coughed softly. At sixty-nine years old now, he wasn't getting any younger and Dana wondered how much longer he could possibly keep up with his hectic schedule. It was enough to make even *her* feel tired, and she was more than thirty years his junior. 'Well,' Krugman said, 'since it's more important that we get the goods on Joseph Tucci than it is to send Mario Garabaldi off to prison for murdering a man that nobody's going to miss anyway, I'd say the only thing we can do for now is continue tailing Garabaldi. Keep on his ass like white on rice. Do you know where he lives?'

'Yes, sir,' Dana said – they'd given her the dossiers on Baldarama and Garabaldi back at the NYC field office. Each one of their files was at least two inches thick and, when Dana finished the paperwork on Garabaldi's latest murder, his would be that much thicker.

'Where are you now?' Krugman asked.

'About an hour away from Garabaldi's house.'

Krugman paused. Then he said, 'Well, I know it's late, but why don't you guys head over there now and see what his next move might be? Remember, Agent Whitestone: this is a marathon, not a sprint. I know it sucks sometimes, but we need to keep our eyes on the overall prize here. Does that make any sense to you?'

'Yes, sir. Of course it does.'

'Good. Other than that, how are things going for you? I haven't heard from you in a couple of days and I was beginning to worry.'

'Everything's great, sir,' Dana lied. 'I'm sorry I haven't been in contact lately, but this new case is taking up most of our time now. Not that we've gotten very much done up to this point, I'm afraid.'

Krugman grunted. 'A lot of hurry-up-and-wait going on for you two?'

'You don't know the half of it, sir.'

Krugman sighed heavily. 'Says you. I was out in the field once myself, so I know how tedious the job can be at times. Anyway, keep me posted on Garabaldi's movements. I want to bring down the entire Gambino family from top to bottom, and from what I understand about Mario Garabaldi he's just the sort of guy who might provide us with an opening. I know that you and Agent Brown are up to the task. That's why I reassigned you to this case in the first place. Do me a favour and don't make me look like an idiot on this one, OK?'

Dana winced, reading Krugman's meaning between the lines as easily as if he'd come right out and called them incompetent. Not only had she and Brown made themselves look like idiots on the Chessboard Killer case, they'd made Krugman look like one, too. 'I'll do my very best, sir,' she said.

'That's all I ask, Agent Whitestone. I'll talk to you soon.'

Dana hung up the phone and turned in her seat to face Brown. 'Krugman wants us to hold our fire on Baldarama's murder for now. He wants us to continue following Garabaldi and bring down the whole kit and caboodle, not just one of the pieces.'

Brown closed his eyes briefly before opening them up again. 'Well, I'm not surprised. Krugman goes by the book. Always has.'

Dana felt her cheeks flush, reading Brown's meaning just as easily as she'd read Krugman's. She wasn't angry with her partner, though. Brown had every right to be annoyed with her. He'd been absolutely right and she'd been absolutely wrong. It was as simple as that. And now it was time for Dana to apologise. 'I'm sorry I jumped down your throat earlier,' she said. 'I was flustered and I let it get to me. It won't happen again.'

Brown didn't say anything in response. But after a moment or two, he reached out a hand and placed it on her left knee.

Gooseflesh rippled across Dana's body. Despite her initial inclination to remove Brown's hand, she let it remain there all the way to Mario Garabaldi's house. After a while, she reached out and put her hand on top of his. Guilt and shamc flooded hot through her veins, but it wasn't enough to overcome the tenderness she felt for him inside.

I guess we're all just looking for someone to hang onto when the going gets tough, Dana thought. *Even me.*

Especially *me.*

CHAPTER TWENTY-NINE

The first punch caught Beatrice square on her nose, splintering the bone in half a dozen different places and sending a sickening gush of blood pouring down her face. Her clear brown eyes widened in complete terror. Two more quick punches closed up the whore's surprised eyes for her, dropping her unconscious to the floor.

Still naked and fully erect, Michalovic straddled the prostitute and began raining down punch after vicious punch on her ugly face as hard as he could, his heart rate never rising above eighty the entire time. Gradually, what had once been a woman's face became an unrecognisable soupy mess that not even her mother would have been able to identify at the morgue.

As Michalovic continued to put all his weight behind each of his powerful punches long after the stupid bitch had stopped breathing, he wondered idly why O'Hara had murdered Don Yuntz – and why the stupid idiot had left behind a copy of *Chess for Dummies* at the man's apartment. Was he *trying* to get them caught here? So they'd got one of the most experienced FBI agents and her partner pulled off the case, but that didn't mean they could rest easy. The FBI, the NYPD, the media, the people of New York – they were all baying for blood. It was important that Michalovic and O'Hara stayed in control, stuck to the game.

Michalovic breathed in evenly and forced himself to stay calm while he continued to batter the unconscious woman's face. Technically, he supposed, O'Hara's recent extracurricular activities constituted straying from the very specific rules of their game, which in turn meant that Michalovic could now rightfully claim the five million dollars each had put up for the winner of the contest. Michalovic had no plans to do that, however. Far from it. As he'd established earlier – way back when this game had first begun in the glittering lobby of the Fontainebleau Hotel – money had nothing at all to do with what was going on here between himself and O'Hara. This final contest was strictly for *fun*. And if O'Hara thought that Michalovic wasn't wise to the Irish-American's plan to kill him in revenge for the night when the Russian had broken every bone in O'Hara's father's body in an attempt to get him to sign over the rights to a plot of land out on Long Island on which Michalovic had planned to build a brand-new shipping port, he was sorely mistaken about that. Michalovic hadn't meant to *kill* the stubborn bastard. It wasn't *his* fault the old fart's heart had simply given out due to the excruciating pain. It had just been *business*. What was so hard to understand about that?

Michalovic shook his head and finally stopped punching the prostitute's face. His knuckles were bruised, scraped and bleeding by now. Breathing heavily from the intensity of his efforts, he rose to his feet and walked over to the desk before unzipping his duffel bag and extracting a hacksaw. The weight of the sturdy tool felt wonderful in his hand – American-made, no doubt. Quality stuff.

The hard floor in the motel room – the same floor off which he'd repeatedly bounced Beatrice's head with each one of his vicious blows and the very reason he hadn't wanted to do it with her on the bed in the first place – provided the necessary base. Calmly, Michalovic began to hack off the woman's head. The fine-toothed tempered blade – purchased from a Home Depot in Manhattan just hours earlier – was the ideal tool for the job. Michalovic grimaced from the surprising amount of muscle it took to get the grisly deed done, gritting his teeth and working the blade carefully back and forth across the woman's throat, and then back and forth again. A little bit of overkill, perhaps, but he'd paid for a half-and-half here tonight and he wanted to get his money's worth.

On the third movement of his arm, a line of blood squirted up from the woman's severed jugular vein. Michalovic stopped his sawing and wiped away a smear of blood from his eyes with the back of his right hand. Oh, well. Nothing to be concerned about here. Practice made perfect. And one day soon, the practice of this particular manoeuvre would prove quite invaluable. For one day soon, it would be Edward J. O'Hara's neck under the razor-sharp teeth of this very same saw.

CHAPTER THIRTY

Two long hours of driving down the dark, mostly deserted highways later, Dana and Brown beat Mario Garabaldi to their shared destination by a full twenty minutes. From their hidden position across the street from his house, they watched as the lowlife thug finally returned home from Albany in his shiny black Lincoln Towne Car.

Garabaldi pulled into the long, winding driveway of his faux-Tudor home – a far from modest two-storey affair that featured an expensive-looking brick façade – and left the expensive car running as he hustled inside. Five minutes later, he emerged with an electric chainsaw held in his right hand and hopped back inside his car.

The mobster backed carefully out of his driveway and drove away, not noticing Dana and Brown who were hunched down low in their seats in the Ford Focus. A moment later, they followed him at a discreet distance, weaving their way through the heavy Manhattan traffic as best they could while trying to keep up with Garabaldi, who – in addition to being a stone-cold killer – also seemed to have something of a lead foot. Fortunately for them, Garabaldi never caught sight of his tail.

Half an hour later, he finally brought the Towne Car to a stop in front of Luigi's Deli on Colfax Avenue – the same deli at which he and Baldarama had conducted their business earlier that morning. Dana and Brown parked up forty yards away, easing their own car between a delivery van and a brand-new Mini Cooper with a United Kingdom flag painted on the hood. The street was deserted.

Garabaldi got out of his vehicle and flicked his still-burning cigarette into the road before popping the trunk with his key-chain control and emerging a moment later with a large black garbage bag in his arms, struggling beneath the bag's heavy weight all the way into the deli. Thirty seconds later, he returned for the electric chainsaw and went back inside.

Brown cursed under his breath. 'This is worse than an episode of the fucking *Sopranos*,' he snarled. 'Twenty to one that's Joey Baldarama's body he's going to chop up in there.'

Dana didn't say a word. Once again, they couldn't do a goddamn thing about it. Krugman had told them to hold their fire, and she knew better than to disobey the Director's orders.

Brown cracked his knuckles in frustration. 'What should we do?' he asked. 'I want to go in there and bring that bastard down so badly I can taste it. He doesn't have his little buddies around this time to save him.'

Dana turned to her partner and shrugged. She was upset too, but their instructions were clear: leave Garabaldi alone for the time being and concentrate on bringing down the entire Tucci family. 'Nothing we *can* do,' she said. 'I want Garabaldi too, but our hands are tied on this one. Krugman wants us to just watch for now. Says we can bring him in later.'

Brown cursed again, louder this time.

In the distance, Dana imagined she heard the faint whine of an electric chainsaw starting up.

CHAPTER THIRTY-ONE

Four days after the phone call from Pierre LeBlanc that changed her life for the better, Betty Arsenault looked around her new home on Fourth Avenue and smiled. All the boxes were finally unpacked and all the contents had finally found their own places throughout the seven rooms of her new digs. From the crown moulding to the extra bedroom that she was planning to use as a home office to the significant upgrade in neighbourhood safety for her children, it was about a gazillion times better than her old place over on Second. Not only that, but for the first time in months Betty actually had a *job*. A *real* job. One she actually got *paid* for.

Betty felt a warm glow spread throughout her entire body. A feeling that had seemed nearly impossible ever since she'd lost her previous job at a trucking company way back in November in an ugly dispute over some misplaced paperwork.

A second, more powerful ripple of emotion spread through Betty's consciousness at the realisation of the wonderful unexpected second chance at life she'd been given. Things were finally starting to look up for her now. She hadn't felt this good in *years*. Not to mention the fact that she could easily imagine a future for herself at Settle Systems Group.

Though today had been her first day on her new job – and although things had seemed a bit confusing at times with all the new information she was expected to learn – Betty knew that she was up to the task. Besides, she was determined to make this situation work, come hell or high water. Honestly, there wasn't much choice in the matter. At almost forty-five years old now, the chances of her ever getting a fresh start somewhere else didn't seem very likely. Like it or not, it was make-or-break time.

In her more wistful moments, Betty couldn't stop herself from imagining a rise up the ranks. Who knew? Maybe someday she could even leave the secretarial pool behind and snag herself a nice little promotion to the position of a mid-level manager or something. God knew the company was large enough to accommodate her. Its four thousand workers made it one of the largest computer-technology outfits in all of New York City.

Yep, the sky was the limit for her now. Now it was time for Betty to shoot for the stars instead of simply struggling to stay out of the gutter. She owed it to her children. She owed it to *herself*.

Betty's new Droid cellphone sounded in her pocket and brought her back into the present. The phone had been a welcome gift to her from Settle Systems Group, and she'd set her ringtone to 'Billionaire' by Travis McCoy and Bruno Mars. Twenty-four thousand dollars a year certainly seemed a far shot from that, of course, but it never hurt to dream, now did it?

Betty dug out the phone from her pocket and struggled with the answer function for a moment before finally figuring it out. Sliding the digital green bar across the bottom of the phone, she said, 'Hello?'

A familiar voice sounded in her ear. 'Miss Arsenault, it's Pierre LeBlanc. I'm just checking in to see how your new position is working out for you.'

Betty's pulse quickened. Her ears rang. Her stomach churned. Now that she had a job, she wanted to keep it. So she knew that the stakes were raised when it came to anything connected to it.

Including this phone call.

Ironically, though, Betty's intense desire to please her superior only worked against her here, made her voice come out haltingly and without self-confidence. 'The job is absolutely wonderful,' she said, a little too quickly, hoping she could cover up her nervousness by speaking in short bursts. 'Thank you so much once again for the opportunity, Mr LeBlanc. I can't tell you how much I appreciate it. I can't tell you how much it means to me and my family.'

Thankfully, Pierre LeBlanc didn't seem to notice the heightened nervousness in Betty's voice. Or, at the very least, he didn't comment on it. Either way, though, Betty reckoned that she had dodged a bullet. For now. 'Excellent, Miss Arsenault,' LeBlanc said. 'I'm so happy to hear that. And, please, there's absolutely no need for you to thank me. You're more than qualified for the job.

You weren't the only candidate we interviewed for the position. You were simply the one whom we wanted the most.'

LeBlanc's words put Betty at ease at once, even if he were only saying them to be nice. Gradually, she felt her pulse begin to slow a little. Maybe there wasn't anything for her to be nervous about here. Maybe she should try to have a little more confidence in herself. Other people seemed to, including Pierre LeBlanc.

When Betty spoke again, her voice sounded stronger even to her own ears. 'That's very nice of you, Mr LeBlanc. Today was only my first day on the job, but I love it there already. The people are so nice.'

'Excellent,' LeBlanc said. 'Anyway, listen, Miss Arsenault, I know you're off the clock right now, but do you recall in our initial conversation how I mentioned there might be some package deliveries involved from time to time?'

'Yes, of course.'

LeBlanc paused and cleared his throat. Apparently, this time it was *his* turn to feel uneasy. 'Good. Well, I'm afraid that our courier has already left for the day, and seeing as how you live closest to the package's destination I was wondering if you might be able to deliver it for us.'

Betty frowned, not quite understanding what her living closest to the package's destination had to do with anything. It still meant she'd need to travel across town to the office first in order to pick up the parcel. Not to mention the fact that she'd finally gotten her kids to settle down and start their homework, which had always been a struggle roughly along the lines of World War III.

Still, it wasn't as though Betty was going to say no to LeBlanc. Certainly not on her first day. 'Of course, Mr LeBlanc,' she said. 'I'll get over to the office right away.'

LeBlanc laughed uncertainly. 'There's no need for that, Miss Arsenault. I sort of figured you'd say yes, so I took the liberty of dropping off the package at your building on my way home from work. I hope you don't mind very much.'

Betty breathed a deep sigh of relief. *Mind?* Of course she didn't mind. That shaved an hour and a half off her travel time right there. 'Of course not, sir,' she said. 'That's just fine. Where would you like the package delivered?'

LeBlanc told Betty the address, and Betty frowned again. The address was just one block away from her new home. Why hadn't LeBlanc just taken it over there himself since he'd already been in the neighbourhood anyway?

Betty shook her head, knowing it wouldn't do to question her boss. He knew what he was doing, hadn't achieved his own lofty position by accident. Besides, if she was lucky, she might even get an hour or two of overtime in her pay to show for it, and she could certainly use the extra money. And she'd be back home before the kids even had a chance to figure out she was gone in the first place. It was a win-win situation for her any way she looked at it. 'I'm on my way now,' Betty said. 'I'll have your package over there in a jiffy, Mr LeBlanc.'

'Thank you, Miss Arsenault. Have a wonderful evening. And, oh, Miss Arsenault?'

'Yes?'

'Stay safe out there.'

Betty hung up the phone, puzzled by LeBlanc's last statement. But then she brushed it off. To heck with it.

It was time to earn her money.

CHAPTER THIRTY-TWO

Micah Brantley rocked back and forth on the edge of his bed at the rehab facility that he'd checked into a few mornings previously. Sweating heavily, he looked up at the large round clock hanging on the wall, the one whose second hand ticked so loudly he thought it would make his skull collapse.

Five-twelve p.m.

Micah had shot up a speedball directly before arriving at the rehab facility, of course, but enough time had passed since then to make the potent combination of heroin and cocaine just a distant memory – one that was fading away a little bit more with each maddening tick of the clock on the wall. Now he had the shakes.

Micah cursed softly under his breath and forced himself to stay on the bed, knowing that if he got to his feet he'd start punching the walls and kicking the door. Not that it would have made much difference. The walls in his room had been padded with a thick rubberised material at least three inches thick, and the door was constructed of reinforced steel – also padded. No windows, of course. Typical detox accommodations through and through.

Bad as things were for him right now, though, Micah

knew that prison would have been a million times worse. Everybody *loved* a celebrity in prison, didn't they? The inmates made it a point to target high-profile cons such as himself in an effort to make a name for themselves. But who had connected Micah to the rape and murder of that stupid little slut back in college, anyway?

Micah tried in vain to remember the conversation he'd had with the mysterious caller several days earlier. Sadly, though, he couldn't remember much. The drugs had turned his brain into mush. The one thing about the conversation that *did* stick out in his memory, however, was that the man who'd called and woken him from his nap had threatened to go to the police with all the details on what Micah and his friends had done one night on spring break at Syracuse University fifteen years earlier. Miraculously, despite the nearly continuous supply of speedballs he'd shot into his system directly after hanging up the phone, he'd managed to keep at least *some* of the mystery man's words in his mind long enough to drag his sorry ass out of bed the following morning and make it to the rehab facility in time.

The caller's ominous words echoed in Micah's mind again:

'Eight a.m. sharp. You'd better be there, Micah. Because if you're not, you'll pray you were.'

Micah ran his dry tongue across his desiccated lips and willed himself to hold on until six p.m. At six o'clock, he'd receive a cocktail of diazepam, klonopin and Tylenol to help him deal with the excruciating detoxification process. Besides, thinking this much made his head hurt. Always had. He just needed to hold on a little bit longer now. After that, everything would be OK.

Micah looked up at the clock again.

Five-thirteen p.m.

One *fucking minute?*

Just when he'd thought he'd literally lose his mind, a knock sounded at Micah's door. A moment later, a key rattled in the lock and the door opened up. It was Smith, the orderly who'd given Micah a dirty look earlier in the day. The orderly who'd been giving him dirty looks ever since Micah had first arrived at the godforsaken rehab facility. A petite blonde woman who looked to be about forty-five years old followed in behind. 'You've got a package delivery here, douchebag,' Smith said, shaking his head in disgust. 'God knows why you get special treatment, but I guess that's what you get for being a celebrity, huh?'

The woman crossed into the room and handed Micah a yellow envelope cushioned on the inside with bubble wrap. 'From Settle Systems Group,' she said, then immediately turned and left the room.

Smith shot Micah another dirty look before stepping back out into the hallway. 'See ya tomorrow, big guy,' he said, lifting the set of keys that was attached to his belt by a thick silver chain. 'You might want to wipe off some of that sweat from your forehead, though. Never know when you'll receive female visitors, eh? Try to remember, sweetheart: you always want to look your best for your adoring public.'

Micah gritted his teeth when the orderly shut and relocked the door. Then the sound of his footsteps receded down the long hallway. When they'd finally faded into silence, Micah tore open the envelope with his teeth and pulled out a yellowed newspaper clipping. It was a section of the sports page from the *New York Times*. A forty-point headline had been stripped across the top:

BRANTLEY POWERS NY PAST CHICAGO;
KNICKS ADVANCE IN PLAY-OFFS

Micah skimmed the article that he practically knew by heart. In glowing terms, it detailed the career-topping night he'd had way back in 1998. At the bottom of the article, someone had scrawled a message in black magic marker:

FROM YOUR BIGGEST FAN. ENJOY. EAT THIS AFTER READING OR DON'T EXPECT ANY MORE PACKAGES.

Tears of frustration clouded Micah's vision as he looked into the envelope again. Nestled at the bottom, a syringe loaded with a clear liquid stared back at him.

A speedball.

Micah blinked hard, not quite believing his eyes. In his darkest hour, a bright, shining light had been delivered right into the heart of his prison. It looked as though Smith had been absolutely right about his assessment, even if he'd only been saying it to get a rise out of Micah: celebrity *did* have its privileges. And now Micah would enjoy one of them.

Fuck waiting until six o'clock, he thought. *I need to feel better* right now.

Balling up the newsprint in his right hand, he shoved the wad of paper into his mouth and chewed only twice before swallowing it down whole. Then he reached back into the envelope for the syringe.

Sliding the sharp needle deep into a vein on his left arm, Micah depressed the plunger. A cold rush of euphoria immediately flooded throughout his entire body.

A moment later, his eyeballs rolled up into the back of his skull before he fell off the bed and began a violent seizure.

CHAPTER THIRTY-THREE

Dressed in only a cotton bathrobe and slippers that had been monogrammed with the initials of which he'd always been so very proud – initials he'd soon *avenge* in the bloodiest of fashions – Edward O'Hara opened the door of his apartment at The Dakota at six a.m. on Sunday morning and leaned down to retrieve the bulky morning edition of the *New York Times* on his welcome mat before taking the newspaper with him back to his sumptuous wood-panelled study.

Even though the process would take anywhere from six to eight weeks before all the paperwork was in order, workers had already begun to pack up some of O'Hara's non-vital belongings in anticipation of his impending move over to John Lennon's old apartment. A bit fanboyish, perhaps, but he liked to stay ahead of the curve on this sort of thing.

O'Hara shooed three Hispanic women out of his study with some rudimentary Spanish – they might have been from El Salvador, but he'd be damned if he could remember – before sliding back his office chair and sitting down behind his massive desk. Propping up his slippered feet on the desk blotter in front of him, he scanned the front page of the *Times* and smiled when he saw the box in the top left-hand corner of the page that served as a window into the paper, informing readers of some of the more interesting stories they could find inside:

FORMER KNICKS STAR DIES AT REHAB FACILITY

The tersely worded teaser pointed readers to the sports section of the paper – the 'C' section – but according to the rules that he and Michalovic had spelled out O'Hara supposed the Russian's manoeuvre *technically* met the requirement that their capture moves should appear no later than the 'B' section of the *Times*. By making it into the teaser window, Michalovic had cut it close but he'd made it. The lucky prick. Michalovic still retained ownership of his five million dollars, at least for now. But O'Hara knew his oppon - ent wouldn't prove anywhere near as fortunate in the coming weeks. One way or another, O'Hara would *win* this deadly game they were playing, regardless of what the coin flip had decided back in the gleaming lobby of the Fontainebleau Hotel.

O'Hara patted the front pocket of his robe to make sure that the Saint-Gaudens he'd stolen from Michalovic was still there before he opened up the paper to the front page of the sports section and read the headline and story positioned in the right-hand two columns. It was right next to an article about the New York Yankees' season opener, which they'd dropped 3-2 to the lowly Cleveland Indians thanks to some late-inning heroics from Shin-Soo Choo, the Tribe's South Korean-born right fielder.

O'Hara shook his head in disappointment upon learning of the Yankees' opening-day loss, having always been an avid local sports fan, especially of the Bronx Bombers. After a moment, though, he simply shrugged. To hell with it. There was absolutely nothing to be worried about here. He knew the Yankees would soon acquire the pesky ballplayer via trade or – at the very latest – during the following year's free-agency market. After all, that was the Yankees' *modus operandi*, wasn't it? If they didn't already have the best players, they simply went out and *bought* them. Especially the ones who'd played well against them in the past.

O'Hara nodded approvingly, admiring his hometown ball club's business acumen, which had led to an unprecedented twenty-seven World Series titles – the most in the history of the Major Leagues. O'Hara himself had used his own money plenty of times over the course of his life to purchase exactly what it was he needed to win, too. It was simple economics, really. The law of the jungle. Survival of the richest.

Folding the newspaper lengthwise, he read the headline sitting on top of the story about Micah Brantley's tragic death:

TROUBLED KNICKS GREAT FOUND DEAD
By Raymond C. Garcia
New York Times staff writer

Former New York Knicks basketball player Micah Brantley was found unconscious in a drug-rehab facility on Fifth Avenue in Manhattan early last night. Four hours later, he was pronounced dead at Laura Michele Memorial Hospital, also in Manhattan.

Preliminary blood tests revealed evidence of cocaine and heroin in Mr Brantley's system. Hospital staff struggled to revive Brantley for more than two hours, but those efforts ultimately proved unsuccessful. Dr Mohammed Mobati, the lead surgeon on duty at the time, said more tests would be run throughout the day.

Though once in top physical shape, Mr Brantley's health had deteriorated considerably in the years since his banishment from the National Basketball Association in 2004 following a third failed drug test, the league's equivalent of the 'three strikes and you're out' law often applied to felons across several parts of the United States.

Mr Brantley was thirty-eight years old.

A brief memorial service is planned for 4 p.m. Wednesday at Madison Square Garden. The general public is invited to attend. Donations to the New York City chapter of Narcotics Anonymous are requested in lieu of flowers.

The article ended with contact information for the reporter and additional details of the memorial service that O'Hara had no plans to attend. As far as he was concerned: good riddance to bad rubbish. The world was far better off without Micah Brantley, anyway. He and Michalovic had done everyone a *service* here – not that O'Hara expected any congratulatory phone calls for their efforts. Human trash or not, the New York sports world had *loved* Micah Brantley, had held him up as some sort of superhuman being.

O'Hara shook his head in disgust. There was absolutely no reasoning with sports fans, no accounting for taste. You stuck with your team through thick and thin and you loved them, warts and all. No ifs, ands or buts about it. Anything else and it meant you'd never *really* been a fan in the first place.

O'Hara tossed the newspaper back onto his desk and leaned back in his chair while he considered his next move. Five minutes later, he'd worked out his response to Michalovic – and it was an absolute beauty. Furthermore – as this next manoeuvre would be a capture move as well – it would need to be splashy enough to make at least the 'B' section of the *Times*. But without the assistance of celebrity to help him out, O'Hara knew he'd need plenty of blood if the murder were to be featured in a proper slot in the newspaper.

No problem there. The next piece he'd be moving had simmered for many years in her thirst for revenge, which made her the ideal pawn to use here. And it didn't hurt matters that there'd also be an element of kinky sex involved in the slaying, either. After all, much as they did with beloved sports stars, the general public *salivated* at the prospect of anything perverted. Drooled all over it like one of Pavlov's dogs. Why was anybody's guess. Maybe it made them feel better about themselves, better than the people they read about.

O'Hara put his feet back down on the floor and leaned forward in his seat to pick up the phone on his desk. The time had come to remind his pawn of what had happened in her Manhattan apartment on a stormy night twenty-five years earlier – and to offer her the chance to finally exact the revenge she'd been lusting after all these years.

Sex sold – no denying that simple fact – and now it was time for O'Hara to sell some of it himself.

Amber Coletta picked up her phone after three rings. Clearing his throat, O'Hara quickly set into motion the train of events that would ultimately lead to Betty Arsenault's gruesome death, the Michalovic pawn who'd been put to work at Settle Systems Group. 'Mrs Coletta,' O'Hara said, getting straight to the point, 'I have some disturbing information about your husband's murder.'

A shocked silence followed. Then, 'Who is this?'

'It doesn't matter who this is,' O'Hara said. 'Do you want the details or not?'

'Robert's been gone a long time. Last I heard, the woman who killed him had died, too.'

O'Hara waved a hand in the air. 'That may be true, ma'am, but I can give you the woman's daughter. I can give you the illegitimate child she had with your husband. If you're not interested, I can—'

Coletta cut him off. 'Of course I'm interested. Don't be ridiculous. What's her name?'

O'Hara grinned. It hadn't taken him long to reel Coletta in – which bode well for the future. Obviously, he was operating at the top of his game – exactly where he *needed* to be operating. 'Her name is Betty Arsenault,' O'Hara said. 'She'll be at the StayClean Drug Rehabilitation Centre at precisely seven p.m. tonight. That gives you twelve hours to prepare. If I were you, I'd give serious thought to doing to her what her mother did to your husband. Just a suggestion, but you certainly can't ignore the poetic justice of it all.'

Coletta paused. After a moment, she said, 'That's not a bad idea. Not a bad idea at all.'

O'Hara shook his head, irritated. The woman clearly wasn't thinking things all the way through, and he *hated* sloppiness. Always had. 'Aren't you at all worried about getting caught?' he asked.

Coletta laughed without humour. 'I'm sixty-nine years old, whoever you are. I've got diabetes, glaucoma and Stage Five skin cancer. I assure you, getting caught is the least of my worries.'

'Fine. So be it, then. Good luck to you on your mission tonight.'

Hanging up with Coletta, O'Hara then dialled Betty Arsenault's number. When she answered her phone, he lowered the bass level in his voice and said, 'Ms Arsenault, this is Lieutenant Vernon with the New York City Police Department. We have information that you delivered a package to the StayClean Drug Rehabilitation Centre last night. As we're questioning everyone who was in the building yesterday due to the fact that a client of the centre died after receiving a fatal dose of drugs, we'll be questioning you, too. Routine procedure, I assure you, and you're not in any trouble for anything. But is there any way you could meet me at the facility at seven p.m. tonight?'

Arsenault sounded shaken up. 'Of course, lieutenant,' she said, her voice quavering. 'Seven p.m. tonight. I'll be there.'

O'Hara hung up the phone again and smiled. Instant karma certainly had its benefits, but there was nothing quite as satisfying as serving up a nice big plate of ice-cold revenge.

Better yet, soon enough Sergei Michalovic – the heartless monster who'd killed O'Hara's father more than thirty years earlier over a stupid piece of land that the idiot had never even bothered to develop – would get a chance to sample a heaped helping of that revenge, as well.

Sample it until the motherfucker choked on it.

After all, that was the American way. And if Michalovic wanted to be a citizen of this country so fucking badly, that was something he'd just need to learn the hard way.

PART V

ENDGAME

'All I want to do, ever, is just play chess.'

Bobby Fischer

CHAPTER THIRTY-FOUR

Dana and Brown were in Café Lalo on West 83rd Street the morning after the vicious murder of Joey Baldarama out in the dark Albany woods, sipping on piping-hot mochaccinos and discussing the injustice of not bringing Mario Garabaldi in. Outside, a hard rain slapped against the sidewalks and streaked the windows of the coffee shop with swirls of running water.

Dana stared out at the rain and decided that was *precisely* what she felt like right now: as though she was viewing the world through a window streaked with running water. Up looked like down to her; east looked like west; right looked like wrong. She struggled in vain to reconcile her moral compass with the fact that they'd let Garabaldi get away with the crime of blowing out a man's brains right in front of their eyes in exchange for bringing down the entire Gambino gang. In an Old Testament world, where you took an eye for an eye, they were practising New Testament ideals and simply turning the other cheek. It was enough to drive her to distraction.

Brown blew a cloud of steam from the drink in front of him and looked across the table at her. 'I'm not happy about it, either, Dana,' he said. 'But orders are orders, and our orders are to stand down on the murder for now. We'll get Garabaldi in the end. For now, just try to enjoy your coffee, would you? Damn things cost eight bucks apiece.'

Dana smiled thinly across the table at her partner. She'd have *loved* to enjoy her coffee right now, but the truth of the matter was that her expensive drink tasted more like water to her: bland and completely flavourless. *All* her senses felt that way right now: *numbed*. Especially her sense of right and wrong. Still, she knew that she needed to have faith in Bill Krugman's decision. If the Director thought it best to take a wait-and-see approach with Garabaldi, he was probably right. After all, he hadn't risen to his senior position with the FBI simply because he'd known somebody on the inside. And she suspected that her frustration wasn't just to do with this investigation. She still couldn't quite let go of the Chessboard Killer case, playing it over and over in her mind. Why couldn't she and Brown crack it? Was she really losing her touch? She sighed. She needed to concentrate on this case, the one she was actually assigned to, and do as she was told. 'I'll try, Jeremy,' Dana said. 'But it's not going to be easy. Any word from your guy down in DC about what's going on in the Chessboard case?'

Brown shook his head. 'Not a thing. Says he'll be sure to let me know just as soon as any new information becomes available.' He paused and nodded down at her barely touched drink. 'Coffee doesn't taste so great to you right now?'

'It doesn't taste like anything to me right now.'

'Hmm. Mine tastes a bit like mud.'

'Lucky you.'

Brown laughed humourlessly. 'Yeah. Well, anyway, try not to let it get you down, OK? It's just the way the system works.'

'Well, the system sucks, then.'

Brown nodded again. 'Amen to that. But try to remember that we're the good guys here, OK? Try to remember that we're doing the right thing, even if it feels wrong to you.'

Although Dana gave him credit for trying to make her feel better, his attempt wasn't quite working. Still, at least he'd cared enough to give it a crack. Another great thing about him. He always put others' feelings in front of his own. The mystery woman he'd married probably loved that about him.

From there, they each slipped back into their own thoughts for a little while. For Dana, it was a rainy day back in Cleveland, Ohio thirty-five years earlier – a day that resembled this miserable day in New York City enough to give her chill bumps, as though a pair of long-dead ghosts had floated through the coffee-shop window and wrapped her up in their freezing embrace. In her mind, a four-year-old version of Dana was seated on the living-room couch next to her parents, James and Sara, and discussing how she had lied to them that morning about breaking one of her mother's prized vases.

*

'Well, if you didn't break it, who did?' James Whitestone asked as the cabinet-style television in the middle of their living room played a rerun of *Leave It to Beaver* with the volume turned off. 'Your mother and I certainly didn't do it. Sort of narrows down the list of possible suspects, wouldn't you say?'

Dana shrugged her slender shoulders, which lifted her flowered sundress three inches above her skinned knees. 'I don't know. Maybe the cat broke it.'

Sara Whitestone suppressed a grin. 'We don't *have* a cat, Dana. Do you maybe want to reconsider that story? Another lie doesn't make the first one any better, you know. It only gets you into more trouble.'

James Whitestone stifled a grin of his own and put an arm around his wife's shoulder. The glow in his warm brown eyes made it clear that his love for Sara had only grown stronger after seven years of marriage. 'Do you know the difference between right and wrong, Dana?' he asked.

Dana frowned in concentration, her little face puckering up. 'Sure I do,' she said, holding up one hand and looking at it, and then doing the same with the other. 'This is my right, and this is my wrong.'

James Whitestone burst out laughing. He just couldn't help himself. 'I'm afraid it's not quite that simple, pumpkin.' He shifted on the couch and turned to his wife. 'Do you want to maybe field this one, sweetheart? I don't think I'm up to the challenge. It sucks, having a kid who's smarter than you are.'

Sara straightened on the couch and looked her

daughter directly in the eye. 'Right is when you do something God would want you to do,' she said, 'and wrong is when you do something God *wouldn't* want you to do. Does that make any sense to you, honey?'

Dana considered the question carefully, turning the query over in her mind as only a four-year-old could. After a moment or two of considered thought, she responded with a question of her own. 'Does *God* always do the right thing?'

'Of course He does,' James Whitestone said. 'He *is* God, after all.'

Dana nodded. 'Then why did He make me break Mommy's vase in the first place? He could have stopped me, you know. He *is* God, right? You just said so yourself. He *never* makes mistakes.'

Sara sighed. Sometimes her daughter could be too precocious by half, and she only hoped it didn't get Dana into trouble later on in her life. 'God didn't *make* you do anything, little lady,' she said sternly. 'And I'll take that last statement of yours as a confession of your guilt. It would have been much easier on you if you'd just told us the truth in the first place, but now I'm afraid you'll be going to bed early tonight as your punishment.'

Dana shrugged again, not quite having reached the age where going to bed early represented a life-and-death proposition. 'Oh well,' she said. 'I'm tired, anyway. Besides, now I know my right from my wrong.'

'What the fuck are you doing here?'

Brown's voice jolted Dana out of her reverie and back

into the present. Looking up, she saw none other than Mario Garabaldi standing over their table in the coffee shop.

Garabaldi slid out a chair without asking permission, taking a seat and smiling at Brown, who was squaring up to him, his hand automatically resting on the gun concealed at his side. 'Whoa, take it easy, big guy,' Garabaldi said. 'I'm not here to hurt you, I'm here to make your lives a little bit easier, that's all. There's no need to go all Clint Eastwood on me.'

Dana was too stunned to speak. Fewer than two feet away sat a man she knew was guilty of cold-blooded murder, and she couldn't do a damn thing about it. What was more, he knew who they were, that was obvious. And why in the hell did he seem so nonchalant about the whole thing? By confronting them in the coffee shop he'd walked directly into the lions' den, and he couldn't possibly know about Krugman's order that she and Brown should go easy on him over Baldarama's murder for now. Could he?

When Dana finally managed to talk, she didn't even try to disguise the contempt in her voice. It dripped like venom off her tongue. 'What in the hell do you mean, you're here to make our lives easier?' she snapped. 'We should arrest you right now just for being so goddamn stupid.'

Garabaldi toyed with a plastic swizzle straw on the table in front of him. Unlike his previous night's tracksuit get-up, he was now wearing a long black trench coat over a tailored grey suit. Dana had very little doubt that a designer label had been stitched into the inside pocket. Clearly, he'd dressed for work today. Shifting his gaze over to Dana, Garabaldi said, 'Arrest me for what, sweetheart? Looking this good?'

Dana held his stare. Bile burned the back of her throat. 'Your time is coming soon enough, Garabaldi. That much you can count on.'

Garabaldi brought his right palm to his forehead in a mock gesture of surprise. 'Oh, you're talking about my little conversation with Joey Baldarama outside Luigi's Deli, aren't you?' The mobster shook his head and chuckled. 'Well, I'm afraid that's not going to cut it, Agent Whitestone. It'll never hold up in court. You two should really work on your cover. You don't make very convincing plumbers.'

The bile rose higher in Dana's throat. If Garabaldi and Baldarama had been feeding them false information outside the deli it meant that all their hard work on the case had just been flushed down the toilet. Not to mention the fact that it made her and Brown look like fools. *Again.* 'You knew we were there?' Brown asked, his jaw clenched. 'Then why did you two jerks keep talking? Do you *want* to go to prison? Even if you weren't giving us anything accurate, you still broke about fifteen federal laws while you were at it. Ever heard of RICO statutes? Obstructing justice? We could bring you in right now, Garabaldi. We've got plenty to bury you with – that is, if we could find out where Joey Baldarama is, of course. *You* don't have any idea of where he might be, do you, Mario?'

The looks on the faces of everyone seated at the table made it clear that all three of them knew for a fact that Garabaldi had blown out his partner's brains in the woods fewer than twelve hours earlier. But the gangster seemed puzzled by the thinly veiled accusation. 'No idea,' he lied. 'Maybe Joey took a vacation or something. I wouldn't know.'

'Yeah, a permanent one,' Dana said, gritting her teeth. 'One that I doubt he *planned* to take.'

Garabaldi tied the plastic straw he was fiddling with into a tight knot and shrugged his broad shoulders. 'Maybe this, maybe that. Who the hell knows? Anyway, do you want to waste all our time here talking about someone else, or do you guys want to hear how I'm going to make your lives easier?'

Brown pressed together his lips into an even tighter line. 'Why don't you enlighten us?'

Garabaldi widened his grin into an approximation of an axe blade. 'I'm going to help you guys bring down the entire Gambino crime family,' he said. 'Including Joseph Tucci himself. I want to turn state's evidence.'

CHAPTER THIRTY-FIVE

Five minutes after Garabaldi had left the coffee shop, Dana relayed to Bill Krugman down in Washington, DC the mobster's offer to turn state's evidence.

'You've got to be kidding me,' the Director said when Dana had finished bringing him up to speed. 'He actually came up to you guys while you were sitting there in the coffee shop?'

'Yep,' Dana said.

Krugman's laugh was hollow. 'Un-fucking-believable. He had you guys pegged the entire time.'

'Looks like it.'

Krugman took a deep breath and let it out again in a resigned sigh. 'It doesn't matter,' he said. 'Don't worry about it. This is just what we need. Garabaldi can give us the inside look we're after. Where is he now?'

'Not sure,' Dana said. 'We got his cellphone number. He said he wants us to call him after we talk to you.'

'What kind of deal is he looking for?'

Dana gritted her teeth. But much as she hated cutting deals with criminals – almost as much as she hated knowing there were people out there in the world actually capable of taking another person's life in the name of business – she also knew it was sometimes a necessary evil in their line of work. Besides, as Krugman had told her earlier, she needed to keep her eyes on the overall prize here. By letting Garabaldi off the hook for now on Baldarama's murder, they could shoot for Tucci at the top of the power structure and bring down the entire house of cards, not just grab one of its lower-level operatives. Besides, Dana knew that it was far better to bring down the entire Gambino crime family than it was to apply her own oversimplified definition of right and wrong to this case. She wasn't four years old any more. And the aim of Krugman's strategy seemed simple enough to understand: cut off the head of the snake and the body died. 'Garabaldi wants limited immunity for his testimony and to serve a nominal prison sentence for Baldarama's murder,' Dana told Krugman. 'He said he'll do three years at a medium-security penitentiary and not a day longer. After that, he wants to enter the witness-protection programme. Says he'll consider going anywhere warm near water. Preferably Hawaii.'

Krugman paused. After a moment, he said, 'Let's just hope he isn't playing you. We'll keep it simple. Five years on the murder that you and Brown witnessed. Not a day less. And we'll need a paper trail leading directly to Tucci or else the deal is off. Garabaldi also needs to show you guys what he did with Baldarama's body. No guarantees on his placement in the witness-protection programme. We're not a travel agency.'

Dana switched off the phone and relayed the Director's deal parameters to Brown. 'Do you think

Garabaldi will go for it?' Brown asked when Dana had finished going through the details.

'Only one way to find out,' Dana said. 'You still got his number?'

Brown dug out his wallet. He read off the number the mobster had scribbled down on the back of a business card for Luigi's Deli while Dana punched it into her cellphone. Garabaldi answered his own phone ten seconds later, and Dana told him what Krugman had just told her.

Garabaldi grunted when she'd finished speaking. 'Uh-uh,' he said. 'I already told you guys: three years and not a day more. Call your boss back. I'm not—'

Dana cut him off. 'Listen, Garabaldi,' she said through gritted teeth. 'I'm not sure where you got the idea that you're calling the shots here, but you're not. Let me explain how this will work: you're going to take the deal, and you're going to like it. No bitching about it, no moaning about it, no complaining about it. Most of all, no *negotiating*. You're getting a sweetheart deal here and you know it. The only thing you need to do from your end is not fuck it up. Think you can handle that? Either you'll take the deal or word gets back to Tucci that you tried to rat him out. Understood?'

Garabaldi chuckled into the mouthpiece, and Dana got the distinct feeling that he'd once been a naughty schoolboy with a long history of charming his way out of trouble. Wasn't going to work here, though. 'Whoa, slow down, honey,' Garabaldi said. 'Take it easy. I was just fucking around with you. What else do I need to do? Just tell me and we'll get this circus on the road.'

Dana said, 'You also have to show us what you did with Baldarama's body.'

'No problem. You guys still at the coffee shop?'

'Yep.'

'I'll be over there in twenty minutes.' Garabaldi paused. Then he added, 'Order me up a frappuccino to go, would you?'

CHAPTER THIRTY-SIX

An hour and a half later, Mario Garabaldi finally pulled up to the kerb in front of Café Lalo. As passers-by cut between him and Dana and Brown on the still-wet sidewalk, the nattily dressed gangster activated the heavily tinted window on the passenger side of his Lincoln Towne Car and leaned over from the driver's seat. Grinning up at them, he said, 'Where's my frappuccino?'

Dana and Brown didn't bother answering. Still, had Dana been holding a drink in her hand at that precise moment she was pretty sure she would've thrown it directly into his pompous face, whether or not it had been made with boiling water.

'Fine,' Garabaldi said after a short pause, shaking his head and still smiling up at them. 'I guess I'll just have to go without my caffeine today.' He raised his eyebrows. 'Well? What are you guys waiting for? I don't have all day here. Follow me, and try to keep up this time, would you?'

On the short walk back to their Ford Focus, neither Dana nor Brown said a word. Finally getting inside their vehicle, which was parked at the side of the road a hundred yards away between a gleaming Rolls-Royce

Phantom II and a battered El Camino with no hubcaps, they pulled on their seat belts just as 'Toes' by the Zac Brown Band came on over the car radio. Brown leaned forward in his seat and switched it off. 'Doesn't exactly fit with the mood,' he muttered.

Dana was behind the wheel this time as they drove up behind Garabaldi thirty seconds later. She flashed her headlights twice to let Garabaldi know he could proceed. Lifting a hand to his rear-view mirror, he eased his vehicle back out into the heavy mid-morning traffic and drove away.

'Why do I have a feeling this guy enjoys pulling our strings?' Brown asked while they followed close behind, cutting off a bread truck in their attempt to keep up.

Dana took a left onto Lombard Street ten seconds after Garabaldi had done the same thing and pursed her lips. 'I'm just hoping this works out. The less time we have to spend with this guy, the better, as far as I'm concerned. He gives me the creeps.'

Twenty minutes later, Garabaldi finally pulled his shiny black Towne Car into the parking lot of an abandoned warehouse in Brooklyn. A rusted metal sign hanging over the front door identified the building as the former home of Kimble & Sons Manufacturing. Dana and Brown got out of their car and stood together as bright sunlight streamed down from high overhead in the clear blue sky. Dana sighed at the most recent schizophrenic shift in the weather. Maybe springtime was here to stay for good this time.

Didn't feel like it, though.

Garabaldi finally got out of his own vehicle and flicked his still-burning Pall Mall onto the parking-lot blacktop before extinguishing it beneath the heel of his black shoe. He immediately lit up another smoke and jerked his head toward the warehouse's entrance. 'C'mon,' he said. 'Joey's body is in there.'

Dana and Brown followed Garabaldi inside the warehouse, keeping a few feet behind him the entire time, just in case. Dana reached into her blazer and flicked off the safety on her Glock against the unlikely possibility this might be some sort of set-up. Then again, you could never underestimate the treachery of the criminal mind. Especially not one as obviously messed-up as Mario Garabaldi's. Just hours earlier, he'd blown out the brains of one of his colleagues. At the very least, he wasn't the kind of guy you'd want to turn your back on.

The interior of the warehouse was dark and forbidding, like something out of a horror movie. Old machinery parts had joined the scattered remnants of broken-out windows and several dozen empty beer cans littering the cement floor. A mouldy sleeping bag had been laid out on the ground right next to a rusted-out hibachi, indicating to Dana that the building had most probably served as a non-sanctioned homeless shelter sometime in the not too distant past. Dusty rays of sunlight struggled through the intermittent holes dotting the ceiling and illuminated the eerie scene.

And then there was the familiar smell.

Dana covered her mouth and nose against the overpowering stench of rotting flesh while Brown did the same two feet to her right. Taking out a linen handkerchief from the inside pocket of his blazer, he spritzed it with a thin mist of cologne from a small container before handing the cloth over to her. Dana gratefully accepted it.

For his part, Garabaldi didn't seem even to notice the stomach-turning odour. He'd probably grown accustomed to the smell of death by this point in his life. After all, this hadn't been his first rodeo. Not by any stretch of the imagination. Unlike those who rose to the top position in the Mafia, you didn't get to the rank of enforcer by keeping your hands clean. Quite the opposite.

Dana slid her gaze down to Garibaldi's hands. They looked clean, no doubt scrubbed pink in the shower earlier that morning. All trace of his cold-blooded deed washed away. A diamond-studded pinkie ring that looked to be at least two carats decorated his left hand. 'C'mon,' Garabaldi said. 'It's over here.'

Dana and Brown followed him to the north side of the warehouse, trekking through old cardboard boxes, stray nuts and bolts and bits of scrap iron. Dana felt something sticky under her feet and looked down. An army of ants converged upon a stain of long-ago-spilled soda, seeking sustenance in the sticky goo. Finally, Garabaldi came to a stop two hundred feet from the main entrance. A huge pile of dead rats rose four feet from the filthy floor. On top of the pile sat Joey Baldarama's severed head.

Baldarama's eyeballs had disappeared, having been consumed rapidly by an efficient clean-up crew of rodents and insects. Disgusting white maggots already wriggled in his empty eye sockets.

Dana swallowed back the acrid flood of stomach acid she could taste in her mouth. This was part of the job she never got used to. 'Where's the rest of him?' she breathed through the handkerchief.

Garabaldi laughed, obviously completely at ease with the atrocity he'd committed. 'Oh, that's all of him,' he said, waving a hand toward the foul pile. 'His whole body's in there. It'll probably take you guys some time to put him back together again, though. Sort of like Humpty-Dumpty now, ain't he?'

Dana and Brown ignored Garabaldi's tasteless joke. Shifting uncomfortably, Brown nodded to the pile of dead rats and wrinkled his nose in disgust. 'What did Baldarama rat about?' he asked.

A confused look flashed across Garabaldi's lined face. 'What do you mean by that?'

Brown coughed against the intense smell, his clear brown eyes watering. 'The message here isn't exactly subtle,' he said. 'A pile of dead rats; a rat in the family. So what exactly did Baldamara rat about?'

Garabaldi dropped his latest cigarette to the floor and again crushed it out beneath his heel. 'Oh, Joey didn't *rat* about anything. He was a stand-up guy, always had been, ever since the beginning, back when we were kids knocking over drugstores together. See, that's the thing: Tucci wanted Jocy dead simply because that's what Tucci does. If there ain't a rat in the crew, he makes one up. He does it to keep the rest of the fellas in line, to show them what could happen if they start singing like little birdies. It's sort of like maintenance.'

'So why are *you* singing now?' Dana asked. 'Aren't you worried about what Tucci will do to you if he finds out you're cooperating with us?'

Garabaldi wrinkled up his face. 'Isn't it *obvious* why I'm singing here? I'm singing because it doesn't matter what the fuck I do at this point. My turn's coming eventually. It's only a matter of time now. But at least this way I have a *chance* of staying alive, even if I end up getting whacked in prison. If I make it through that, though, it's all gravy from there.'

Dana shook her head. In an odd way, the gangster's words seemed to make sense. And if she and Brown could use his testimony to bring down Tucci and the entire Gambino crime family, all the better for them. *Cut off the head of the snake and the body dies.*

Dana stared over at Garabaldi while still holding Brown's handkerchief to her mouth and nose. 'But if you and Joey Baldarama were friends since you were kids, how could you bring yourself to kill him?'

Garabaldi snickered. 'Easy. Yeah, Joey was my friend, but this wasn't personal, see. Not even close. It was strictly business; just like everything else in the mob. Besides, it's not your enemies you need to look out for, it's your friends. Haven't you ever seen any Mafia movies in your life? That's just the way it goes.

Kill or get killed. I don't make the rules; I just play by them. Just like you guys do.'

Dana and Brown didn't say anything in response. Although neither of them could fathom Garabaldi's lifestyle nor the choices he made, Dana knew it was their job to figure out exactly that.

After a moment or two of further silence, Garabaldi lit up a fresh cigarette and snapped shut his gold Zippo. 'Anyway,' he said. 'I don't know about you guys, but I'm fucking starving. Who's in the mood for some lunch? I'm buying.'

CHAPTER THIRTY-SEVEN

After arranging for the excavation of Joey Baldarama's chopped-up body from the pile of dead rats in the abandoned warehouse by a team of FBI forensics experts now stationed in New York City, Dana returned home to her room at the Fontainebleau Hotel to freshen up.

She looked around her beautiful suite and sighed, knowing that she'd miss staying here. On the drive back to the hotel, word had come down from Bill Krugman that she and Brown – who'd been staying in the room next door – would be moving their base of operations out to the Motel 6 in Queens the following week. Made sense, and not just financially. Although she and Brown were the ones doing the surveillance on the mob here, they never knew who could be watching *them* in return. Garabaldi had proved that. So it was logical that they should shake things up a little, vary their routine. It could mean the difference between being the hunters and becoming the hunted, which could often prove to be a very narrow dividing line when dealing with the mob. In any event, better safe than sorry.

Dana went over to the mini-fridge in the corner of her living room and opened it up before peering inside. A selection of candy bars, several different kinds of soda and a veritable bonanza of alcohol products stared back at her. There was Stoli vodka, Bud Light, Miller Genuine Draft, Jim Beam. Nestled in the centre of them all, her very favourite stress-buster of them all – Jack Daniel's.

Dana's mouth went dry at the prospect of a drink with the good stuff added. Still, no matter how much time had passed since her last alcoholic drink, she knew that she'd be right back at Step One if she gave in to the temptation now. So instead of grabbing the Jack and guzzling down the wonderful liquid in four quick swallows, she wrapped her fingers around an ice-cold Coke and pulled it out before closing the door of the fridge again. The muffled sound of glass clinking against glass filled her ears, almost mocking her, daring her to drink her fill.

Dana cracked open the can of Coke and took a long swallow, imagining that it contained a shot of Jack Daniel's. The carbonated beverage froze the back of her throat and sure as hell *tasted* like liquor to her. The alcoholic's brain at work, Dana supposed, doing its best to justify the reintroduction of booze to her system. But Dana had fought like hell to cut alcohol out of her life and she'd be damned if she'd lose out on all her hard work now simply because she'd had a rough day at work.

Then again, most people's workdays didn't feature severed human heads sitting on top of piles of dead rats.

Dana took another long drink of her Coke and placed the can down on the table next to the television set, which was tuned in to CNN's *Headline News*. As fate would have it, the impeccably coiffed anchor was engaged in a panel discussion about the Chessboard Killer and all the bloody crimes that had ripped across New York City like a tornado ripping through an Oklahoma trailer park. Just Dana's luck. Shaking her head, she muted the volume and phoned Bill Krugman down in Washington, DC. The Director sounded out of breath when he picked up.

'Is this a bad time to talk, sir?' Dana asked. 'I could call back later.'

Krugman was panting. 'No, no,' he said. 'I just got off the treadmill, that's all. Seven miles every day, whether I feel like it or not. I need to do *something* to keep up with you youngsters. Anyway, what's up?'

Dana filled Krugman in on the day's events as quickly as she could, right up to the point in the day when Garabaldi had taken her and Brown to see Joey Baldarama's severed head. 'Garabaldi says Tucci ordered Baldarama's murder just because he could,' Dana told Krugman. 'Technically, that constitutes homicide in the legal sense. Just like how they convicted Charles Manson for masterminding the Tate-La Bianca murders, even though Manson didn't have a direct hand in any of the murders. With Garabaldi's testimony, we could probably have Tucci indicted the same way. What do you think?'

Krugman finished catching his breath. 'I think it's certainly a nice fallback plan, but for now let's keep looking at the bigger picture. It's not often that we get a rat as high up in the food chain as Garabaldi, so we should use him while we have the chance. Make the most of our opportunity here.'

'So what's the plan, then?'

Krugman grunted. 'The plan is the same as it's always been. Use Garabaldi to topple the whole goddamn thing. Garabaldi is the loose thread on the sweater. Just keep pulling on him, Agent Whitestone. The entire Gambino crime-family operation will unravel eventually. Mario Garabaldi definitely represents the weak link here.'

'So what exactly do we need from Garabaldi?' Dana asked.

'We need a paper trail. A nice long paper trail that leads directly to Joseph Tucci's front door. I want to know what businesses they're using as fronts to push the drugs. Where and how they manufacture the domestic drugs. Where and how they smuggle the foreign drugs into the country. We'll need names, places, dates, receipts – anything we can use to tie the crimes to Tucci. Let's nail this bastard and his entire operation while we have him in our cross hairs, Agent Whitestone. We may never get a shot this clean again.'

Dana closed her eyes. That drink of Jack Daniel's was sounding better and better to her by the second. What had once looked like a simple means to an end – using Joey Baldarama's murder to arrest Tucci on the grounds that he'd orchestrated it – had just turned into a whole hell of a lot more work for her and Brown. Then again, what else was new? Still, Dana needed to remember that they weren't going after a one-man band here, some guy running an illegal bookmaking business out of his apartment on the weekends, taking bets on college football games in between phoning out for pizzas with everything on them. They were going after the mob, *la cosa nostra*, the big boys. The ones who shot back at the good guys when they weren't too busy shooting at each other. And if they could pull this one off they just might salvage something of their reputations.

Dana hung up the phone with Krugman and opened the door of her hotel suite. Stepping out into the long corridor, she walked along to the room next to hers and knocked lightly on Brown's door. Brown opened it a moment later, wearing nothing but a white towel wrapped around his waist while he used a second towel to dry off his short brown hair.

Dana averted her eyes and studied the carpet. If anyone ever asked her about the particulars, she could safely say that its pattern was brown with yellow swirls. 'Sorry,' she said. 'I didn't know you were taking a shower. I'll come back later.'

Brown laughed. 'Don't worry about it, Dana. What's going on?'

Dana looked up and ignored the glimmer of hope in his eyes. She just couldn't go there, even if she wanted to, not now. She brought Brown up to speed on Krugman's instructions. When she'd finished relating all the details, Brown shook his head. 'Sounds to me like a lot more work just opened up for us. Give me five.'

'Sure.'

Fifteen minutes later, they met again downstairs in the lobby. The atrium-like setting was awash in sunshine. Huge glass windows surrounded them on all sides. A glass ceiling towered a hundred feet above their heads. Potted plants covered the marble-tiled floor. Frazzled-looking travelling salesmen hustled to and fro.

Thankfully, now that Brown was fully clothed it was *much* easier for Dana to concentrate. From what she'd seen up in his hotel room, her partner hadn't skipped too many workouts lately. Dana only wished she could say the same about herself. Even Bill Krugman was leaving her in the dust these days with his daily seven-mile treks on the treadmill. If Dana were *really* lucky, she might be able to squeeze in seven miles a *week*.

Brown dug out his cellphone from his pocket and phoned up Garabaldi, letting him know what the FBI needed from him. After a brief exchange of words, Brown switched off his phone and turned back to Dana. 'Garabaldi says he's already got a ton of paperwork for us to go through. Apparently, it was one of his jobs to keep the books. Says it's all coded, though. Says he'll need to walk us through it so that we'll know what it means.'

Dana frowned. The last thing she had any interest in was spending any more time with Mario Garabaldi than she absolutely needed to. Still, what choice did she have in the matter? None.

Dana tried to fight the intense feeling of frustration flooding through her. Although she'd tried her best to ignore the chatter – *scuttlebutt* they called it in the FBI –

rumour had it that she was now considered Bill Krugman's top lieutenant, the current strained nature of their relationship notwithstanding. Talk around the FBI had it that Krugman was grooming Dana to take his place at the top one day, though another person would probably serve first after Krugman had stepped down. At thirty-nine years old, Dana wasn't considered anywhere near old enough yet. Still, between the Cleveland Slasher case, the failed Chessboard Killer investigation and the mob case she and Brown were dealing with now, Dana sure as hell *felt* a lot older than her years. And if this case went the way the Chessboard Killer one had she wouldn't even get to the first interview.

'Where do you want to conduct this thing?' Dana asked. With all the FBI field offices scattered throughout the city packed with overworked agents, she and Brown had been conducting their business in one of the Fontainebleau's conference rooms. Not exactly the most secure set-up in the world. And if they were going to be handling sensitive information, Dana knew they should consider finding someplace a little more private. No telling when a meeting of Manhattan's leading stamp club had been scheduled for the same room and they'd be forced out of the space.

Brown shrugged. 'I don't see that we have many options. I know we're scheduled to move on next week, but what do you think about staying here on our own dime? The door to the conference room locks, and I doubt very much we'll do any better anywhere else.

This place has got twenty-four-hour security, too, so I'll bet that if we tipped the guy up front he'd keep an eye out for us.'

Dana tucked a loose strand of blonde hair behind her right ear. It wasn't textbook procedure, but she and Brown already had their work cut out for them as it was without playing musical hotel rooms. 'Doesn't matter to me,' she said. 'I'll run it by Krugman later, but I doubt he'll raise a stink about it. What time are we supposed to meet Garabaldi, anyway? I want to get this over with as quickly as possible.'

Brown checked his Tag Heuer watch – a gift from Dana on his thirty-fifth birthday. She winced when she saw that he was still wearing it. Then Brown looked up again, but not at her.

Dana followed his gaze to the revolving glass doors of the hotel's entrance. Dressed in a Pierre Cardin ensemble complete with a pink handkerchief tucked into his breast pocket, Mario Garabaldi was pushing his way into the prestigious hotel.

Brown turned back to Dana and raised his eyebrows. 'How does right now sound to you?'

CHAPTER THIRTY-EIGHT

Sergei Michalovic logged on to his MacBook Pro in the ridiculously well-appointed living room of the Presidential Suite at the Fontainebleau Hotel and laughed out loud when he read the brief article detailing Betty Arsenault's grisly death at the hands of Amber Coletta, the Stage Five skin-cancer patient serving as Edward O'Hara's queen piece:

> WOMAN MURDERED OVERNIGHT; SEX TOY SHOVED DOWN THROAT
> Nick Brandt
> *New York Post*
> Only in New York City.
>
> Just days after former professional basketball player Micah Brantley died from a massive drug overdose at the StayClean Drug Rehabilitation Centre on Fifth Avenue in downtown Manhattan, a woman's dead body was discovered on the sidewalk outside the facility with a large pink dildo shoved down her throat.
>
> The victim, Betty Arsenault, a 45-year-old mother of three, was shot once through her heart, police sources say. There are no suspects at this time.

Anyone with information about the murder is asked to contact NYPD headquarters located at 1 Police Plaza in Lower Manhattan.

Story still developing. Check back often on the *New York Post* website for updates.

New York City's only *reliable source of information.*

After that deliciously kinky opening salvo, the murders unfolded fast and furious over the course of the following week, sending panicked New Yorkers scurrying out of the city in droves. To begin with, Michalovic and O'Hara swapped eleven more positioning moves in rapid succession, relaying their non-capture manoeuvres via the online edition of the *New York Times*, which allowed real-time advertising.

After the non-capture moves came the next series of capture manoeuvres – the really fun part of the game – with each of the deaths duly noted in newspapers across the city and the world, though law enforcement hadn't yet connected the deaths to Michalovic and O'Hara's exceedingly interesting little game.

The first murder involved O'Hara's painting contractor, Jack Aaron, who'd been put to work at the same apartment complex where Anna Baker had opened up a child-abuse investigation on D'Andre Williams at Michalovic's urging. Without knowing it, Aaron had executed the *CXD4* move – and in the process Michalovic's kind-hearted social worker, when he'd offered the elderly woman a sandwich containing a combination of peanut oil and finely ground peanuts:

HEIRESS DIES FROM ALLERGIC REACTION
By Raymond C. Garcia
New York Times staff writer
Reclusive peanut-butter heiress Anna Baker, 81, died last night after consuming a sandwich containing – of all things – peanut butter.

Unbeknownst to the general public, Baker had suffered from a peanut allergy her entire life, an oddly ironic fate for a woman worth an estimated three hundred million dollars from the SmoothGold peanut-butter empire started by her ancestor, Jeffrey Baker, in 1855 . . .

To answer his opponent's decidedly clever move, Michalovic had sent Arum Colby – known to everyone involved with the Russian mafia as a man willing to do anything if the price was right – to dispatch the hapless Jack Aaron a short while later:

PAINTING CONTRACTOR SHOT EXECUTION-STYLE
Nick Brandt
New York Post
A painting contractor linked to the recent death of peanut-butter heiress Anna Baker was shot once in the back of the head on a deserted stretch of highway in Long Island late last night.

Jack Aaron, 51, who unknowingly handed Baker a sandwich containing peanut butter earlier in the week – to which the heiress was reportedly allergic – was not charged in connection with Baker's death, though police aren't ruling out retaliation as a possible motive in Aaron's own death . . .

From there, the deaths became even more interesting, as the next few kills featured something of a religious flavour. To kick off the chain of highly publicised events, O'Hara employed the *BXE2* manoeuvre to take out a high-ranking bishop in the Catholic Church in a shockingly cold-blooded murder that easily found its way onto the front pages of both the *New York Times* and the *New York Post*. At the same time, Michalovic employed the countermove *BXE2* to take out O'Hara's piece in lightning-quick retaliation, planting a sharpshooter in the crowd since he'd known exactly when and where to strike – due to the fact that he'd underwritten the entire cost of the event where both clerics had died right in front of the disbelieving eyes of thousands of onlookers.

HOLY WAR TURNS DEADLY; TWO SLAIN
By Raymond C. Garcia
New York Times staff writer
Long-simmering tensions finally came to a sen - sational boil Tuesday afternoon when an enraged Bishop Terrance Manwaring – pastor of Living Waters Protestant Church in New York City –

rushed the stage where Bishop Martin Eastman, leader of the Catholic Church in New York, was delivering a speech. Bishop Manwaring shot Bishop Eastman once in the temple at point-blank range during a rally that featured free food and drink for those in attendance, which, according to police sources, more than doubled the original number of people expected to attend.

In the ensuing chaos created by the shocking murder, an armed member of the horrified crowd took aim and shot Bishop Manwaring once between the eyes, presumably in retaliation. Due to the sheer size of the overflow crowd, no suspects were apprehended at the event. New York City Police said they will continue to study video footage of the event in an effort to identify a suspect.

Bishops Manwaring and Eastman, who'd traded vicious verbal jabs with one another in the press over the course of the past several months – with each man insisting that his own interpretation of the scriptures was the correct one – had a long-standing rivalry ever since both men were ordained as priests back in 1963, sources close to both clerics say.

According to preliminary police reports obtained by the *New York Times*, Bishop Manwaring became enraged upon learning that Bishop Eastman had arranged for a massive rally just two blocks away from Bishop Manwaring's own church.

'(Manwaring) said he was going over there to kill the (expletive),' said Father Joe Simpson, Bishop

Manwaring's second-in-command. 'He just grabbed a gun out of the sanctuary safe and rushed out the door. He had a really strange look in his eyes. Everything happened so fast that I didn't have time to stop him. I was on the phone with the police when I saw the news break on television. I feel horrible about all of this.'

Bishop Anthony Hess, second-in-command of the Roman Catholic Church in New York City, was ushered in as Bishop Martin Eastman's replacement following the assassination of his superior.

'It's a tragedy,' Bishop Hess said late last night when reached by telephone. 'We can only assume this is God's will, though I'm absolutely heartbroken by the death of my good friend and mentor. Still, I will do my best to continue serving our congregation in the truest spirit of Bishop Martin Eastman. May God bless him, and may his eternal soul rest in peace for ever.'

Michalovic closed the lid on his MacBook Pro and lay back on his comfortable leather recliner, preparing mentally for the upcoming series of kill moves that would now be taking place. Reaching into his pocket and flipping open his cellphone, he dialled a familiar number. After seven rings, the voicemail clicked on: *You've reached Edward O'Hara. Please leave your name and number and I'll return your call shortly.*

Michalovic worked the lever on the recliner and put his feet back down on the floor. 'Edward,' he said, rising to his feet and pacing his suite. 'I'm just calling to confirm our meeting tonight here in the Presidential Suite. Unless I hear otherwise from you, I'll be expecting your presence at precisely seven o'clock.'

Michalovic paused, then with a smile added two of his favourite American expressions in his concluding remarks. 'By the way, is there any way you could bring along a few more of your Behikes? Seems I've developed something of a taste for those particular cigars. As a matter of fact, as soon as this final game of ours is complete, I'm giving serious consideration to buying out the remainder of the Behikes on the European market. I'm quite sure you don't mind. After all, all's fair in love and war, right? In any event, I'll see you here at seven o'clock tonight. Be there or be square.'

CHAPTER THIRTY-NINE

On a cold Tuesday night not long after the most recent series of brutal murders had really begun in earnest, Edward O'Hara drew a deep breath and flexed his aching shoulders. From his hidden position in an abandoned warehouse on the west side of Manhattan – a warehouse that had been equipped with a long bank of television monitors and a state-of-the-art loudspeaker system that could be operated from the small back room in which O'Hara had stationed himself – he pondered his forthcoming moves.

The high-tech set-up provided the most efficient environment in which to conduct these next kills, of course, but it didn't mean that the Irish-American's spirits were high at the moment. Far from it. Much as O'Hara didn't like it, he and that vile monster Sergei Michalovic would need to work together on this next series of murders due to the complicated nature of the rapid-fire capture moves. Still, O'Hara's presence was the only one required here tonight, so that was certainly a good thing. For it had gotten to the point now where the strong odour of Michalovic's expensive cologne – a scent in which the man seemed to *bathe* daily – had become enough to turn O'Hara's stomach. No small feat. Because O'Hara had always been a man with an especially stout constitution.

Shaking his head to chase away the thought, O'Hara's mind drifted back to his most recent meeting with the Russian. During that meeting, Michalovic had smoked no fewer than *three* of O'Hara's precious Behikes while the two had engaged in their ritualistic positioning of pieces on the Russian's living-room chessboard.

'OK,' Michalovic had said calmly, illustrating his points by moving each one of the chess pieces in question. 'Here's how it will go from here. We'll start with our new friend, Bishop Anthony Hess, who was elevated to his position following Bishop Martin Eastman's very public murder. By the way, Edward, very nice move on that one. I was duly impressed, to put it mildly. Very nicely done, indeed.'

O'Hara had smiled thinly in response to the Russian's maddeningly condescending tone. Still, it was no matter. If it were the last thing he ever did in this life, O'Hara would *bury* the Russian, slipping a Behike or two into the man's inside jacket pocket for the asshole to puff on in the afterlife. 'Thank you, Sergei,' O'Hara had answered, fighting to keep his own tone civil. 'Your countermove was rather impressive as well. To tell you the truth, I wasn't expecting such a rapid response. Care to let me in on the identity of the shooter in the crowd?'

Michalovic had shaken his head and laughed while he'd fiddled with one of the rooks on the chessboard. 'No, I don't think so, Edward,' he'd said. 'You're much too fine a player for me to be able to afford such a handicap. You'll know the shooter's identity when the time is right. Besides, a magician never reveals his tricks. I'm sure you understand.'

With that, Michalovic had taken another long drag on his mooched Behike, blown out a huge cloud of blue smoke and continued. 'In any event, where were we? Oh, yes. The next piece I'll be moving in the game – Bishop Anthony Hess – is, as we both know, scheduled to engage in a modified game of Russian roulette with your next piece, Daniel Dierkson. Tell me, Edward: have you made the arrangements for this yet from your end?'

O'Hara had nodded in response, at the same time resisting the urge to ball up his right fist and punch the Russian square in the mouth as hard as he possibly could. But, true to his word, O'Hara had already phoned Dierkson – a convicted child molester – and had laid out his ultimatum in order to ensure the man's attendance at the warehouse the following night: play a game of Russian roulette with the Catholic bishop or else have his past exposed to the day-care centre at which he now worked. 'Yes, Sergei,' O'Hara had said, managing to keep his fists at his sides, at least for the time being. 'My piece is firmly in place. And yours? Is the game ready to proceed from your end?'

Michalovic had smiled and stubbed out his Behike in the large glass ashtray sitting on a highly polished end table next to the chessboard before reaching back into the rapidly emptying box of cigars. Snipping off the tip of a fresh one, he'd flipped open his gold Zippo, casually fired up the long cigar and snapped shut the lighter again. 'Of course, Edward,' he'd said. 'My pieces are *always* in place. You should know that by now. If not, then you'd better learn it fast. The game is almost over now. Just a few more moves for each of us until it's complete – for better or worse.'

From his back room in the abandoned warehouse, O'Hara gritted his teeth and leaned forward to operate one of the cameras scattered throughout the cavernous space. Using a small plastic joystick, he brought into sharp focus the images of both men seated at a small table in the middle of the main room. A single naked light bulb dangled from a frayed electrical cord above their heads and provided the only light. A shiny silver pistol lay on a small white towel between them.

Leaning back again, O'Hara propped up his feet on the table of television monitors in front of him and watched the game unfold.

'I believe you're supposed to go first,' Bishop Anthony Hess said, his voice trembling. Sweating heavily, he was wearing his full black priest outfit, complete with a stiff Roman collar around his throat – a collar that might just as well have been a hangman's noose right now. 'The man on the phone told me that you're supposed to go first. He was very clear about it.'

Daniel Dierkson reached across the table and retrieved the silver pistol, fighting back an intense wave of anger at the impossible position in which he'd been put. Dierkson had struggled like hell with his sickness over the past decade, but the drunken mistake he'd made with eight-year-old Penny Morgan ten years earlier in the back seat of her father's Buick Regal had risen up to bite him in the ass again. Dierkson's own outfit of dirty blue jeans and an *I Love New York* T-shirt – purchased from a street vendor for just three dollars – made for quite the contrast in clothing styles between himself and the cleric. Still, the priest was absolutely right – the man on the phone had told him the exact same thing: *Dierkson* was supposed to go first in this game. Dierkson sighed. Oh, well. At least this way he still had a fighting chance to continue his life with the past remaining where it belonged: *buried*.

Flipping open the pistol's cylinder, Dierkson saw a single bullet nestled inside one of the chambers. Drawing a deep breath, he snapped shut the cylinder and spun it several times. There could be only one winner in this game, and there was only one way to find out who it would be.

Lifting the muzzle of the pistol against his temple, he closed his eyes and squeezed the trigger.

CHAPTER FORTY

Over the course of the next week or so, Dana and Brown ploughed through the voluminous paper trail that Mario Garabaldi had been supplying them with – at the same time trying to ignore the recent and highly publicised spate of bizarre murders across the city that Dana couldn't help thinking might be connected to the Chessboard Killer slayings in some way. Still, Brown's source on the inside had told him that the inter-agency task force assigned to the investigation didn't believe there was a link, so that was where things would stand until further notice.

Dana sighed. She didn't agree with the task force's decision – not one little bit – but she didn't have a voice in the case any more. Such was the consequence of her and Brown's failure to put a stop to the murders themselves. And Mario Garabaldi had given them *plenty* to stay busy with in their investigations of the mob.

He'd given them receipts, betting logs and contracts – some of them literally *stained* with the blood of particularly tenacious negotiators. The task seemed nearly impossible at times. Some of the items were even indecipherable. Still, at least they were making *some* progress. Sadly, though, it wasn't nearly enough. Not enough to topple the entire house of cards, at least. Dana knew they'd need to capture Joseph Tucci on tape speaking about his complicity in Joey Baldarama's murder if they wanted to start the process that would bring down the entire Gambino family from top to bottom. In order to do that, though, Garabaldi would need to wear a wire while he went in to speak with his boss.

The gangster seemed philosophical about the proposal. Dana and Brown weren't surprised at his ready compliance. Nothing about Garabaldi surprised them now. If he had a death wish that was his problem. As long as he got them the goods, what did it really matter? And they were watching his back, after all; perhaps he felt that was comfort enough.

'Why the fuck not?' Garabaldi said, chewing on a wooden toothpick with his feet propped up on the table in front of him as he, Dana and Brown met in a corner conference room at the Fontainebleau Hotel. 'What do I have to lose at this point? I never liked that bastard Tucci, anyway. And I'm a *great* actor. Just wait, you'll see.'

With that, Garabaldi flipped open his cellphone and called up his contacts list before punching a button and placing the phone to his ear. 'As a matter of fact,' he went on, putting his feet back down on the floor and brushing an imaginary piece of lint from the shoulder of his pinstriped silk suit, 'I'll arrange for a sit-down with that greasy motherfucker right now.'

CHAPTER FORTY-ONE

The deafening gunshot – rigged to be amplified via the loudspeaker system by a small computer chip embedded in the butt of the pistol – echoed throughout the abandoned warehouse and made both of Bishop Anthony Hess's eardrums ache. Stunned, he looked in abject horror at the nightmarish scene that had just unfolded right in front of his disbelieving eyes.

Just three feet away across the small table, Daniel Dierkson's brains had emptied from his head through the enormous hole in the left side of his skull. A waterfall rush of blood streamed down from the man's nostrils and collected in a rapidly expanding pool of red liquid at Hess's feet. 'Jesus Christ!' the bishop screamed.

Edward J. O'Hara smiled and leaned forward in his chair, positioning the microphone directly in front of his mouth. 'Settle down, Father,' he said. 'You're still alive, aren't you? You *won* this game. The first round of it, at least.'

Hess jumped at the unexpected sound of O'Hara's disembodied voice, bolting out of his seat and sending his wooden chair clattering down onto the filthy cement floor. He looked around frantically for the source of the voice – the same voice from the previous day's phone call, the same voice that had laid out the ultimatum that Hess should show up at the warehouse the following night or else have his elderly mother's severed head delivered to him in a burlap sack. 'I did what you told me,' Hess whimpered, still scanning the darkness. 'Can't I just leave now? You told me I could leave after I did what you told me. I've done that. Now you have to leave my mother alone. You *promised*.'

O'Hara grunted into the microphone. 'Sit back down, Father,' he said sternly. 'Yes, you did as you were told, but the game's not quite over yet. Not for you, and not for me, either. We still have a few more moves to go. Now, have a seat, please.'

Tears filled Hess's eyes. His voice cracked. 'Why should I? Why can't I just leave? I only did this because you told me the other man was a criminal who hurt little children. And because you were threatening the life of my mother.'

O'Hara laughed into the microphone, sending his voice rippling through the speakers again. The time had come to spring his surprise checkmate move on the perverted priest. 'Is that a fact, Father?' O'Hara said, still chuckling. 'Well, I heard some more facts from the altar boys you molested while you were serving as the pastor of a Catholic church in Southbridge, Massachusetts in the early 1980s. Now, like I said before, please sit *down*.'

Hess's jaw dropped. Nausea swirled around in his stomach. Leaning down, he righted his chair and settled back down into it, resisting the urge to throw up. His face had gone as white as a sheet, creating the perfect contrast to his black clothing. 'I didn't *hurt* anyone,' Hess sobbed, leaning forward to rest his elbows on the table and burying his face in his hands. 'I didn't hurt them.'

O'Hara shook his head. 'Of course you didn't, Father,' he soothed. 'At least, that's the way you'll be remembered if you do exactly as instructed from here on. If you choose *not* to do what I tell you, however, I'm afraid I'll need to release to the press the thirteen sworn affidavits I have in my possession that testify to your guilt. The thirteen sworn affidavits from your now-adult victims. Now, listen to me very carefully, Father. There's a drawer on your side of the table. In it, you'll find another gun. This particular gun has bullets in each one of the chambers, so there's no way you can miss. You know what you need to do; now do it. It's as simple as that.'

Hess hesitated for a moment before leaning back in his seat. Heart in his throat, he slid open the drawer in front of him. As his tormentor had promised, a small black pistol nestled inside.

Hess wiped bitter tears from his eyes. But he knew he'd been caught red-handed. He *was* guilty of the crimes of which he'd just been accused. And there were more than those thirteen, too. A lot more. Now the time had come for him to pay his penance. Somewhere, deep inside his heart of hearts, he'd always known that this day would come. He was no different from the man slumped opposite him.

Lifting the gun to his temple, Bishop Anthony Hess pulled the trigger. A tremendous bang echoed throughout the warehouse. A split second later, his splattered brains mingled on the floor with those of convicted child molester Daniel Dierkson to create a sickening grey-and-red-infused stew.

Edward O'Hara flipped off the bank of television monitors in front of him and rose to his feet. Distasteful as the task might be, it was time to clean up.

And after that, things *really* ought to get interesting.

CHAPTER FORTY-TWO

An hour and a half after their most recent meeting with Mario Garabaldi in the Fontainebleau Hotel, Dana and Brown were hunkered down again in their 'Jimmy's Plumbing' van outside Vito's Place, a bar in Little Italy. They listened in as their informant played a deadly game of cat and mouse with his boss where the stakes were nothing less than the turncoat's own life. Outside the bar, armed toughs stood guard on the busy street, smoking unfiltered cigarettes and speaking to each other occasionally with their hands covering their mouths.

Rife with static from a bad connection caused by the storm front looming over the area, Mario Garabaldi's voice crackled in Dana and Brown's headphones. 'I'm here to see the boss,' Garabaldi told one of the toughs.

A deep voice sounded in response. 'We'll need to pat you down first, Mario. You know the drill. Spread your arms and legs wide. Don't make any sudden moves or I'll blow your fucking brains out. Just like you did to Joey, right?'

Dana's breath caught in her throat. If the mafioso patted Mario down, there was always a possibility – however slight – that he'd find the microphone that she and Brown had hidden inside the metal buckle on

Garabaldi's belt. Thankfully, though, the next voice to come across the line belonged to none other than Joseph Tucci himself.

Tucci's strong voice cut like a sharp knife through the din of the noisy bar. 'No need for that, Salvatore,' Tucci said. 'If I can't trust Mario here, fuck, I can't trust anyone.'

Dana let out her breath and cupped her headphones even tighter against her ears. A series of footsteps was followed by the scrape of wood against a tile floor as Garabaldi pulled back a chair and sat down at Tucci's table.

'So?' Tucci asked. 'What's so goddamn important that you needed a sit-down with me, Mario?'

Dana breathed another sigh of relief when she heard Garabaldi's confident answer. True to his word, this foot soldier for the New York City mob delivered his rehearsed lines without so much as a single hitch in his voice. Murdering lowlife or not, he had actually told the truth back in the Fontainebleau Hotel. Dana raised her eyebrows at Brown, impressed. Much as Garabaldi disgusted her, even she had to admit he was a damn fine actor. 'The FBI contacted me and said they want me to play informant,' Garabaldi told his boss, somehow managing to sound casual about the whole thing. 'I ain't no fuckin' snitch, though. I told them to go fuck themselves just as soon as they came up to me. After that, I came right to you. That's what you've always told us to do in these situations, right?'

'*Are* you wearing a wire, Mario?'

'Fuck, *no*, I ain't wearing *no* wire.'

'You cooperating with the feds?'

'No way.'

'You sure about that?'

'Positive.'

Tucci paused. Dana heard the snap of a lighter before he spoke again. 'I'll need you to prove that to me, of course. That OK with you, Mario?'

Garabaldi grunted. 'Anything you need from me, boss. You know that. Just tell me what to do and I'll do it.'

Even from the back of the van, Dana could practically *see* Tucci waving a manicured hand in the air while he relayed his instructions to Garabaldi just as casually as if he'd been ordering a glass of red wine. 'I'll need you to kill somebody for me, Mario,' Tucci said. 'If you *are* working with the feds, then it's illegal for them to let that happen. It's the only way I can know for sure whether or not you're lying to me. I'm sure you understand. And Mario?'

'Yeah, boss?'

Tucci breathed out slowly. 'If you don't do this for me by the stroke of midnight tonight – and not a second later – I'll kill your rat ass myself.'

CHAPTER FORTY-THREE

Six hours after his decidedly tense meeting with Joseph Tucci, Mario Garabaldi stood in the middle of a field that was a twenty-minute drive from Manhattan. The blood coating the machete in his right hand slid down the razor-sharp blade and dripped onto the face of a rival gangster, Antonio Bellazo, an enforcer with the Columbo crime family and one of its most feared soldiers. No doubt an all-out mob war would break out as soon as news of this brutal gangland slaying got back to the Columbo organisation.

That was when both gangsters started laughing.

'Goddamn it,' Dana yelled. 'Cut!'

Garabaldi and Bellazo grinned back at Dana while she hit the STOP button on her video recorder. 'Sorry about that, Agent Whitestone,' Garabaldi said, still chuckling. 'It's just that this shit is funny to me. Fuck, it looks so *real*.'

Dana shook her head in irritation and resisted the urge to shout again. Fifty feet to her right, Brown was conferring with a group of hastily assembled special-effects personnel. 'That's the whole point, Garabaldi,' she said, speaking carefully and through gritted teeth. 'If it *doesn't* look real, then it's going to *become* real for both of you. Is that what you guys want?'

Antonio Bellazo wiped fake blood from his eyes with the back of his right hand and shook his head. Just hours earlier, Dana and Brown had plucked him off the streets of Brooklyn and relayed to him the parameters of the deal that would keep him out of jail for the rest of his life: either play along with this mock execution at Garabaldi's hands or else prepare himself for a nice long stay in a maximum-security cell at Sing Sing prison in Ossining, New York. 'Hell, no,' the Columbo enforcer said. 'What do you want us to do now? Take it from the top again?'

Dana closed her eyes. She honestly didn't know how professional directors did it. Then again, she very much doubted whether the talent they worked with was anything like Mario Garabaldi and Antonio Bellazo. 'Yes,' Dana said tensely. 'That's exactly what I want you to do. Now, let's try again. In three, two, one . . .'

Two hours and thirteen maddening takes later, Dana finally had what she and Brown needed. Following a quick editing job from the professionals, the video she'd just shot would be delivered into Joseph Tucci's hands, thus satisfying the mob boss's directive that Garabaldi should murder Antonio Bellazo in order to prove his loyalty. Dana just prayed that the ploy would work. She knew that both her and Brown's careers were on the line here.

Dana pressed the rewind button on her digital

recorder and watched the manufactured events unfold again. A dummy recorder had been propped up on a nearby tree stump to provide the needed misdirection, and the footage had been shot at such an angle that it would appear as though Garabaldi himself had taped the grisly events.

Garabaldi's voice boomed over the surprisingly powerful speakers attached to the sides of Dana's high-tech recorder when she pressed the PLAY button.

'Sorry, Bellazo, but I'm here to deliver a message from Joseph Tucci,' Garabaldi said, taking a menacing step toward his adversary. 'This is what happens to rat-fucks like you.'

Amazingly, the fear in Bellazo's eyes actually looked real. Tied to the thick base of a large oak tree, he was perspiring heavily, a thick line of sweat glistening on his Neanderthal brow. 'C'mon, man,' Bellazo whimpered, staring up at the approaching Garabaldi. 'I've got money. I can pay you. Just name your price. You don't have to do this.'

'Fuck your money,' Garabaldi snarled in response. '*Here*'s what I think of your fucking money.' With that, Garabaldi sprang forward and brought the rubber machete down on Bellazo's exposed neck as hard as he could. Right on cue, blood from a plastic tube hidden inside Bellazo's shirt squirted out, operated by Brown via a hand-held remote control.

Dana pressed the STOP button again and removed the memory card from her video recorder before handing it over to Garabaldi and holding his stare. 'Take this directly to Joseph Tucci,' she said. 'If you're not dead by midnight, I'll know it worked.'

Garabaldi smiled and took the memory card from Dana's hand. 'Oh, it's going to work,' he said. 'Don't you worry about that. Like I told you guys before, I'm a great actor. Anyway, what are you guys going to do with Bellazo now? You ain't going to keep him on the streets, are you?'

Dana ignored Garabaldi's question, irritated that he'd even had the temerity to ask it. He was getting way too comfortable with her and Brown, and the less he knew about what was going on here the better and the safer for all of them. So there was no way she'd let him in on the fact that Bellazo would soon be entering the witness-protection programme. As a matter of fact, at this very moment a chartered plane was waiting for the Columbo-family enforcer on a darkened runway over at JFK International Airport. Just to be spiteful, Dana had arranged for Bellazo to be relocated to Hawaii. And if she had her way, Mario Garabaldi would eventually wind up somewhere deep in the heart of Alaska – far, far away from any semblance of civilised society. 'Don't you worry about what's happening to Bellazo,' Dana said. 'You just worry about your own problems, Garabaldi. You've got plenty of them, that's for damn sure. But if you try anything funny – if you even *think* about double-crossing us – I'll hand your dumb ass over to Joseph Tucci myself.'

Garabaldi grinned and tucked the memory card into his shirt pocket. 'Ah, c'mon, Agent Whitestone,' he said, winking. 'You'd never do something like that to me. I can tell that deep down inside you like me way too much to ever give me up. Another time, another situation . . . who knows? Maybe you and me could've had something really special together.'

CHAPTER FORTY-FOUR

The bright rays of early-morning sunshine streaming in through his bedroom windows and falling onto the left side of his unshaven face roused Mario Garabaldi from his deep slumber at seven a.m. the next day.

He let out a loud yawn and sat up straighter in his king-sized Tempurpedic bed to stretch his aching back, twisting his body and groaning like a piece of rusted-out machinery as he pivoted at his stiff hips. The sound of popping vertebrae filled his ears, blissfully releasing the tension coiled up in his muscles.

Still groggy and in that bizarre no-man's-land where everything seemed a bit surreal, Garabaldi rubbed at his tired eyes before glancing down at the empty section of bed next to him. No severed bloody stallion's head had kept him company throughout the night, so that was certainly a good sign. From all appearances, it looked as though his mock execution of Antonio Bellazo had worked like a charm. Or at least well enough to pull the wool over Joseph Tucci's eyes and allow Mario to continue breathing fresh air for the next day or so.

The gangster smiled and dragged himself out of bed with another groan before making his way into the bathroom. Half an hour later, steam rose in swirling clouds from his broad shoulders as he emerged from his shower and stepped into his walk-in closet. Designer suits – all featuring major labels – surrounded him on three sides. A shoe rack four levels high supported three dozen pairs of dress shoes crafted from the finest Italian leathers available. An impressive collection of silk ties hung from an electric carousel positioned against the far wall.

Garabaldi breathed in deeply through his nostrils in satisfaction at the sight of his haute couture. Most of his fancy clothing had fallen off the backs of trucks over the years – *the Mafia discount*, they called it. Still, the chances of him retaining access to the mob's exclusive shopping club once he entered the witness-protection programme were slim to none. As a matter of fact, the only item of clothing he'd be likely to receive from *la cosa nostra* in the near future was a custom-fitted pair of heavy cement shoes before the animals dumped his dead body into the swirling brown waters of the Hudson River. So – that being the case – Mario knew that he'd need to find an alternative source of income if he wanted to continue indulging his major clothes fetish. No problem there, though. In a shoebox tucked into the closet's crawl space sat half a key of heavily cut cocaine separated into tiny plastic baggies – easy money once he distributed the white gold out on the streets. All he needed to do now was keep Dana Whitestone and Jeremy Brown off his ass long enough to actually sell the stuff.

Removing a baby-blue Roberto Cavitti ensemble

from a hanger, Garabaldi dressed before slipping his feet into a pair of nine-hundred-dollar Marco Pellini shoes and knotting a medium-width red tie around his tanned throat. The money that the cocaine would bring in would provide a nice little windfall, of course, but he wanted to avoid getting a real job once he got to Hawaii so he'd need a *tornado* of cash before heading off into the witness-protection programme. Fortunately for him, though, he knew exactly how to make that happen.

Picking up his cellphone from his bedside table, Garabaldi punched in a number. Just one last major score – *just one more* – and he'd be sitting pretty in tailored suits for the rest of his life.

CHAPTER FORTY-FIVE

The early bird gets the worm, right?

Or, in this case, the murdering, lowlife Mafia gangster.

After following Mario Garabaldi back to the bar called Vito's Place in Little Italy the previous night and ensuring that he'd come out again in one piece, Dana and Brown had conducted an all-night surveillance session outside his house to guard against the very real possibility of a mob hit on the turncoat mafioso. Thankfully, though, the hit had never materialised. But now both Dana and Brown were absolutely exhausted. It was only adrenalin keeping them going – and the determination to pull this off. To *redeem* themselves.

Dana's cellphone sounded in her pocket as she and Brown drove back to the Fontainebleau Hotel at shortly past eight o'clock in the morning. While Dana had been busy filming the mock-execution scene with Garabaldi and Bellazo, Brown had used the time wisely when he wasn't helping the movie personnel by planting a small bug in Garabaldi's cellphone, which transferred his calls to Dana's own phone. Better safe than sorry – and this way they could keep an eye on

Garabaldi and his movements even when he wasn't directly in their line of sight.

Dana turned in her seat and rolled her eyes at Brown when the theme song from the *Godfather* movies poured forth from her cellphone. 'Very funny,' she said. 'I never knew you had such a great sense of humour.' From his seat behind the wheel, Brown smirked.

Flipping open the phone, Dana placed it to her ear. A deep voice tinged with a slight foreign accent came across the line.

'Mario,' a man said. 'I'm so glad you called. I was beginning to worry about you. I thought maybe you'd chickened out of our upcoming deal.'

Garabaldi snorted into the mouthpiece. 'Highly fucking unlikely, Mr LeBlanc,' he answered. 'I need the money like you wouldn't believe. I'm going away for a little while after this, so I'll need to sock away every last bit of cash I can. Anyway, when is all this shit going down? I've got a couple mosquitoes buzzing in my ear, so the sooner this happens the better.'

The man on the other end of the line chuckled and cleared his throat. 'Very well, Mario,' he said. 'If that's the way it needs to be, then that's the way it needs to be. Still, I was hoping we might wait a few more days to ensure the security of our deal. That said, if you think we should act now, then by all means, that's exactly what we'll do. Now, listen to me very carefully. At precisely three o'clock this afternoon I'll call you on your backup cellphone with further instructions on how to proceed. Be in Yonkers at three o'clock and I'll let you know where and when you can find your payment for your end of the deal. Does that sound reasonable to you?'

Garabaldi sounded puzzled. 'My backup cellphone? What in the fuck is my backup cellphone? This one here is the only one I've got.'

The man on the other end of the line chuckled again. 'Not any more, it isn't, Mario. Open up the drawer on your bedside table. Inside it you'll find a prepaid cellphone. Untraceable, of course. That's the phone on which I'll be calling you at precisely three o'clock this afternoon.'

Garabaldi's voice exploded in Dana's ear. 'How in the fuck did you get inside my house without me knowing it?'

The man on the other end of the line tutted. Judging from the tone of the voice, he was clearly the kind of man used to being in charge. Another Mafia operative? Someone close to Joseph Tucci? If so, why had he allowed Garabaldi to live? 'That's not important at the moment, Mario,' the man said. 'The important thing here is that you do exactly what I tell you to do. If you follow my instructions precisely, you'll stay alive and you'll be outfitted in your precious designer suits for the rest of your miserable life. Do we understand each other?'

Garabaldi coughed softly. Apparently, it wasn't a fight in which he wanted to engage now that he'd had some time to think things through. 'Yeah, whatever. But why do I need a backup cellphone?'

The man on the other end of the line blew out a slow breath. 'Elementary, Mario. You need a backup cell-phone because the federal agents you're working with are listening in to our little conversation *right now*.'

CHAPTER FORTY-SIX

The line went dead and Dana flipped off her cellphone.

She cleared a lump from her throat and filled in Brown on the details of the call, trying desperately to ignore the pounding of her heartbeat. Didn't work. Somehow, Garabaldi's mystery caller knew that she and Brown had planted a bug in the mobster's cellphone. But *how*? Had they been watched even then, back in that field?

'Jesus Christ,' Brown said when Dana had finished bringing him up to speed. 'So, do you want to bring in Garabaldi or what? The man said the backup cellphone is untraceable but we're dealing with killers and liars here. I don't think it's a very good idea to just take their word for it.'

Dana chewed on her lower lip and tried to think things through. It wasn't easy. Her brain felt like mush right now. But Krugman had been very clear about his directive to topple the entire Gambino family, and while the man on the other end of the line *might* have been closely connected with Joseph Tucci, she wasn't willing to push in all her chips on that particular bet. 'Let's just wait and see who Garabaldi is going to meet,' she said. 'If it *is* someone high up the chain of command we'll scoop up both of them then and there. If it's *not*, Krugman's going to have our asses for going against his orders. But I don't see how we have any choice.'

Brown nodded. 'Makes sense.' Flipping on his signal, he executed a quick U-turn.

Dana raised her eyebrows. 'Where are we going?'

Brown tightened his grip on the steering wheel and pressed his foot down hard against the accelerator. 'Back to Garabaldi's house,' he said, letting out a loud yawn as the Ford Focus's engine produced a low whine beneath the hood and the battered vehicle gradually picked up speed. 'Like it or not, looks like we're not getting any sleep today.'

Dana flexed her aching shoulders. 'You OK with that?'

Brown nodded. 'Yep. Besides, we'll have plenty of time to sleep when we're dead, right?'

Dana didn't answer him. She was right out of even gallows humour now.

CHAPTER FORTY-SEVEN

Dana and Brown established their tail on Mario Garabaldi twenty minutes later, just as he was backing his Lincoln Towne Car down his long driveway.

Brown breathed out slowly and waited for two buffer vehicles to get between them before following Garabaldi down the busy street. 'We cut it close, but we made it,' he said, looking sideways at Dana. 'So, are you ready to do this?'

Dana let out a humourless laugh. 'Yep. Can't wait.'

For the rest of the day, they trailed Mario Garabaldi around town, struggling to keep their eyelids open the entire time. While the task proved mildly interesting at times – a visit to a dog-racing track in Newark, lunch at an Italian restaurant in Manhattan and a trip to an Asian massage parlour in the seediest section of Yonkers for dessert – Dana couldn't help but think back on all the missed chances during the Chessboard Killer investigation. Struggle as she might, though, she still couldn't quite piece together the motive for the slayings. She only hoped the agents who'd taken their places on the case were having better luck than they'd had. As Dana had noted earlier, she didn't care *who* caught the killer or killers, she just wanted the murders to stop. *Now.*

From their position across the street from the Asian massage parlour – shielded by a huge bread truck that featured on its sides the freshly scrubbed faces of smiling children eating sandwiches for lunch around a wooden picnic table – Dana and Brown watched Mario Garabaldi emerge from the building half an hour later, looking thoroughly refreshed and smoking one of his unfiltered cigarettes. Popping the locks on his Towne Car with his key-chain control, Garabaldi opened up the driver's-side door and slid his stout body behind the steering wheel.

'Looks he just got a—' Brown started to say, but stopped suddenly when Garabaldi stomped down hard on the gas pedal and tore out into traffic, nearly causing a deadly pile-up at the intersection of Westminster Drive and E. 119th Street. 'What the fuck!' Brown yelled, slamming the Ford Focus into gear and kicking down violently on the accelerator in an attempt to catch up with the mobster.

Through the back windshield of the Towne Car, Dana watched Garabaldi press a cellphone against his ear. 'He's getting his orders now,' she said, feeling her heartbeat notch up several levels in her chest. 'This is it.'

Brown pressed his lips together in a tight line, then clenched his jaw when he was forced to slow down in order to navigate the jumble of honking cars littering the street in Mario Garabaldi's wake. 'I just hope we're there in time,' he said.

'Me, too, Jeremy,' Dana answered. Adrenalin coursed through her. 'Because if we blow this one, I have a funny feeling that our careers are finally over.'

CHAPTER FORTY-EIGHT

Pressing his ample belly as flat as he could against the warm tar covering the roof of a five-and-dime drugstore in Yonkers, Edward O'Hara peered down through his binoculars at the two men standing in the narrow alleyway a hundred feet below. Once again, he and Michalovic needed to work in tandem to pull off this next series of moves. After this, though, all bets would be off.

Tasked with placing the untraceable cellphone in Mario Garabaldi's home the previous day, O'Hara had made one minor but *extremely* important alteration that would ensure his victory in this game. An alteration that would ensure his *revenge*.

One of the men standing in the alleyway below wore a red bandana tied tightly around his shiny bald head; the other's headgear was blue. O'Hara smiled to himself as the hot sun overhead softened the tar of the sizzling rooftop, staining the front of his white T-shirt and oversized designer jeans. As planned, both his and Michalovic's pieces were firmly in place.

As fate would have it – or at least as *Michalovic and O'Hara* would have it – O'Hara's chess piece, Donte James, was a member of the infamous Bloods street gang.

Had been his entire life. For his part, Michalovic's piece, Lawrence Bowman, had long ago pledged his undying loyalty to the Crips. Predictably – with the two men representing rival factions in a bloody gang war that had stretched on for *decades* now – the scene degenerated quickly into violence.

'What the fuck are you doing here?' Donte James growled, taking a menacing step toward his sworn enemy and twisting his face into an ugly sneer. 'You *trying* to get your stupid ass murdered or something? Where Timson at? *He* was the one I was supposed to meet here. Not your gorilla ass.'

O'Hara swept his binoculars over to the alleway's entrance fifty feet away from where the heated argument was taking place, at the same time pressing the redial button on his cellphone. Ten seconds later – summoned by the vibrate function on his prepaid cellphone – Mario Garabaldi flipped open the untraceable device and placed it to his ear. 'Yeah?'

O'Hara cleared his throat softly. 'Listen to me very carefully, Mario,' he said, lifting his wrist and checking his watch. 'In the next thirty seconds or so, Lawrence Bowman will take out a gun and shoot Donte James dead. When that happens, you must immediately take out Bowman. No questions asked. There's no time for that now. Understood?'

'Which one's Bowman?'

O'Hara gritted his teeth. 'The nigger wearing blue,' he snapped. 'Shoot him immediately after he kills the one wearing red.'

Garabaldi grunted. 'Gotcha. And my payment for this? Where's it at?'

O'Hara's pulse quickened. This was it. The part of the games he lived for. The capture moves. 'Your payment's already in your hand,' O'Hara said. 'It's hidden in the back of your phone. Remove the back cover and you'll see what I mean.'

O'Hara watched Garabaldi slip off the plastic cover from the back of his phone. A moment later, the gangster held up the Saint-Gaudens Double Eagle that O'Hara had stolen from Michalovic at the beginning of this contest. 'What the fuck is this?' Garabaldi snapped. 'This thing's only worth twenty dollars. You think I work that cheap?'

O'Hara closed his eyes. 'The coin's worth nearly eight million dollars on the black market, you fucking idiot. Now just do as you've been told. This is it. What I've been waiting for all this time.'

Just then, the deafening crack of a gunshot echoed through the alleyway below. O'Hara jerked his binoculars to the right. Lawrence Bowman stood over Donte James's dead body, a nine-millimetre pistol still smoking in his hand.

On cue, a second shot rang out from the entrance to the alleyway.

O'Hara took in a deep breath and steadied himself. Now the game could *really* begin. In fewer than two hours, Sergei Michalovic would lie dead on the floor of his fancy suite over at the Fontainebleau Hotel.

Taking out a .45-calibre pistol from the front pocket

of his designer jeans – the same gun that had been used in the Bobby Fischer killings – O'Hara aimed it directly at the back of Mario Garabaldi's head.

CHAPTER FORTY-NINE

Dana and Brown were halfway past an alleyway dividing a Chinese laundry from a drugstore in downtown Yonkers when the unmistakable sound of gunshots filled the air.

'Jesus!' Dana screamed. 'Stop the car!'

Brown slammed down hard on the brakes, bringing the Ford Focus to a screeching halt in the middle of the street. Dana was out of the vehicle before it stopped moving, her Glock gripped tightly in her right fist, the safety switched off. She met Mario Garabaldi just as he was exiting the alleyway, a still-smoking gun held in his own meaty fist. He looked shocked to see Dana standing there.

'What the fuck?' Garabaldi stuttered. All the blood drained out of his face and turned it a ghostly white. 'You motherfuckers followed me again?'

Dana ignored his question and levelled her Glock squarely at the centre of his broad chest. 'Drop the gun, Garabaldi!' she yelled.

The gangster shook his head, clearly still in a state of shock. Nonetheless, he did as he was told, letting the gun slip from his fingers and down onto the ground at his feet before he closed his eyes in disgust. 'So, now what?' he asked. 'Where do we go from here? Does this mean our deal's off?'

Dana was about to answer him when the muffled sound of another gunshot rang out. A split second later, Mario Garabaldi's skull exploded on his shoulders.

Dana's breath caught in her throat. She tried to move but her feet felt as though they'd been nailed to the sidewalk. For several agonising seconds she couldn't even breathe. Her eyes worked all right, though.

She swept her gaze frantically down the long alleyway to see if she could identify who'd fired the shot. No luck. There was no one there. No one *alive*, at least. The thought that the shot could have come from above finally made her move. Crouching behind a dumpster, she peered out, still clutching her gun. A hundred feet away she saw two black men laid out on the ground and bleeding heavily. The unseen assailant who'd just shot Mario Garabaldi was nowhere to be seen, however. Dana almost threw up. She and Brown had fucked up again.

Brown hunkered down beside her and put a comforting hand on her shoulder. 'I didn't see who did it, either,' he said, breathing hard and peering round the dumpster. He stared up at the rooftops above. The silence was almost as shocking as the gunshot had been. 'Probably came from up there, but whoever did it must be long gone by now.'

They remained behind the dumpster for a few moments just to be sure, then they both stepped out into the open. As Dana covered him, Brown approached

Mario Garabaldi's prone body. Grey brain matter leaked out of the gangster's right ear and collected in a disgusting pool next to his head. Brown pressed two fingers against Garabaldi's throat.

He looked up at Dana and shook his head.

Dana's mind raced. 'Pat him down,' she said. 'See what he's got on him.'

Brown did as he was instructed. Reaching a hand into the mobster's pockets, his fingers came out holding a shiny gold coin. 'Well, now,' Brown said, turning over the coin in his hand and studying it closely. 'What's this?'

He paused and looked up at Dana again. 'I don't know about you, partner, but it looks to me like we've finally found ourselves a clue.'

CHAPTER FIFTY

Back in the hotel suite at the Fontainebleau Hotel an hour later, Dana flipped open her cellphone and punched in a number. Maggie Flynn's voice came across the line after three quick double rings. 'Maggie Flynn, FBI Headquarters. How may I help you?'

Dana drew a deep breath and brought Flynn up to speed on the details of the coin that Brown had discovered in Mario Garabaldi's pocket. Much as she hated knowing that she and Brown had screwed up again, she needed to find out what she could about the coin and she knew that Maggie Flynn would be up to the task. There was a reason why her nickname around the FBI had always been Google. 'I'm on it,' Flynn said. 'I'll call you back just as soon as I find out anything interesting.'

The promised return call came less than two minutes later. 'That's no ordinary coin you guys have got there,' Flynn said, clearly impressed. 'As a matter of fact, the damn thing's worth a bundle.'

'How much are we talking?' Dana asked.

'Nearly eight million dollars.'

Dana's jaw dropped. '*What?* Who the hell does it belong to?'

'Russian shipping tycoon by the name of Sergei

Michalovic,' Flynn said. 'Bought it at auction back in 2002. Quite an interesting history behind it, too.'

Dana's heart almost stopped beating as something in her brain clicked into place. Had it really been this simple? Had the killer finally made his first mistake? Trying to keep her voice steady, she asked, 'Sergei Michalovic? Are you sure that's the guy's name?'

'Yeah. Why do you ask.'

Dana let out a slow breath. 'Because that means his initials would be SM – the same initials as the pattern we found in the skulls of the Bobby Fischer victims.'

'Oh my God,' Flynn said.

Dana's body trembled. 'Yeah, I know.' Finally, finally, after all this time, they might just have unearthed *the* vital clue that could solve the Chessboard Killer case – and Dana wasn't on it any more. She needed to think clearly, needed to get in touch with the others, needed to call Krugman.

'So, now what?' Flynn asked, cutting through Dana's fractured thoughts. 'What else do you need from me?'

Dana was about to answer her when the beep of an incoming call sounded on her cellphone. 'Hold on a sec, Maggie,' she said. 'I've got another call coming in. I'll switch back over to you in a minute.' Hitting the button to transfer lines on her cellphone, Dana said, 'Hello?'

A tiny, scared little voice came across the line. 'It's me,' a little girl said. 'You said I should call you if I ever needed someone to talk to.'

Dana raised her eyebrows, puzzled. 'What's your name, sweetheart?' she asked.

'Molly. Molly Yuntz don't you remember me?'

Dana's heart broke inside her chest. 'Of course I remember you, honey,' she said. 'What would you like to talk to me about?'

Molly Yuntz paused. Finally, she drew a deep breath and said, 'I know who the Chessboard Killer is.'

Dana's ears rang. Her mouth went dry. Her palms flooded with sweat. 'Who, Molly?' she asked. 'Who is it?'

The little girl started crying, sniffling into the phone. 'It's my brother,' she sobbed. 'Jack said that he'd never kill anybody, but he lied to me. A bad man called. He made Jack do it. I was listening to their phone call. Jack never would have hurt anybody on purpose. It's not his fault. It's the bad man's fault.'

Dana tried her best to calm down the little girl. She needed details here. Molly Yuntz wasn't making any sense. Her brother was only fourteen years old. He *couldn't* have committed the murders. He was much too young, lacked the necessary resources. And who was the 'bad man', anyway? Sergei Michalovic? 'Where is your brother now, honey?' she asked.

The little girl's reply struck Dana like a bucket of ice water in the face. 'He's at the Fontainebleau Hotel,' she said. 'Room 800. I wasn't supposed to look, but I found the room number in his chess notebook. Is Jack going to be in trouble for this?'

CHAPTER FIFTY-ONE

Huddled around the ornate chessboard in the middle of the Russian's glittering suite, Sergei Michalovic and Edward O'Hara positioned chess pieces handcrafted from solid ivory.

'So, Edward,' Michalovic said, grinning in excitement while he slid the pieces into their proper slots for the final sequence in their game. 'This is it, huh? The end of our beautiful little game. The moment for which we've both been waiting all this time. Tell me, are you prepared for it?'

Still wearing his tar-stained clothing, Edward O'Hara didn't smile back. Moving his hand around to the back of his jeans, he felt the .45-calibre pistol tucked snugly against the small of his back and curled his fingers around the corrugated grip. Slipping out the gun, he levelled it directly at the middle of Michalovic's forehead. 'Oh, I'd say I've been ready for this moment for a *very* long time now, Sergei,' O'Hara said. 'I know it was you, you know – the man who killed my father over a worthless piece of land you never even bothered to develop. I've known it ever since the day I met your worthless ass at that joke of a black-tie gala honouring the chairman of the Securities and Exchange Commission. Unfortunately for you, however, payback time has arrived.'

Michalovic laughed straight in the Irish-American's face. 'Settle down, Edward! Before you fire that gun, there's something you need to know.'

O'Hara's finger twitched on the trigger. Pure hatred flooded his entire being. 'What's that?' he spat.

Michalovic stretched and clasped his hands behind his neck. 'I've already found your replacement, Edward. As a matter of fact, once you're dead and gone and safely removed from this world, he and I shall continue to play our exceedingly interesting games. He's a wonderful student, really he is – something of a child prodigy, as it were. Pity you won't be around to see his development, though. *Your* time's up, Edward. Consider this your checkmate. *Now*, boy! *Do it now!*'

CHAPTER FIFTY-TWO

Dana threw her cellphone down on the plush carpet and bolted out of her suite, tearing up the concrete steps in the fire-escape stairwell as fast as her legs would carry her. There wasn't time to make any calls. She needed to act *now*. Brown had been coming out of his own suite and after yelling 'Dana, what is it?' raced after her.

On the penthouse floor, Dana threw open the heavy metal door and stepped out into the long hallway. Just then, the sharp crack of a gunshot echoed from the far end of the corridor. 'Fuck!' Dana yelled. She turned around to face Brown. It was up to them now. 'I'll bring you up to speed later,' she said, breathing hard. 'Turn off the safety on your Glock. We need to move. Now!'

Brown looked puzzled for a moment, but he knew better than to question her. 'C'mon,' he said. 'I'll take the lead.'

Twenty seconds later, they stood in front of the set of massive double doors leading into the Presidential Suite. Brown drew a deep breath and stepped back. Gathering all his strength, he lunged forward and put his weight behind a powerful kick that landed just above the lock. The wood cracked in a deafening explosion of splinters and the door sprung open, giving them a clear view into the suite.

Jack Yuntz stood in a doorway leading off the living room. A small silver handgun smoked in his right fist. Thirty feet away, a large man with a single bullet wound to the right side of his skull was slumped over the couch. Next to him, a silver-haired man wearing a tuxedo reached into his jacket pocket. The hand that came out was holding a huge black gun.

Everything was a blur after that as Dana swung her Glock in the silver-haired man's direction. Before she could squeeze the trigger, though, another shot rang out from the interior of the suite. The silver-haired man crashed down hard onto the chessboard over which he'd been standing, scattering the pieces across the bloodstained carpet.

Brown stepped inside the suite and levelled his Glock directly at Jack Yuntz's head. 'Drop the gun, son,' he said, calmly but firmly.

The look on Jack Yuntz's face seemed inhuman as he did as he was instructed. He dropped the gun and stepped out into the main room. Dana shook her head, unable to believe what she'd seen. The boy was only fourteen. He must have been desperate, forced into playing a deadly game. Is that what Molly had meant? Had he found out the identity of the Chessboard Killer? Were there two? Were these two men here their killers? There were so many unanswered questions.

That was when a small smile played across Jack Yuntz's thin lips. Dana almost missed it, but it had been there, fleetingly. Her stomach lurched. She'd seen that exact same smile dozens of times before. He might have been only fourteen years old, but Dana knew she'd just witnessed the birth of a killer – the youngest she'd ever seen. She just hoped there was time to turn him back into the boy he'd once been – before it was too late.

Brown holstered his Glock and began walking toward Jack. 'Stay right there. Don't move.'

Dana still held her Glock in her hand. Something about the boy's look had made her extra cautious. He might have been a minor but she'd seen him kill a man, his hand steady.

Brown advanced still closer to the boy and reached out a hand to grab him by his arm. Before Dana knew what was happening, the boy reached around with his other arm to the waistband at the rear of his jeans. In one fluid motion, he jammed a sharp pair of scissors deep into Brown's exposed throat.

Brown fell to the floor, choking on his own blood. Fear, disbelief and confusion flashed across his terrified face. 'Jeremy!' Dana screamed.

She covered the fifteen feet between them in a flash, aiming the barrel of her Glock directly at the centre of Jack Yuntz's narrow chest while Brown gargled away on his own blood. A minor or not, the bastard had just stabbed her partner. Brown's trembling fingers reached for the sharp metal in his neck before they fell away again to his sides. Dana retched, knowing it was already too late.

Raising his hands high over his head, Jack Yuntz

smiled that horrible smile again.

Dana breathed hard and squeezed the trigger of her Glock, exerting two pounds of pressure, then three. Four. At five pounds of pressure the gun would go off. All she needed to do was just pull the fucking trigger.

Bitter tears blinded Dana's eyes while she listened to Brown take his last gurgling breaths. Blinking hard, she loosened the grip of her index finger on the Glock's trigger. Even though her partner – the man she'd *loved* ever since she'd first met him – was dead and what she wanted more than anything in this world right now was to make the person who'd just killed him pay for it with his own life, Dana wasn't a killer. Certainly not a *child*-killer. There were good guys in this world and there were bad guys. Like it or not, she was one of the *good* guys. Always had been. Always would be. 'Why'd you do it?' she sobbed, casting her blurry gaze down at Jeremy's lifeless body while still keeping the gun trained on Jack's heart. 'Why did you have to kill him? I *loved* him.'

The boy laughed at her. His tone sounded joyful. 'I killed him because I knew he'd just get in our way later on, Agent Whitestone.'

Dana stared at the boy again. 'What do you mean by that?' she asked quietly.

Jack Yuntz laughed again. 'What I mean by that, Dana Whitestone, is that *our* game isn't quite over yet. Won't be until I'm twenty-five or so and out of whatever half-assed reformatory they send me to after this. I've researched similar cases, done my homework. That's what they *always* do when a troubled child such as myself snaps and takes someone's life. Two murdered parents; a never-ending succession of foster homes – I could go on and on. But it's cut and dried and you know it. If I were you, I'd get busy on my *own* homework before that day arrives. After all, I want you to be as well-prepared as you possibly can be for when we finally meet again.'

Vomit flooded into Dana's mouth. She swallowed back the acrid taste. Heartbroken as she was, she needed to know how Jack Yuntz had figured out the pattern of murders in the Chessboard Killer slayings, because it was clear that was just what he'd done. And exactly how deeply had he been involved in all this? Had he been there at the start? Could she be sure that the two strangers lying in their own blood were their Chessboard Killers? Or were there in fact three killers? Or just one: Jack? Nothing made any sense any more.

The boy waved a hand in the air. 'It wasn't all *that* difficult,' he said, grinning wider now and obviously happy for the chance to share his genius with her. 'It just so happens that these two clowns were recreating a game played by my all-time favourite chess master. The most famous game in the history of chess. The problem with this pair of idiots, though, was that they didn't study all the possible variables involved. Until I came along, they never even *considered* the possibility that a third player might like to participate in their game. After I pieced out the opening moves, it was a fairly easy proposition to figure out which game they were playing. Amateur shit, really, to tell you the truth.'

Dana bit down hard into her lower lip. Tears slid down her cheeks. 'What game's that?' she asked. 'What game were they recreating?' She needed to keep the boy talking. He was the only person who could tell her at least half of what had been going on and once he was in the system he could quite easily clam up. If he was telling the truth, that was, which Dana believed he was. He was *proud* of what he'd done and in a horrible, twisted way, it all made horrible, perfect sense.

Jack Yuntz widened the grin on his face until it was as sharp as an axe blade. 'Why, Garry Kasparov versus IBM's computer "Big Blue", of course,' he said. 'Back in Philadelphia fifteen years ago. Garry Kasparov won that game – just like *I*'ll win the game we play when we meet again in ten years or so, Agent Whitestone.'

Holding out his thin wrists, Jack Yuntz smiled mischievously at her. 'So, Dana,' he said, 'are you going to handcuff me or not? The sooner I can begin my sentence for these crimes, the sooner you and I can complete our own little game. Sound like a plan to you or what?'

EPILOGUE

A week later, Dana knelt on the ground and traced her trembling fingers over the incised lettering on Jeremy Brown's marble gravestone at Calvary Memorial Cemetery in downtown Los Angeles, pressing down on the soft grass underneath her while she held on tight to the engagement ring that Jeremy had been carrying around with him in the front pocket of his jeans on the day he'd been so brutally murdered.

Dana closed her eyes and again felt her heart break into a million tiny pieces. Turned out that her partner hadn't still been married, after all. Instead, Jeremy had been a widower who'd lost his young bride to breast cancer when they'd both been just twenty-one years old – just three months after they'd graduated together from San Diego State University with matching criminal-justice degrees. Dana might've known that if she'd ever bothered to ask Jeremy about it directly – but she hadn't. Instead, she'd assumed the worst and had been dead wrong about the whole thing. And now she could never ask Jeremy *anything* ever again.

Dana fought back chest-racking sobs, still unable to absorb the fact that they'd been staying in the same hotel as one of the Chessboard Killers. She and Jeremy had scoured the entire city, but they hadn't thought to check out their own lodgings. The irony was enough to make her brain explode.

To make matters worse, Jack Yuntz had been absolutely correct when he'd boasted of the likelihood of receiving just a slap on the wrist for his horrific crimes. It had taken a federal judge fewer than two hours to rule the boy clinically insane before remanding the young killer to the custody of The Squires Boys' Home in Albany, New York. The expected duration of Jack Yuntz's sentence? Ten years. Exactly what he'd predicted. Dana no longer believed that he could ever be turned back into the innocent young boy he'd once been. He was far too gone for that now.

Jeremy's gravestone featured the FBI shield and motto. The words positioned under them seemed far too few and far too insignificant to describe a man who'd defied description his entire life:

JEREMY ALLEN BROWN
BORN 3 MARCH 1976; DIED 19 APRIL 2011
BRAVERY, FIDELITY, INTEGRITY

More tears filled Dana's eyes. Less than six months after she'd lost her mentor, Crawford Bell, and her best friend, Eric Carlton, she'd lost yet another person whom she'd loved with her entire heart. Like the others before him, Jeremy had gone on to the next world and had left Dana all alone in this one to figure out things for herself. She didn't know if she ever could, but she knew that she had to try. After she'd stopped off at home in Cleveland, she was expected back in New York City the following day to begin her debriefing session with Bill Krugman about the Joseph Tucci RICO case that she and Jeremy had constructed, as well as help to put together the final pieces of the Chessboard Killer investigation. Jeremy wouldn't have expected anything less from her. He'd have expected her to move on, to do her best to live a happy life despite the many heartaches along the way. He'd have expected her to stand up, brush the dirt of his grave off her knees and get back out there to do the only thing that she had ever been any good at doing in this life.

So that was what she did.

She stood up, brushed the dirt of Jeremy's grave off her knees and walked back to her car.

What *else* could she do? She had a flight to catch. And, like it or not, life was waiting for her.

ALSO AVAILABLE IN ARROW

Kill Me Once

Jon Osborne

Introducing a new breed of serial killer . . .

Nathan Stiedowe is seeking perfection – and he has been learning from the best. Recreating some of the most sickening murders in history, his objective appears chillingly simple, but his true motive remains unclear.

On the trail of this sadistic monster is FBI Special Agent Dana Whitestone. Driven by the brutal childhood slaying of her parents, Dana's relentless pursuit of the most evil and twisted criminals has seen her profile many violent cases. But never has she encountered a maniac as demented as Stiedowe, or a mind as horrifyingly disturbed . . .

'Terrifying, suspenseful and genuinely original, *Kill Me Once* will chill you to the bone' Karin Slaughter

arrow books